The Inside of Rainbow

A Novel

Bridget L. Rose

Pitstop Series

Team Names

Velocità Rossa

Alfa

Adrenalina

GRENZENLOS

Hawker

Klein Racing

Spark Racing

This book is dedicated to everyone who's struggling with anxiety. This story is for you. We may have anxiety, but we won't let it define us or take away from our worth, you hear me? You deserve all the good things in the world.

Content Warning

This book contains explicit scenes of sex, vulgar language, violence, scenes of grief, and themes of anxiety and scenes with anxiety attacks.

Author's Note

In this book, you will meet Scarlette. She struggles with an anxiety disorder in the same way I personally struggle with it as well. Everyone's experience is different, and Scarlette's is mine. Her doubts, her triggers, her fears, and her symptoms are my own. I wrote this story as a way to assure people like me that it's okay. You're not alone. It can feel lonely, I know, but there are so many people out there going through a similar thing, just like I am. You're stong, much more so than you probably think. Having anxiety does NOT take away from your worth. Having anxiety does NOT make you weak. Having anxiety does NOT make you less of who you are, and who you are is amazing. Don't let anyone tell you otherwise, especially not your own head. I know it can often be our greatest foe, so you must become a fearless knight, and take the beast head on.

If no one else has said it to you before, let me be the first: anxiety is nothing to be ashamed of. I am proud of you for living with something so destructive and still finding ways to get up in the mornings. You're strong, a force to be reckoned with, and I hope you never lose sight of your worth.

Chapter 1
Storm

Peace. I never feel at peace except when racing down the highway on my bike. The rest of the world disappears into a blur as I find harmony in the speed of this heavy machine in my grasp, under my complete control.

I like being in control. It steadies me in the chaos of my life. *Work?* Forgotten. *Drama with my family?* Vanished. *All the fucking chores waiting for me at home?* Not important. Nothing's important except for the calmness of this moment.

Riding my bike is my happy place.

But every ride has to come to an end eventually. I have to return to my responsibilities and figure out what the hell I'm going to do about the huge bomb my dad dropped on me this morning. Maybe avoiding it for a bit longer isn't that bad. I could keep going, keep riding until... well, until I permanently escape this hell of a small town I call home.

My best friend, Elias, points two of his fingers toward the closest exit, and I give him a single nod of my head. I follow behind, slowing my speed as we reach the neighborhood area. He gestures to the drive-thru of the only fast-food place in our town, and I shake my head when I realize that's why he was so eager to get off the highway. That *idiota* is hungry.

Elias orders some food for both of us while I wait in the parking lot, inspecting my bike. Something felt a bit off earlier, and I want to make sure everything is in order. I didn't spend almost thirty grand on this Kawasaki to have it fall apart on me now.

I pull my helmet off my head and place it on my seat, bending down to check the left side, then the right, front, back, and as much of the underside as I can see. Nothing looks out of place, so I straighten out my back again and let out a sigh. I'm starting to imagine things. *Great.* Just what I needed at this point in my life.

"Here ya go. Smile for me, and I'll give you your food," Elias teases, but I pull my lips into a thin line.

"You have three seconds to hand over my burger." I don't tell him what happens if he doesn't. We both know I'd smack the back of his head the first chance I'd get.

"I'm just messing with you, Mr. Grumpy, don't worry," he says and hands me the bag with my food in it. I mumble a 'thanks' before I pop a fry into my mouth. "I do have one question I've always wanted to ask you." *Of fucking course.* Elias always has some sort of ridiculous question to ask.

"I swear, if it's something as stupid as you look, I will punch you," I say, and he bursts into laughter.

"No, no, I promise this is a genuine question," he assures me.

I lean the bag with my food against my helmet on my bike, waiting for him to ask it. My arms cross in front of my chest, my breathing even as I get ready to kick his ass.

"When you have sex with someone, do you also always look this unhappy, or do they get you to smile a little?"

A sigh slips past my lips before I make my way toward where he's standing. Like the coward he is, he runs around his bike and away from me, laughing at his own joke like it was the best one he's ever made.

"Okay, okay, I'm sorry," he says when I catch up to him. Lucky for him, he's still wearing his helmet, so the smack doesn't hurt him as much as I wish it would.

"Come on, Storm, tell me what's bothering you," he pleads after I've gone back to eating my food.

Storm. A nickname he decided to call me exclusively because I guided him to safety when we were out for a ride and it started to pour down like the world was going to end. It was one of the scariest moments of my entire life. But nothing could ever compare to—

"Storm," Elias repeats, this time his voice sounding serious and sincere.

"Yeah?" I ask because I was spiraling into the black hole inside of my chest, and it usually takes a few hours for me to completely snap out of it again.

"What did your dad want this morning?"

My dad... my role model, guiding compass, and an absolute piece of shit when it comes to money. That man is the greediest person I've ever met.

"You know what, man? I'm not hungry anymore. I think I'll just head home. See you there?" I ask, but knowing my best friend, he's not going to leave me alone until he's found a way to cheer me up.

"You want to go ride for a while longer?" he says, and I suck in a quiet, sharp breath.

"Yeah," I reply because sadness is starting to creep into my chest, and the patience to deal with suppressing it doesn't exist in me today.

"Okay," Elias replies, squeezing my shoulder to comfort me. "Only if you smile at me though." Another sigh leaves me, then— "Ow, I'm not wearing my helmet anymore!" he complains.

"Stop asking questions that are none of your business."

Especially because I don't want him to know the last time I had sex with anyone was the day before my ex decided I was no longer good enough for her and fucked one of my former close friends. Yeah, he and I aren't very close anymore. All of this happened six months ago, and I've moved on since then, but I haven't been able to be that vulnerable with anyone else. I can't bring myself to open up to that level of losing control.

"Ah, right, your vow of sexual abstinence, I almost forgot," he jokes, but I'm too surprised by his words to scowl at him.

"I don't have a vow of abstinence," I blurt out, and Elias lets out another amused laugh, stuffing his burger into his mouth a second later.

"Yeah, right," he replies with a full mouth, and I shake my head. "When's the last time you even looked at a woman?" I cock an eyebrow at his question.

"I had lunch with Mamá yesterday." Elias rolls his eyes in response.

"We both know that's not what I meant," he replies with a snort, and I shake my head once again.

"I do not have a vow of abstinence, I just haven't found anyone I feel connected to recently, which by the way is, *again*, none of your fucking business."

I slide my helmet on, fasten the clasp, and then swing my leg over the true love of my life. For once, Elias stays quiet as he finishes his meal and then gets on his bike as well.

Elias gives me a honk once he's ready, earning himself yet another shake of my head. I don't know what kind of annoyance pills he took this morning but, fuck, he's bugging the hell out of me.

He zooms past me on the way back to the highway, and I smile under my helmet, something I only do for myself, right before I speed past him. Elias forgets that everything he knows, I taught him. I was the one who showed him how to even get on the bike. He doesn't stand a chance against me when it comes to riding, and he never will. This is second nature to me. It's what I want to do for a career.

Now, after what my dad has asked of me?

I have no idea what the hell I'm going to do.

Chapter 2
Scarlette

"Let's go, Lettie," my best friend Violet says as I drag my suitcase out of the trunk of her car. "I have a million things to do before we can go out for dinner tonight," she adds, but I roll my eyes at her.

Vi was the one who decided to go for dinner. I wanted to get settled in and ready for my first day at work the day after tomorrow. Although this town is small and pretty much isolated, Moonville has one of the most affordable universities in the country when it comes to an engineering degree. Since I will be paying for it all by myself, this was my only option. Move to a town no one's ever heard of, get a job at a multi-billion dollar company to make some money, and then try to find some time between those things to actually have a social life. Then again, that is at the very bottom of my priority list. Getting my degree is the most important thing in my life. Once I'm an engineer, I will do everything I can to become a race engineer in Formula One. It's been my dream since I was six years old.

"You know what? Let me carry that. You're going way too slow," she complains and pushes me out of the way to carry my suitcase inside. I laugh at her impatience.

We've been close for most of our lives. My mom and Violet's dad used to hate each other in primary school, but now, they are best friends. Vi and I have been inseparable since we were babies and now she moved to this small town because I wanted to go to university. Granted, she is also taking courses and found work at the animal sanctuary twenty minutes outside of Moonville, her dream job.

Violet and I planned on taking a year off to earn some money for a degree, but then a year turned into two because I had to help my family pay the bills after my parents both lost their jobs. They're back on their feet now, and I finally got the chance to chase my dream career again, even if I have to do it all by myself. I don't mind it actually. It makes me feel independent in the best way, no matter the pressure on my shoulders.

"I'm sorry you had two weeks to get settled in already," I say, and Violet spins around, her strawberry-blonde hair flying from the dramatic motion.

"Well, someone took forever to move out of her parents' house," she replies, making me laugh at her.

Both of us know it wasn't my decision to stay an extra two weeks with my parents. I needed to sell the love of my life, my motorbike, to be able to pay tuition. I cried for a day, something I hadn't done in years. I usually try to find the positives in life because there is so much darkness in the world as is. A smile rests on my lips whenever I'm around somebody to brighten up their days. It's something I learned from my parents from a very young age. They needed me to be their light through the tough times. It also distracts people from the faint scar running a few centimeters above my lips to a little under them.

My biggest insecurity...

"Stop it. It's beautiful, just like you are," Vi says, and I cock an eyebrow.

"How did you—" I cut off when she offers me a sad smile.

"Because you always get that same look when you think about it. You almost died as a kid, but that scar shows you survived. And you can barely see it, so stop it. No negative thoughts about something I love about you," she explains, and I return her smile.

"I love you," I reply, and Vi gives me a wink before carrying my suitcase up the stairs of the little house we're renting.

It has two small rooms, an antique-styled kitchen, one bathroom, and a little living room. This house may not be much, but it is absolutely perfect for what we need. There are lots of windows on the walls, light gray furniture came with the place, and Vi has done an amazing job adding photos, vases, figurines, and light blue throw pillows to make it feel more like our home.

"The oven isn't working properly, and the sink in the bathroom leaks," Violet informs me as she places my suitcase on the chair opposite my twin bed.

"Alright, no problem. I will take care of it later," I assure her, dropping my backpack on top of my light red sheets.

"No, you can do it tomorrow. There is no rush. Please, just get settled in, and I will pick you up for dinner later. Love you," my best friend says before hurrying out of the house.

I drop onto the bed, sucking in a sharp breath and relaxing my face into a neutral expression. My feet bring me to the small closet on the right side of my room, and I start packing away everything. My mom calls me to ask how the short trip here was, and we end up chatting for a while. Apparently, Dad cried after I left this morning, which she only tells me because she loves to guilt-trip me, whether it is using her own feelings against me or someone else's.

When I first told her I was moving to a different town, she spent three hours asking me how I could do this to her, that she needed me now more than ever. I felt guilty at first—even now I still do—but it was time. I can't spend the rest of my life taking care of my parents.

"When do you think you will come to visit us?" I almost sigh into the phone. Instead, I force a little laugh from my lips.

"Mom, I just left today. Can we worry about that later, you know, after I started uni, my new job, and have managed to somewhat settle in?" I ask, hoping if I list everything I have to do, she will back off.

"But we will still get to see you again someday, right?" *Oh my God, she can be so dramatic.*

"Of course, but let me figure things out first, Mom. That's all I'm asking."

Moving out was the most selfish decision I've ever made, but no part of me regrets it. I'm chasing my dream. I'm trying to find a way to make myself permanently happy. I've done everything to be able to have this opportunity, and I will not, under any circumstances, give it up again. It would destroy me.

"I'm worried about you, Scarlette. With your anxiety attacks, I don't think—" I cut her off then.

"I've lived with them for three years now. I know how to handle them and what to do." It's half a lie, but also half true.

My anxiety attacks are brutal. At first, they started because of intrusive thoughts that terrified me. They sent me spiraling until an attack swept over me and shut down my whole system. Nowadays, they come whenever they want, with no actual trigger necessary. All I know is I will have one of my many symptoms—heart racing, hands shaking, uneven breathing, a nervous feeling spreading, etc.—and then break down into an attack. It takes me a while to get out of them, but I know how to take care of myself. Plus, they're not as regular as they used to be. They only happen a couple of times a month, not four times every day like when they first started.

"You took your lavender oil with you, right?" Mom asks, and I roll my eyes, thankful she can't see me.

"Yes, Mom. I will be fine, don't worry."

We hang up moments later, and I sink onto the floor, dropping my head into my hands. I'm nervous enough about starting university next week and my job the day after tomorrow. I don't need her to remind me of my anxiety. I don't need her to remind me I could get an attack at work any time and lose my job because they could deem me incapable of doing it properly.

Oh no, what if that really happens? What if they fire me on the first day because I can't control my anxiety attacks? What if—

I stop myself.

Everything will be fine. I will be fine.

I've worked my butt off to get here, and I will do my absolute best.

Hopefully, it will be enough.

Chapter 3

Storm

"Did he tell you he's buying a farm to get lots of horses?" Elias asks, and I shake my head at him.

"Why would I be upset with my dad about something like that? I like horses and he has more than enough money."

Dad owns the biggest, most successful company selling airplane parts in the whole country. He controls most of Moonville, and I fucking hate it. I hate how he keeps making more and more money while other people in Moonville—hell, the fucking world—get poorer by the second. It's why I'm so angry at him for what he's suggested. It's why I don't want to talk to anyone about it, not even Elias, and I tell him everything.

"I don't know, man. I've been playing the guessing game for the past two days, wishing you'd finally open up and share your deepest, darkest secrets with me, but nothing! You've said *nothing*, and it's driving me crazy," he says and slams his hand on the table. I cock both eyebrows, surprised at the way he's feeling.

"I'm sorry, Elias, but I haven't figured out how I feel about what happened with my dad. It's not fair of me to dump it all on you and expect you to have some kind of great solution," I explain, and my best friend leans back on his side of the booth, raising his hands into the air in frustration.

"But I have the best solutions. I'm like your guiding compass, I always have the right answers," he replies, which sends me into deep thought.

He's right. For the entire duration of our friendship, he's always had answers to my problems. Fuck. He really is my guiding compass. I can never, ever admit that to him. He will not let it go until the day we die, and I don't want to spend the next, hopefully, sixty years listening to him telling me how great he is.

"Fine, you want me to share my dilemma with you? I will share it. Ready?" I ask, and an excited smile brightens up his brown eyes. "Dad wants me to take over his company by the end of the year," I blurt out without giving it another moment of hesitation.

Elias' face slips into shock.

"But you hate what he does," he says.

"Yeah."

"And your dream is to become a professional motorcycle racer," he goes on.

"I'm aware."

"And you've been training so hard to make it happen," Elias states, and I sigh.

"Are you just going to list things I already know? Because it's not helping," I reply while he slides his hands into his hair and tugs on the roots of his curls.

"I'm sorry, this is much worse than I thought it'd be. My brain was making up the mildest scenarios, but this? This is a much bigger load of shit I could have ever come up with, and I have a wild imagination," he says, and I give him an agreeing nod. "Paulo knows you hate his company. Why would he want you to take over?" Elias asks, making me shrug.

I'm not even qualified for the type of position my dad wants me to fill. If anyone could take over, it would be Elias. He has a business degree and has always been passionate about what my dad does. He's also mentioned many times that he'd like to run his own company one day. Elias would probably do a much better job than my father ever could. If my best friend hadn't started working at the animal sanctuary instead, I would have suggested he takes over the company.

"Because he wants the business to stay in the family and he wants to retire." At fifty, my father has decided he's had enough of work and since he's so goddamn rich, he can do it too. "The problem I'm facing is, Mamá is convinced this is a great idea," I start, and Elias gives me a knowing look.

"And you can't say no when Mommy asks," he says, earning himself an eye roll from me.

"My mother has done everything for me. She worked several jobs when I was still growing inside of her, she gave up her career because it didn't earn her enough money, and she never, ever complained. Yes, she may have married one of the richest men in the world when I was two, but I can't imagine what she went through the three years before that. She barely survived so I could live," I say, and Elias frowns, manifesting the guilt he's feeling from his previous comment.

"And you also think you owe it to Paulo, don't you?"

I look away, not prepared to answer his question. Yes, I do feel a certain responsibility to the man who raised me and treated me like a son ever since I came into his life, even though I wasn't biologically his. He never made me feel like I wasn't his family, and I owe him more than I can ever give back. Taking over his bloodsucking company and doing exactly what he wants me to do with it would be one way to repay him, but it would make me miserable.

"I have no fucking clue what to do," I admit, sucking in a sharp breath and letting the sensation send a burn through my chest.

"I know you think you owe him a lot, but you can't change your morals because of it. You don't agree with what he's doing, don't do it yourself," Elias says, and I nod several times, still agreeing with him.

"*Mamá me va a odiar*," I say, letting out a shaky breath. *Mom is going to hate me.*

"Listen, man, you're going to the National Championship next season. Hawke just sponsored you. This is your passion. Getting into MotoGP is your dream. Don't let him take that from you," he replies, slapping his hand on the table to make sure he has my full attention.

"You know, this was actually very helpful. Thank you. I appreciate it," I tell him, and he lets out a taunting laugh.

"Don't sound so surprised. I told you I always have a solution to your problems," he says, wiggling his somehow perfectly shaped eyebrows at me.

I'm convinced he spends an hour a week on them and then gets mad at me because mine always look better than his. I won't ever tell him I get them done, not because I'm ashamed, but because I know he will want to come with me every single time. I'm open to a lot of things, but not spa days with Elias. Nope, not going to happen.

"Okay, change of subject. Why did you want to go out for dinner tonight?" I ask, bringing his attention to me after he started doodling on a napkin using the pen he brings everywhere.

"Because there is actually something I need to discuss with you," he says, and I slap my forehead with the palm of my hand.

"You wanted to discuss something but bothered me about my thing?" He nods with a wicked grin on his face. "You don't make sense to me, *hermano*," I reply, taking a sip of my water.

We came here with our bikes, which means neither one of us is going to drink any alcohol. I made a strict rule with myself when I was young that alcohol would be off-limits as soon as mounting the bike would be a possibility afterward. Elias adapted this rule quickly, neither one of us willing to risk our lives for a brief buzz.

"Yes, I need to tell you about this drop-dead gorgeous woman I met at work two weeks ago. I want to ask her out, but I have no idea how. I don't even know if she's interested in me, and I don't want to come off as a creep," he explains, his hands waving around in the air as he articulates with them.

"So, in other words, you're asking me how to not be yourself?" I tease, the corner of my mouth twitching ever so slightly at my joke. It stops soon.

"I'm glad you find this entertaining, but, man, I mean it. Violet is stunning with that strawberry blonde hair and those big, brown eyes. She's an angel sent from heaven. She's the breath of oxygen when you're drowning. She's—she's walking right this way. Holy shit, hide me!" he says and raises the menu to cover his face.

I scrunch my eyebrows together, wondering where his confidence has vanished off to before turning around to see how beautiful she is for myself.

But Violet isn't the one who catches my gaze.

The woman next to her does.

And I'm incapable of looking away.

Because holy shit.

Wow.

Chapter 4

Scarlette

I can't breathe. I've forgotten how sometime between walking into the restaurant and making eye contact with the... I don't even have words. *Most beautiful? Sexiest? Most gorgeous?* All of the above would suit best because this man, he's not just handsome. He's more than that. He's breathtaking.

Even though he's sitting, I can see how lean but muscular he is. His skin is dark gold, and his hair sits on top of his head in brown waves. A birthmark the size of an almond is painted on his left cheek; so beautiful, so unique. Those full lips of his have a scowl lingering on them, but his eyes, they are my favorite. The closer we get, the more I study them. The left one is a rich coffee brown. The right one is a mix of that same color and green, half-half.

I'm mesmerized by him, which is why I can't look away, not at first. Even when he tears his eyes from me, I study his muscular backside and the line of his shoulders, my heart pumping against my ribcage at a speed that shouldn't be possible. It makes me wonder why my body is reacting like this. It never has before, not because of an attractive person catching my eye at a restaurant. This isn't normal. Maybe I'm getting an anxiety attack.

The waiter leads us to the booth next to the man I want to keep looking at and the guy he's with. I have a perfect view of him from where I am, which is going to be a big problem. He's too attractive, and I need to stop being a creep, but when

I glance his way again, his eyes are on me already, curiosity sparkling in them. His gaze sends another wave of heat over me, making that stupid organ in my chest work overtime.

"Lettie, you're drooling," Vi says, and I tear my eyes off the stranger.

"Actually, my heart is racing," I reply and give my best friend a look she recognizes. She laughs in response.

"I think you're confusing anxiety with horniness," she says, and I kick her against the shin.

"Keep your voice down," I hiss, but Vi only bursts into laughter.

"Why? It's normal to be horny, especially because in twenty years, you haven't had sex once," she reminds me, making an upset frown slip across my face.

"Yeah, well, I was busy."

Busy taking care of my family. Busy juggling school and work. Busy being a curvy woman around childish men who couldn't handle me. Women weren't interested in me either. Then again, I didn't have time for that yet, something Vi loves to remind me of.

"He's really hot. You should ask him for his number." Heat rushes into my cheeks, probably painting them a deep red.

"Are you crazy? I can't just ask a random guy for his number!" No matter how good-looking he is. I'm not that brave and won't pretend to be either.

"Fine, I will ask," she says and gets up before I can stop her.

"Vi!" I bark, but she's already at their table. I watch her eyes go wide as her attention drifts to the other guy.

"Elias? Hey, how are you?" she asks, smirking at him like he's a piece of meat she'd love to dig into.

I raise my eyebrows in surprise at her behavior. She's had feelings for Anna, a mutual friend of ours, for over a decade. Violet hardly ever allows her attention to drift to anyone else, except when she's looking for someone to hook up with. I'll have to ask her what it is about Elias that is making her look at him in a way I've never seen on her before, with pure, raw emotion. Lust, want, need, desire, admiration, it all wanders onto her soft features.

"Do you and your friend want to join us?" Elias asks, and I hope to God my best friend will decline.

"Sure. Scarlette, come over here," she encourages me, and I think about divorcing her.

A nervous feeling spreads through my chest, but it's so familiar to me now, I only curse at it inside of my head. I gather my things and walk over to the other table, offering a sincere apologetic smile to the stranger I ogled. His hard expression softens at my face, his shoulders falling at the same time.

"I'm sorry they're doing this. You probably just wanted a quiet evening," I say, still smiling at him like I do with most people. Sweat starts collecting at the back of my neck when he doesn't respond, merely gives me a strained nod, and then grabs his water to take a sip from it. "Okay then," I whisper to myself and settle in the seat next to him since Violet chose the one next to Elias. Sensing my discomfort, she starts talking about where they met.

"Elias works with me at the sanctuary. He mostly takes care of the marine animals while I take care of the mammals," Violet explains and nudges Elias in the side. His cheeks flush a wonderful pink.

Elias is cute, handsome even. He has dark brown eyes, black hair like me, and an inviting smile. Unlike the gorgeous man beside me, he keeps grinning, his full attention on my best friend. It's clear as day he likes her. Elias hasn't stopped looking at her once since she sat down. I also feel eyes burning my skin, but I do my best to listen to Vi as she tells me more about work. I last about a minute before my head turns in his direction.

"What's your name?" I ask, trying to make conversation and ignoring the awkward feeling spreading through my chest. His beautiful eyes scan my face, making me even more nervous. I drop my gaze to his hands and almost gasp. Defined, strong, veiny hands that could probably do a lot of wonderful things to my bo—*woah*. Maybe I *am* horny.

"Storm." It's all he gives me. So, naturally, I keep talking.

"Oh, that's a cool name. Which one of your parents chose it? Or is that too personal of a question? I apologize, I'm merely curious. It's a very unique name, I like it. I don't think I've ever met anyone called Storm, or Thunder or Lightning for that matter," I rant, letting out a little giggle at my joke. He watches me with curiosity, a robotic look on his face.

"You're very bubbly," he says, his voice low and rough. I enjoy the way the words sound falling from his lips, but I'm unsure if I like them put together like that.

"Is that supposed to be an insult?" I challenge, crossing my arms in front of my chest and leaning away from him. Panic briefly slips across his face before his features fall back into a scowl.

"Not at all. I'm just wondering how great your life must be for you to be this bubbly," he says, not condescending but genuinely interested. I, on the other hand, am starting to get irritated with this breathtaking stranger.

"That's quite a judgy way to phrase it," I reply and shake my head, turning to my best friend, who is deep in conversation with Elias. Her face is bright and happy, sending a wave of those feelings through me too. I love seeing her this way.

"I apologize. It wasn't supposed to come out that way." I don't give him a response anymore. He may be stunning and I like the way my body vibrates from his proximity, but I won't let him make me feel bad about being who I am. "Have I upset you?" he asks, but I shake my head.

"Oh, so you think it's possible to upset a bubbly person?" I challenge. He tilts his head, almost looking amused if his features weren't set in a firm expression.

"I never said being bubbly is a bad thing," he reminds me, and I cock an eyebrow at him.

"What if I said you're dull? What if I said I was wondering how miserable your life must be if you look so unhappy all the time?"

Oh, he doesn't like that I flipped it on him. I can tell by the way he turns away and pulls his phone out of his pocket to show me he's done talking to me. Meanwhile, this conversation, confrontation even, has triggered my anxiety. My hands have started to shake, and I get up from the table before storming outside.

Really? Right now?

I sink to the floor at the side of the restaurant, my heart racing, lips trembling, and body shaking. Everything starts to spin when I don't offer my lungs and brain enough oxygen, but at least I'm out of sight. I don't like being vulnerable like this. I don't like the way my face contorts, the way I lose myself in the panic. My mom and Violet are the only people I've ever let see me this way, but it wasn't by choice either. They found me when I fell into an attack, and I needed them more than I was willing to go through it by myself. Nowadays, I don't care if I'm alone anymore. I snap out of it eventually.

"Scarlette?" Vi's voice comes from the entrance minutes later. I've managed to calm down enough to face her.

"Yes?" I ask, straightening out my dress. At least this time I didn't cry. Most of the anxiety attacks I get make me burst into tears, but not this one. *Thank God.*

"Where did you go? What did Storm say? Elias told me he can be an asshole sometimes, so whatever it was, don't take it personally. He's like that with everyone apparently," she says, but I raise both of my eyebrows.

"Everything's fine. We just didn't see eye-to-eye on something, nothing to worry about. He's a stranger anyway, and I'm not interested in him." At least not anymore. He caught my attention, but that's all it was.

I won't waste another second thinking about this man.

Chapter 5

Storm

I really fucked up. There she was, more beautiful than any woman I'd ever met, and I fucked it up. Scarlette was a combination of gorgeous, cute, sexy, and funny, and I said the shittiest thing I could have ever come up with. And the worst part of it all, I cannot stop thinking about her. It's been thirty-six hours, and I've not been able to have a single thought other than her. Fuck me. I keep replaying the way her blue—bluer than I've ever seen—eyes studied mine, my mouth, and my hands. *She really liked my hands.*

I couldn't help staring at her scar when she wasn't looking. It fascinated me, took my breath away. The line was so faint, but, somehow, the way it contrasted her sunshine personality was wonderful. So fucking wonderful, I haven't been able to stop thinking about it. She's like a rainbow, something so beautiful made out of her bubbly personality and the rainy world around us. *Oh God, why am I even thinking about this?* Scarlette is just a woman. I've been cheated on by one of them. I don't want to have feelings for anyone ever again.

I stop my bike, letting the cold, hard realization sink in. I couldn't turn off my thoughts. I didn't escape all of my problems like I always do. Scarlette had me riding with every worry and regret still at the front of my mind.

Goddamn it. Am I fucked?

Is this how things will be from now on? No, of course not! I met her once. We got into a fight. I'm overreacting. I'll probably never see her again. That thought settles me. Yeah, I won't see her again, I'm sure of it. I never meet new people, and yesterday was a coincidence. It means nothing.

I walk into Dad's huge building, sucking in a sharp breath. For the first time in hours, I let myself dread the conversation I'm about to have with him. This is awful. He's going to think I'm the least grateful son in the world. Then again, we tried working together years ago. I offered him ideas to be more environmentally conscious and give back to the community, but he's so goddamn cheap, he dismissed them without a second glance. The people he works with are just as bad, and I don't want any part of this anymore. His money is something I haven't taken since I was eighteen, found a job, and moved out of my parents' home.

My head is swimming with dread now, but then, everything vanishes. When I see her sitting at the desk outside of my father's office, I forget about the rest of the world, letting it pulverize inside my mind. She looks... there are no words. There never will be words good enough to describe her beauty. Her long, wavy black hair is loose, contrasting her light blue eyes. Her curvy body is covered by a white blouse and a dark blue skirt, and I get lost in the thought of touching her for a moment too long. I can't help but imagine running my hands, the ones she likes so much, all over her, memorizing the feel of her. Claiming her lips, burying myself— *What the fuck is wrong with me?*

I shake my head, feeling my breathing hitch uncontrollably. What has she done to me? Well, whatever it is, I won't let it happen any longer. It can't go further than this. So, when I approach her, I place a scowl on my face.

"I'm here to see my father," I say because, unfortunately, he's made it a rule for me to announce myself to his assistant before I'm allowed to enter his office.

Scarlette's eyes go wide at the sight of me, the pen she's holding between her fingers dropping onto her notebook. Her lips part ever so slightly, making images of me slipping my tongue between them fill my head. *For fuck's sake!*

"You're Paulo Rodrick's son? Your name is Storm Rodrick?" she asks, but I give her an unimpressed glance. It's the opposite of how I really want to look at her.

"No. Now, can you let him know I'm here?" I sound impatient, which is probably why she rolls her eyes at me.

"Yes, sir," she replies, and my knees go a little weak.

Scarlette stands up after my father doesn't react to her call button, striding toward his office with so much grace, I'm staring after her probably with a bit of drool coming from the side of my mouth.

"He's most likely in the washroom. Mr. Rodrick should return soon," she says while sitting back down at her desk and focusing on her screen.

Silence fills the space between us, and I settle down in the seat across from hers. Something inside of me is telling me to be close to her, make conversation with her to hear the softness of her voice, watch her lips as they shape the words. Part of me also wants to know what the hell she is doing here, at this awful company.

"I can't believe you work here," I blurt out, catching her full attention.

"What is that supposed to mean?" she challenges, and I love seeing the fire inside of her come out into the open, wrapping around me until my skin is trapped by flames.

"I wouldn't work here," I say, but it only confuses her more.

"You know what? You've been judging me without knowing anything about my life, so let me tell you something, mister. It is none of your business, respectfully." Scarlette turns back to her computer, and I let out an unamused snort.

"Don't you feel guilty working for a company that is just taking more and more money without giving anything back?" I ask, and she starts chuckling at my question. It surprises me so much, I lean back in my chair.

I don't want her at this job. She should be anywhere else. Hell, I'd open my own company and pay her triple she's earning here to get her out of this place.

Wait... what? What the hell?

"Listen, Mr. Judgy, I need this job to finance my education. It is the only one that pays me enough because my parents cannot help me out. I've worked several jobs to provide for them, and now I've finally found one allowing me to have the time to study and still earn enough money. So, please, leave me alone," she says, leaning toward me to make sure I hear her clearly.

I can see in her eyes that she wants to tell me to fuck off but a) she probably doesn't swear and b) she's scared of losing this job. After what she just told me, I can't believe how much of a dick I am. I should really hold back, but something about her makes me... it makes me incapable of controlling my emotions. They're all over the place. Some of them are drawn to her, others are telling me to stay the fuck away, to not set myself up for vulnerability like I did once before. My heart doesn't want to get hurt again after fully healing itself only months ago.

"I don't like you working here," I blurt out. There is something seriously wrong with me. Do I have no self-control when it comes to speaking my mind with this girl?

Ms. Rainbow smiles at me.

"Well, it's a good thing I don't care what you think then," she says, still smiling. I know better than to believe she means it in any other way than a condescending one. It threatens to bring a smirk to my face, but I manage to keep it at bay. I will not start smiling in public because of this woman. It's not happening.

"I bother you, don't I?" I say, and she lets out a sharp laugh.

"That's an understatement, but yes, you bother me a lot," she replies while I study her closely, trying to understand why I don't like her having negative feelings about me.

"You bother me too," I say, and she gives me a happy grin.

"You just made my day by saying that." Her attention shifts to her screen, but I know she's having a hard time not looking at my face by the way she's gripping the pencil sharpener next to her keyboard. "Stop staring, it's weird," she blurts out when my attention has been stuck on her mouth, her scar, for a little too long.

"Hmmm," is all I reply, shifting my gaze to some of the other people walking around the office.

They're all dressed in ridiculously fancy clothing. My father insists on them only wearing suits and other formal attire. Once I've finished rolling my eyes at the extravagance of it all, I bring them back to Scarlette, who is already staring at me. I cock an eyebrow, intrigued.

"Hypocrite," I say, causing her cheeks to flush a deep red.

"Buttface," she mumbles under her breath, but I can hear her loud and clear, and fuck me, it takes everything out of me not to burst into laughter. *Buttface? Ay, qué preciosa.*

"Is that how you address the son of your boss? Maybe I should speak to my father about your kindergarten-level name-calling," I tease, so her eyes form thin slits as she studies me.

"You are a wonderful human being, do you know that? Your smile really brightens up a person's day." Oh, she's going for sarcasm now. This woman is heaven. I'm about to respond when I'm interrupted.

"I hope you haven't been waiting long, *mijo*," Dad says, smacking me on the shoulder as soon as he's close enough. I tear my eyes off Scarlette, the last thing I want to do right now, and bring them up to the man who raised me.

"Not long at all. I've met your new assistant. She's very welcoming," I tease, feeling amusement settle in my gaze as I glance at her. *Uh oh, too close.* I turn my head back to Dad.

"That's great. I'm happy to hear that, Scarlette. Do you mind grabbing me a coffee from the office kitchen?"

She's on her feet and rushing to get my father's coffee as soon as possible.

"I hope to see you again soon," I call after her, watching her back tense as she walks away. Her reaction tugs on the left corner of my mouth, and I barely keep it from lifting.

I'm so screwed.

Chapter 6

Scarlette

My first three days at work go well, and after his appearance on Monday, Storm hasn't shown his face in my life again. It would be fantastic if he wasn't on my mind 24/7 either. I'm so frustrated with him, with his behavior, I don't get a minute of peace from the replays of him in my head.

"Are you ready? I don't want to be late," Violet says from the front door, and I hurry over to her, my bag under my arm and a smile on my face.

I'm genuinely excited to start university. It's the biggest step toward becoming a Formula One race engineer I've ever taken. The only thing I haven't quite figured out is how to build connections with people in F1 because without them, I'm screwed. Having no connections means I'm a nobody. Being a nobody means no one knows who the heck I am so they can't hire me, which is bad. Actually, it's horrible. I should start putting more time into finding opportunities to get my foot in the door.

"Did you remember to pack water? You know how bad your anxiety gets when you're dehydrated," my best friend reminds me, and I force a smile.

I hate it when she does this, her and Mom. They remind me of these things like I don't live with my mental health problems myself. I appreciate them looking out for me, but it upsets me how little faith they have in my ability to take care of myself.

Then again, for a while I was struggling badly. Maybe they're right to be pushy about this.

"It's packed, don't worry. Let's go," I say, walking toward her car.

We drive ten minutes until we arrive at a castle-style building, the University of Moonville. Like most of this town, it's antique. Everything about it is old and rusted, but it has a charm to it. I adore it, not that I would like to imagine spending the rest of my life in this small town, I think it would be my worst nightmare, but it's great for now. It's exactly what I need.

The castle is a faded white, cracks everywhere. There are pillars upholding the structure, and I feel a bit lost, as if we'd just stepped into a different realm or time period. Considering how ancient and priceless this building looks, it's surprising how low the tuition is. It should be a crime, but when we walk inside and I take in my surroundings, I'm glad it's not.

It's made completely out of stone. Paintings of landscapes hang in rows on the walls, decorating the simple façade. People rush past me, crowding the long hallways. It's a combination of modern-style decorations and an antique structure, which reminds me a bit of the type of school someone in a fantasy show would go to. It's mesmerizing.

"Come with me," Violet says, and I follow behind her, grabbing the hand she extends to make sure we don't get separated in the crowd.

We stay together, holding up our schedules to find our classes. I go to my Introduction to Engineering one, she goes to her Biology course. I give her a kiss on the cheek, and she gives my butt a slap when I walk away, dragging a laugh from my lips. I hurry to my class, hoping I can still make it. Everyone is gathering inside, finding a chair in the lecture hall. I settle down in one at the back, wanting to mind my own business and give my anxiety a small break.

"Scarlette Roots?" an unfamiliar voice says, and I lift my head, forcing my gaze to the person demanding my attention. My eyes meet a tall blonde man with piercing blue eyes and a warm smile.

"How do you know my name?" I ask, curious.

"My name is Aaron, and I was assigned to help you find your way around the university," he says, and I cock an eyebrow, surprise bringing an unsure smile to my face.

"Am I the only student special enough to get someone to help them around?" I challenge, earning myself a cute grin from him.

"You saw right through that, didn't you?" he asks, and I lean back in my chair, nodding while my cheeks burn from smiling.

"Yes, but it was nice, thank you." I pull out my notebook, but Aaron remains in front of me, a shy look on his attractive face. "So, how do you know my name?" I ask again, trying to get an answer.

"Well, you know what they say about small towns. Everyone knows everyone, so as soon as someone new shows up, people start talking," he explains, and the thought makes my skin crawl. People are already talking about me. How unsettling.

"Ah, I see," I reply with another smile.

"Would you like to sit with me and my friends? We're all either on the soccer team or buried in schoolwork. Maybe you relate to one or the other so we have something to talk about," he offers, pointing at a group of people on the right side of the room.

"That's really nice of you, but I don't want to intrude—" Aaron cuts me off before I can finish my sentence.

"You're not, I promise, but I also understand if you're not interested. If you change your mind, we'd be happy to have you," he says and walks away to give me the space to make a decision.

Aaron is very kind to invite me, but too many worries cross my mind.

What if I'm so awkward around these people, they will wonder what's wrong with me? What if I say something stupid? What if they make me feel like an idiot about it afterward? What if they stare at my scar, like most people, and I will get uncomfortable?

All of those questions are byproducts of my anxiety, which is why I practically jump out of my chair to join Aaron and his friends. I love soccer and burying myself in work is my forte. I should fit right in.

"Everyone, this is Scarlette. Scarlette, this is everyone. Grayson is our top player, and he's well-known for being the least dedicated academically in our group," Aaron says, pointing at a guy with black hair, green eyes, and sharp facial features. Then he shifts my attention to the next person. "This is Bex. They are our goalie and the funniest person you will ever meet. They're everyone's favorite in the whole group." I smile at Bex, who returns it and then shifts their attention back to their notes. "We have Andrew, Victoria, and Nate, who are absolute nerds, so stay on their good sides," he suggests, the last part of the sentence merely a whisper that makes me chuckle.

"Noted," I assure him with a smile.

"Okay, last but not least, we have Halo, because he's such an angel,"—Aaron gives me a look that says this nickname is pure sarcasm—"Logan, and Xavi. They are all on the soccer team as well. I'm the team captain," he adds at the end, and I turn my body to study his. His muscular, broad frame is lean, stunning.

Then, out of nowhere, images flood my mind. Visuals of Storm's eyes as they look at me with so much confusion, it's almost amusing. He can't figure me out, and I like that. I like how he tries to understand me, but I don't make it that easy for him. His full lips are constantly shaped into a thin line to keep from revealing any emotion. It makes me wonder how his face would look if he smiled, smirked, grinned, anything. I want to see it, want to experience it.

30

"Hey, where did you go?" Aaron asks, but I simply shake my head.

"Sorry, nowhere. I was trying to memorize everyone's names," I lie but do it well enough to convince all pairs of eyes staring at me that it's the truth. The blonde man next to me smiles.

"Don't worry. You have the entire semester to get them right," he assures me and squeezes my arm before settling down next to Victoria, a girl with beautiful long, brown hair and green eyes. She flashes him a warm smile, and he intertwines his fingers with hers. *Cute.*

"Yeah, they're pretty disgusting, but you'll get used to it. And, if you want, we can also start making out to make people uncomfortable. You know, even it out," Halo teases, and I finally understand where he got the nickname from. I laugh at his comment.

"Wow, so keep a five-meter distance from Halo," I say out loud as I lift my notebook and pretend to write it down, a smile on my face while I tease him.

He bursts into a deep laughter, and I can't help but join him. He's quite attractive, which is probably why he's so cocky. He has brown hair and icy-blue eyes. Like Aaron, he's lean but muscular. Unlike Aaron, he doesn't seem to be very tall. Halo must have people falling at his feet, I'm sure of it.

"I'm in love, Scarlette," he jokes, and I shake my head, sitting down in the seat next to Aaron.

Our professor walks in moments later. He's short, trained, and bald. His eyes are almost transparent in their gray shade, and, for some inexplicable reason, his bright smile carries something else with it, something I'm not sure I trust. When his gaze catches my inquiring one, I feel an uncomfortable heat settle in my cheeks. I have no reason to dislike him, and still, I get a very negative feeling about him, especially when he smirks at me. *Yeah, I'm definitely uncomfortable.*

"Welcome to Introduction to Engineering. My name is Jason Holden. For the next four months, I will be here to guide you through this new, exciting chapter of your life. I hope you're ready," he says with a small chuckle, sending weird shivers down my spine because he's staring specifically at me throughout his speech.

I'm going to switch classes.

The thought enters quickly, but I push it away immediately. Switching classes is not an option since this is the only Introduction to Engineering one. Not to mention, I'm probably just overreacting to a strange gut feeling. Whatever it is, I'm sure it will pass.

For now, I want to focus on starting my new life, including making friends with this group of people.

Is it possible I will actually have time for a social life outside of Violet?

Oh man, I can't help but smile at the possibility.

Chapter 7

Storm

Mom and Dad were furious when they found out I'm not taking over the company. They called me every single synonym for selfish and ungrateful there is in the English language, Mamá even switching into Spanish, our mother tongue, to throw more at my head. It hurt. Fuck, it hurt more than anything has in a while, but I swallowed all of the words and left the house. I went on my bike, drowned everything out, and then... Scarlette's beautiful goddamn face popped into my head.

She didn't leave for the entire duration of my ride, and I almost exploded from anger. It's infuriating how obsessed I've become with the hope of seeing her again. Every conversation we have is a disaster, but I feel this need to have another with her anyway, to study the way she gets upset with me. To have the heat of her rays envelop me. The thought is so tempting, I wonder if it's worth stepping into my father's building just to be near her.

It's been a week since I've seen her. The last time I went to meet my father, his other assistant was working, and I almost yelled at him for not being Scarlette. I'm so fucked, she's the first thing I think about in the morning, takes up most of the rest of the day, just to be in my head when I'm trying to fall asleep. It makes me angry. I shouldn't have her on my mind. I shouldn't linger on her smile or the desperate need somewhere inside of me to touch her soft curves, feel them under my fingertips.

People can't be trusted. I'm not getting into another relationship, it's not happening. I've tried dating. It's not for me. I may only be twenty-one, but one experience was enough to shatter my whole idea of what a relationship was supposed to be like. I knew they didn't all last forever, but they're not supposed to end this way. They shouldn't end in a mess.

Scarlette wouldn't do that, my subconscious thinks, and I almost stumble backward. I can't know that for certain. What is my mind trying to do to me? I don't like her. Nope. I just haven't had sex in a while, and I'm attracted to her. That must be it.

No, it's not.

I'm starting to not like my mind. It's feeding into my wish to see her, bicker with her, get her so frustrated, her cheeks are flush with heat. I hope I'm on her mind. Goddamn it, what if I'm not? What if she met someone at university? Why the hell do I care so much? I'm known as the town grump, the guy who doesn't give a shit about anything except his family and his career. I don't need to be known for anything else, especially not pining after a woman I always fight with. A woman so mesmerizing, I can't get her out of my mind. It's been almost two weeks since I've met her, a week since she's last seen me. She's definitely not thinking about me.

Shit.

I want her to think about me.

Before I can stop myself, I grab my helmet and my keys, walking toward my bike outside Elias' and my home. I know she's working and no longer care about dealing with my angry father in order to see her. I really don't know what has come over me, but it doesn't matter. I just want to lay my eyes on her. Then I can go back to my life, train later if I find the energy after the day I had at work.

I park my bike in one of the spots designated for visitors in front of the large skyscraper. My feet keep pushing me forward, but I welcome their ability to bring me to her. Excitement courses through me as I wait for the elevator to take me up to the very top floor. It feels like I'm about to vibrate because I'm so close to her now, it sets me on fire. I feel alive with the anticipation of seeing her light blue eyes and black hair, her smile and her scar. The thin line slicing through her lips somehow makes her sexier, if that's even possible.

The elevator doors slide open, sending my heart into a frenzy. Scarlette is talking to Dan, the guy from marketing I've hated since I just saw him smiling at her like she's the most beautiful person in the world. I mean she is, but it bothers me. Actually, it infuriates me. I stalk toward them, sinking into the chair across from Scarlette's and waiting impatiently for her to finish her conversation with that jerk.

Finally, her eyes meet mine, and she sits to pay attention to me.

"Here to see your father?" she asks with a smile I know she's forcing. Scarlette is wearing faint yellow eyeshadow to match her dress and the flowers she put in her braids. *God, she's so breathtaking.*

"Yes," I lie because I know at this time of day, my father takes his half-hour break. There are still twenty minutes left until he returns, which means I have twenty minutes to study Scarlette's features.

"He isn't here right now, but feel free to wait in his office. He should return soon," she replies, still offering me that fake smile to be polite.

"My father hates it when I wait for him in his office." It's another lie, but I want to stay out here, stay close to her.

"Okay," is all she replies, turning to her computer while I keep my eyes fixated on hers.

"You enjoying your work at this bloodsucking company?" I want to see her fire, the heat of her passion when she fights with me.

"Very much," she says with a fake smile. I tilt my head in response.

"Do you steal candy from toddlers in your free time too?" She snickers at that, and it's the sweetest sound I've ever heard.

"I don't particularly care for children, so I don't know what you're trying to achieve by asking that question," Scarlette replies, grinning at the screen because she got a glimpse of the shocked expression that slipped across my face.

"Hmmm." She rolls her eyes at my response. My gaze fixates on her scar, wondering how it would feel to trace it with my finger. I shake my head. Jesus, I need to get the thought of touching her out of my head.

"What? Did that answer not satisfy the image of me you've crafted in your head?" she asks, and I shake my head because that's exactly what I was thinking.

"It didn't. I saw you as the type of person who would love a big family." She crinkles her nose in response.

"God, no. I'd rather be the cool aunt to Violet's children." This woman is full of surprises, good surprises too. "Maybe find a partner to grow old with down the road," she adds, speaking more to herself than me as she gets lost in her thoughts. I can't help my next words, no matter how hard I try to hold them back.

"Your taste in men is questionable," I blurt out, earning me a genuine chuckle from her.

"You mean Dan?" she asks, and I give her a strained nod, anger making my usual serious face even more so. Scarlette fully smiles at me then. "You are unbelievable," she says, shaking her head.

"I don't like the way he was looking at you," I reply and almost slap my mouth to keep it shut. *Did Elias slip me some truth serum this morning?*

"You do realize he's happily *married* to his husband of five years, right?" This sends a wave of heat up my neck until it settles in my face. "Holy crap, are you blushing?" she asks, teasing me for the way I misread the way he looked at her. I frown, which only brightens up her features more. *Esa mujer me tiene loco.*

"I don't blush, *arcoíris*," I reply, and she cocks an eyebrow at my nickname for her.

"What did you just say?" I don't give her a response. Instead, I change the subject altogether.

"So, what are you studying at uni?" I ask, grabbing her stress ball from the desk. She watches me with confusion.

"None of your business," she says with a smirk, and I almost smile. Goddamn, this woman is hot.

"Hey, Dan?" I call out because he's close enough to hear me. When he realizes who is addressing him, he straightens out his back and approaches me with a respectful stance and smile.

"Yes, sir?" He seems scared of me, which I guess I understand considering what expression my face is pulled into all the time.

"Don't you find it so impressive what Scarlette is studying?" His young face reveals uncertainty.

"Engineering?" he asks, and I turn my head toward Ms. Rainbow.

"Yes, engineering," I say, fighting back a grin. It's the hardest thing I've had to do in a long time. Scarlette flashes me an annoyed frown. "That's all, Dan," I add, allowing the poor guy to leave. I could sense how uncomfortable he grew with this exchange between her and me.

"What do you even want from me? Is it amusing for you to drive me crazy?" she asks, and I lean forward, my interest piqued.

"I drive you crazy?" I ask, my eyes lighting up before I can stop them. Scarlette merely shakes her head, her black curls dancing with the action. *Puñeta*. Why? Why is she this gorgeous?

"Yes, very much so. Now, can you leave me alone? I have to figure out how to fix this annoying laptop. The screen keeps freezing on me," she complains, turning to the device and pressing some buttons that won't help her.

"Here, let me see," I say, my voice turning soft as I walk around the desk and guide her chair further against it. "May I?" I ask, and she looks up at me, nodding once.

Then, I trap her between my arms to reach her keyboard and work on unfreezing the screen for her. My head is right next to hers as I force my gaze to fixate on the computer. There are a hundred better ways to do this, but when I smell the lavender scent coming off her, filling my nose, and then spreading through my bloodstream, I know I've made the right choice by putting us in this position. I also realize the same thing when I notice her staring at me from the corner of my eye. Half her bottom lip is tucked between her teeth, and her chest rises and falls too rapidly.

She's attracted to me.

Fuuuuck.

I shouldn't like that as much as I do, but I could pop a bottle of champagne right now. Just knowing her body responds to me sends the sweetest sensation through my system, lighting every cell and atom of mine on fire. It makes me linger, my body close to hers but not quite touching. I want to touch her, but I can't. I shouldn't. I won't. Not until she asks me to.

Wait.

Even then, I'm not touching her! I'm not putting my heart on the line again. Something's seriously fucking wrong with me, which is why I step away, fighting back the nauseous feeling bubbling up in my throat. I shouldn't have come here, shouldn't have gotten so close to her. What was I thinking? Now the scent of her is burned into my memory, and I doubt I can get it out any time soon.

"There, that should fix it for now," I mumble and walk over to where I left my phone, wallet, and keys on the desk. I have to escape, get as far away from her as possible.

"Thank you," she almost whispers, but I don't look at her again. I'm on my way home to take a shower and calm my pained muscles. They're exhausted from the amount of restraint it took to step away from Scarlette.

"*Mijo*? What are you doing here?" Dad asks, somehow making this situation even worse than it already is.

"Nothing, sorry. I was just leaving," I say and swiftly move past him, toward the elevator. My father follows.

"Did you want to talk?" he asks, but I shake my head.

"Just get Scarlette a new computer. Hers won't last much longer and she's getting frustrated," I say, pressing the button to go down.

"Scarlette? Wait, do you like her?" I let out a harsh, unamused snort.

"Don't be ridiculous," I say, but not even the most naïve of people would believe me.

Jesus Christ, I like her. I know hardly anything about her, but I like her.

Kill me now.

Chapter 8

Scarlette

My head is still spinning. Storm is the most infuriating man I've ever met, but my mind hasn't found a way to stop turning since his body trapped mine, since he came so close to touching me. I wanted more. It's been two days, and I've thought about nothing but how badly I wanted him to put his hands on me. He smelled like sandalwood, and it drew me in, had me imagining things I have never imagined a specific person do to me.

"Why don't you just ask him out?" Violet says, and I look up at her, furrowing my brows. I was zoning out again, which has happened too many times recently for her not to notice.

"Who?" I ask, trying to play dumb. My best friend flashes me an irritated eye roll.

"Storm. You're so into him, anyone could see it," she says, and I actually burst into laughter.

"I think you're seeing things. That man is aggravating. We haven't had a normal conversation since we met, and I doubt it will ever change," I reply, tugging my feet under my butt and shaking my head.

"So? He doesn't have to become your boyfriend. Just go get some," she says, and I laugh again.

"You're being ridiculous."

I don't have time for a boyfriend, let alone the complications it would carry. Plus, I don't think I'm the type of person who could be with someone just for sex. I need to be able to trust the person I plan on being intimate with. Storm looks like he'd be fantastic in bed, but the way we're going, I'll never ask him to touch me.

"Can we change the subject? You wanted help solving a math problem you got in your Economics class, and I'm your woman for the job," I say, smiling brightly at my best friend.

Engineering requires high-level skills in mathematics, but I actually enjoy it. I love the way I get to work toward a specific problem with only one possible outcome. You either have the right answer or you don't. I was never good at all that interpretation stuff English requires. My imaginative side is very overpowered by my logical, rational one.

"Yeah, please, help me. I'm struggling," she admits with a nervous laugh, and we spend the next hour figuring out her homework.

I explain the math as simply to her as possible, making sure she understands a step completely before moving on to the next one. Luckily, I have a lot of patience when it comes to helping Violet with something, especially something I adore. People have always given me weird looks for admitting how much I love physics, math, and science in general, but I don't mind. This is my calling. Becoming an engineer is who I'm meant to be. I'm certain of it.

"You're annoyingly smart, much more so than I am," Vi eventually blurts out, but I nudge her shoulder with mine.

"So are you, just in a different field! Don't compare us, it takes away from your accomplishments, and that would be a shame. You're a remarkable woman, Violet." My best friend looks up at me, disbelief in her eyes.

"You really are just pure positivity, aren't you?" she asks, and I beam at her.

"The world is bleak enough as is. I might as well light it up, even if it's only by a little bit," I reply, standing up to get us some water before we keep studying.

"I have to tell you something you won't find any positivity in," Vi says after a moment of silence, hesitation clear as day in her voice.

"Tell me."

Violet's brown eyes search my face, a frown tugging down the corners of her wide lips. *Uh oh.* Whatever she wants to tell me, it can't be good.

"Your mom keeps calling and checking in with me to see how you're doing. She thinks you can't handle this new change with your anxiety," Vi explains, and understanding washes through me.

"Well, I get it. I made her life very difficult with my mental health struggle, and now she's worried I'm playing down how I'm actually feeling. It's understandable," I reply, sinking back into my seat. Violet stares at me in disbelief again.

"How are we best friends? If my mom was snooping around behind my back, I'd be furious. Hell, I'd fucking scream at her. You can't let her do this," she says, but I place my hand on her shoulder, the softness of my touch calming her a little.

"You don't know how hard my anxiety attacks were for my mom. She had no idea what was happening to me, and it was scary for her. She felt helpless," I explain, but Vi still gives me that same frown as before.

"Your anxiety attacks should never have been about how your mom felt. Sure it was difficult, but they are yours, your struggle, your battle, not hers. Never hers." My eyes drop to the table while her words settle in my chest.

I disagree. When you're the person throwing everyone's life upside down with whatever mental illness decides to dig its claws into you, it's impossible not to think about how it's affecting the people in your life. It makes you feel like a burden, which only worsens the situation. I saw what my mom went through in the first six months of my anxiety. I saw how much it tore her down to be unable to help me, so now, she needs to know how I'm doing from everyone around me. She thinks I'd lie to reassure her, but I wouldn't do that. Except for the one big anxiety attack and a few small ones here and there, I've had no problem. There is always a small hint of it in the back of my mind, lingering in my chest. That's just how it works. I've learned to accept it as a part of me.

"Oh, shit, I forgot to tell you something else. Elias is stopping by later to bring me my purse. I left it at his place yesterday by accident," she says, and I smile at her.

"So, you're over Anna?" I ask, and my best friend's eyes widen with realization.

"I haven't thought about her since I met Elias. Holy shit," she replies, staring off into the distance with a little smirk tugging on the corner of her mouth. "There's just something about him, about the way he makes me feel, that causes everything else to vanish. We've only hung out so far, no kissing or touching in any way, but maybe I should make a move. I really like him," she says right as the familiar sound of a motorcycle engine roars in front of our house.

Wait.

There are two.

One doesn't make that much noise, and I almost slap my forehead when I look out the window to see Storm pull off his helmet. His hair sticks all over the place, but he gets it under control with a single slide-through of his hand. My heart is accelerating more and more with each second, making breathing unbearably hard. I can't decide what's hotter, him or the red Kawasaki he just rode up our driveway. Either way, my body is reacting in ways I'm not proud of, a too-familiar ache settling between my legs when he drops his helmet on the seat, the muscles in his arms flexing.

"One night, and I'm convinced he'd take care of all your needs," my best friend whispers in my ear before ripping the door open and sprinting into Elias' arms.

He catches her with ease, laughing from the bottom of his heart. He's happy with Violet, I can tell.

Meanwhile, I step outside too, walking over to his green bike to study it. It's a Kawasaki Ninja 1,000, but his is an older model, probably 2017 or 2018. I run my fingers over the seat, bringing them to the throttle to feel the rough plastic under the tips of them. I miss my bike. I know it was for the best I sold it, necessary even, but I miss it so much.

"You ride?" Elias asks, and my eyes briefly shift to Storm, who is leaning against his bike with his trained arms crossed in front of his chest. His eyes are on me while a scowl rests on his full lips. My eyes briefly linger on his birthmark before I turn to his friend.

"I used to. I had to sell my bike for tuition," I explain, forcing myself not to look at Storm again. I fail. I catch him staring off into the distance with a bothered look on his face. I can't read him, and it annoys me. The need to see into his mind, to understand him, nearly knocks the air from my lungs.

"Damn. What bike did you have?" Elias again. He's more interested in my life than Mr. Stone over there, which sends a stinging pain through my chest. I ignore it, smiling as I shift my head back to the man that makes my best friend happy.

"A black Kawasaki Ninja 600," I reply, my fingers stuck on the throttle. I haven't figured out a way to let go yet.

"Fuck, you hear that, Storm? *Ella monta motocicletas.*" I don't catch that last sentence, but soon realize it was in Spanish. The brooding man next to me nods his head.

"*Lo escuché,*" Storm replies, his voice low, seductive. The way the Spanish falls from his lips makes a wave of heat settle everywhere inside of me.

"Would you like to ride it? I don't mind," Elias says to me, but I shake my head immediately, bringing back my smile.

Tears sting my eyes as my emotions overwhelm me. I've given up a lot for my dream, and it's worth it. It merely hurts sometimes, especially when I stare at a bike that isn't mine, knowing I won't be able to afford one for the next five, if not ten, years of my life.

"I appreciate the offer, but I should go back to my school work. It was nice to see you guys," I say, inhaling deeply to get rid of the tears.

It doesn't work, so I walk away, unwilling to let myself bring down their mood. I hate letting negativity infiltrate my mind, but sadness sometimes needs to take charge for a little. It's up to me then to try and push past it, no matter how difficult it gets. I don't win every fight, but I do my best, which is all I will ever ask of myself.

"Scar?" Storm's voice fills my ears, and I'm so surprised at his nickname for me, sadness vanishes from my chest. I spin around, sensing Violet's eyes going wide from beside me. "Take my bike, I will take Elias'. Come for a quick ride with me," he says, holding out his helmet for me to take.

I don't know what compels me to go, maybe the instant regret I felt for turning down Elias' offer. Maybe it's simply missing how carefree I feel on a bike. No. It's not the carefreeness I miss. It's the feeling of belonging, the sense of being in my happy place.

I shouldn't take Storm's helmet, shouldn't mount his bike before slipping on the gear—he even hands me a motorcycle jacket with armor for my safety. The inside of his helmet smells like him, sandalwood, and I take a deep breath, letting it wash through me.

Storm watches me for a moment, and then does something I would have never expected from him. He steps toward me, closing the distance between us, before reaching for the straps and tightening them, ensuring the helmet sits properly. His fingertips are so close to my skin, it's almost impossible not to lean into him to have them on me. I manage to fight off that urge before it consumes me.

"Be careful. Mine has a lot more horsepower than your old one," he says once he's satisfied with my protection.

It's almost sweet how he makes sure I'm safe. One might even think he cares. I know better. Whatever reason he has for letting me ride his bike, I don't trust it. But I'm also too giddy to question it.

"Yes, sir," I reply, earning myself a strained nod from him.

He's always so serious. I wonder why he never smiles, but I don't linger on it. He doesn't give me a moment to as he mounts Elias' bike, putting on his friend's helmet.

"Follow me," he calls out loud enough for me to hear, and I give him a thumbs up.

I haven't been this freaking excited in a long time. I'm so happy all of a sudden, it hits me like a tsunami right in the chest. I let it wash over me until every part of me vibrates from joy, joy Storm has brought me.

How strange...

Chapter 9
Storm

Never in my entire life have I let anyone get on my bike, ever. So, I don't quite understand what the fuck just happened, or why I'm so okay with Scarlette riding it. As a matter of fact, I've let myself smile under my best friend's helmet ever since she overtook me on the highway, speeding down it and enjoying her zoomies. My eyes stay on her ass for a moment too long, but I can't help myself when she wiggles it from side to side from excitement. I let out a laugh under my helmet, speeding up to overtake her.

She doesn't let me.

Scarlette goes even faster, causing my heart rate to dip and the color to drain from my face. She knows what she's doing, I'm well aware of it, but the thought of anything happening to her almost sends me into cardiac arrest.

"Slow down," I scream after her, hoping she will hear me.

She turns her head back, watching me do the hand movement—extending my arm to the side and pressing down on an imaginary brake pedal several times—to tell her to decrease her speed. I've entered panic mode, something I haven't felt in a long time on my bike.

"Pull over," I call when we're next to each other, and Scarlette obeys immediately, following me to the side of the highway.

Fear has consumed my body, making it shake. We weren't even going that fast, but something has come over me, and it won't go away as I rip my helmet off my head and storm toward her. I'm not angry, but every part of me is undeniably terrified of anything happening to Scarlette. *Why?* Fuck, I wish I had even an inkling of an idea.

"What are you thinking? You could get yourself killed!" I yell, and she takes a step back, removing my helmet from her head too.

"Storm, I'm fine—" I know she isn't finished talking, but there is no logic or rationality left in my brain. If anyone else had gone as fast as her, including me, I wouldn't have minded. Sometimes we just need to let go a little of the restraints, but not her. She can't put her life in danger like that.

"That was reckless. You know the other drivers on the road don't look out for bikers! You know how fucking easy it is to get mowed down by a truck!" I'm screaming, I'm so upset with myself for caring so much and not having found a way to ease the panic weighing on my chest.

Scarlette stays quiet for a moment, anger and understanding on her beautiful features. I would be angry with me too. I'm acting like a dick, but I don't care. Nothing can happen to her, especially not after I was the one to offer her a ride on my bike.

"I'm sorry if you were worried about your machine. I shouldn't have—" I cut her off again, this time shock replacing everything else. *That's what she thinks I'm worried about?*

"I don't give a damn about the bike, Scarlette! You just can't go that fast, you will get yourself killed," I say, rubbing my face with my right hand.

My whole body goes rigid when her hand slides onto my arm, comforting me... She's comforting me. Shit, I have to sit down. I have to do something. My legs have turned into jello, the adrenalin wearing off now because she's touching me.

All because her fingers are sending a wave of heat through my body, settling so deep inside of me, it reaches places I've never dared to imagine were real.

"I didn't mean to scare you," she says, and I have to step back, breaking the contact between us. It gives me back control of myself. "It wasn't my intention, but I'm fine, Storm, I promise. I've been riding bikes since I was five years old, it's like breathing to me, okay?" Her words make perfect sense. They also send a wave of guilt over me. I shouldn't have overreacted when she knows what she was doing. I'm such an asshole. "You don't have to yell at me anymore," she adds in a low whisper, and I let out a frustrated groan. Correction. I'm *the biggest* asshole.

"I'm sorry, Scar," I blurt out, taking another step toward her despite my better judgment. A frown lingers on her usually happy face, and I want to kiss it away, replace any negativity with only the purest of emotions.

"That's the second time you've called me that," she says, her lips still pulled downward.

"You don't like it?" I ask, taking another step toward her. Her eyes fly to mine, meeting my hungry gaze. So blue. Her eyes are so blue, like a pastel sapphire stone.

"Is it because of my name or because of this?" she says, drawing her finger over the length of the scar cutting through her lip.

"Both," I admit because that faint line has been drawing me to her mouth from the moment we met. I've wanted to trace it with my lips, show her just how beautiful I think it is.

"Then I don't like it," she replies, stepping away from me the same moment I decide to give in to the urge of touching her cheek.

"Why?" She's about to shove the helmet back on when she hesitates.

"Because I hate this reminder of the darkest moment in my life. Hate how visible it is on my face. It can't be hidden with makeup, and it has people staring at me wherever I go," she says, causing my eyebrows to scrunch together.

"You think everyone stares at you because of your scar?" I know without a doubt it isn't true, not with a smile, glow, and body like hers.

"Can we leave now? Spending time together usually doesn't get us anywhere but an argument and after all of the excitement, I desperately need to sleep," she says, but I'm baffled by how blind she is to her own beauty.

"Answer my question, please, Scar." She lets out a huff.

"I tell you I don't like it, but it doesn't matter to you, does it? You will continue to call me by a nickname I despise, won't you?" I take a step toward her and then another until she's pressed against my bike, my face close to hers. I'm not touching her, but, God, I want to.

"Something as beautiful as your scar deserves to be worshipped. Do you understand me?" She's frozen as every tension leaves her body. Scar was ready to fight my words, but not anymore. They've surprised her, softened her walls.

"You make no sense to me," she whispers as I battle with the urge to kiss her lips. Our breaths are both heavy, so close to each other I can almost taste her, but I keep my distance to keep her comfortable.

"And you none to me. I should dislike you for working for my father, dislike you for challenging me, frustrating me." Her shoulders return to their tense state.

"Then why don't you?" she asks, her chest rising and falling so abruptly, it almost distracts me from hiding my emotions in the way I've practiced for years. The only times I don't control them are under my helmet and in the bedroom. I'm not about to let her change that.

"Who says I don't?" I say, and she drops her head.

I hate myself, but it had to be done. She can't be attracted to me, she cannot want me. I don't know if I will ever be able to trust another person enough to give my heart to them. Scarlette is getting closer to giving me that false sense of security with every second I spend in her presence, but I have to let self-preservation kick in now.

"Let's get you home," I say, but she's already ahead of me, mounting the bike and driving away. Waiting for me seems to be the last thing she wants to do. I can't blame her either.

When I get back to her place, she's already inside her house, allowing disappointment to settle inside my chest. This is what I asked for, but it's not what I want. For fuck's sake, I want Scarlette, and it's becoming a big problem. I can't want her. She'll break me if I let her in. I just patched myself up, I can't go back.

"What the fuck did you say to her, *pendejo*?" Elias asks when I pull his helmet off, throwing it to him.

"I'm going home."

I grab my own helmet, cursing under my breath when her lavender scent fills my nose. I try not to think about the fact that only a minute ago, Scarlette was sitting on *my* seat, riding *my* bike. It doesn't do anything but give me a headache and make me nauseous with guilt.

Without my jacket on, the wind freezes my arms, but I welcome the pain. It overpowers the emotional one I've inflicted on myself. It also distracts me from overthinking what I've done. Well, at least until my limbs have frozen and everything numbs. Then the thoughts come crashing back in.

I know nothing about this woman, but we've been at each other's throats from day one. How that doesn't turn me off the idea of seeing her is beyond me. If anything, it makes me want to be with her more. I love my bike, but it doesn't come close enough to making me feel alive anymore, not like Scarlette's smile and our bickering does.

I really, undoubtedly like her beyond return.

No amount of fear is going to keep me from seeing her again. I want to get to know her, find out every little thing that makes her happy. Every smile she offers the world, I want to witness. The fire inside of her, I want to fuel. The softness in her eyes, I want to soak in it. She's got me wrapped around her finger, and there is no unwinding myself from her grasp anymore. I can try to stay away to protect myself, but what's the point of living if I deny myself the chance of caring for someone, especially for someone as remarkable as Scarlette?

It's like a switch flips in my mind, forcing me not to care about getting my heart shattered by her. Any second in her presence is worth the pain that comes with it or after. Anything is worth being around her, getting blinded by her sunshine, getting to see the rainbows she leaves in her wake.

God.

I hope I didn't fuck everything up for good.

Chapter 10

Scarlette

"Who is your favorite driver?" Halo asks, tugging on my sleeve from excitement. He's practically bouncing up and down in his chair after I told him why I want to become an engineer.

"Leonard Tick," I reply, and he leans away, slapping the table ever so gently.

"Shut up! He's mine too," he says, shaking his head in disbelief.

Halo and I've been spending a lot of time together in the last week. After Aaron introduced me to his friendship group, they have all done their very best to be welcoming. Bex is one of the kindest, most forthcoming people I have ever met, and I like them a lot. The others have also been quite nice to me, but Halo? He's been unbelievable. Every chance he gets, he makes me laugh or smile, and he seems to enjoy the fact that we're both what others call "sunshine" people. We're always in a good mood, smiling at everyone, the complete opposite of some people.

Yes, I mean Storm.

That grumpy, rude man had some nerve. He listed things he dislikes about me while simultaneously looking at me like he wanted to rip my clothes off and have me right there on his bike. I wouldn't have minded, wouldn't have said no, but then he said something so infuriating, I had to leave. I've known him for a month, and since the day he said those things to me, I've seen him three times.

The first time, I managed to avoid him and hide inside my house. Elias dropped off some food he'd made for Violet, and both of them came with their bikes. The second time, Elias came to pick up my best friend for a ride. I was outside fixing a broken gutter and couldn't run inside quickly enough before his words stopped me.

"You want to be my backpack?" Storm asked me, and I shot him a smile I didn't mean the slightest bit.

"I'd rather eat a snail," I replied, and he gave me a look that said 'are you serious right now'. It made me smile so hard, I almost laughed.

"What if I told you I'd be the backpack?" he offered, but I shook my head.

"No, thank you. I'm never riding your bike again, especially not with your arms around me. I have no desire to have you touch me," I said, well, I lied, but it made his frown deepen and his eyes sparkle with disappointment.

He might not want to show any emotions apart from anger and indifference, but his eyes always give him away. I wonder if anyone's ever looked at him as closely as I have to realize how much he gives away without meaning to.

The third time I saw him was at the office. He sat down in the chair across from mine again, one of his favorite things to do, but he didn't say anything as he waited for his father. It irritated me how he was just there, watching everyone in the office, excluding me. It drove me absolutely mad, but I didn't point out my frustration. I let him sit there until Mr. Rodrick showed up. I think my boss is convinced there is something going on between his son and me, but he keeps things professional, which I appreciate.

"You, Scarlette, you are perfect," Halo says, interrupting my thoughts and bringing me back to reality. It takes me a moment to reorganize my mind until I remember we were talking about our favorite Formula One drivers.

"Is that why you're in love with me?" I tease, but he nods eagerly.

"One million percent, gorgeous, one million percent," he replies, popping one of my strawberries into his mouth.

I offered for him to take as many as he wanted, which is the only reason why I'm okay with him taking food without asking. It's one of my biggest pet peeves when people just steal food off my plate. I will *always* happily share, but, for the love of God, just ask me. It's all I expect.

"How many people have you fallen in love with this week?" I ask him while he stares after a gorgeous brown-haired guy.

"A few," he replies, winking at me before returning his full attention to my face.

"Well, I'm almost honored to be one of them," I say, letting out a genuine laugh.

I'm not interested in Halo. He's hot beyond a doubt, but he's also a player, which is not the kind of person I'd ever see myself becoming interested in, at least not at this point in my life. As a friend, he's great and makes me happy.

"Don't worry, Scarlette, you're my favorite out of all of them," he adds, and I shoot him a suspicious grin.

"Yeah, I'm sure," I say, popping a strawberry into my mouth. Halo brings his fingertips to my cheek, wiping away something I can't see. Nonetheless, this small, little moment has my heart racing and my hands trembling ever so slightly.

"Make a wish," he says as he holds up the eyelash. A smile tugs on the corner of my mouth.

"I don't believe in making wishes," I reply, the memory of every single one of my birthdays slipping into my head.

I used to love blowing out the candles and letting a wish float around in my mind as I did it. Then, my parents lost their jobs. I had to press pause on my career, work tirelessly for two years, and now I took a job I don't like. Storm was absolutely right. I don't believe a company like the one I'm working for fits in with my morals, but I don't have a choice. Tuition comes first and the only way to afford it is by taking every hour Mr. Rodrick spares me. So, I've stopped making wishes. They never come true, not without me working my butt off to make anything happen.

"You don't believe in wishes?" the gorgeous man next to me asks, disbelief all over his face.

"No," is all I answer before picking up another strawberry. He gives me a frown as he turns to my eyelash.

"Fine, I will make a wish for you," he says, blowing it off his thumb and screwing his eyes shut. "There. You will see. It will come true," he adds with a wink, and heat rushes into my cheeks in response.

Asher "Halo" Henderson is way too charming.

The rest of the day goes by dreadfully slowly, but by the time I walk outside, I'm calling Violet, asking her where the heck she is. She was supposed to meet me outside of my classroom, like she does every day, to pick me up and drive me to work. It's a deal we made. I do most of the cooking and chip in for gas, she drives me around.

"Hi," she says into the phone, sounding too chipper for my liking. She's up to something.

"No. What have you done?" I ask, the sound of her giggle filling my ears.

"I made a deal with the devil. Muhahahaha," she replies, and I suck in a sharp breath.

Storm.

"He's going to drive you to work. He called me and said he was on his way there anyway, and it would be no problem to take you with him. Before you protest, I've already left to go to Elias' house for our first official sleepover," she says, and I don't even bother holding the phone away when I let out an inhuman growl. "Down, girl. Storm really wanted to pick you up, and I couldn't deny him after he bribed me with a box full of my favorite candy," she explains, but I hang up on her.

Unbelievable. My best friend has lost her mind if she thinks I will be climbing on Storm's bike, feel his body pressed up against mine, have my arms around him, and feel his muscles so hard and tight... *God.* This isn't healthy anymore. Every part of me aches with need and desperation to have him exactly where my mind was just picturing him, and it's not going to happen. I refuse. Anyone but Storm.

My eyes find him as soon as I step out of the building, leaning casually against his bike with his trained arms crossed in front of his muscular chest. Everything inside of me somersaults and jumps at the sight of him, begging me to approach him. It's almost as if every cell in my body turns to metal and he is the magnet.

"Hey, *arcoíris*," he says as soon as I'm close enough to hear.

Then it happens. It does so too quickly for me to register it fully, but I see it. I see the right side of his mouth briefly slip into an amused smirk. He hardens his features soon, but I got a glimpse of what a smile could possibly look like on his face, and it was the most breathtaking thing I've seen in a while. It has my mind blank, deprived of all the things I wanted to throw at his head for showing up here, for going behind my back and bribing my best friend to abandon me. If the walk to the office wasn't an hour long, I'd already be on my way, but I don't want to be late.

"I'm not getting on your bike," I finally manage to blurt out in a moment of clarity.

Storm doesn't look upset, but he doesn't look happy either. He's so neutral, so indifferent, I wonder why he does this to himself. Showing emotions, especially positive ones, is my favorite thing to do. I don't like to keep things bottled up. I tried to do that in the past, but all it got me was crippling anxiety.

"Come on, love, please don't fight me on this. I even brought you a gift to be nice," he says, turning around to grab something he put on his seat. When he holds it up for me, I almost gasp. It's a small bundle of lavender, tied together with a glittery purple band that slips into a bow at the front.

"Lavender?" I ask, swallowing hard. "Do you know about my—" I cut off, unwilling to tell him myself if he doesn't know. Storm cocks an eyebrow.

"About your love for it? Yes, Scar, I smell it on you every time you're close to me," he replies, and I let out an inaudible sigh of relief. I take the bundle from him, bringing it to my nose so the scent can wash over me, spreading a familiar calmness down my spine.

When I first started getting my anxiety attacks, I did a lot of research to figure out how to help my body when it overcharged with fear. Lavender was one of the most common suggestions because of its calming qualities. I tried it once and now I put a little bit of my special lavender oil on my wrists, neck, and chest every morning. It gets me through most days, but it also carries a sense of nostalgia with it. It helped me when I first needed it most, and it's gotten me through more difficult days than I could have kept count.

"Don't call me that," I whisper, still staring at the bundle. I need to regain some strength, and fighting him on my nickname will do so.

"Scar," he says, tilting my head toward him with his index finger. Electricity shoots through me, sending a wave of heat through my body, originating where his finger is on my skin. He looks serious as he stares into my eyes. "I like my nickname for you too much to stop using it," he adds, and the magical spell breaks.

"I loathe you," I reply, and he narrows his eyes at me.

"*No creo que sea verdad, mami,*" he says, and I let out an annoyed groan both because I can't understand him when he speaks Spanish but also because I never want him to stop. It twists my insides in all the best ways. *Why do I like it so much?*

"Bye, Storm, or whatever your real name is," I say and attempt to walk away, but his words stop me.

"Be my backpack, Scar, just this once. Please." I shake my head.

"Actually, I'm too heavy to be a backpack, sorry," I reply, but he grabs my hand before I can walk away. He pulls on me until I'm against his chest, my hands moving up his torso. He's so hot and hard, I forget how to breathe for a moment. He isn't holding onto me either. Nope. My hands are on his pecs for no reason apart from the needy ache between my legs telling me to keep them there.

"Bullshit. You're perfect," he says, sending another wave of heat through me. "Please, let me drive you," he begs, and I suck in a breath when I remember my body needs oxygen to live.

"But we don't like each other. Why do you insist on taking me to work?" I ask, mostly confused. He's saying all of these sweet things after he told me he should dislike me and might actually. I know he's not into me. His behavior shows the complete opposite of how a person is supposed to act around someone they like. *Right?*

"Maybe not, but I still want to drive you to work. Get on the bike, love, please." His gaze holds mine, and I can't help the smile slipping across my face.

"Has that 'please' you love to throw around ever gotten a 'no' before?" I ask, watching him lift his tongue to the roof of his mouth in response.

"No," he says, the hint of a smirk creeping back onto his face.

I drink it in as much as I can, the way his eyes sparkle and his jaw unclenches. We're too close, my hands still pressed against his torso and his hanging by his side. When I realize, I almost stumble back.

"Then let me be your first," I say as I spot Halo walking toward his car. I will not give Storm the satisfaction of getting his way with me. Plus, the way his jaw ticks from anger when I return the lavender bundle and he sees where I'm going is priceless. "Halo!" I call out, and he turns to me, his face brightening at the sight of me.

"Scarlette, sunshine of my life, how may I help you?" he asks, wrapping his arm around my shoulder as I approach.

"Want to help me annoy that guy with the bike?" I say, and he glances behind me to see who I'm talking about. A smile tugs on his lips.

"Storm?" I nod, making him let out a low chuckle.

"He's been getting on my nerves," I say, leaving out the part about how attracted I am to the grump in the process.

"You want a kiss?" Halo asks, and I look up at him in surprise.

"On the lips?" I've kissed two people in my life, but neither of them was really into it, so I don't have a great amount of experience in this department. Halo chuckles again.

"Yes, gorgeous, on the lips. To make him jealous," he clarifies, and I suddenly feel excitement course through me at the thought of Storm watching me kiss another man.

Will it bother him? Probably. After the reaction he had over Dan, I'm certain of it. For some inexplicable reason, he doesn't like seeing me with other men. *Why do I like the thought of it so much?*

"Yes, but a quick warning, I've never really kissed anyone before." I don't know why I'm sharing this with Halo, but he's my friend, and telling him things like this is comfortable.

"Don't worry, I have enough experience for the both of us," he says, trapping my body between him and his car. "Just pat my chest twice any time you get uncomfortable," he adds, and I swallow hard.

"How long do you plan on kissing me?" I ask, and he grins. Man, Halo is too attractive. His face is chiseled, his features defined. His cheekbones sit high on his face, his lips are full—the top one less so than the bottom one—and his gaze carries pure sex in it.

"However long you think it will take for him to be jealous," he replies, running the back of his fingers over my cheek. Heat rushes into both of them in response.

And then, his mouth is on mine. Halo doesn't waste a second, kissing me in a way I've never been kissed before. He's demanding but in a sweet and gentle way. His hands have moved to my jaw, tilting my head up so he can easily claim my mouth. My knees have turned to putty, everything inside of me has lit on fire, and I can't help my hands from moving to his hips. Halo's tongue swipes over my bottom lip, and I part my lips for him without thinking. He gives an approving groan, slipping his tongue into my mouth so briefly, it leaves me dizzy.

"You think that's enough?" he asks as he pulls back, the kiss not having affected him in the slightest. I, on the other hand, am still in a haze.

"Yeah," I manage to croak out, and Halo gives my cheek a sweet caress.

"I really don't know why people haven't kissed you properly before, Scarlette. You taste as sweet as candy," he says, making me swallow hard. A nervous laugh escapes me, only making him grin. "You need a ride to work?" he asks, and I manage to meet his inquiring gaze again.

"If you don't mind," I reply, and he gives me one more swift kiss before opening the door.

"Not in the slightest. I'm going to be the most desirable man on campus now after the show we just put on, so I owe you," he says, and another nervous laugh leaves me.

"I'm glad this was mutually beneficial," I reply, my cheeks hot with fire and lust. I can't believe I've never taken the time to explore this side of life with anyone. One kiss and I feel exhilarated.

"It was. Look at Storm. He's furious," Halo says, and I glance in Mr. Stone's direction to see less of his usual façade. Halo is right, he's angry, and I'm smiling from ear to ear at his response.

"I'm going to buy you a coffee," I say to my friend as he drives out of the parking lot, waving innocently at Storm as we drive by him.

I laugh so hard, it takes me several minutes to control myself. Storm loves to mess with me, but this time, I stood my ground, no matter how nauseous I am from guilt.

I won't let him mess with my head, not again.

Chapter 11
Storm

Jealousy. Pure, raging, unfiltered jealousy courses through my veins, and I let it. I let it consume every little part of me. I'm convinced I've never been this angry in my entire life, but it's exactly what she wanted. It's why she let the university's fuckboy, Asher goddamn Henderson, stick his tongue down her throat. God, I'm furious. I don't want anyone else's hands on her, and I'm angry because everyone else has a right to when she allows them. That's why I'm really upset. She isn't mine, and nothing has bothered me as much as knowing that in a while.

I feel like punching a fucking wall. The scene of them kissing repeats itself over and over again in my mind, and it's making me want to do violent things to my bike. Kick it, throw it over, anything to release the tension inside of me, which only frustrates me more. I've long considered my bike to be the love of my life, but right now, it's just a piece of machinery I could use to let out my frustration.

Why did she do this to me?

I wanted to bring her a bundle of lavender. I admitted I find her perfect. I allowed myself to be so vulnerable around her, constantly begging her for anything, and she treats me like I'm the worst person she's ever met. Maybe I am... Maybe we've argued and bickered so much now, she thinks that's all I'm good for. Fuck, I've approached this all wrong. If I hadn't pushed so much, I wouldn't have pushed her right into the arms of Halo. Damn it! I'm stupid.

The worst part of it all, I made plans with Dad to be able to have an excuse to drop Scar off there, and now I'm going to have to see her at the desk after what she just pulled. I think about canceling on my father, but our relationship is rocky enough at the moment as is. My complicated situation with Scarlette does not justify brushing him off without giving him any notice. I won't be that disrespectful.

The drive to the building is long enough to calm my racing thoughts but too short to take me to my usual happy place. Instead, I cook in my own anger the whole way there. Eventually, I come to the horrible conclusion that she's not interested in or even attracted to me. I dipped my toe in the water to see if there is anything except for extreme dislike, but she pushed me from the edge, not drawn to me in the slightest.

But then why did she touch me like that? Why did her hands slip up my torso, sending the sweetest wave of electricity through me?

Every single time her body comes close to mine, everything in me screams with a special type of desire. I want more. Every time she presses those fingers against me, I crave more of it. More contact. More proximity. More of her scent and smile and fire. Just more of the rainbow I see every time I look into her blue eyes.

Out of every fucking person in this small town, my mind has to focus on this infuriating woman. I groan under my helmet, then I scream. I stop in front of my dad's building, parking my bike and jumping off it to let out another yell. It's muffled because of my helmet, but an elderly woman still turns her head toward me, probably thinking something's wrong with me. At this point, I couldn't even deny it. Scarlette has sufficiently driven me to the brink of rational thought and action. Soon, I'm going to be making all my decision emotionally, and that cannot happen.

My feet bring me into the expensive building, and, suddenly, everything pisses me off. The extravagant chandeliers hanging from the ceilings are ridiculous. The bright white walls irritate me. All the fancy technological equipment is unnecessary, especially because I know how pricey all of this is. The only thing I like about this building is the openness and the windows everywhere. Even those piss me the fuck off at the moment.

She isn't at her desk. For the first time since she started working here, Scarlette is not sitting at her desk when she's scheduled to work, but I do notice the brand new computer my dad must have put there. If I was in a better mood, I would have probably had to fight back a smile. Instead, I'm growing angrier by the second. Everything irritates me, and I just want to go home and take a bath. It might be the only thing capable of calming me right now. Baths are the closest I feel to my happy place when I'm not on my bike.

I walk toward my dad's office, ready to tell him I'm not feeling well and asking if we could reschedule. But when my eyes catch her, standing in front of Dad with a beautiful smile and elegant posture, I freeze. This is the big problem I'm facing. Seeing her anywhere when she's smiling like nothing is wrong in the world causes two reactions inside of me. One, I want to be around her constantly so that whenever she offers the world this type of smile, I will be one of the few lucky people to experience it. Two, I want to tell her she doesn't always have to be so goddamn happy. I can tell it's a defense mechanism on a deeper level, a way to shield herself from the bad. She needs to be reminded it doesn't have to be this way.

Scarlette deserves to get her breaks too. It must be exhausting to constantly be joyful around others, and I want to become her permanent break, allow her face to do whatever *she* wants it to, not what she thinks will please the people she surrounds herself with.

"Dad," I say, my tone soft, as I walk into the office. My father's face lights up at the sight of me.

"*Mijo*, come in," he replies, waving me inside completely. "Scarlette and I were just talking about the race weekend in Monaco in four weeks' time. Did she tell you she wants to be an F1 race engineer?" he asks, and I cock an eyebrow.

Damn. I was already impressed because she's taking on a male-dominated field and I know she will be a force to be reckoned with, but this? This is next-level badass. It makes me like her even more. *Fuck me.*

"No, we haven't gotten to that part yet," I say through gritted teeth, and Scarlette shoots me a weird look before rolling her eyes.

"Well, then I think we should all go to the race together. I even have some connections to the Grenzenlos team principal Robert Fuchs. I think it would be great for Scarlette to mingle a little considering she's working toward a job there. I will take care of everything, of course," Dad says with a smile, and Scarlette's eyes go wider than I've ever seen anyone's go. Ah, yes, his connection with Robert Fuchs. The one he got because they share the same private jet company. *Rich assholes.*

"Oh, sir, you don't have to do—" He cuts her off.

"Don't be silly. Anything for my son's girlfriend," he says with a smile, and I forget how to breathe.

Scarlette hesitates. *She fucking hesitates.* I would have expected her to jump at the chance of this silence to deny this statement, but she stares at my father with an uncertain expression lingering on her face. I wait. I'm too fucking intrigued about her reaction to do anything but stand there, biting my bottom lip to keep from smiling. This is a huge chance for her, exactly what she needs to get into the circle of people she will be working for in the future. It's a once-in-a-lifetime opportunity she can't pass up, which is probably the reason for her next words.

"Thank you, sir." Then she walks over to me, shooting me a desperate look. "Did you hear that, babe?" she asks, and I frown at her nickname for me. She places a hand on my chest, pleading with me.

"Yes, love. I heard it loud and clear."

I drag my arm around her waist and pull her against my chest, too fucking content with this situation. Little Ms. Rainbow needs the big, bad Storm now. This is too precious, especially the way she gasps at my small display of affection. I shift my attention to my father, giving him a slight nod. What he's offered, paying for this weekend, is pennies to him. It's the reason why Scarlette didn't turn down the offer and why I don't feel bad for going along with it.

"Thank you," I say to him before leading Scar out of the room. "I'll be right back," I assure him, earning me another full-faced smile.

He made an assumption about us dating, which is why he's so happy to hear it's 'true'. Little does he know Scar and I couldn't be further from two people dating, falling in love. Well, at least one of us is.

I guide Scarlette all the way to an empty office with a window that overlooks the parking lot. I see my bike waiting for me and drag a hand down the length of my face, a sigh slipping past my lips. This is very amusing to me, but things have just gotten exponentially more complicated between us. She wasn't interested in me, but now she is pretending to be in front of my father to get something out of it. I should be pissed. Instead... I see an opportunity to make her like me.

"Why did you go along with this?" she asks when a few moments of silence have passed between us.

"Because this is important to you," I reply as if it's the most obvious thing in the world. To me, it is; to her, it's a surprise.

"I should make things right and come clean to your dad," she says, starting to leave the room. I settle against the desk, crossing my arms in front of my chest and watching her closely.

"Or, you could let him believe it, go with me to the Monaco Grand Prix, and get the connections you need for the job position you want in the future," I say, my eyes on her round face as she contemplates my suggestion with confusion.

"And what do you get out of this arrangement? Because we sure as heck won't be a couple in private." *Heck? Oh my God, Scarlette.* I can hardly keep myself from smiling.

"And with that you mean you don't want to cuddle or fuck, am I correct?" Her breathing hitches and I let the smirk settle on my face. I don't care anymore. Let her see how sweet I find her reaction.

"Or kiss or anything sex-related. We'll be nothing more than unfriendly acquaintances. Is that really what you want?" I nod without giving her another response. My face has fallen back into its carefully carved scowl. "Why? You don't gain anything from this then! Nothing physical, nothing personal. What's your goal, Julián?"

My body tenses for two reasons. The first is the fact that she found out my real name and is using it now. The second is the fact that she pronounced it perfectly, not in the English way everyone else uses it. No, her Spanish pronunciation of my name was flawless. Okay, I'm speechless now.

"Is it just to mess with me more?" she asks, and I almost shake some sense into her.

How can she be so blind to the way I crave her warmth? Can she not see the way my very being is drawn to her whenever she enters a room? Is she so appalled by me, she doesn't want to consider the possibility of me liking her?

"Mess with you? I came to your university to drive you to work, even brought you a bundle of lavender because it reminded me of you. Then you stalk off and have Halo stick his tongue down your throat. Who's messing with whom, Scar?" This shuts her up.

"We would never make a convincing couple, Storm," she says, and I take a step toward her.

"Yes, we would, and it starts with you using my real name, love. I'm Julián to you now, not Storm, okay?" Scarlette nods, and I close the distance between us more. "Then, you're going to have to stop looking at me like I'm your worst enemy, at least while we're around other people." I take another step in her direction. Her heart is racing, and I wish I knew what was going through her head. "You need to give at least the impression that you want to touch me, that you can't wait to get me alone and have me naked," I say, my voice merely a whisper. She stares at the floor.

"That shouldn't be too hard," she mumbles so quietly, I almost miss it. Almost. Fuck, I'm filled with excitement now.

"Good," I say, raising my hands to either side of her on the wall. "Because I will get something out of this. My parents will get off my back to find someone, and I will have my peace and quiet," I lie, but she seems to believe me as she nods. My eyes shift to Dan as he passes by the door of the office, his gaze stuck on us the entire time he walks by. One less person we will have to convince.

"Julián?" Scar asks, and I can barely hold myself back from kissing those sweet lips for saying my name right.

"Yes, *arcoíris*?" I'm so close to her, our breaths intertwine.

"I think we should establish ground rules, like you not looking at me like this when we're alone," she says, and I realize I've been staring at her mouth for the past thirty seconds.

"Okay. Ground rules," I blurt out, fighting every cell in my body to step away from her again.

"Is there anything specific you'd want in the rules?" she asks, making me smirk again.

"Anything you want, love, it's yours."

Chapter 12

Scarlette

"Should we write these down?" I ask, getting nervous now. This is reckless and selfish on my part. I don't even know what it is on Julián's—still weird to call him by his real name and not a nickname.

"If you'd like," he says, sitting down in one of the seats at the desk. His usual scowl is back on his face, but he gave me two smirks earlier, faint but on his face nonetheless. They made my heart race at an unhealthy speed.

"Okay," I reply, taking the chair next to his.

I'm nervous. I made a stupid decision earlier, and now, we're going to pretend we're dating so his father will help me. My gaze meets his, seeing amusement sparkle in his eyes.

"You're enjoying how flustered I am, aren't you?" I ask, and he leans back, turning his chair to face me completely.

"Yes." It's all I get, but it causes a low groan to leave me.

"Rule number one," I start, pulling up the notes app on my phone to write them down. "No more bickering or fighting in front of people," I say, and Julián nods in agreement.

"I'll behave if you will," he replies, and I roll my eyes, ignoring his comment.

"Rule number two: we keep the PDA to a minimum. I don't need you to hold my hand or hug me all the time. I am not the type of person who likes that," I lie because I'm pretty sure with him, if this would be real, I'd constantly want his hands on me.

"So, no kissing?" he asks, causing heat to rise up in my chest and neck, and then settle in my cheeks.

"No," I reply, pretending to be focused entirely on my phone despite his eyes trailing over my body.

"Fine."

He lets out a yawn, stretching his arms into the air until his shirt lifts and allows me to catch a glance at his V-line and the trail of hair running from his belly button down to his boxers. Holy fu—

"If you change your mind, you let me know, Scar."

"Why? So you can tease me about it?" I challenge, and he leans forward, placing his elbows on his knees.

"No," is the only thing he says. It drives me crazy.

"You are infuriatingly vague, do you know that?" I ask, but his eyes are fixated on my lips again, causing my head to spin.

"Yes," he replies. One of his hands drops to my knee before he pats it. "Next rule, love. Stop getting distracted," he says, and I let out a laugh I don't mean. God, he's frustrating at times. All times.

"Rule number three: as soon as we get back from Monaco, this ends," I go on, and his jaw tenses, ticks with something I can't read.

"Hmmm," he says, clicking his tongue. "Rule number four: you have to stop thinking I do everything to tease you. I don't. This is important to you, and getting my parents off my back is going to help me too," he goes on, and I nod absentmindedly.

It's good this is beneficial for both of us. It also explains why he went along with this considering how rocky our acquaintanceship has been. A month of chaos has already passed between us. This agreement might be what we need to at least start tolerating each other enough to keep from fighting all the time. Maybe we will even like each other as friends, who knows?

"Do you know anything about Formula One?" I ask, bringing myself back to the moment.

"Yes, love, I know everything about it. I watch it every race weekend," he says, and I beam up at him.

"Who is your favorite driver?" This is not a conversation we need to have, but I'm curious.

"I have a feeling you have a very strong opinion on this and my answer will be heavily judged. I decline to answer," he says instead, and I burst into laughter. He watches me with amusement and pride.

"Okay, I'm making this rule number five: you have to at least tolerate Leonard Tick because he's my absolute favorite," I add, and Julián nods in agreement.

"He's the best driver on the grid, maybe to have ever walked this Earth." *Stop it.* I search his face to see if he's messing with me, but there is sincerity in his features and tone.

"Julián, Julián, Julián," I say because we've shared a wholesome moment, and it's one of my favorite things now.

His face grows even more serious as he leans forward to take the phone out of my hands. He's careful enough to ensure I could keep it if I didn't want to give it to him, which surprises me. This man hasn't demanded anything of me. He's been gentle, even as we fought, and it makes me think he might care for me. The thought is so ridiculous, I shut it down immediately.

"Do we tell anyone?"

This question shuts me up for a brief moment. I don't keep secrets from Violet. She's the one person I have never lied to in my entire life. The question alone sends a shiver down my back.

"I can't keep this from Vi," I say out loud, even if it's more to myself. Julián gives an agreeing hum.

"I won't be able to lie to Elias either." They're best friends, maybe brothers on some level like Violet and I are sisters.

"So we tell them, but only these two. Plus, if we tell one, the other would probably hear about it anyway," I say and earn myself another agreeing nod.

"But only those two. Not our parents, friends, or anyone else." It's my turn to nod then. "Good," he adds, inhaling deeply. His torso rises so much, it shows off his broad chest and shoulders. He isn't too wide, but lean and muscular anyway. He's... perfect.

"Good," I repeat to distract myself from the way I keep ogling him.

"Okay, real rule number five: no kissing or dating anyone else. If we want to make this seem real, you can't go around asking Halo fucking Henderson to kiss you," he says. It's my turn to lean back in my chair then.

"Why did that bother you so much?" I'm amused, but he isn't. He's the opposite.

"I think we should go on a few dates to ensure people believe we're actually dating. After today, they'd probably need to see me stick my tongue down your throat to believe it, but we can also make that happen a different way." If I didn't know better, I'd really think this man was jealous. His unique eyes travel over my face, sending a wave of heat to my cheeks.

"And how do we do that?" I ask, taking back my phone as he hands it to me. Julián stands up, straightening out his shirt before leaning down just enough to cause my breathing to hitch with his proximity. God, he's hot and smells so good.

"I'll pick you up on Friday and we will go on a date. Then, next Monday, we will go to the first soccer game of the season. It's your university against the neighboring town's, right?" he asks, and I barely manage to nod.

"Okay, Friday and Monday it is," I manage to croak out, my voice breaking because his face is hovering over mine, and I'm struggling to contain the urge to beg him to kiss me.

"I'll be at your place at seven on Friday." I nod in response. "And for Monday, love, wear a tank top, please," he says, and I cock both eyebrows, snapping back to reality.

"I'm not letting you tell me what to wear," I reply, and he lets out a sigh.

"Please, Scar, I will bring something for you, and it requires you to wear a tank top or a very light shirt. This will be the only time I will dare ask you to wear something for me," he says, and I frown.

"Only if you stop calling me 'Scar'." For the third time in half an hour, he smirks. My heart does multiple somersaults.

"I need to have a nickname for you if we're going to be dating, *arcoíris*," he replies, placing his index finger under my chin and titling my head up.

"Is that Spanish for, I don't know, enemy or something?" I ask, but my voice is pathetically weak. I wish I knew why his touch has me feeling dizzy, but I can't figure it out. Julián lets go of me as he steps back.

"No." This man and his one-word responses are driving me wild.

"You know what? I'm already regretting agreeing to this and we haven't even been fake dating for ten minutes. Jesus. Let me get to work before I'm late to start," I say, jumping out of the chair. I expected him to back away but instead, my chest presses against his.

"Careful now, love, you don't want to break the rules already, do you?" he asks, but right now, I've forgotten about everything we've just written down.

"What rules?" I blurt out before I can stop myself, and the back of his hand lifts to caress my cheek for the briefest moment.

"Remember. Let me know when you want to change them," he says and makes his way toward the door. My mind unwinds, clarity spreading through it.

"'When'?" I ask with an amused chuckle.

"When, Scarlette. I won't do ifs with you."

And with that vague statement, he leaves the office and me to my spiraling thoughts.

Chapter 13

Storm Julián

I've been driving around on my bike for an hour just to do one very simple thing: smile. My cheeks burn from the exhaustion of twisting my facial features into the most brilliant smile I've placed on my face in years. Scarlette and I have made a deal which will make me hers and her mine for the duration of four—granted, it's a very short time—weeks. For now. Four weeks for now, but I'm hoping I can convince my father to take her to more races. That'll be a problem for later. My mind is set on getting her to like me back in the next few weeks, no matter what it takes.

The way I feel about her is exhilarating. She's breathed life back into my lungs, and I've become addicted to her proximity, her scent, her smile, her fucking everything. And she wants me too. I can feel it, sense the way her breathing accelerates when I'm near, and see the way goosebumps spread over her skin when mine grazes hers. She's attracted to me, this much is clear as day now, but I don't want her to only feel that toward me. I want to earn her trust. I want to learn how to make her happy so I can do it all the time. I want to be the man she deserves. It may have taken me a bit to get here, but I've built a house now, and I'm not leaving until I'm everything she needs, or, of course, if she kicks me to the curb.

At this moment, though, I'm still grinning, still too happy to return my soul back to my body. It's floating in the clouds, enjoying the carefreeness Scarlette has offered me. Yes, there are a million things I have to do today, tomorrow, and the day after, but they don't seem to matter at this point. My training might be the only thing battling with my mind about my priorities, but I will make time for it, I always do. I have a race next Saturday after all.

Mamá demanded I come over for dinner when she heard I have a girlfriend I didn't tell her about, and, naturally, as soon as I told Elias where I was going, he said he was joining. He loves Mamá. My dad too, in a way, but not like he does my mother. Elias lost his parents in a car crash when he was five years old. His grandfather raised him afterward, but Mamá became someone very special to him. She became the mother he never thought he could have again. Mamá, being who she is, welcomed him without a moment's hesitation. Her heart holds so much love, my dad's too, I've never minded sharing my parents with him. If anything, I've always adored how close we all are.

I park my bike in front of the double garage next to my parents' house, staring at the mansion. Extravagant, expensive, topped off with pillars upholding the structure on the sides. It's ridiculous. Absolutely and undoubtedly ridiculous, but Dad is a big fan of things that cost a lot of money. I've never bothered asking him why he feels this way. I know he grew up in a poor neighborhood in Colombia and working his way to the top is something he's very proud of, as he should be. But it doesn't change the fact that I think he shouldn't keep all that money to himself.

Mamá grew up in Puerto Rico where she met my sperm donor and moved with him because he got a job opportunity here. Then he decided he had enough of his family and left a week after Mamá found out she was pregnant. *Fucking asshole.*

The sound of my best friend's motorcycle roars in my ears, and I turn to watch him park it right beside mine. He slips off his helmet, storming toward me before bombarding me with questions.

"Why did Mamá call me and say you and Scarlette are dating?" he says, and I scrunch my eyebrows at him. This is the first time he didn't say 'your mom', but fully embraced the title she told him to use ages ago. An invisible string tugs at the corner of my mouth.

"Because I am," I reply, making him sweat a little by not giving too many details at first. He hates it when I do this. I love it.

"*Te voy a matar,*" he says, and I cross my arms in front of my chest, keeping my amusement hidden. *I'm going to kill you.* I mean, he can try, but we both know who the stronger one is.

"*Qué dramático.*" I click my tongue, watching anger shoot across his face. This is too good not to keep going, but he will lose it if I push him too hard. "It's a long story, and you might want to sit," I suggest, so he sits down right on the spot, not bothering to move to the stairs a few steps beside him. I shake my head.

Then, I share the story of today, all the way from going to her university to pick her up to us setting ground rules for our ruse. Elias watches me closely, waiting for any type of reaction, but I've practiced indifference on my face for too many years. No one knows why I've become so hard on the outside. No one, not even Elias, knows why every time I smile, guilt spreads through me. I've never shared what happened with anyone. The plan is to take this experience to my grave.

"You're fake dating Scarlette?" he asks to clarify.

"Yes," I reply.

"You're not actually dating her, though, so there will be no touching, kissing, or sex," he says, again to clarify the situation. For which one of us? I'm not sure.

"Yes," I reply. Elias lets out a strained laugh.

"Why? Why would you agree to do this? What's in it for you? I get Scarlette's intention, but yours? Your parents haven't been on your ass to find someone new. They understand you've been hurt, that you have trust issues now," he says, and I decide to sit down across from him on the floor, watching his perfectly-plucked eyebrows rise up his face.

"I like her a lot, man." *Puñeta.* Five words I didn't mean to say but because I hold no secrets—but one of course—from my best friend, they spilled from my lips anyway. I would die for this guy. How could I ever keep this from him?

"You don't even know her," Elias replies, but for some reason, I take offense.

"I know she's twenty, worked her ass off to support her parents because that is how much she loves them. Prioritized them over her dream, however, gave up everything, including a bike she adored, to set it into motion now. I know she's a generally happy person, but on the inside, she's probably exhausted from being positive all the time. Her scar is something she finds ugly, but I plan on changing her perception of it by worshipping the faint mark, just like the rest of her stunning body. There is a fire inside of her so full of passion, it drives me wild. At the same time, she's kind and sweet, but not afraid to tell me to fuck off. She smells like lavender, doesn't swear, loves Formula One and wants to become a race engineer for it one day, and her eyes have a little bit of yellow around her pupil, like a ring of sunshine."

My rant comes to an abrupt end when I see my best friend's eyes widen with shock. Yeah, I wasn't planning on this defensive response, but it feels like I know Scar. Granted, there are so many things I don't, but that's why I agreed to this deal. I want to get to know her, study every little reaction she offers me. I'm willing to take anything she has to give. My walls were up so high when I met her, but now that she's torn them down, they've vanished for good.

"Holy fuck. I'm speechless, Storm. You've made me speechless." I've made myself speechless too. I don't know what else to say, which is why I'm glad when the front door opens, and Mamá appears in the doorway.

"*La comida está lista,*" she says, and Elias jumps to his feet. She doesn't need to tell him twice that the food is ready.

My best friend's arms wrap around Mamá, his lips moving to her cheek to assault it with kisses. She laughs in his arms, enjoying the affection from her son—that's the way she's always seen him. Elias' mom and mine were good friends before the accident. I don't know if they ever had a conversation about what they'd do in case anything should happen to either of them, but Mamá has done more than Juliette would have ever asked of her. Plus, she taught Elias Spanish, allowing him to grow up bilingual.

I walk over to her once Elias is inside, most likely searching the kitchen or dining room to see what Mamá has prepared for us. My arms slide across her back as I lean down, hugging her close to my chest.

"*Te extrañé,* Mamá," I whisper before pressing a soft kiss to her cheek and stepping back.

I really missed her, so much. It's been over two weeks since I've taken some time to see her, which is unacceptable. Between training, work, and the chaos with Scarlette, I've barely had time for a moment to breathe. Plus, after our fight about me not taking over the company, things felt weird between us.

"*Yo sé, mijo,*" she replies, placing her hand on my cheek. Some of the tension washes off my shoulders as she comforts me. "*Vámos, la comida se está enfriando,*" she says, and I give her a slight nod. God forbid the food gets cold before Elias has had a chance to inhale a plate. He would be mad at me for weeks if I was the reason for that.

"Elias, don't forget to wash your hands," I tease, and he lets out a snort so loud, I can hear it from the kitchen.

"I already did, dickhead," he replies, and Mamá lets out a soft gasp.

"Elias," she warns, and I press my lips together in response.

Mamá has barely ever gotten angry or loud with us. After everything she went through, she's made it her mission to give us the best life possible. She doesn't want us to experience anything like the hell she went through.

"*Perdóname,* Mamá," he calls, and she smiles as she shakes her head.

I press a kiss to her temple before stepping away and into the kitchen where my best friend is. His hands are dripping, and he winks at me as he pops a piece of carrot into his mouth. Then, Dad walks through the door, and we all sit down for dinner where my parents throw question after question my way. Elias steps in and answers most of them, earning himself multiple glares and frowns from me. He doesn't care. He's too excited, and, if I'm being honest, it takes a bit of the weight off my shoulders. I don't have to lie to my family this way, which, deep down, I know is the reason he's doing it.

After dinner, he and I clean up the kitchen before joining my parents in the living room to watch a movie. This is the typical type of evening we've had thousands of times, but this, being around them, never gets boring.

It *will never* get boring.

Chapter 14

Scarlette

Violet stares at me with utter disbelief. I can't blame her. All of this must have sounded ridiculous. Julián—to her Storm—and me fake dating, all of our rules, and the reasons that motivated this decision from both sides. It all must have sounded like a big pile of unbelievable bullcrap, especially because it came out in a quick rant. There is no way I made any type of sense, but her brown eyes still show understanding.

"And you took sex off the table, not him?" she asks, and my eyebrows pull together in response.

"Really? After everything I've just told you, that's where your mind got stuck? On me telling him we won't be physical?" I ask, and my best friend throws her hands into the air out of frustration.

"Yes! Why, Lettie, why? You are so fucking attracted to this man, why would you take sex off the table? I know you're horny by the way you always look at Storm. So, tell me, what is the reason you said no to being intimate with him?" she says, and I sink into the couch, wrapping my arms around myself.

"We don't like each other. Storm and I always bicker, and I don't have the level of trust with him I'd need to have with the person I have sex with for the first time. Trust is important to me," I say, and Violet gives me a compassionate smile.

"Why else?"

God, I hate how she sees through me all the time, but we both know trust is earned, and Julián is more than capable of earning it if he wants to over the next four weeks. Something else made me hesitate.

"I've never been naked in front of anyone, okay? The only person who has ever seen me was my gynecologist," I blurt out, causing both of us to let out a laugh.

"You're not ready to have sex?" Violet asks, squeezing my shoulder.

"I am, but not with Julián Alvarez," I say, making my best friend's eyes go wide.

"That's Storm's real name?" I nod in response. "Fuck, it's sexy." *Yes, it is.* That was my first thought when Halo let it slip in the car on our way to work, not that I told my new friend what went through my head.

"He said I should let him know if I change my mind about the rules," I say, and her eyes go wide in response.

"Because he wants you to change them! Oh my God, please tell me you're not that blind to his attraction for you," she says, and I let out a breathless laugh.

"Listen, when he and I can have one meaningful conversation without being at each other's throats, maybe I will see what you see." I run my fingers through my long, black hair, sucking in a sharp breath.

"You know, being at each other's throats isn't always a bad thing. It's one of the most pleasurable body parts," she says, trailing her hand over the sides of her neck. I roll my eyes and shake my head.

"Your ability to make everything dirty is beyond me," I reply, giving her an easy smile.

"Okay, now, let's talk about important things. Game plan for the weekend in Monaco," she says, and I sit up straight, grinning from ear to ear.

We talk for an hour, constructing a simple plan for me to make a great impression in front of Robert Fuchs, the Grenzenlos team principal. Before this morning, I had no idea how I would ever be able to make connections in Formula One. From the expenses of going to a race weekend all the way to meeting the people in charge, I was pretty hopeless about it all. This is my dream, but I had no place to start.

Now?

Now I have an 'in' I cannot give up under any circumstance. This is probably the only chance I will ever get, and I'll make it work with Julián.

We will make it work.

"Um, Lettie?" Violet's voice fills my ears as I finish up the assignment from my Introduction to Engineering class. I've been working on it for the past two hours, which means I'm tired, hungry, and in need of a break.

"Yeah?" I ask, running my hands over my face.

"Come out here right fucking now," she calls out, and I let out a strained breath.

Whatever it is, I don't want to see it. I want to curl up in bed and prepare myself for the public performance Julián and I will give during our date tomorrow. It's been three days since we agreed to fake date, and he's texted me a few times, asking if I was still comfortable with the arrangement. I don't know what he's trying to do, but if it is to get me to like him, it's unfortunately working.

"I hope this is worth it," I say to Violet as I step into the kitchen. Shock is all over her face.

"Oh, this is so worth it, you have no idea," she replies, pointing outside the window above the sink. I follow her finger, my heart sinking into my stomach at the sight in front of me.

My bike.

My black Kawasaki Ninja 600 with a single red stripe running across the sides.

I run outside before my mind has a second to catch up. It can't be real. This must be a sort of hallucination my mind has fabricated from my lack of sleep and hyperfixation on my assignment for two hours. Tears have already shot into my eyes, but they don't roll down until my finger grazes the throttle and I find the knick in the plastic around the grip. This is mine. This is really my bike.

My knees give in until I'm on the floor, spotting a present next to the bike. I would open it, try to find out what hides inside, but everything around me has become a blur as emotions overwhelm my heart, soul, and brain. This can't be real. I refuse to believe this is real. Selling my bike was one of the most painful things I've ever done.

How is it here?

Tears keep streaming down my face as I kneel in front of my bike. I can't see it through the haze in front of my eyes, but I reach out to touch it, making sure it's really here. There is no doubt in my mind. But it still doesn't make sense. A bike like mine, even used, costs eight thousand dollars. It was cheaper than a car when I first bought it three years ago, but nowadays, everything is expensive for me. I have no savings, and all of the money I'm earning is going toward rent, food, university, and other living expenses. I don't even have enough money to buy myself a new jacket. The one I have has a massive hole on the side, but that is a problem for when the temperatures drop. But at least I have one. And I have a roof over my head, food on the table, an opportunity to get a good education, and a job. I'm grateful for it all, but this is the very reason I don't understand how my bike is here. My parents could have never afforded to buy it back for me.

"Scarlette?" Violet's voice streams into my ears, gently dragging me back to reality.

"How is it here?" I ask, looking up at her while more tears drop down my face. Her gaze shifts to the box next to me.

"Can I open it?" she says, and I manage to nod, bringing the tips of my fingers to the fender I had to buy after I broke the first one.

There is so much history I have with this machine. I went on my first date on it, intimidated the guy so much, he left, and then I drove to a froyo place, enjoying the fact that I dodged a bullet. This bike carried me to work and back every single day. It let me cry on it more times than I can remember, and I never, ever had to hide when I sat on it. The smile I keep on my lips for the people around me, to spread positivity, it didn't have to stay on my face when I was riding. There is no other place in the world I am as happy as when I'm on that bike.

But this? This isn't right. However it came to me, I cannot accept it.

"'*Arcoíris*'?" Violet says, butchering the word completely, but I understand. It's loud and clear in my ears, and it drains the color from my face.

"This fucking man," I blurt out, causing Violet's eyes to go wide. Yeah, I have never sworn in my entire life, but I'm angry. I've never been this damn angry.

I slip on the helmet that was in the box and then the jacket, mounting my bike a second later.

"Where the hell are you going?" my best friend asks, and I turn to her.

"To return my bike," I say and drive off.

Chapter 15

Julián

I'm exhausted. Sweat is dripping down my forehead and back, which is why I rip my shirt off and sink onto the front steps leading up to my porch. Elias drops onto the one below mine, trying to catch his breath. We go for runs four times a week. I have to stay physically fit in order to endure the toll motorcycle racing takes on the body.

"This time you really pushed me too far. I think I'm going to pass out," he says, and I cock an eyebrow.

"I never asked you to train with me," I remind him, but he waves away my comment, completely out of breath. I roll my eyes in response.

The roaring of a motorcycle tears my head upward, and then I watch her ride the bike up my driveway with grace and control. Fuck me. My body catches fire at the sight of her curvy body on that black bike. Every cell inside of me comes alive, and, suddenly, I'm standing. I'm beyond tired, but she's breathed so much energy back into me by simply being herself, I'm walking toward her now.

She rips the helmet off her head before storming over to me and slamming it into my stomach. It's not hard, but it knocks the air out of me anyway. Scar is angry, but I don't understand how getting her bike back led to this emotional frustration. I was only trying to do something nice for her...

"What the hell were you thinking?" she yells, but I'm frozen in place. *Did she just swear?* "How dare you buy back my bike, dangle it in front of me when you know I could never keep such a gift!" she goes on, and I take a step back, confusion settling in my chest.

"I thought you'd be happy," I say, which knocks her back a little. Her eyes have been on my torso since she first took her helmet off, and I suddenly become very aware of how shirtless I am. If she wasn't so upset with me, I might smile.

"How could I be, Julián? I cannot keep it! Where did you even get the money to buy it?" she asks, and my hands twitch from the need to touch her face and wipe away her frown. She's keeping that goddamn bike because it will make her happy. End of story. Now I only need to convince her of that.

"It didn't cost me a thing," I assure her because it's true.

In a way, this was Dad's idea. He offered me the money to buy it for her so she could get to work more easily. Considering he makes what this bike costs in the span of ten minutes, I didn't hesitate to take his money. Plus, Scar needs it and I want to make her happy.

"Julián," she says, and I can't help myself. I take a step toward her. Place my hand on her cheek. Caress her skin softly until the tension in her shoulders subsides visibly.

"It's yours." She shakes her head.

"I'm not accepting this. Your dad is already paying for everything in Monaco. I'm not a charity case in need of money. Maybe we should call off this deal altogether. It's obviously not working," Scar says and steps back, sending a wave of panic through me.

"My father is a billionaire, love, one that keeps getting richer and continues to ignore my suggestions to give back to the people. He's selfish when it comes to his money, so, sometimes, I ask him for some and invest in people who need it. The fact that he agreed to do all of this for you shows me there is some humanity left in him when it comes to money," I say, a realization that has just dawned on me too.

"But I don't want your charity, Julián. I may not have money, but it doesn't mean I will simply accept an eight thousand dollar bike," she says, and I stare into her blue eyes, studying the ring of gold around her pupils.

"You need it for work. Think about it like a company car," I suggest, but it deepens her frown.

"It's not in my contract." I barely keep myself from smacking my forehead with the palm of my hand.

"You are so stubborn," I blurt out, walking over to her bike and placing the helmet on the seat. Her gaze burns my skin in the best way possible, and when I turn around, I find uncertainty in her eyes. Uncertainty, but also lust for my half-naked body.

"How did you find it?" she asks, wrapping her arms around herself in a hug. The setting sun is shining onto her face, turning her skin golden and her eyes into two shining crystals.

"I asked Elias to give me Violet's number. I asked her where you sold your bike and found out it was to a high school friend. She was easily convinced to sell it back to me," I explain without hesitation. I don't care if she knows how ridiculous I am to have spent this much effort on getting her bike back. Maybe it's for the best even. She'll finally see how I feel about her.

"I don't want to owe you anything," she says, and I lean against her bike, crossing my arms in front of my chest.

"You owe me nothing. You will never owe me anything. Would you like to have that in writing?" I need her to stop fighting me on this and just take the bike.

"Yes," she replies with a small smile.

I close the distance between us again, my hand slipping around to her back pocket, pulling her phone out of it. I'm careful not to touch her anywhere that would make her uncomfortable, but when she presses into me in response, I can't help but smirk. Any excuse to touch me, she takes, and it's the best thing in the whole world.

"I, Julián Alvarez, of sound mind and body hereby state that Scarlette Roots owes me nothing, will never owe me anything," I say after hitting record on the video button. This makes her smile. Not the one she usually places on herself around people, but the one I've been getting more and more recently. The genuinely amused and happy smile.

"This is the last thing you get to buy me, even if it was indirectly," she says, but I shake my head.

"Actually, I want to make this part of our rules. I get to buy you whatever I want, whenever I want to." Her eyebrows shoot up her forehead.

"No," she says, putting her foot down.

"Why? Give me one good reason why not, and I won't put it into our rules." She crosses her arms in front of her chest.

"Because I can buy my own things, thank you very much. I don't need a man to take care of me," she barks, and I lick my lips.

I would love to take care of her, not in the way she thinks though. Scarlette is assuming I want to control her, but she's the one in control of me, and I don't mind it one bit. The only taking care of her I'd want to do is emotionally, mentally, and physically. Desperately so too.

"I agree, but it's not a good enough reason, love, because we both know you deny yourself the simplest pleasures in life for your education. Those are the only things I want to give to you." This makes her think. She knows I'm right, and I'm having a difficult time not smiling at the way her lavender scent fills my nose.

"Why? Why do you want to buy me things anyway? We're supposed to be fake dating, Julián, not actually dating," she says, reminding me. Her words send a stinging pain through my chest, but I ignore it.

"If you don't have a reason, Scar, I'm putting it in the rules," I reply instead of answering her question.

I don't want to tell her I'd do anything to see her happy. I've already put myself out there once, and she went to kiss Halo instead. I'm not doing it again, not until I know she feels something for me.

"Ugh, you're so infuriating. Why can't you ever answer my question?" I almost smile before my next words come out.

"Because you ask a lot of questions," I reply, causing her to narrow her eyes at me.

"And what makes you say that?" Another question. She's teasing me, and I almost drop to my knees to worship her because of it.

"Are you hungry?" I ask, stepping away from her and toward my house. "I'm going to make dinner, in case you're interested," I say, turning my head to see her hesitate. She touches her hand to her stomach, clearly hungry, but then shakes her head. Scarlette is about to say something when I speak first. "Don't think about lying to me right now," I add, causing her mouth to fall open a little.

"I am, but I don't want to impose. Plus, we don't really like each other so—" I cut her off by throwing her over my shoulder and carrying her inside. "Julián! I'm too heavy! Put me down," she says, and I cock an eyebrow.

"Remember what I said the last time you told me that bullshit?" I ask, and her body relaxes a bit on top of my shoulder.

"'You're perfect'," she repeats, and I give an agreeing *hmmm*. Scarlette isn't slim. She has curves and thighs to die for. It's why I think she's perfect.

"You are. I don't know who gave you the idea you're too heavy for something, but if we're going to be fake dating, you can't think that anymore, especially not when it comes to things with me. I'm strong, *arcoíris*, I'm made for beautiful women of your body type," I say before gently dropping her back onto her feet inside of the house. Her cheeks are a flaming red, and I want nothing more than to drink in the color with a kiss.

"I'm not insecure about my body," she defends, and I tug a loose strand of her hair behind her pierced ear. I spot seven piercings on each ear. Gorgeous.

"Good, you shouldn't be."

Chapter 16

Scarlette

My gaze has been stuck on Julián's half-naked body for the past half an hour. I'm hot. I'm so freaking hot, my whole body is vibrating with desire for him. The ache between my legs has gotten its own heartbeat now, controlling the one in my chest. My skin is on fire, and I want him. God, I want him so much, especially after what he said to me as he carried me inside. *I'm strong, arcoíris, I'm made for beautiful women of your body type.* Yes. Yes. Yes. He is so strong, his arms pure muscle and his chest, the one he keeps pulling me against, rippled and hard. I wonder how it would feel to run my tongue along the length of it—

"Love? You alright?" Julián asks, and I let out a shaky breath.

"Yeah, of course. Where is Elias anyway?" I ask with a nervous laugh, which causes him to scrunch both of his eyebrows together.

"You're worried about him?" This seems to surprise him, but it's not the reason behind my question either.

"No, just curious," I reply, rubbing my left arm with my right hand.

"Are you uncomfortable being alone with me?" he asks next, a hint of sadness on his face, which I know he's trying his best to hide.

"No, not at all!" I blurt out quickly. He doesn't look certain. "I promise, Julián, I'm very comfortable in your home." Maybe a little too much by the way I've been ogling him.

"Okay, but I need you to know that if you ever get uncomfortable or you want to leave or anything, you tell me and I will make sure you feel the opposite. Do you understand? I want you to feel as safe as I will always keep you," he says, causing my lips to part ever so slightly. He wants to keep me safe... *why?*

"You confuse me," I say because a person who constantly bickers with another can't possibly hold any feelings for them, right? Then again, I bicker with him, and liking him doesn't sound impossible.

"*Y tú me tienes loco, mami,*" he replies, and I roll my eyes. It irritates me how sexy he sounds when he speaks Spanish, but I can't understand him. Well, nothing but the way he addresses me.

"You have all those sweet ways of addressing me, but I don't have any for you. Last time I called you 'babe' in front of your dad, you almost threw up," I say, and Julián's shoulders shake. I'm convinced he just chuckled, but his back is facing me, so I can't be sure.

"Julián is all you need, love." His voice is firm, showing no signs of the amusement I thought he felt a moment earlier.

"What if I want a pet name for you?" I ask, crossing my arms in front of my chest. He turns around, knocking the breath out of me with his beautiful torso, his dark golden skin smooth and the line of hair disappearing into his pants delicious. My eyes catch the birthmark on his cheek, the desire to run my fingertips over it too strong to resist forever. "What about Juju?" I tease, both of us knowing full well I would never call him that.

"Try another, love," he says, placing his hands on the counter and letting the muscles in his arms flex as he leans his weight onto them.

"What about Stormsie?" I ask, doing my best not to laugh.

"I think 'babe' has been my favorite so far, and I hate it anyway," he replies, scrunching his nose in disgust.

"What about 'baby' then?" I offer, but he doesn't look convinced.

"If you get to call me 'baby', I get to hold your hand in public," he says, handing me another deal.

I fall into deep thought for a second. There is no doubt in my mind I want this man's hands on me all the time. Getting even a little bit of it sends a thrill through my system, one I cannot get enough of. However, I can't stop the next words from spilling through my lips.

"I could just find another pet name," I remind him, and Julián nods in agreement.

"Yeah, you could." But I don't want to.

"Okay, 'baby' it is," I say, taking his deal without admitting I am.

Julián walks around his counter and toward where I'm standing. He watches me closely as his fingers lift to my arm, stopping centimeters before they graze my skin.

"May I?" he asks, and I manage to nod.

His hand trails down my arm, sending a wave of shivers down my spine. Goosebumps spread in the wake of his fingertips on my skin along with a heat I feel moving between my legs. My eyes flutter shut for a moment, but I force them open again, sucking in a quiet, sharp breath as his hand wraps around mine. His fingers intertwine with my own, his unique eyes—one fully brown, one half-brown and half-green—studying my reaction.

"Is this okay?" Julián asks, and I nod again. "Words, *mami*, I need your words." He can have them all.

"I'm very okay with you touching me like this," I reply, my gaze fixated on his collarbone so I don't have to admit it to his face.

"What about this?" he asks, bringing our hands to his naked torso, hovering over it before mine presses against his. Realizing what he means, I push my hand to his chest, feeling his hot skin and hard muscles underneath it.

"We shouldn't touch like this," I whisper, but my whole body is drawn to his, desperate to feel it pressed up against mine.

"Does that mean you don't want to?" he asks, bringing his hands to my hips and guiding me against him.

Before he can do so, a door slams shut.

"Oh shit, sorry, everyone. I'm a bit clumsy," Elias says, and I put distance between Julián and me.

The haze his half-naked body put my mind under clears up, and I move around the kitchen to distract myself. I don't know what the heck just happened between Julián and me, but it can't happen again. We might be in an agreement to benefit both of us, but... *why shouldn't we have another part of it to benefit us both? Put sex back on the table. Make this beneficial for us in more ways than one.* God, the fantasy is so sweet, my knees go weak at the thought.

There was not a lot of trust between us, not as much as I need for sex, until a moment ago. Until he told me he wants to keep me safe and comfortable with him. Until he waited for my consent every single time he touched me. Until I realized, I've always felt safe around him, even when we argue. There has never been a time when his body close to mine has done anything but cause an upwhirl of the most delicious feelings inside of me.

Nope. I can't do it. I can't even begin to imagine a way I would start the conversation with him. Plus, no part of me wants to have sex with the risk of us fighting about something stupid afterward. There might be more trust between us now, but I don't trust us enough to be intimate without falling apart after. This realization might send a stinging pain through my chest, but it also gives me the wake-up I needed. I may not have wanted it, but for the sake of my feelings, it was necessary.

"Dinner is almost finished, love," Julián says, and I give him a nod, looking around his home.

His house is only one-story, but for the two of them, it's more than spacious enough. Everything is modern, almost as if this place was only built recently. They have a single couch, a three-seater, in the middle of the living room with a television across from it and an armchair to the right. They have a veranda leading to a garden, and their bedrooms are down the hall from the entrance. They're right next to each other, which surprises me.

"Don't you hear everything the other person does in their room?" I ask, and Elias lets out a soft laugh.

"Yeah, it's really annoying, especially because Storm talks in his sleep," he says, sending a wave of curiosity through me.

"Is that so?" Julián turns to me as I reappear in the kitchen, shaking his head with an unimpressed look on his face.

"It is! You should hear him. 'Scarlette is so pretty. Scarlette is so beautiful'," he says, imitating his best friend, who throws a towel at him in response.

"Go lay the table, *pendejo*," Julián says, facing his food again. I smile at their exchange before Elias approaches me and grins.

"He doesn't actually say your name in his sleep, only when he—" Julián cuts him off then.

"*Cállate, mentiroso. La vas a hacer sentir incómoda*," he says, and I almost shake him to complain that he's speaking Spanish. I want to understand what he's saying.

"*Perdóname, señorita*," Elias says, taking my hand and pressing a kiss to the back of it in apology. I give him an unsure laugh.

"Okay?" I ask, still confused about what just happened. My best friend's boyfriend gives me no explanation as he takes three plates and some utensils and walks into the dining room.

"I'm sorry about him, love. I taught him how to ride a bike, but manners? I still have some work left," Julián says, and I cross my arms in front of my chest.

"Well, if he's relying on you to teach him, I fear for humanity," I tease, and he knocks the air from my chest when a small smirk tugs at the corner of his mouth.

"*Eres una traviesa, mami*," he says, and I roll my eyes with a frustrated groan.

"Fine, that's it! I'm learning Spanish!" I say, the smirk deepening on his face.

I smile to myself, desperate to find out what he looks like when he's smiling, grinning, or laughing.

I'm going to find out.

Chapter 17

Julián

After dinner, I drove Scarlette home—her on her bike, me on mine. That was yesterday. Today, I'm running around, trying to get everything I need before picking up Scar. Elias has been watching me with amusement for the past hour, not quite sure what the hell I'm doing in the kitchen. He's sitting on the chair at the counter, his head resting on his intertwined fingers, his elbows pushing off the marble.

"You really like her," Elias says, smiling like it's the best thing in the world. I reveal nothing on my face. My words on the other hand...

"Yes."

I go back to baking, ignoring the way his gaze burns a hole in the back of my head. He can be a goddamn pain in the ass, but no part of me is in the mood to argue with him about his nosy behavior.

"Do you think you could eventually fall for her?" I almost sigh at his question.

"Yes."

I'm not quite sure where this answer came from, but there is no doubt in my mind if Scarlette and I continue to see each other, there will be no more return. She will have my heart completely, but there is no stopping myself from doing everything I can to make it hers anymore either. I like her a lot considering we've only known each other for five weeks.

"Holy shit. And you haven't even kissed? Not once?" Elias and his never-ending stream of personal questions. This time, my lips open to let out the sigh lingering on my tongue.

"No."

I've thought about little else besides the fact that I want to kiss her more than anything, especially when she stares at my lips like they're water in a desert. Scarlette wants me, but I have a feeling that she doesn't trust me with that part of herself yet, or many others even. I have made it my personal mission to be someone she can be herself with one hundred percent, to earn every part of her she wants to give me.

"What if she will never be interested in being with you like that?" Elias asks next, and the thought sends a wave of panic through me.

"Then so be it. I will leave her alone after our agreement ends."

Elias' eyes go wide, and I have to keep myself from smacking the back of his head. He's getting on my nerves.

"You won't even tell her how you feel?" he asks, and I turn back to my muffins.

"No." I'm not going to make her feel bad by sharing my feelings with her if she's not interested in me.

"How many more questions can I ask before you slap me?" Elias says, and I look up at him again.

"Minus five," I reply, offering him a small smile, ignoring the guilt in the back of my mind. He jumps out of his chair.

"What the fuck has she done to you? You're smiling now? Even if it was just a little, that means something! Fuck, not even Holly could do that," he says, making my face drop back into a scowl at the mention of my ex-girlfriend's name.

"Don't you have to go to work?" I ask, irritated with him now.

"Yeah, I'm leaving, man. Don't worry. I will let you go back to your quiet baking time," he says, finally disappearing out of the room. I love that guy, but he's right.

When I bake, it's my quiet time, and I wanted to tell him to piss off since he first sat down at the counter.

Now I can get back to finishing the muffins for Scarlette.

Today is our first fake date. I put on a dress shirt for her and spent an hour fixing my hair until every wave sat perfectly. I also drove my car here because I'm not wearing my helmet after the amount of work I've done on my hair. *Ridiculous*. It really is, but Scar has that effect on me. She's making me do all sorts of things I usually wouldn't, like fake dating someone.

"*Relájate*, Julián," I say to myself before knocking on her door.

Never in my entire life have I been nervous for a date. Not a fake date. A regular date. So why the hell am I nervous now? Scar made the decision to pretend to like me either way. It should settle me, but it does the opposite. I want her to like me. I will do everything in my power so she does.

Scar opens the door a second later, my breath getting stuck in my throat and chest at the sight of her. She's wearing a light purple summer dress that hugs her breasts but falls loosely over the rest of her body. It's low-cut and... fuck me. I force my gaze to her eyes, noticing matching eyeshadow painted on her lids and some lipgloss making her lips shiny and inviting. Her hair is in two dutch-braids, lavender sticking in the loops. Oh God. I need to sit, kneel, squat, anything. It isn't news to me that Scar is beautiful, but this, the amount of effort she put into her appearance for our 'date', makes my heart flutter uncomfortably. She's every word for stunning in all languages.

"Is this acceptable?" she asks, staring down at her dress and then giving me a small smile. *Words, Julián, speak.*

"Yes," I croak out because I'm an idiot.

"Oh, good," Scar says, clearing her throat because I've been staring at her like a creep for the past minute, not saying anything through my parted lips. "You look nice," she compliments me and closes the door behind her. I snap out of my trance, barely.

"Thanks." Someone smack me. I deserve it for not worshipping her the way I should, the way I want to.

"So, where are you taking me? I assume somewhere a lot of people go on a Friday night," she says, and I swallow hard to regain the ability to talk. My lips are dry at this point, so I lick them once, grabbing her full attention. Yeah, that does nothing to help me stop fantasizing about kissing her.

"We are going on an old-fashioned rollerskating date," I inform her, and Scar snorts.

"That's funny. No, but seriously, where are we going?" I'm almost offended my idea amuses her this much.

"I'm not joking, Scar. Rollerskating night at the *Moonville Rollerrink* is about as public as we can go. Everyone will be there, all of my parents' friends, potentially even some of yours," I explain, and Scar blushes.

"Sorry. I really thought you were kidding. I didn't know people still went on rollerskating dates," she says with a nervous laugh and stares at the ground. My fingers slip under her chin, so I can lift her gaze back to mine.

"Don't be. Under different circumstances, I wouldn't bring you there either." I'd make her a homemade meal, take her for a ride on my bike, and then find a place to eat dessert.

"Yeah? Where would you take me? A class on how to never smile again?" she teases, and I bite down on my bottom lip to keep from grinning at her. God, she's making it so hard to stop my face from twisting into a smile, but I can't. I can't smile at her, not without years of guilt hitting me like a bus. *Right?*

"Yes, how did you know?" I ask while we make our way to my car, Scar chuckling beside me.

"You have that vibe about you," she explains as I open the passenger door for her.

"How chivalrous and unexpected of you," Scar says, and I frown at her.

"Get in, *mami*," I command, causing another little laugh to escape her.

"So bossy," she says and clicks her tongue before doing exactly as I asked of her and keeping the smile on her lips. Fuck, I've never wanted to kiss someone as much as I want to kiss her.

One day, I think to myself before closing her door and walking over to the driver's side.

Chapter 18
Scarlette

"¿*Qué puñeta?*" Julián blurts out as we walk into the empty rollerskating rink building, his eyebrows almost touching his hairline from shock and confusion. I wish I knew what he just said, but it sounded a lot like swear words.

"Where are all the people?" I ask, my eyes fixated on his handsome face.

The birthmark on his left cheek always catches my attention when I look at him. There is something so beautiful about it, something that makes me want to trace it. I like that we both have marks given to us by life. It separates us from everyone else, and it also makes me feel connected to him.

"*No sé, mami, pero—*" He cuts himself off and turns to me, shaking his head. "Sorry, sometimes I confuse my languages," he says, but it makes me smile at him so hard, he takes a step back to study all of me.

"You're cute sometimes," I explain before lifting my fingers to my lips and pressing them shut. God, what is wrong with me? That's not something fake dating people tell each other.

"Hmmm," is all he says in response before closing the distance between us and taking my hand. "What size shoes do you wear?" he asks, and I furrow my eyebrows. He can't possibly still want to go through with this if there is no one at the rink.

"We won't convince anyone we're dating here, Julián. What's the point of staying?" I ask, but he doesn't answer my question, merely guides me to the counter where a young woman is standing on her phone.

"What size?" he repeats, and I let out a small sigh.

"I don't want to say," I reply, which grabs his attention.

He turns to me, letting go of my hand, which is a relief considering my mind was going fuzzy from his warmth and proximity. I don't like that I want him to put his hands on me all the time. A good fake girlfriend should be able to separate her feelings from what is right, and what is right is keeping my distance from him when no one is here to see us touch.

"Love, you don't have to tell me if it makes you uncomfortable, but, I assure you, having big feet is nothing to be ashamed of," he says, and I cock an eyebrow at him.

"Maybe for men because someone came up with the idea that big feet meant you have a big penis. For women, however, feet, hands, waists, it all has to be small, petite, blah, blah, blah," I say with an eye roll, but Julián surprises me by taking a step closer, our breaths intertwining now.

"You know what I like?" he asks, and I swallow hard as I shake my head. His eyes scan my face as he lets out a thoughtful hum. "I like everything about your body. I like—" Julián is cut off by the woman behind the counter.

"Can I help you two?" she asks now that she's finally realized we're here. The man in front of me curses in Spanish before turning to her with his usual scowl.

"Yeah, we need two pairs of shoes," he says, and I decide to let go of his words without overthinking them.

I won't linger on them. Nope. We are fake dating. That is all. As a matter of fact, I will say my shoe size out loud to remind myself we're not supposed to be interested in each other romantically. We're merely helping each other out. That's all.

"It's adorable that you think your feet are big," he says after I told the woman my shoe size. Her brown eyes study Julián for a moment, appreciating his muscular build and handsome face. *Crap. Why do I dislike that so much?*

"Let's stop talking about them, shall we?" I say, a little annoyed with myself for caring about the way a stranger is checking out Julián. She has every right to. He would have a right to return her interest too. Instead...

Instead, he takes my hand in his and leads me to the benches where we sit down to put on our shoes. My head is spinning so much so that he shifts his body in my direction, a sad frown lingering on his lips. It contrasts the usually angry one he gives most people.

"I'm sorry if I've upset you," he says, sending a wave of surprise through me.

"No, you didn't. I'm just—" *Jealous. I am jealous, even though you aren't mine, and I have no right or reason to be.* Julián places his pinky over mine on the bench, which only irritates me more. "You don't have to be so touchy. There is no one here to convince," I remind him, and he leans back, sucking in a sharp breath.

"Right, okay," is all he replies before standing up and skating onto the rink.

My eyes fixate on the disco ball in the middle of the ceiling while I try to calm my racing heart. This is fine. I don't want us to have a real date. We don't even like each other. He made me the best homemade meal I've ever had, but it doesn't mean anything. His affection and kindness are all part of our deal. He's an infuriating man. I can't forget that, especially not when he's waiting at the side of the rink for me, extending his hand as an invitation.

I don't hesitate.

I stand up and move over to him to slip my hand into his. Music starts blaring through the speaker, and I realize only old songs fill the room. The lights are dark, but the disco ball is bringing a glittery shine everywhere. It might be empty in here, but the man in front of me has the type of presence to fill an atmosphere. I don't need anyone else when he's here, helping me find balance on my skates.

"You had to choose an activity I was terrible at for our first date, didn't you?" I ask with a laugh before realizing what the heck I just said. "Our fake date, I mean," I correct, and Julián's eyes sparkle with amusement, even if his mouth tells me nothing.

"It would have been perfect if people had been here. Me, holding you close and whispering in your ear how well you were doing," he says, my face heating in response to the thought of Julián praising me. Oh my. *Get out*, I yell at the thought. "And then, when everybody was watching, I'd have wrapped my arms around you and held you against my chest while a slower song filled the speaker, one I would have paid good money to have played," he keeps going, leading me along the circular rink. We stay near the railing to make sure I can hold on if I need to.

"I can't believe you're such a romantic, Julián," I reply with a small chuckle, the music so loud, I wish it away. I want to hear his low, husky voice.

"I can't believe no one's here on a Friday night. Unless—" He cuts off and squeezes my wrists, which he is still holding as we skate to make sure he can catch me if I fall. I'm starting to get the hang of it, but I'm not ready for his warmth to leave me yet. "There must be some kind of event at the town center. Do you want to go there? I know you would like people to see us," he says, and he should be right. Instead, I almost scream my response.

"No!" He gives me a confused cock of his eyebrow. "I mean, let's stay here. We can use this as a trial run for Monday," I lie because leaving right now when I have Julián all to myself doesn't sound appealing to me.

He flashes me the smallest of smirks before the corners of his mouth drop again.

"Alright then, *mami*. Do you think you can try skating by yourself?" he asks, and I nod in response. He lets go of me and... and I don't fall. I make it one lap, then two, laughing from the depths of my chest.

We stay for a little longer until we decide to leave and get some food. Neither one of us is in the mood to put on a show anymore, so we get dinner from the nearest drive-thru and sit in his car. We share some embarrassing childhood stories with each other—I convinced him by saying couples grow comfortable and familiar with each other by knowing such things—and I realize something about Julián I find adorable. He's a great listener. He likes to talk to me. Yes, he often gives me one-word answers or vague ones that drive me crazy, but he speaks a lot around me. However, when it comes to me telling a story, he stays quiet and listens closely, asking follow-up questions that show he's paying attention. I do the same when he shares embarrassing stories with me—like the time Elias pulled down his swimsuit trunks at the beach when they were kids. I tried my best not to laugh, but when Julián gave me a warning side glance, I couldn't hold it back anymore.

At the end of the night, Julián walks me all the way to my front door, his hands behind his back. No one's around, so he doesn't have to hold my hand, but there was no one earlier either and he repeatedly took it.

"This was fun," I say, and Julián nods.

"Yeah, it was." There is a thoughtful expression on his face as he stares at the ground in front of him.

"Good practice for Monday," I remind both of us, but he simply sucks in a sharp breath and stares into my eyes.

"See you on Monday, *arcoíris*," he replies and leaves without touching me again. Good. This is the way it's supposed to be. He's not supposed to kiss me good night like this was a regular date, he isn't supposed to hug me either. And I don't want any of that. Nope. No way.

Liar.

I step inside the house, letting out the breath I've been holding subconsciously. We might not have achieved anything tonight in the convincing-people-we're-dating department, but it was a nice 'date'. Unfortunately, I've finished all my assignments and have the weekend off work, which means I will get to overthink every little detail about tonight to prepare myself for Monday.

Great.

Just what I need.

Chapter 19

Julián

My hands are shaking as I stand in front of Scarlette's door with another bundle of lavender and my jersey tucked under my arm. As a part of my sponsorship deal, Hawke offered to make some merch for me with my racing number—fourteen—and my last name on the back. I may not be on the soccer team, but Scarlette will be wearing my jersey. The turquoise color will look amazing on her, not that anything could possibly look hideous if she's wearing it. She's too beautiful.

I manage to knock, my heart racing so unbearably fast, *again*, it feels like I'm going to faint. All these years of me being reserved have vanished to dust. She has me fucking nervous all the time. Standing here, on this hot summer day, waiting for the sexiest woman on the planet to open the door for me, I'm sweating. This is the second time in four days I'm here, but I still have no control over the speed of my heart or the hitching of my breath.

Then, I forget how to breathe entirely.

Scarlette opens the door, standing in front of me in a white tank top that does nothing to contain her chest. I almost stumble backward when my eyes trail down her body to see her thick thighs hidden beneath a black skirt. She put on some black eyeliner and nude lipstick. I barely manage to keep myself standing upright let alone form any coherent words. The only thing that somehow slips past my lips is the worst thing I could have possibly said to the goddess standing in front of me.

"Ummm." I want to punch myself.

Instead of being upset with my nonsense, she starts laughing, blinding me with her sun rays for a moment. I blink several times, trying to make sure I'm not imagining her response. Nope. She's standing in front of me, cheeks flushed with color and a smile lingering on her lips after she's finished laughing.

"'Ummm' good, or 'ummm' bad?" she says, and I'm mesmerized she even has to ask this question.

"Ummm, you look incredible," I manage to reply, earning myself a shy smile from her. Yup, I'm going to melt into a puddle of happiness if she keeps looking at me like this.

"Thank you. So do you," she says. *Holy fuck. Are we having another moment?* I think we are, a good, non-chaotic moment. I want more of them. More of her. "Are you blushing again, Julián?" Up until she just said it, I hadn't realized how hot my face has become from her compliment. I clear my throat, my frown set in place.

"No," is all I say before lifting the lavender bundle. Her eyes go soft at the flowers. "Don't give them back to me again. They're yours, okay?" I say, and Scar gives me a small nod in response.

"I'm sorry about last time."

Her apology knocks the air out of me. I wasn't expecting it. Hell, I can't even remember the last time someone apologized to me for hurting my feelings. Whenever Elias and I fight, we simply go our separate ways for a few hours and then come back as if nothing had happened. Mamá and Dad don't apologize. The last time we fought, they threw every hurtful thing at me, but they never took the time to make it up to me. No one has ever bothered to string together those three little words for me: I am sorry. Not even my ex-girlfriend bothered to apologize after she cheated on me.

I'm sorry about last time.

I can barely hold myself back from kissing her.

"You don't have to be," I croak out, overwhelmed by emotion. Scarlette steps forward, placing her hand on my shoulder. I stare at the point of contact, a little upset at how friendly her touch is. I don't want her hand there, not when I've felt it against my chest before.

"But I am. I know we bicker, but you were trying to do something nice for me, keep trying to do something nice for me, and I was a jerk. Forgive me," she says, and I can't stop my fingers from lifting to her cheek, my thumb tilting her head back to capture her full gaze.

"Nothing to forgive, love," I reply, letting go when I realize how close I've let myself get to her. She made it explicitly clear we do not touch in any other way than the friendly one she just offered me. "I'm also sorry, truly. I don't want to upset you," I blurt out, realizing how one-sided this apology about both our behaviors was. Unacceptable. I don't ever want her to think anything is one-sided between us.

"Maybe this thing between us will work after all, Julián." Her smile is bright, contagious. It takes everything out of me not to let her get under my skin so much that I smile back. It's one of the hardest things I've ever had to do.

"It will," I say because I'm prepared to give her everything to make her dream happen, and us. I want to make us happen.

"What's that?" Scar asks, tugging on the jersey I brought her. I let her take it from my grasp. She studies the front, a fourteen written across the chest, before spinning it around, realization dawning on her features.

"You're sponsored by Hawke? Are you in a racing sport?" she asks, surprise and shock lacing her features.

"Yes, love. I race motorcycles. It's actually something I wanted to discuss with you. I have a race on Saturday, and, as my girlfriend, fake or not, I would like for you to attend," I say, and she lets out a snort.

"Of course, I will be there! This is so freaking cool. How come you haven't told me about this before?" I don't have an answer for her right away because I'm not certain why.

"I don't know," I reply honestly after a moment of silence and hesitation. She gives me an excited smile before slipping on the jersey. It's way too big for her, but I wanted to make sure it's comfortable.

"I love this. Now I finally understand why you wanted me to wear a tank top," she says, but I only give her a small nod in response.

She shakes her head with a grin. God, she's always so goddamn happy. I love it as much as I want to hug her and assure her not being okay is perfectly fine too.

"I have a feeling you like spoiling me." Fuck, I do. I adore giving her everything she could ever need. I crave the smile she gives in response to something as silly as me asking her to wear my jersey. I need the warmth spreading through my chest from making her happy.

"Maybe," I say, holding out my hand and then leading her toward my bike when her fingers slip between mine. She hesitates when she sees where we're going. "You're perfect," I remind her, causing her shoulders to drop.

"You have to stop saying that, Julián, or I'm going to think you actually like me," she teases, but I don't find it funny at all that she still has no fucking clue how beyond like I am. I *adore* her.

I sigh and shake my head, walking over to her bike to grab the helmet off it and hand it to her. It's black like her machine, a stripe of red running around it horizontally. It's badass, just like the woman I bought it for. The urge to kiss her before sliding the helmet on her head has me breathless, but I push past it, ignoring it.

"Thank you," she says, but the way the words fall from her lips lets me know she doesn't just mean putting the helmet on. She means everything I've done for her, which is nothing.

"My pleasure," I reply, giving the underside of her helmet a quick pat with my finger so she looks up at me. "Ready to play having the hots for me?" I ask, and Scarlette's shoulders shake from her chuckle.

"Ready to play being irrevocably captured by my presence?" I cock an eyebrow at her question.

"Yes." Because her presence has always captured me, irrevocably, irreversibly, and irresistibly.

I won't have to play any part today. I'll be myself and everyone will believe how deeply I've already fallen for this bike-riding, lavender-smelling, engineering woman.

I'm fucked, but I've never minded it less.

Chapter 20

Scarlette

Julián guides my hands around him when we're on his bike, resting them below his pecs but above his belly button. My breasts are pressed against his back, and I'm convinced he can feel the way my heart is racing against him. I'm not anxious. I haven't been truly anxious in a week now, which either means I'm figuring myself out or a big anxiety attack is coming soon. Either way, my heart isn't racing because of that. It's pounding in my chest because I'm nervous. Nervous because of how good it feels to have his hard back pressed up against me. Nervous because we're about to make another public appearance as a 'couple', and I worry someone will see through our pretense. Nervous because a million things could go wrong, but, for some inexplicable reason, I'm happy.

Being here with Julián while he drives us safely to the soccer game has me filled with a joy I can't explain. The same goes for wearing his jersey. There is no reason for me to keep smiling because of the way his sandalwood scent somehow lingers on the fabric or how wonderful it feels against my skin, all soft and comfy.

At a red light, Julián squeezes my knee, turning his head to nudge my helmet with his. I let out a small laugh, patting the sides of his helmet. We keep going until we're play fighting, and a wonderful feeling washes through me. He's laughing. I can't hear it well, can't see the way his face twists into it, but I feel the vibrations of his laughter go through me. The sensation weighs heavy on me, but on him too, I can feel it by the way he leans back and against me. Without thinking, I slide my arms onto his chest, lying them on each of his pecs. We're already acting like a couple, and there is no one even around for us to convince. It makes me feel... whole.

"Careful, *arcoíris*, you're close to breaking the rules," he says loud enough so I can hear him through the layers of his and my head protection. Simultaneously, he lifts his hands to wrap around mine. He wants me to keep them there, despite what he just said, and I'm more than happy to oblige.

"Stupid rules," I whisper to myself so he doesn't hear me.

Our moment is interrupted by the light turning green, and I let my arms fall back to where he initially placed them. He lets his bike roar once, sending a thrill through my heart and a smile onto my lips. I can't believe Julián races motorcycles. I will have to ask him about it later, like if he's trying to get a spot in MotoGP, how Hawke found him, what league he's currently racing in, and more questions I'm sure I will still come up with later.

"We're here," he says when we've been standing for a few seconds and I've made no attempt at getting off his bike.

"Oh, sorry," I reply, hopping off with a lot more grace than I would have expected. I give myself a mental pat on the back.

Julián reaches for my helmet after he parked the bike, and I smile at the way he wants to do those little things for me for no apparent reason. He pulls it off my head, straightening out my black hair once he's finished. I grin up at him, catching his usual scowl and wishing for the hundredth time he'd give me anything, any little smile he can muster. I would complain, but if there is a reason for him not wanting to show that side, I'm not going to put him on the spot and force it to feed my curiosity.

"How bad is it?" I ask when he doesn't stop staring at my hair and running his fingers through it.

"You just had a few strands tangled," he explains, but I sense it. I sense him lying.

"You like touching my hair," I blurt out, and he freezes for a split second, his features hardening, his jaw tensing.

"Yes." It's the only answer I get, but I don't need more. I simply smile to myself as he turns to put our helmets on his bike.

"Won't they get stolen?" I ask as he takes my hand, something we apparently do now. I don't mind it one single bit. As a matter of fact, there is something about the way his hand envelops mine, sending a wave of heat and electricity through me, that has me breathless. He always has me so breathless.

"No, love, they won't. Moonville is one of the safest towns in the country. Everyone knows everyone, so if someone were to steal them and anyone else saw, I guarantee you the person responsible would have the Chief of Police, Mark Matts, in front of their door an hour later." I nod at his explanation, a bit dizzy because of how close he's holding me.

"That's good," I say moments later, and Julián looks down at me, stopping dead in his tracks.

"Are you alright?" he asks, causing both of my eyebrows to lift up in surprise.

"Yes, why?" I meet his inquiring gaze, but he seems genuinely concerned now.

"If you've changed your mind, we will leave, *mami*." His words bring an unstoppable smile to my face.

"Simple as that?" I ask, and he steps back, a firm expression slipping across his features.

"Simple as that."

Having his hands on me right now would seal this moment as perfect, but he's too far away, and I know I'm being silly. We have an agreement, rules in place to keep up our boundaries. He doesn't want to date me any more than I can trust him.

But I can trust him, can't I?

He's never given me a reason to distrust him, but he's given me a hundred to believe his intentions. That's the problem. I'm starting to like him, especially because of the wholesome moments we've been sharing today and at the rink.

"Do you think people will believe we're dating if the only thing we do is hold hands?" I ask, a little weak in the knees as I think about what I'm saying. Julián gives me a small smirk, and I have to do my best to keep standing.

"Why, love? Do you *want* me to do more?" *God, yes, please.*

"I'm just asking," I tell him, looking at the ground with heat rising up my neck. I didn't think suggesting for him to touch me more would have this much of an effect on me, but it does. It sends my heart into a frenzy and turns my cheeks a deep red.

"What do you want, *mami*? *Dime*," he says, and I assume the last word means 'tell me'. I melt on the inside.

"Too much," I admit, sucking in a sharp breath and letting it out through gritted teeth. Julián takes a slow step toward me, causing my heart to skip a beat. His gaze trails along my face, settling on my lips.

"Do you want to change the rules?" he asks, and everything inside of me screams to tell him 'yes'. *Yes, yes, yes.*

"I d—" I'm cut off by someone calling his name.

"Storm? Is that you?" the person asks, and I turn around to face a couple walking toward us.

"Fuck no," I hear him growl under his breath, making me take an instinctive step toward him. He's so surprised by my reaction, his eyes widen. I don't care. Something about these two people approaching us has made him feel uneasy, and I don't like it. I want to comfort him.

"Who are they?" I whisper when I'm close enough to Julián so he can hear me. His eyes are on me, studying me closely.

"My ex and the guy she cheated on me with," he replies just as the couple stops in front of us. My heart sinks into my stomach from his words.

"How have you been?" the guy asks, smiling at my fake boyfriend. His long brown hair is tied into a bun and he has bright green eyes. The woman next to him is blonde with brown eyes and a tired look on her soft features.

Julián tenses beside me so I take another step toward him, bringing my back to his front until we're pressed against each other. I feel him loosen up, one of his arms slipping to my waist to drag me even closer to him. Sensing he doesn't want this conversation to continue any longer than it already has, I force a smile to my lips, pretending to be polite. I'm not nice when it comes to people who've hurt Julián.

"I'm sorry, we don't have time to entertain a conversation with you," I chime in, and Julián squeezes my side. "Have a terrible evening," I say, pressing a single kiss to Julián's cheek and then grabbing his hand. "Come on, baby, let's go," I add and lace my fingers through his before pulling him toward the grandstands and leaving the other two behind while they catch their jaws off the floor.

When we're out of sight, Julián leads me to an empty hallway in the university, trapping me between him and the wall. His scent fills my nose, his racing heartbeat mimicking mine. With his hands on either side of me, and his breathing so uneven, I realize how horrible that must have been for him. I raise my hands to his cheeks, feeling his sharp features against my palms.

"It's okay," I assure him, but he shakes his head.

"No, it's not. What you did for me, it's—" He cuts off, and panic fills my chest. I let my arms drop back to my sides.

"I'm so sorry if I overstepped. I thought that was what you needed," I explain, and Julián's mouth opens, growing closer to mine.

"Fuck, *mami*, it was everything I've ever needed. You didn't overstep. You were fucking perfect." The distance between our mouths disappears more and more with every moment. "You just knew what I needed. How, love? How did you know?" he asks, grabbing my hands to place them back on his cheeks.

"I could feel it," I admit, and he drops his head, letting it land on my collarbone. Without a single doubt, he can hear how fast my pulse is going.

"You could feel it?" he asks, his breath hot on my skin, lighting every part of me on fire. I slide my fingers over the back of his neck, intertwining them there. Shivers run down my spine as the aching between my legs forces me to press them together for any sort of relief.

"Yes," I croak out while the tips of his fingers run up my bare legs, my skirt lifting a little too. I've never been this turned on in my entire life. Everything aches, begging me to let him touch every part of me.

"Is this okay?" he asks while I bite back a little moan.

"More than."

"Do you feel what I need right now?" he asks then, his nose brushing my collarbone.

"Your mouth on me," I say, and he chuckles against me. It weakens my knees to the point where he has to hold me up by my hips.

"Yes, *mami*. That is exactly where I need my mouth. All over you," he says, and I let out a small whimper when his nose grazes the most sensitive area on my neck. "Right here. This is where I want my tongue," he adds, brushing his nose over the same spot again. "Do you want that too?"

"Yes," I blurt out before he even finishes the sentence. Another chuckle from him. God, I wish he'd show me his face.

"You better be sure, love, because one taste won't be enough for me," he says, still holding me up because I'm incapable of doing it myself anymore.

"Scarlette? Are you in here? We're all waiting for you," Bex's familiar voice fills my ears, and I snap out of the moment.

"Coming," I call back, and Julián drops his head against my neck in defeat.

"I swear, every single time," he says and then lets out a small groan. His head falls back, but his hands move to cup my face, grabbing my full attention. "Next time, there won't be any interruptions. Next time, when you tell me you want the same things I do, I will take hours, days even, to give it all to you, love."

His words have made me speechless. So all I do is nod. His hands drop from my face, making me feel the loss of his touch in the depths of my bones. He lets out a sigh and then clicks his tongue, shaking his head as he holds out his hand for me, turning to look the other way.

This has bothered him. He wants me, he almost had me, and we were interrupted. Again. The first time it was Elias, then his ex and her new boyfriend, and now Bex. I don't know if it's only physical for him or if there is something more, but all I know is that I'm enjoying every single second passing between us.

Dang it.

I really like him.

I really like Julián "Storm" Alvarez with every piece of me.

Chapter 21

Julián

Everything, every single part of my body, is on fire. I got so close to her, had her wanting me, and then we got fucking interrupted. *Again.* It took all of my willpower to step away from Scarlette when I knew she needed more, needed my tongue all over her as I promised. I heard her heartbeat, heard how its fast pace matched mine. I saw the way her breathing hitched, smelled the way her body craved my touch. I almost got to taste her, which, without a doubt, I know would have been the end of me. I would have had it all right then and there. After the way she protected me from my ex, the way her usually happy personality didn't reveal itself in front of them, was perfection. It was the best present I could have ever received. I just wish I would have gotten to unwrap her a little too.

Instead, I'm leading her to the grandstand where her friends are, trying to ignore the fact that she's the only one who has fought a battle for me in over a decade. I'm trying to ignore how her hand fits in mine like I was made for her, like every crease and indent in my skin were crafted for her to fit into. I'm trying to ignore the way my head's still spinning and the heat is swooshing through my veins in response to touching her. God, I need some distance from her to calm my body and, at the same time, I need to be even closer.

"Hey, Lettie!" Victoria Bennett says as the most beautiful woman sits down next to her, offering her a hug I wish was meant for me. I long for the feeling of her arms wrapped around me for the first time, to know how it is to be held by Scarlette, to hold her in return.

"I'm so excited," Scar states, wiggling in her seat. Her eyes shift to me, her face bright with happiness. I want to caress her cheek, press a soft kiss to her joyful lips, but instead, I grip the bench we're sitting on.

"The first game of their university lives. I can't imagine how nervous they must be, especially Aaron," Victoria says, and I stare down at the field, finding her boyfriend and team captain standing with the rest of the players.

Living in this small town my entire life has had two unfortunate outcomes. One, I seem to be fucking stuck here. Two, I know almost everything about everyone. It's annoying. I don't desire the knowledge of Aaron's romantic promposal to Victoria last year, which was the day they became a couple. Elias is the one who always collects all the gossip and then spreads it to me, despite all of my efforts to keep his mouth shut.

I shake my head, returning to the moment just in time to see Halo fucking Henderson winking at Scar next to me. Every jealous bone in my body catches on fire, desperate to storm down to where he is and put him in his rightful place. Scar already has a man, one who will worship her like no other ever could. We might be fake dating for now, but he has to understand that I will do *everything* to be right for Scarlette. *Everything*.

"You're so tense," she says, leaning her chin against my shoulder and taking my hand in both of hers.

The way she keeps showing me affection is driving me wild. Once we're alone, I'll have to ask her if she wants more. I have to know. When I'm certain it's only her and me, I will offer myself to her in every single way she desires. God, I'm so far gone, so far past the boundaries I set for myself after Holly, it scares me a little. It scares me how okay I am to be vulnerable again.

"Why are you so tense, baby?" Scar asks loud enough for other people around us to hear. I almost groan at the fact that I enjoy the way she addresses me but wish it would be in private, for my ears only.

"Because Halo is a fucking flirt, and if he doesn't reign it in, people are going to think you're dating him and not me," I whisper, when in reality I wanted to tell her that I want no other man winking at her, even breathing her way. It's a bullshit feeling I'd never act on, but I can't help the jealousy. We're not dating. If we were, it would be different. I'd feel secure knowing I was hers and she was mine.

"Are you jealous?" she teases, making my jaw clench with an aching force.

"No," I grit out, but we both know it's a lie.

"Look at me," she demands, and I obey, tilting my head to meet her amused gaze. "I only have eyes for you," Scar says loudly, making Victoria and some of their friends turn our way.

I can read in their confused and slightly disgusted faces what they're thinking. Storm is the town grump. He never speaks to anyone who isn't his family or best friend. His face is always pulled into a scowl, unhappy about everything. They can't fathom why a person like Scarlette, joyful in everything she does, would choose to be with me. If only they knew she wasn't really mine.

"The way he looks at you bothers me," I admit, and Scarlette chuckles, running her fingers down the length of my arm. She merely grazes my skin, but it lights me on fire nonetheless.

"Then do something about it," she says, leaning in until her face is right in front of mine.

"Not here, not with everyone watching, love." The first time I kiss her, she will know it is because I want to, not to prove to everyone we're dating.

"Okay," she mumbles, facing the field again. Her breathing is so uneven, I stand up in response. I need to give my body a break from all this aching she's responsible for. I think I might actually explode from heat if I don't put some distance between us right now.

"I'll be right back. I forgot something at my bike," I lie, walking toward it and leaving behind a confused Scarlette.

"Storm Alvarez is your boyfriend?" I hear Victoria ask as I walk away.

"Yes, all mine," Scarlette replies, sending my heart into another frenzy. At least she didn't have to lie to her friend about one part.

I am all hers.

When I make my way back to my seat, the game hasn't started yet, but there is a middle-aged man without hair in front of my girl. I've never seen him before, which means he must be new to Moonville too. He's speaking to Scarlette, but only when I get a bit closer, I realize how uncomfortable this man is making her. The usual smile on her face has long vanished, her shoulders are tense, and the way she leans away from him sends me into high alert.

I rush over to her.

"Maybe you could stop by my office so I could give you a few tips on how to improve your work on the assignments," the man says, and I realize he must be her professor. Scarlette gives him an unsure, polite smile.

"That's okay, I will figure it out by my—" The professor cuts her off before she can finish the sentence. It sends a wave of anger through me. I almost run to her.

"I really think you would benefit from my guidance, Ms. Roots," he says, and I stand in front of him, straightening out my back. I could spit on this man's head, something I find very appealing at the moment. He looks up to meet my furious gaze.

"I don't think that'll be necessary. Scarlette is far more intelligent than you could ever understand, and she will figure out what she's done wrong by herself. She does not need your guidance, and I suggest you stop bothering her about it, professor," I say, a threat in my warning.

"I'm sorry, and you are?" the bald man asks, and I tilt my head down, anger pulsing through me.

"Your worst nightmare if you do not leave Scarlette alone," I reply, holding his gaze until he looks away and shakes his head.

"I don't know what you think was going on here, but I was simply offering a student some guidance," he says, and I cross my arms in front of my chest, watching him.

"At a soccer game, outside of the classroom, and without accepting her answer when she said 'no'?" I ask because everyone here can see how creepy this guy is. The short man flinches backward a little.

"She didn't say 'no'." Oh, I want to beat the shit out of him.

"She may not have used that exact word, but she said no. Now leave her alone before I call campus security, or decide to take things into my own hands. I don't think you want to find out what kind of a person I am when I'm angry, *pendejo*," I say, slow enough so he can understand me clearly. Scarlette raises her hand to mine, taking a hold of it as her professor walks away without another word.

I look down at her, realizing Victoria and her other friends weren't here when he approached. I sit down beside her, and she grabs my arm, pressing herself against it. I wiggle it out of her grasp to slide it over her back and bring her body against my chest instead.

"Ever since the first class of the semester, I've had a bad feeling about him. I didn't tell anyone because it was just a gut feeling but this, what happened now, confirmed it. He always gives me weird looks too. It makes me very uncomfortable," Scar admits, pushing her cheek against me, seeking comfort. Under different circumstances, I'd be giddy as hell right now.

"When you feel like you cannot tell anyone, you tell me, okay? You always tell me, love, especially when it comes to this kind of situation," I say, and she shifts her head to look at me. It would be so easy to kiss away her frown in this position, too easy to make her happy again if my lips on hers had that effect.

"Why? We're not actually dating, you know?" she reminds me, and I can't help myself. I brush my nose over hers. Her cheeks flush a bright pink before a smile returns to her features.

"Because I will always believe you, no matter if we're dating or not, and I will make sure that slimy man stays the fuck away from you," I say, earning myself another smile from her. I want to enjoy the way she looks at me, how close she is, but I'm still fuming over what just happened.

"Julián?" she asks, and I hardly manage to keep my eyes open. They always want to flutter shut at the way she pronounces my name perfectly.

"Yes, *mami*?" I reply, keeping eye contact. It sends a wave of heat through me.

"Next time we make a public appearance, no more drama, okay?" she asks, and I grab her chin between my fingers, desperate to show her as much affection as I can while she's comfortable with me doing so. She waits patiently, running her fingers over my chest now.

"Next time, we will have dinner, at yours or my house. I can cook. It can be just the two of us," I say, earning myself a full-faced smile from her.

"That sounds really nice," she replies, leaning away from me.

"Stay," I beg, surprising both of us. Her head falls back against my chest while I wrap my arm tighter around her.

This is good. Here, she will be safe from any harm. I can protect her like this. It also keeps me from finding her professor and ensuring he will never look at her again. How would I do that exactly? I'm not quite sure. Probably threaten to get him fired or punch out a few teeth. Both are very possible.

My dad owns most of Moonville, and I'd do anything to protect Scar.

Chapter 22
Scarlette

Today is race day for Julián. After he dropped me back home on Monday—our team won by two goals—he promised to pick me up at ten in the morning so we could go together to where the event is. We've spent the past week texting every single day, even calling sometimes at night just to talk. We speak about everything and sometimes nothing at all. It's wonderful.

I've just finished getting ready, adding some simple makeup, and putting on his jersey again, when the doorbell rings. It's my day off school and work, but Violet went to work very early this morning. So, I make my way to the door, confused because it is still too early for Julián to pick me up.

"Lettie!" my mother says as I open the door, her arms wrapping around me as soon as she's able to. "How are you, sweetie?" she asks, and I stumble out of her grasp.

"Mom, what are you doing here?"

This is bad. This is possibly the worst thing that could have happened today. She does not know I'm pretending to date Julián, or even that I'm actually 'dating' him. I didn't lie to her nor did I tell her the truth. I simply avoided her. I didn't take her calls for the past week but texted her to say I'm busy. Since this agreement between Julián and me was only supposed to last for four weeks, I didn't see a problem keeping this from her. I didn't expect her to show up here, uninvited, and on the day I was supposed to cheer on my fake boyfriend at his very real race. And tomorrow, we were supposed to have dinner. *Crap! What am I going to do now?*

"I was worried about you. I thought maybe your anxiety got worse again and that's why you—"

She cuts off at the sound of a bike engine roaring up my driveway. Her head spins around until she sees my gorgeous fake date parking his machine and then pulling off his helmet. Julián freezes when he sees my mother, unsure whether I want him to approach or not. It's right then that I notice how wide my eyes have gotten. Panic. It's filling me like a glass under a streaming faucet.

"Who is that?" Mom asks, shooting me a look I know too well. It's her way of saying 'He's so hot' without having to speak the words.

I hesitate in my response. Julián hesitates walking over. It's almost as if time freezes, taunting me by dragging out this uncomfortable moment. I try to speak, but except for a weird wheezing sound, nothing else comes out. Mom raises an eyebrow at me at the same time as Julián starts walking toward us. She will see through it the second he doesn't kiss me. I know it. Mom is a big believer in affection.

"Scarlette, he's holding a bundle of lavender! Is he your boyfriend? You have a boyfriend you didn't tell me about?" Her first question is filled with excitement, the second one tainted with disappointment.

"Yes," I lie before overthinking things any further.

She turns her head away, looking at Julián, and I use that opportunity to mouth two words I never wanted to tell him this way. *Kiss me.* His eyes narrow before understanding washes over him.

"Hi, *arcoíris*," Julián says when he's close enough for me to hear, sending a wave of heat into my cheeks. He stops in front of my mother, holding out his hand with a neutral expression on his face. "Mrs. Roots, it's a pleasure to meet you. I'm Storm."

Dang, he really did understand my panic. I could kiss him for it, which I guess will happen sooner now than I thought.

After they shake hands, he moves over to me, bringing the smallest smile to his lips. I want to drink it in, the way his features brighten ever so slightly, trace them with the tips of my fingers. He doesn't give me a moment to linger on it when his hands move to my neck and he leans down, pressing his lips to my... *right cheek?* I notice then that his entire body is covering me so all my mother saw was him kissing me, just not where in the face exactly. Smart. Disappointing, but smart.

Julián leans back quickly, the pad of his thumb tracing where his lips have left a trail of heat and electricity on my face.

"Here, love," he says before handing me the bundle of lavender. "I read that you can make your own lavender essential oil with these. I thought maybe it could be a fun project for us to do," he says, sending a wave of emotion through me. It lingers deep in my heart.

"I'd love that," I blurt out, barely holding back from letting my feelings drop down my cheeks. "Thank you," I say, and he slips his arm around me, guiding me against his side where he presses a kiss to my forehead. My eyes flutter shut in response to his affection.

My mother has to be convinced now. No one goes to such lengths if they don't have some feelings for the other person. *Right?*

"What brings you to our small town, Mrs. Roots?" Julián asks causing my eyes to open again, staring up at him as he holds me close.

"My daughter has been ignoring my calls, so I thought I would check on her," she replies, and I tense when she shoots me a glare. He squeezes my side, nodding a little at my mother's words.

"I'm afraid that's my fault, ma'am. I've been keeping Scar rather occupied," he says, and Mom lets out a slight laugh.

"You finally got laid? Good for you. Only took twenty years," she says with a laugh that sends a terrible shiver down my back.

I want to die. The embarrassment is so horrifying, for a moment, I'm convinced I might actually pass away. Julián has tensed immensely beside me, his eyes have dropped to my face, and his lips have parted in surprise. Yeah, I want to crawl into a hole and die. Get away from this horrible situation Mom has thrown me into.

"Anyway, are we going to stand out here all day?" she asks, shifting my attention back to her.

"No, Julián and I have to go. He has a motorcycle race today," I state, breaking a bit of the tension.

"I thought his name was Storm," Mom says, and I give her my full attention.

"To everyone else, he's Storm. To me, he's Julián," I explain, but Mom gives me a strange look I don't have the patience to decrypt.

"You're welcome to join us at the race, of course," he adds, and Mom claps her hands together.

"Excellent. Give me a moment while I use the washroom," she says, pinching my butt as she passes by me.

As soon as she is out of sight, I step away from Julián, letting more embarrassment heat up my cheeks. This is by far the worst way he could have found out I was a virgin. I saw that conversation going a hundred ways, none of them involving my mother being the one to share this with him.

"Scar?" he asks, and I screw my eyes shut.

"Yeah?" I reply, turning away from him to hide my pink cheeks.

"Must I speak to your backside, love?" he says, and I run my hands over my face, not willing to answer yet. I take a deep breath, letting it back out a moment later.

"Yes," is all I respond. Great. I'm turning into him.

Julián appears in front of me then, his hands holding my arms to keep me from spinning around once more. It's almost as if he knew I'd do that, which I most certainly would have. There is no way I can look into his eyes while we talk about this. Everything else sex-related, sure. But not this.

"This," he says, running his hands over my arms. "It's all new to you?" I nod. My throat has dried up, making it impossible to speak. "Is that why you wanted sex off the table?" he asks, but his question brings back my more confident side.

"No, I took sex off the table because there was no trust between us," I reply, and his eyes go wide with understanding.

"But you trust me now, otherwise you wouldn't have said yes to me on Monday," he points out, and I nod once more. "Jesus, *mami*, the things I've wanted to do, said that I want to do, you've never even experienced anything close to it." For some reason, the way he says it makes me angry.

"Yeah, well, so what? I was busy. My parents lost their jobs, and I had to take care of them for two years. Sex wasn't high on my priority list," I bark, and Julián's eyes go wide with shock.

"Love, that's not what I meant. I'm simply surprised," he says, but I'm so done with the spotlight being on me and my inexperience, I brush him off.

"Whatever," I say, annoyed with him now. He grabs my wrist, dragging me to his chest. Frustratingly enough, I melt into him. "I don't want to talk about this anymore. I think I was embarrassed enough," I say, spitting the words a lot more harshly than necessary.

"Let me teach you," he says, causing heat to spread between my legs, weakening my knees and causing the ache to reappear. My eyes fixate on the birthmark painted across his cheek, so beautiful and unique, just like his differently colored eyes.

"I don't need you to teach me. I know how sex works," I scoff, but Julián cups my face for the second time today, his throat working as he swallows hard.

"Then let me show you how good it feels," he says, his lips dropping to my mouth.

A moment before they meet, Mom walks back outside. I step back, hearing Julián say something in Spanish. I'm convinced it's swear words. This is getting ridiculous. Every time he and I grow closer, we get pulled apart. Considering that we are supposed to be fake dating and PDA would be a good way to make sure people believe us, we are constantly interrupted.

This is the longest foreplay of anyone's life.

"Let's go?" Mom asks with a knowing smile, causing me to glare at her.

"Yes, let's go," my fake boyfriend chimes in, taking my hand and leading me to Mom's car.

This is going to go horribly wrong.

Chapter 23
Scarlette

M om said she wanted to sit in the back so Julián could be next to me. He's taken this opportunity to watch me the entire drive. It's a good thing Mom brought her car because she hates being on a motorcycle, but I don't know what she's trying to achieve by sitting behind me. Maybe she wants to watch the way my fake boyfriend is looking at me right now, the longing and lust in his eyes that he's selling way too perfectly.

"Eres la mujer más bonita en todo el mundo, mami," Julián says after a while, making me furrow my brows at him.

"What does that mean?" I ask, but he simply reaches out to touch my cheek, running the back of his index finger over it. "You're not going to tell me, are you?" I say with a small smile, and he shakes his head, his serious expression hardening his features.

"No." It's all I get before he breaks skin contact and continues to study my face.

"So, how did you two meet?" Mom asks, trying to make small talk. I keep my mouth shut, shooting Julián a side glance.

"Violet and my best friend, Elias, are dating. They introduced us. Scarlette also works for my father, so I get to see her often," he says, never looking away from me.

"And what do you do, Storm?" she goes on, and he shifts his head to focus on her face.

135

I know what he sees. Mom is an older version of me, except she has a slim built and brown hair instead of black. My dad is the one with my hair color. Mom also has blue eyes, and her bottom lip is slightly less full than her top, just like mine. We have the same sharp nose and round face.

"I tutor English to children who immigrated here from South America," he replies, and I feel my face soften. I didn't know that. He hadn't shared his job with me yet, but it makes me like him even more. "It's great for them because I speak Spanish too, so they feel more comfortable with me," he explains, and my insides turn. "I work a few hours a week at the local middle school, but my main job would be racing, I guess. I make some money every race weekend."

"That's nice, honey. You sound like you have figured everything out in your life already, and this early on. How old are you?" Mom asks, and Julián gives her a tiny smile.

"Twenty-one, ma'am," he replies, earning himself a raise of her eyebrows.

"Only? You seem quite mature for your age," she goes on, and I would love to step in and end this conversation because Mom's intentions aren't pure. I know they're not. She's trying to find a flaw in Julián.

"I have an incredible mom to thank for that." God, I really like him so much.

"And how do you like Moonville? Have you lived here your whole life?" *Mom, stop asking questions.* That's what my look says when I catch her glancing at me in my mirror.

"I didn't like Moonville, not until Scarlette showed up here." No, he needs to stop talking. When he speaks, I want to fall into his words, let them envelop me in the emotions and safety they provide. "*Mi arcoíris*," he adds softly, only loud enough for me to hear.

I catch Mom looking approvingly out the window, silence finally filling the car again. Julián goes back to studying every little thing about my face, and I shift in my seat. I've never had someone wanting to see every detail about me, find things I may not even have discovered about myself.

"What do you see?" I ask quietly at a red light, and then it happens.

His face stretches into a soft smile, wider than any he's ever offered me before. Creases appear in his cheeks, turning him even more gorgeous than he already is, if that's possible. His eyes light up with happiness, and my heartbeat hitches in response. Fire spreads over my face until I'm grinning from ear to ear, drinking in every second of his beautiful smile. I might be in love with it.

"You, Scar. I only ever see you now," he replies, sending a storm of butterflies to my stomach.

"That's not what I meant," I whisper, the strength in my voice gone. Julián continues to smile.

"I know."

This man and his short responses bring a wave of frustration to my very being. It also awakens a very interesting question. *Why do I love it so much?* Every emotion and feeling he brings out in me is... *wonderful*. It's wonderful beyond sense.

For two years, all I did was work. I didn't have time for things like falling in love or even experiencing intimacy with another human being. There was someone once, when I was seventeen, but after a kiss I knew she wasn't into, we went our separate ways. With Julián, everything is different. Whatever I feel, he reciprocates it. He makes me feel wanted and sexy and safe.

But I'm scared.

I realize it right here and now that I'm terrified of sharing my anxiety with him. When people find out, when they see what happens to me, they start treating me differently. They see me as damaged, incapable of taking care of myself. I don't want Julián to treat me any other way than he would someone without anxiety. The way he treats me currently, I need that to keep going. If not, I'm afraid I might lose him.

A honk from behind me startles me out of my thoughts. Julián gives me a cock of his eyebrow, confusion settling on his face as he glances at me. He takes my hand in his, sensing that I need comfort. It's irritating how we can feel what the other person needs, and we haven't even spent a lot of time together, especially not just the two of us.

"*¿Qué pasa? Dime*," he says, and I can't help the genuine smile when I realize I understood him. Simple things like this, I can rhyme together. Others, I'm completely lost.

"*Nada*," I reply with a grin, and he squeezes my hand, obviously not believing me.

I don't explain. I know I should. Having anxiety isn't something to be ashamed of, and I'm not. The only problem is the questions filling my mind, questions I cannot stop.

What if he finds out and decides to break off our arrangement?

What if he looks at me differently?

What if it upsets him to see me in an anxiety attack?

What if it affects his life negatively, like it did with my parents?

What if it will change everything?

There is a big part inside of me screaming back at these questions. It's telling me to disregard every single one of those thoughts because Julián would never do any of those things.

No.

He would tell me I'm the strongest woman in the world, with no hesitation or doubt in his mind.

The race starts soon after we arrived at the track. Julián gave me a kiss on the cheek before speaking to someone at the venue and arranging passes for Mom and me. We get to go almost everywhere with them, which surprises me. Unwilling to be a bother, we decided to walk alongside the fences separating the people from the track. Now we've stopped somewhere close to the first corner, waiting for Julián to come racing by. When he does, my heart skips several beats. He's wearing full body armor in Hawke colors and their logo— a hawk grasping onto the word 'Hawke'— plastered across his chest. He zooms past us, and, for some reason, I find it so hot, my skin lights on fire. *My man is a racer.* Except, he isn't really my man. The thought makes the corners of my mouth drop into a frown. He can't be mine. He will probably never be mine.

"I can't believe you didn't tell me you have a drop-dead gorgeous racer boyfriend who is infatuated with you," Mom says, and I shift my focus to her blue eyes, detesting the fact that we will have a conversation about my lie. I don't want to lie to Mom.

"I'm sorry I didn't tell you," I reply, but she looks genuinely upset with me.

"I thought we were closer than that," she adds, and guilt spreads through my chest. I settle on telling her bits and pieces of the truth.

"We are, Mom, I just—Julián overwhelmed me, even if it was in the best way possible. He knocked me off my feet and carried me all the way into a new world full of experiences I never even dreamed of," I start and stare back at the track right as he zooms past again. He's in second place, sending a wave of pride over me. "He's more than sexy and handsome. He's sweet and kind, and he looks at me like I'm the most beautiful woman in the world."

Mom gives me a small smile, studying my face for any sort of lies. She doesn't believe me for some unknown reason, so I decide to give her the one thing she won't doubt. She'll believe me because it's a truth weighing so heavy on me, I haven't even dared to say it out loud to Violet.

"Julián excites me. It feels like he unpaused my life, and I can't get enough of him. Every little detail I discover about him satisfies a part inside of me I don't understand. I can't begin to explain how much I like him," I admit in a rant. Mom studies me with a cocked eyebrow.

"Then why didn't you tell me about him? Why did I have to find it out like this?" She's still upset with me about it, and I can't blame her. I just didn't want to lie to her.

"Because I wanted this to be mine for a little while, all mine," I lie, but she gives me an understanding nod.

We don't speak much after this. I keep my eyes trained on the track, waiting for Julián to race by every few minutes. When the race finishes, I cannot believe it. He won. He fought the whole time, and he freaking won. I jump into his arms the first chance I get because Mom is constantly watching us now, but mostly because I want to. I want to hug him, tell him how proud I am of this accomplishment. I want to hold his sweaty body against mine and whisper what a great motorbike racer he is right into his ear. So I do it. I do it all. And he hugs me close to him, not letting go for several minutes. Ecstasy is shooting through both of us as we simply keep holding onto each other.

Fake dating or not, I know this moment is real, and it's all ours.

Chapter 24
Julián

"Earth to Storm, are you still present?" Elias asks, and I force my eyes to him.

"No," I reply, staring back down at the ground.

We've just come back from a run, but my mind has been stuck on what Scarlette might be doing for the past three days. It's been as long since I've last seen her, and it's driving me wild. It's been three weeks since we agreed to fake date. After the Saturday of my race, Scar and I managed to meet for dinner and dessert dates every few days. However, her mom is still here, living with her in that tiny house, and Scar can't always leave to be with me. I'm happy she gets to spend time with one of her parents. Simultaneously, not getting to see her as much as I know we both want to has been bothering me. Not looking into her pale blue eyes, seeing her scar run through her lips or her stunning body brings an aching pain to my bones. Every part of me craves to be in her presence, especially after what happened in the car two weeks ago.

I smiled. For the first time in years, I smiled in front of someone, and there was no guilt blooming in my chest. It felt right to do it, especially when I saw how happy it made Scarlette. She grinned back at me, overcome with joy at the happy look on my face. I wanted to do it again, and so I did. Still, there was no shame inside of me for doing so. I haven't tried smiling at anyone else since then, but I have a weird feeling Scar is the only one my heart wants to give that look to. On our dates, she pulls them out of me every single time she does something sweet, and it's dangerous because that woman is the kindest, cutest person in the world. It's fucking with my grumpy reputation, which is probably why people always stare at us wherever we go.

We haven't touched much since the Saturday of my race weekend, but I take her hand every chance she gives me. Scar might still think I'm only taking her on dates to cement the foundation of our fake relationship, but nothing about how I feel is fake. She's become one of my best friends, someone I want to be around constantly. God, I miss her so much.

"If you miss her, go see her," Elias interrupts my thoughts, and I let out a heavy sigh. Great, he can read my thoughts now. *Perfecto.*

"I will see her tomorrow when we fly to Monaco for the race," I explain, and Elias gives me a small nod.

"How long will you be gone?" he asks, making sadness creep into my chest.

"Five days."

Then our agreement comes to an end unless I can convince Dad to fly us to another race. Not only would it allow me to keep being with Scar, it would also help further her career. It's a win-win situation, but one I cannot focus on yet. I should give all of my attention to these next five days.

"Why don't you finally tell her how you feel? Make this fake dating situation a real dating situation?" he says, and I sit down on the steps of our porch, letting his question weigh heavy on me.

"Because I don't even know if she considers us friends at this point. She hated me when we first met, and if those feelings haven't changed, me admitting my own could ruin her weekend. I won't do that to her. It's far too important," I explain, making my best friend's face turn serious.

"You're a good man," Elias says, and I furrow my brows.

"Why? Because I'm capable of putting her needs before mine? That's the very least I could ever do for the woman I care more deeply for than anyone else I've ever been with," I reply, shock pulling his features apart until his eyes and mouth have widened to the max.

"You do? You never even spoke about Holly this way," he says.

"Yeah because she wasn't Scarlette. No one will ever be Scar. She's dedicated, loving, kind, beautiful beyond reason, and perfect for me in every ironic way. I'm the dark, she's the light. I'm the broken, she's the healed. I'm the frown, she's the smile. These opposites need each other in order to exist, just like I need her now."

I'm not ashamed to admit any of this. I've never been great with my words, but they come naturally these days. It's fascinating.

"You've only known her for a little more than two months," Elias reminds me, and I nod absentmindedly.

"I've never even kissed her either, but it doesn't change how I feel. It doesn't change how needy she makes me, for her attention and her touch, her warmth and her love. I would never ask for it, but I take any and all she decides to give me."

My best friend gives me another look of disbelief before shaking his head. We talk about our feelings, sure, but it's mostly him sharing, not me. That has drastically changed since Scarlette showed up in Moonville. Everything has. Pieces of me have opened up again, opened to the possibilities she's presented to me.

"You're fucked," Elias says, and I let out a humorless snort.

"Yeah, no shit," I reply, picking up a small rock in front of me and rolling it between my thumb and index finger.

"We're both fucked because the way you feel about Scarlette? I've felt about Violet for a while now. And, man, getting to hold her, be with her, touch her, it's all so overwhelming to me. Sometimes it feels like I can't breathe when I'm away from her, but as soon as I see her, watch the smile cross her face, I'm breathless too." I know that feeling well. The thought even brings a small smile to my face. "Oh my God, she's done it! Scarlette, she's done it!" he cheers, and I shake my head, still smiling a bit.

"She's done a lot of things to me."

Scarlette has done *everything* to me. All of my emotions have been flipped and turned inside out. My brain is stuck on her every second of the day, longing to have any type of words spoken between us. Physically, I'm constantly craving her touch. Holding her, feeling her body in my hands, tracing her features, it all sends a wave of shock through me until every cell is begging, vibrating with the need to be with her. God, I feel myself harden at the thought of her pressing against me, kissing me. These aren't thoughts or reactions I should have, but they're unstoppable at this point. I ache for her. I ache to be in her presence at all times. I ache to have her be mine in every single way I am already hers.

"If you were to date her, would you be able to trust her fully, no jealousy or anything?" Elias asks, and I suck in a sharp breath, letting out a hissed one.

"You mean because of what Holly did?" I ask, watching my best friend nod in response.

"She really hurt your ability to trust someone," he adds, his voice low and barely audible at this point.

"She did, but if I close myself off from the rest of the world because of what she put me through, I will die a lonely man. I don't want to be alone. I enjoy dating. I enjoy coming home to someone at the end of an exhausting day, have someone cheer for me at my races. I enjoy spoiling the fuck out of someone. I didn't want another relationship because the right person wasn't here. In this small town, there wasn't anyone I wanted to be vulnerable for again. Scarlette, *el arcoíris de mi vida*, she makes me want to be everything she desires. Call me a fool, naïve even, but no matter what she needs, I will be it for her. Reciprocated or not, I'm hers," I say, ending my rant and letting in oxygen again.

Everything I've been bottling up since I met Scarlette, all of my fears and desires, has come to the surface now, and I don't plan on suppressing it again. Instead, I tilt my head up to the sunny sky, enjoying the warmth on my skin. Moonville's weather is fantastic. I should take Scarlette to the beach just outside of town when we get back on Tuesday. Tuesday... when we will no longer be a fake couple or anything if she decides it to be so. *Puñeta*. Fear slices through me.

"Storm?" Elias asks, and I shift my head in his direction. A serious look has pulled his lips into a thin line, his eyes filling with dread. "I can't watch you get your heart shattered again," he says, so I place a hand on his shoulder.

"I promise, no matter what happens, I won't shut you out this time," I reply, and his arms wrap around me a second later. Hesitation keeps my arms by my side for a moment before I return his embrace and pat his back.

"You better not." I could never. The two months after Holly cheated on me, I was a mess. And I didn't accept his help. He was always trying to find a way to comfort me, but I needed to work through it by myself. "By the way, I snatched the muffins off the counter and took them to Violet when you left them there three weeks ago. She loved them," he says, draining the color from my face as I lean away from the hug.

"YOU STOLE THEM?"

Once I'd realized I'd completely forgotten them that Monday, I'd planned on bringing them to her the next day. They were nowhere to be found, so I thought maybe I'd left them when I filled gas. I came up with all sorts of scenarios of what had happened. I should have known it was my best friend.

"Hey now, I thought you'd decided against offering them to Scarlette," he says, standing up while I let anger course through me.

"I spent an hour on those muffins for Scarlette, not for you and your girlfriend," I say, too calmly for the way I'm feeling. Elias lets out an uneasy laugh before taking another step backward.

"Yeah, well..." He trails off, walking closer toward his bike. I watch him with half-closed eyes, glaring. "I'm not even sorry," he says, sprinting to his bike and pulling the helmet on top of his head.

"Run," I reply, and he flings his leg over his bike doing just that.

After I've let out several small sighs, I click my tongue and strut back inside the house, taking a much-needed shower. The water calms my nerves, but Scar's face slips into my head, sending a shiver down my back. I let the memory of her running her soft fingers through my hair and down my torso replay in my head, feeling the blood rush to my cock until it stiffens uncomfortably.

I bring my hand to it, stroking it slowly as Scarlette's laugh rings in my ears. Then, the sound of her breathless voice, a little moan leaving her sends more arousal to my dick.

"Oh God," I groan, pumping my length slowly.

I shouldn't do this. I shouldn't jerk off to the memory of her under my complete control when we were at the soccer game, but I need to find some release. It's been a while since I've had sex, and every moment I spend with Scar, my body reminds me how desperate I am to be inside her. Only her.

I pick up my pace, stroking my cock harder now until I feel the release of my build-up inching closer. Pleasure storms through me, settling in my body in waves, originating from my dick and going all the way into my toes. Fire has spread through every part of me, weighing heavy on my body as I continue pumping my hand up and down my length. Fuck, I can't help but wish my hand was replaced by Scar wrapped around me.

Scar...

I wonder if she touches herself to the thought of my touch, my face, my body. I wonder if she wants me deep inside her, right where I crave to be. I wonder if my mouth on her skin occupies her every thought. Does she know how to pleasure herself properly? God, I want to teach her if she doesn't. I want to experience everything with her, show her just how much fun sex can be.

Another image of her, her fingers slipping into her panties as she pleasures herself to the thought of me, washes into my mind, pushing me right over the edge. My cock pulses in my hand, releasing the tension inside of me until relief consumes my very being. I spill into the shower, not giving a damn about anything anymore.

"Fuuuuuck," I say as I stroke myself a few more times, enjoying the orgasm as it pulses through my veins, filling me with a little bit of ecstasy, but not as much as having sex with Scar would. Jesus. I have to stop thinking about it, about her.

I finish showering, then get dressed to walk back into the kitchen and bake a cake for her. Scarlette deserves to be spoiled to the max, and I haven't quite accomplished that goal of mine yet. I think about the smile she'll give me when I hand it to her, making me wonder if I'll get a kiss on the cheek from her too.

I smile to myself as I gather the ingredients.

Chapter 25

Scarlette

It's been minutes, hours maybe. I'm not sure. My body has been shaking from the earthquake the anxiety has awoken within me. My facial features are twitching and contorting in the worst ways possible, but I'm unable to force them into my usual smile. There is no smiling through this. There never has been in the years I've suffered from these attacks.

I'm wheezing. All of the stupid breath exercises I've tried have never helped me control my breathing during this. Instead, I'm sucking in sharp breaths, my lungs burning from the strained action. God, this is excruciating. I'm exhausted. I'm so freaking tired, but my body is under anxiety's control. Not mine. Never mine in these situations. It feels like I'm dying, which only sends more fear through my body. Anxiety feeds off fear. It wouldn't exist within me without it. I've often wondered if I was less scared of my own mind, trusted myself more to get through this, *would I have anxiety? Would these attacks happen like one of them is right now?*

A slight scream leaves me, and I suck in another sharp breath that makes me wheeze. This is the ugliest side of me. I don't ever want anyone to see me writhing in pain from an attack like this. It scares me a little how quickly I've lost control of myself when that thought had scared me so much, it was the reason I got anxiety in the first place. My intrusive thoughts were always about losing control. *What if I couldn't control this? What if I couldn't control that?* It's ridiculous, really, since most things are not in anyone's hands. Humans were not designed to have a handle on everything. Death, life, loss, love, it's not up to anyone to control as they see fit.

My legs are tingling now. Soon they're asleep while my body goes numb. I can't feel my limbs anymore. They're burning, but I can't move them. All strength has vanished as I cry and cry and cry. Tears keep streaming down my face, but I have to stay quiet. Mom is in the other room, and she cannot see me like this. She'll make me move back to her house, or worse, she'll move to Moonville. Neither option is acceptable.

So, I bite down on my cramping mouth, keeping the sobs inside and the wheezing for air to a minimum. Trying to hold back an anxiety attack is difficult. Heck, it's nearly impossible, but I can do this. I can stop crying. I can find the strength in my bones to get up off this cold bathroom floor and get into the shower. I can uncramp my facial features. I can breathe properly again. I can stop my hands from shaking. I can... *I can't do it.*

I'm so tired. I don't want to fight this anymore. I don't want to be like this anymore. This way of living, it's exhausting. These attacks, they drain the life out of me little by little each time. It feels like, even if I want to keep fighting, eventually, my body will give out on me.

My heart can't do this any longer. It can't keep racing like this, thumping aggressively against my ribcage. No matter how hard I fight, my anxiety is killing me from the inside.

But I will keep fighting.

It doesn't matter how many times I land on the floor, numb and scared and hopeless, I will keep fighting for the days I'm fine. They outweigh the bad ones, even if it doesn't feel that way in my worst moments. I may be tired, but it's not always like this. It can't always be like this. It won't.

I reach for my sink, pushing myself up using every ounce of my strength. It seems like an hour since I first felt the panic settle inside of me and ran to the bathroom. It was probably only twenty minutes, but I lose all sense of time during an anxiety attack. It's hard to focus on anything but trying not to let the feeling of 'I'm dying' push me further into the panic.

"Oh, Storm! It's so nice to see you, honey. Come in," I hear my mother say from the entrance, causing a shock to travel through my system.

No, no, no, no. This can't be happening. He cannot see me like this.

I run my hands over my tear-stained face, trying to fix my appearance. When it doesn't work, I turn on the shower, stepping inside and letting the water slide down my body. There is a soft knock on the door, and I call back, telling Mom I will be right out of the shower. She gives me a little 'okay' before leaving me to finish washing.

My head is aching. It's tired from fighting against the anxiety. I take a few breaths, but it continues to throb, my brain letting me know it's done all it could to help me today, which is fine. I don't think another attack will hit me.

Once I feel calmer and better, I step out of the shower, wrapping a towel around myself. There are no clean clothes of mine in here, which is probably something I should have thought of before showering. I let out a small sigh as I leave the bathroom, hoping Mom took Julián outside on the veranda. Considering they're nowhere to be seen while I walk toward my room, she must have.

I close my bedroom door, making my way to the closet after. Right as I'm about to drop my towel, someone clears their throat from my bed. I jump in surprise, clutching the fabric to my body. Julián stands up, raising his hands with a soft expression on his face.

"I'm sorry, love, your mom told me to wait in here, and I assumed if I said no, she wouldn't believe we're dating. I hope that's okay," he says, and I force a small smile at him. His features soften even more. "Scar, are you okay?" he asks, and, for some reason, tears shoot into my eyes in response.

What the heck?

"Yes, fine, why?" I ask, but he's taking three long strides toward me now, cupping my face in his hands to search it.

"What happened, love? *Dime*," he begs, and I'm close to breaking into tears of exhaustion. I manage to smile through the pain.

"Nothing, I'm all good. Now, turn around so I can get dressed," I say with a small laugh, but he's not even slightly amused. His eyes show only worry and concern.

"*Dime*," he pleads, and the resistance inside of me drops ever so slightly.

"I'm having a bad day," I admit in order to tell him some of the truth but not all of it.

"How can I turn it into a good one?" he asks, caressing my cheeks with the pads of his thumbs.

"Hold me?" I ask, tears falling down my face.

This isn't what he signed up for, it isn't what we're supposed to be doing, but there is something about him, about his presence, that soothes me. I wish I could explain it to myself, wish I could understand it, but I haven't understood anything when it comes to Julián since we met.

"Always, *mami*, always," he replies, bringing me against his chest.

I break down in his arms without meaning to. Julián guides me to my bed, dropping onto it before bringing me between his legs and letting me nuzzle my face into his neck. He makes sure the towel is covering me the whole time, smoothing over the material whenever it rides a little higher. He doesn't care that I'm naked. All he wants is to hold and comfort me while I cry against him.

The tears are streaming down my face because I can never be with him. I can never be with anyone while my mental health burdens me. After the next five days, I will have to let Julián get back to his life, despite how much I like him. I will not throw over his life, seeing if he'd want to make our fake relationship a real one. It would be too selfish. I've seen first-hand what my anxiety does to the people around me, and I can't do that to Julián. He deserves better.

"I'm sorry, I'm getting you all wet with my tears," I mumble against his neck, but he simply runs his hands over my arm, pressing me into his hard chest. His scent, sandalwood, fills my nose, sending a wave of calm over me.

Huh... interesting.

"I don't care about that, love. All I care about is holding you."

He's too sweet. I know we started off on the wrong foot and he may have come off as a jerk before, but he's not. At least he isn't that way with me anymore. Everything he's done since we agreed to fake date is be the best boyfriend in the world. He isn't even my freaking boyfriend. *Why is he acting like this? Why is he making me want things I can't have? Why do I want to confess my feelings and have him kiss me and tell me he feels the same?*

"Do you want to talk about the race weekend? Maybe it will make you feel better," he says, and a genuine smile slips across my face.

"It would," I reply as one of his hands drops to my waist, guiding me even further against him. My eyes are closed as I enjoy the way he smells, my nose pressed right against his neck. He smoothes down the towel again, ensuring I'm fully covered.

"Okay, let's see," he starts, bringing his lips to the top of my head and placing a kiss there as he thinks. I smile against him. "We're going to fly out tomorrow, land on Thursday morning, and attend the driver's meet and greet in the evening. My father will most likely introduce you to Robert Fuchs on Friday, and we're going to make sure he loves you, an easy task really," he says, making my heart flutter. "Then, Saturday and Sunday, we will have a great time watching the drivers on the track, racing for the win. Maybe I can even arrange for you to meet Leonard Tick on Thursday," he goes on, and I let out a small snort.

"Yeah, right," I reply, my fingers playing with his shirt.

"It will be a lot of fun," he says, and I suck in a sharp breath.

"Do you think your dad will believe we're dating, even though we're not?" I ask, panic lacing my tone. Julián tilts my head up to him, giving me another small smile.

"Don't worry. He will believe it once he sees us together, sees the way I look at you," Julián assures me, and my lips pull into a grin. He likes me... It vanishes as soon as I realize that we can never be. I can't do it to him.

There is silence for a few moments before he breaks it again.

"Did your professors give you a hard time for missing four classes?" he asks, his fingertips running down the length of my arm while I stay in his. I feel safe here, and everything about him has calmed me.

"No, they were fine with it. They gave me readings to help me stay on track, but they were all quite supportive when I told them what the trip was for," I explain, letting a little bit of excitement course through me.

"That's good," he says, pressing another kiss to the top of my head.

My tears have slowed and my heart has found its proper rhythm again. I'm not stupid. I know it's because of Julián. I also know there is no way I can get used to this.

"Scar?" he asks, his finger gently tracing my scar. I freeze as he does it, not uncomfortable but surprised. I've been insecure about it for years, but he's made me feel like it's the loveliest thing in the world.

I look up at him.

"Julián?" I say with a small smile, and he sucks in a sharp breath. He hesitates, not sure how to continue voicing his thoughts.

"I want to be your friend." I can't help but beam up at him, my eyes fixated on his green-brown ones, one different than the other.

"You want to be my friend?" I ask, my eyes fluttering shut as his thumb runs over the length of the mark going through my lips.

"For now, yes," he says, and I force my gaze back to him.

"And after?" I ask, scared of his answer because either way, pain will shoot through my chest. Either way, I can't have him.

Julián simply places his forehead against mine.

"*Quiero ser tu todo, arcoíris*," he replies, and I let out an annoyed groan.

"Why do you do that? Just say something else," I say with a roll of my eyes. Julián grabs my chin between his fingers to tilt my head to him again.

"But I don't like switching the subject when it comes to this, and I won't lie to you. I will tell you the truth in English soon, I promise," he says, letting go of my face as he pulls me even closer against his chest.

"I will learn Spanish so I can understand you," I say, and then his chuckle travels through me, sending a wave of warmth through my insides.

"So, can we be friends?" he asks, and I bring my hand to his heart, resting it over where it beats inside of him.

"Yes, Julián, I would like that very much," I say, nuzzling my nose into his neck again.

"Good because I baked you a cake, and if you're my friend, you have to lie to me about whether you like it or not," he replies, causing me to burst into laughter. I lean back to see a bright smile on his face.

All laughter seizes within me, getting stuck in my chest. I reach out to trace his features. They're even more beautiful when they're pulled into a smile. There are creases in his cheeks, one of them slightly hidden underneath his birthmark. His full lips are stretched wide, revealing his perfect, white set of teeth. There is something twinkling in his eyes, something I'm sure if I keep looking at, I will become addicted to.

"You're so beautiful," I mumble, still tracing the lines in his cheeks.

"Yeah? You think so?" he asks, lifting his hands to wrap his fingers around my wrists. The hint of his smile remains, making me happier than I've been in a while. Strange how one person's smile can somehow brighten up another's entire existence.

"I do," I admit, getting lost in the way he's holding onto me, the warmth radiating from him.

Julián's mouth falls open as he attempts to respond, but a knock on the door tears us out of our intimate moment.

"Scarlette? Storm? I've made some coffee, if you would like to join me," Mom says, and I suck in a sharp breath, dropping my hands from his face and attempting to get off the bed. Julián holds me back, cupping my face.

"Do you want to change the rules?" he asks, the serious look back on his face. I melt into his touch for a second, feeling so safe with him it hurts.

"What I want is overpowered by what is best for you, so, no."

Then I get up and rush to grab some clothes. I disappear into the bathroom before joining my mother and Julián on the veranda. I avoid explaining my vague answer. I'm not capable of sharing what the heck I meant by that, so I will keep my distance from him as much as possible. Shouldn't be too hard. It's not like we will spend five days on top of each other, starting tomorrow.

Chapter 26
Julián

Scarlette's mom walks me to my bike as my fake girlfriend takes care of the plates we dirtied. I offered to help, but Stephanie took my arm, saying she'd like to bring me to my bike. Sweat drips down my back, and I'm not sure if it's from the hot fall sun or because of Scar's mom looking up at me as if she knows something I should know too. Her blue eyes reveal worry, making me nervous.

"Listen, there is something I'd like to discuss with you since I'm sure Scarlette has not taken the time to mention it," she starts, and my heart stops beating.

"You really know how to scare a man, ma'am," I reply, and she starts laughing my comment away.

"Don't be silly." I wasn't kidding, but okay. "Has Scarlette mentioned anything about her mental health struggle with you?" she asks, and I stop dead in my tracks, furrowing my brows. Worry courses through me, the desire to run inside and pull her into my arms again almost too strong to resist.

"No, ma'am," I say, turning to give her my full attention. "Don't you think she should be the one to open up to me about it?" I challenge because this woman has overstepped her daughter's boundaries one too many times.

"No, because she won't. She's ashamed, but she shouldn't be. I merely want you to know since you will be going away with her for a few days, and you should be prepared for this scenario." Okay, now I'm terrified.

"Tell me then," I say, pushing my hands into my pockets to keep them from shaking.

"Scarlette gets terrible anxiety attacks. She will never let you see her this way, but if she disappears in the bathroom for a while, it's usually because she's having an attack and wants no one to see. It's embarrassing for her, but I need you to be there for her, alright? She has a lavender oil you can massage into her skin, it will calm her. She also takes other remedies that usually help her settle." I nod along to her words, trying to process this information.

Scarlette gets anxiety attacks.

She deals with them alone because she's ashamed of them.

She smiles through her mental health struggle.

I'm going to be sick.

I want to go hold her, tell her I've got her and will always be there for her, but it's not my place. Stephanie is sharing this with me to prepare me in case Scar has an attack while we're in Monaco together. I make a mental note of everything Stephanie just told me when something clicks in my head.

Scar always smells like lavender.

It's her way of staying calm.

My face and body soften at the thought, but at the same time, I want to punch a wall. I don't want her to struggle with this. She doesn't deserve it, no one does. Elias used to get anxiety attacks when he was a teenager, so I'm used to seeing them. I'm also tired of the people I care about having to struggle with their mental health when they are the happiest people I've ever met. It's not fucking fair.

"What are her triggers?" I ask, hoping we can avoid them altogether this weekend.

"She doesn't always have one. Sometimes it's her own thoughts, sometimes she gets too nervous and then falls into an attack. Other times, we will be having a nice dinner, and then all of a sudden, her hands start shaking," she explains, and I suck in a sharp breath.

"What are her other indicators?" I ask, wishing I could discuss this with Scar. Stephanie looks behind her, almost as if she's suspecting her daughter to be eavesdropping.

"Hand shaking, uneven breathing, heart racing, sometimes she will have ticks, almost like muscle cramps, but that's mostly when she's trying to suppress her anxiety. Don't let her suppress it, it will make her attack so much worse," Stephanie warns, and I nod. Done. I will do everything I can for Scar, no matter what. "But you will notice when her attack starts. She will zone out most of the time, become almost unresponsive."

I want to cry. I haven't cried in years, but right now, in the midst of this conversation, I feel like bursting into tears and screaming like a little kid about how unfair it is. I don't want my beautiful rainbow to go through this. Fuck. She truly is a rainbow. My rainbow. The storm of her anxiety combined with her happy personality radiates all colors of it all the time.

"I will take care of her, make sure she has everything she needs," I promise, reaching for my helmet. I want to hide under it, let out how I truly feel.

"I know you will, but she won't let you, Storm. I raised my daughter to be independent, but I pushed her so far into it, she doesn't accept any help."

But she let me help her. Earlier, she let me hold her when she was feeling down, and the thought sends a wave of bliss through me. Maybe I'm different for her. Maybe she cares for me in the same way I do her.

"Don't worry, ma'am, Scar is safe with me, always. In any way she needs me," I say, flinging my leg over my machine.

"'Scar'," she says, smiling to herself. "I doubt she likes to be called that," Stephanie adds, causing the corner of my mouth to curl ever so slightly.

"She used to hate it, but I'm pretty sure she loves it now," I say, waiting for this conversation to be done so I get to drive off and process all of this information.

"You're good for my daughter, Storm. What you two have is so real and pure, I hope neither of you will screw this up," she replies, and my shoulders fall at her words.

We're not real. I want nothing more than for Scar and me to forget about this fake dating shit and just try dating for real, but she doesn't. It's not in her plans, but I know one thing for sure. What Stephanie just told me doesn't change anything, especially not my feelings for my rainbow. She's perfect to me, and I will ensure this week will be the best of her life.

Chapter 27
Julián

Scarlette is sitting next to me on the plane, looking around her seat with awe on her face. My father, as extra as he is, got us first-class tickets. For once, I don't mind. I want Scar to be as comfortable as fucking possible on this flight. Which she seems to be. Her face is pulled into her usual smile, but, after yesterday, I know she has her bad days. I know she isn't always happy, and my heart almost explodes every time I think about the way she let me hold her. The way she *wanted* me to hold her. I comforted her, let her cry, and it was one of the best moments in my entire life when she settled against my chest and started to feel better.

"This is all so extravagant," she says, covering her mouth with one of her hands. A small laugh escapes her before she swallows it down again. "Do you think it's too late to get a refund for my ticket? I don't want to know how much money your father spent," she adds, and I cock an eyebrow at her.

"Come on, *mami*, you want to back out now?" I ask, and she looks at her television, shaking her head.

"I feel bad," she says, and I let out a small sigh.

"Don't, love, that man has more money than he would be able to spend in three lifetimes," I reply, which seems to reassure her a little. Her blue eyes skip to my face, another smile dancing onto her face.

"I'm so excited," she says, wiggling in her seat and clutching the airplane pillow to her chest. "I've never really flown before, you know, only once when I was eleven," she admits, bringing her beautiful eyes back to my face. Surprise widens my own.

"Only once?" I ask, trying to make sure I understood her properly. She nods. "Are you scared?" Scarlette grins at me.

"Why? Do you want to hold my hand?" she teases, and I smirk at her in response.

A wave of awe crosses her face, just like every time I give her a smile or smirk, and I make a mental note to keep doing so. The usual guilt I feel is so far gone, I wonder if it was ever there. It's a bad idea to think too deeply about it because then it resurfaces and hits me like a brick.

"Are you asking me if I'd like to touch you? Because the answer is always going to be yes," I reply right as my father walks by us. He lets out a nervous laugh.

"Okay, now, children, hands to yourselves on this flight, please. I don't want to get kicked off the plane," he says, shooting me a warning look. I give him a strained nod, wishing him far away from here.

Scarlette's cheeks are a bright red when I shift my attention back to her, making me chuckle. The sound drags her out of her embarrassment, lighting up her gorgeous features again. God, I could get lost in them. Sometimes, I do.

"Can I ask you something?" she says after a few moments of her merely studying my face. She pulls her legs against her chest in the enormous seat, and I lean my head against the back of mine, watching her intently.

"You can always ask me anything that crosses your mind, love," I reply, and Scar chews on her bottom lip for a second, thinking.

"Do you look like your mom? Because I don't see much of your dad in your face," she says, making my heart thump rapidly in my chest. My beautiful rainbow had to go straight for the big one.

"Paulo isn't my biological father," is all I manage to explain. I don't want to tell her the rest, not while we're fake dating. Hopefully, soon, we will be more, and then I will share it all with her. For now, I pray she won't ask more of me.

"Ah I see," she replies with a smile before... letting it go. She simply lets it go. Anyone else I've ever met would have asked a million questions. Not Scarlette. No. Somehow she senses everything I ever need.

Instead of bombarding me with things I don't want to answer, she turns to her little screen, tapping around on it. No movie interests her, so she pulls out her phone, plopping one of her earphones in and then holding out the other for me.

"I don't know if you want to, but I feel like you can get to know someone well by getting to know the music they like," she says, but I'm already putting the other one in my ear, waiting patiently for whatever song she puts on first.

The next three hours, she plays me all different kinds of music genres. Anything from From Angels to Devils to Kane Brown comes through the little speaker. Amazement fills my chest because she remembers the lyrics to every song. Her mouth forms every single word, and I study the way her lips move to shape them. Three hours. And I could spend a thousand more. Scarlette is right. This is helping me get to know her even better. It shows me how similar we are because I also listen to every genre, a bit here and there. It depends on the artist, which seems to be the same for her.

Eventually, Scar falls asleep, but I continue to listen to her music. I enjoy the fact that she can't skip songs this way, so I get to hear the unfiltered ones, the ones she might only listen to by herself. It feels like I get to know her soul this way, and it's the most beautiful thing I've ever felt. Lewis Capaldi's song 'Forever' streams into my ears, breaking my heart a little.

"You are a lot more complex than I could have ever imagined, love, aren't you?" I guide a strand of her hair from her face, smiling to myself as I watch her.

Fuck me.

I could watch her forever.

I lo—

Not yet.

Not fucking yet, heart.

When we arrive at the hotel in Monaco, Dad and Scar are deep in conversation about the race weekend. I walk to the receptionist, my usual scowl resting on my face. It makes them do a double-take of me, much like any reaction I've ever gotten. My unapproachable facial expression turns people away from me, but, often, they can't help but stare. A smile then slips onto their faces, and I realize they find me attractive. Today is no different. The receptionist eyes me before giving me a subtle smirk. Heat rises up my neck. I don't like these reactions, I never have.

"Mr. Rodrick," I say, hardening my features. The receptionist gives me a small nod before turning to the computer.

"So, that would be two rooms, correct?" I nod my head.

"Yes," I reply, swallowing hard. Scar and I will be sharing a room. We will be on top of each other for the next five days.

The receptionist hands me the keys after a few moments, and I walk over to where Scar is standing with my father, smiling brightly at him. God, sometimes it hurts to look at her. It hurts because my heart does a million somersaults in my chest, excited that my gaze is on her. There is so much we don't know about each other yet, but it feels like I've known her for a hundred lifetimes simultaneously. It's weird.

I like it.

"Here you go," I say to Dad as I hand him the key.

Scar shifts her smile to me then, tilting her head to the side and wiggling her eyebrows. I let out a small chuckle in return, causing my father to freeze. He doesn't say anything, but I know how surprised he is to have heard this little sound from me. We're both paralyzed, me because of his reaction, him because he's never heard me chuckle before.

"Let's go," Scar says, taking the pressure off my shoulders.

Her hand slips into mine, and I let out a strained breath, my muscles relaxing in response to her warmth. She needs to stop feeding into my needs.

Dad gets off the elevator on his floor, but Scar keeps her hand in mine, leaning her head against my shoulder as a little yawn escapes her. She woke up an hour after she fell asleep on the plane, and I couldn't sleep at all. We're both in desperate need of rest.

The doors of the elevator open, but I notice her eyes are closed now.

"*Mami*, do you want me to carry you?" I ask, but she shakes her head, another yawn slipping past her plump lips. I should really stop staring at her mouth so much.

"No, just pull me," Scar says with a laugh, but I stand in front of her then, bending my knees a little.

"Hop on," I demand, making her snort. "You have three seconds or I will throw you over my shoulder and carry you that way," I say because there is no way I would ever pull her when I can carry her like this.

"Jesus. So bossy. Do you get cranky when you don't sleep? Because I totally get that. Violet gets cranky when she doesn't get her eight hours. I'm the opposite. I get either very quiet or bubbly." She starts laughing. "Bubbly. Remember when you called me that and I got so upset?" she asks, more laughter leaving her lips. I stop the door from closing before spinning around to face her. She finds this extremely amusing, which is the only reason I smile as well. I love this side of her. Fuck it. I adore every side of her.

"On my back, love. Come on," I say, and she obeys, jumping up and onto my back. I wrap my hands around the backs of her legs, holding her firmly against me as her hands slip across my neck and then down my chest.

"You have such a nice body," she mumbles, drunk on sleep deprivation at this point. I suck in a sharp breath, my body reacting in ways I'm not proud of. "Shit. Ignore that. I didn't mean to say it out loud," she says, but I'm grinning to myself.

"You're swearing now, *mami*?" I ask, causing a giggle to leave her.

"Maybe? You know, I swore off swearing—" She stops to laugh. "—because my dad used to throw bad words at my head as a child, especially after he got drunk. He wasn't a good dad when I was younger." My heart sinks into my stomach, shattering into a million pieces at the same time. I stop abruptly in front of our door, dropping Scar onto her feet and spinning around. She looks lost in thought, tears stinging her eyes.

"Is he the reason you have this scar?" I ask, fearing the answer.

I almost punch the fucking wall when she nods. A few curse words leave me, all in Spanish to make sure she doesn't understand them. My beautiful fake girlfriend brings her eyes to me, a smile tugging on the right side of her mouth.

"You're a good man, Julián, a great fake boyfriend, an even better friend."

Why? Why does she have to say these sweet words to me? I can't handle them, can't handle the fact that I haven't shared my darkest secrets with her because I'm terrified of what she will think.

"I like spending time with you," she admits, staring down at the ground. I tilt her chin up by placing my fingers underneath it and slightly pushing upward.

"Not sleeping makes you extremely truthful, doesn't it?" I ask, and Scar starts giggling. The sound makes me weak in the knees.

"Yes. You better open the door before I tell you what happy-maker I brought in my suitcase," she says, her face dropping into shock.

"Scar?" I ask, but she shakes her head. "What did you bring in your suitcase?" I say, and she lets out a nervous laugh.

"Definitely not the type of toy you're imagining," she says with an embarrassed huff, grabbing the key out of my pocket. "Just forget I said anything. My brain is trying to make me confess scandalous things," she adds, slipping the keycard into the hole.

Fuck me. She brought her vibrator. She brought her fucking vibrator, and our room only has one bed.

The biggest smile spreads over my face.

Chapter 28

Scarlette

I'm still trying to push past the embarrassing moment we just had when I step into the middle of the room and... there is only one bed. A big bed, huge even, and just as expensive-looking as the rest of the hotel. My breathing hitches as I think about the millions of things we could do in this bed together. I might be a virgin, but I've seen and read way too many things to not imagine every single way Julián could make love to me on this bed. Then my mind thinks about the thousand ways he could fuck me on it, making my knees weak and my clit ache. I could really use a minute alone with my vibrator... the one I indirectly told him about! *I'm such an idiot.*

"There is only one bed," I croak out, feeling Julián's hands as they slip over my shoulders to take off my jacket. Shivers run down my spine.

"Yeah. Is that okay with you? If not, I will go change the room right now, or sleep on the couch. Anything you want," he says, but neither of those options sounds in any way appealing to me.

"It's fine. I mean, we're just going to sleep, right?" I ask, earning myself a small chuckle from him.

"We will do whatever you want us to do in that bed." Because I'm in charge. Julián wants me, but he needs me to know I'm the one in full control. He takes me any way he gets me, and I have to stop this before it goes any further.

"Sleep. Sleep is good. As a matter of fact, we need it to survive, and I need it to stop telling you everything," I say with a laugh, grabbing my backpack and stalking into the bathroom.

I suck in a sharp breath, looking at myself in the mirror. Today is one of those days my scar has decided to be front and center in my face, as if it had decided there is nothing better than being visible. I wish it would bother me more, but Julián has made me feel beautiful about it. He's done a lot of irreversible things to me, like the way my heartbeat is still between my legs as the images of him naked on top of me slip into my head. My imagination should get a raise. It's working overtime a lot these days.

I pick up my phone, dialing the number of the one person that can give me clarity right now. Her voice streams through my speaker a moment later.

"Hey, babe, how was your flight?" Violet asks, and I suck in a sharp breath, keeping my voice barely audible.

"There is only one bed," I whisper, and Violet squeals into the phone.

"Then do him! Fuck, Lettie, just have sex with him. You both want each other, crave each other even. Have sex with him, it'll solve all your problems," she says, but I shake my head.

"I can't," I reply, clutching the sink as nervosity fills my chest.

"Why? What is it really, Scarlette? Tell me the truth," she begs, and I feel tears stream down my face. I turn on the sink to make sure Julián cannot hear my next words under any circumstance.

"I think if we have sex, I'm going to fall for him," I admit, sinking onto the rim of expensive bathtub. I'm already so close, but being that intimate, it would push me right over the edge.

"Oh, honey. And what would be so bad about that?" My best friend can be so oblivious.

"I'm broken, Vi. I've already ruined my parents' lives and yours with my anxiety. I can't ruin Julián's too," I say, running my hand over my face.

"Listen to me now, you stubborn woman, you did not ruin my life or your parents'. You are not broken. You have anxiety, which is nothing to be ashamed of. Storm would understand if you told him. Hell, the way he looks at you, he'd kiss you so hard and assure you the same thing I am right now," she says, and I let out a small laugh.

"He doesn't like me like that. Yes, he's attracted to me, but the rest is just fake dating stuff," I reply, feeling my heart drop in response to what I'm saying.

"Oh my God, please tell me you're not that naïve, Lettie. Please. Otherwise, I'm going to come there and smack some sense into you," she spits into the phone, and I laugh again.

My heart is racing as we say goodbye, and I turn off the water, stepping outside of the bathroom. Julián is taking his shirt off just as I walk in front of the bed. He gives me a small smile when I'm next to him, but I don't return it. My body is aching with need, need to touch him, kiss him, or lick him. I'm not quite sure which one I want the most.

"Scar?" he asks when I close the distance between us.

"Julián?" I reply, feeling my heart race even faster. "May I?" I ask before lifting my hands to his chest.

"Always."

I'm wet and desperate as I lift my fingers to his rock-hard abs, tracing his ripples. God. He's so hard and hot, it makes my head spin. I lay my palms flat against his lower abdomen, right on top of his V-line. His dark golden skin contrasts my light one, and it looks right to me. Everything about us together looks right to me.

I notice his breathing racing, but his arms are on each side of him. I've never had the chance to explore a man's body before. I desperately want Julián's to be my first.

"Is this okay?" I ask, running my fingers over his stomach. He nods in response.

I raise my hands to his hard nipples, slowly running my index fingers over them. When my eyes skip to his face, I notice his are half-closed, watching me with desire. My lips pull into a small smile as I lean forward to press a kiss to his left pec, stepping on my tiptoes to reach. The heartbeat between my legs sends waves of unease over me. Pressure. It's unbearable pressure I would love to ease. His breathing hitches loudly when I remove my lips from his skin, dragging them down to his nipple.

"*Mami*, I'm going to come right here in my pants if you don't stop," he says, breathless.

"And what would be so bad about that?" I ask, leaning back to stare into his different-colored eyes. He grabs my face between his hands, forcing my gaze to stay on his.

"Because the first person out of us to orgasm will be you, not me," he replies, running his hands down the sides of my body. "*Quiero mi lengua en tu piel, mami*," he says, making me groan out of frustration.

"Translate," I demand, and he chuckles, leaning down until his nose is brushing over my neck. Shivers run all over me, dancing in response to his proximity.

"I want my tongue on your skin, love, all over it actually," he says, and I snake my fingers around his nape as he guides me backward, my back hitting the wall.

"I want that too," I reply, pushing off it again to bring my chest against his.

He grabs my leg, wrapping it around his hip until my clit pushes against his hard cock. *Oh sweet pleasure, that feels way too good.* Julián lets out a small groan before running his hot, wet tongue over the soft spot on my neck. A moan slips past my lips.

"Fuck," he curses under his breath before picking me up and bringing me to the bed. He lies me down on it, standing back to admire the view of my fully clothed body while a smile lingers on my face. "*Tú eres perfecta, mami.*" *That* I understood, and it makes my insides warm instantly.

"Do you always speak Spanish when you're in the bedroom?" I ask with a smile, but Julián shakes his head.

"No, but I like how your body reacts to the words, even if you can't understand them all," he says, painting my cheeks a deep red. He notices how my body reacts to him... He knew all along how desperately I crave him. It should bother me. Instead, I reach for the hem of my shirt, tugging on it to pull it off.

A knock on the door stops me.

"Leave!" Julián barks and I let out a small chuckle. I stand up, pressing my hands to his chest to calm him.

"Who is it?" I ask, attempting to walk to the door when he grabs my wrist to keep me next to him. His features are soft as he looks at me, the complete opposite of how he looks at everyone else.

"Bellhop, miss. I have your luggage," she says, and I step on my toes to plant a kiss to Julián's cheek before opening the door for the woman requesting entry.

She quickly places our luggage in the large, expensive room with a balcony I only notice now and a couch area with a television in front of it. *God, how did I not notice how huge this room is?* Because I was focused on the fact that Julián and I will share a bed for the next five days.

"Thank you," I say as Julián hands the bellhop a tip.

Just as the woman walks out of the room, Mr. Rodrick appears in the doorframe. Julián and I really can't catch a break. I force a smile onto my face as my boss steps into the room, grinning like a happy child. His brown hair is mostly grey, his brown eyes deep and dark as he studies his son. He isn't very tall, not like Julián, but they're both a lot more so than I am. Then again, I'm quite short.

"Are you two ready to go to lunch and then the Meet & Greet after?" he asks, sending a wave of panic through me. I completely forgot about that.

"Just give me ten minutes. I have to shower," I say, rushing into the bathroom with my suitcase. Like the rest of the room, it is huge and has enough space to open my luggage and search through my clothes for something to wear today.

A smile dances onto my face when I realize how excited I am. It's really happening. I'm going to get my foot in the door leading to the sport of Formula One.

Chapter 29
Julián

"So, you seem happy," Dad says, smiling in that way I find extremely irritating. It's the one where he wiggles his eyebrow insinuatingly. I can't be bothered to decipher its meaning right now.

"I'm not," I reply honestly, letting out a sharp breath of air. "Scar and I cannot spend one uninterrupted moment together before someone barges in, and it is frustrating me to the point where I would like to punch my way through that wall," I rant, causing my father's eyes to widen in response.

"I apologize, *mijo*, I didn't you two were trying to—" He cuts off, looking for a good way to phrase what he really means. "—have a moment. I'm sorry. I didn't want to interrupt, but we need to get going," he explains, and I nod absentmindedly.

"I know. It's not your fault. It just seems like we'll never *have a moment* to ourselves," I say, and Dad raises his eyebrows, surprised now.

"Wait. So you two haven't had—" Again, he cuts off, simply waving his hands around to show what he means. I look up at him, then my eyes drop to the floor again.

"I won't be discussing that with you, Dad," I reply, getting up from the bed and walking over to my suitcase to pick out a dress shirt and pair of black jeans to wear.

"You will have plenty of time to be alone, I promise. I will even schedule it in if you'd like me to," he says, and I frown at him. Dad starts laughing at my expression, raising his hands in mock surrender. "I'm teasing, *relájate*," he adds, but I'm still not smiling.

It isn't funny. Having her perfect body in my hands, desperate to kiss her and be with her but then getting interrupted is not funny.

"Okay, I get it. You only smile at Scarlette, only laugh with her too. I'm going to try not to take that personally," Dad says, pretending to pull a knife from his chest and laughing.

Damn, I can't help but grin a little. It feels so easy to do now because I know how happy it makes Scar to see me this way.

"*Dios mio*," he adds, giving me a shocked smile. "*Mijo*, your smile is so nice." I roll my eyes at him.

"Don't get used to it. I reserve them all for Scar," I say, and he shakes his head, still grinning.

"You're in love. For the first time in your life, you're in love, and with one of the most wonderful women in the world." I let out a scoff at the first part of his sentence.

"I'm not in love. I just really like her," I defend, thinking about his words for a moment.

I'm definitely not in love with her. I see myself there, eventually, but for fuck's sake, we haven't even kissed yet. Maybe that'll be horrible. Then again, she had me rock hard as soon as she trailed her fingers over me and I almost came when she kissed my chest. God, she has more control over my body than any woman I've ever been with. Shit. *I almost fucking came when she touched me.* That's a hard pill to swallow.

"Sure, *mijo*, whatever you need to tell yourself," Dad says, running one of his hands over my shoulder before squeezing it and letting go again. "I will wait in the lobby for the both of you," he tells me before leaving the room.

I get dressed, slipping on my jeans and dress shirt before fixing my hair to the best of my abilities. It doesn't look too bad actually, something I wouldn't worry about as much if Scarlette wasn't with me. I want people to look at us and understand why we're 'dating'. They should see us and think, "Holy shit, what a hot couple!" because that's what I would be thinking. Any couple with Scar in it would be the hottest, but she's not with anyone else. She's with me, at least for now, and it sends a wave of happiness and pride through me.

She isn't yours, my brain reminds me, and I let out a small sigh. I hate my own mind sometimes.

"Okay, I have no idea how to dress for fancy restaurants in Monaco, so you have to tell me if this is appropriate," she says, calling out from the small slit in the bathroom door.

"Come, *mami, muéstrame*," I say, hearing her laugh nervously from the bathroom.

"Does that mean 'show me'," she asks, waiting for my answer.

"*Sí*," I reply, and, finally, she opens the door, stepping into the room and...

Fucking hell.

Her body is covered by a long dress, hugging every single one of her goddamn curves. It's a simple white at the top, flowy and colorful in the lower half. Her arms are covered by tight, white sleeves. Her long, black hair is wavy and loose, a little bit of makeup on her face. Her blue eyes stand out against the dark eyeshadow she put on, her lips full and covered with lip balm. They look so beautiful, I want to plant mine against them and get lost forever.

"Scar," I start, running my hand down the length of my face. She stares at her dress like there is something wrong with it, making me shake my head. "You are stunning, gorgeous, beautiful, sexy, elegant, and graceful all at the same time, and so much more." I should really start cutting back on the honesty around her, but she makes it so easy, so comfortable, to share every single thought I have.

"So are you," she says with a little laugh, closing the distance between us to put her hands on my chest.

"You like this part of my body, don't you?" I ask, earning me a blush from her.

"I like every part of your body," she whispers, and I tilt her head up, studying her shy eyes.

"You haven't even seen all of me, *mami*," I say, seduction dripping from my words.

"I know, but I've *felt* most of you before," she admits, running her fingers down to my pants and tugging on the belt loops. "And I would like to see all of you too. Maybe later, when everything is quiet and calm, you can undress me and then yourself." Blood shoots into my cock until it's unbearably hard, pressing against my tight pants. Scarlette looks up at me through her thick eyelashes, and I cup her face tightly.

"You want to change the rules?" I ask for the hundredth time, praying she will say the words I long to hear.

"Yes, I want to change the rules." There they are. God, they sound even better than I thought they would.

"I need you to be sure, *mami*, sure about me being your first, sharing this part of yourself with me," I say, still holding her face to keep her gaze on me. I always want her eyes to be on me.

"Hmmm, you're right. Maybe you should tell me why you'd be right for me," she teases with a smile, but I'm prepared to tell her everything I've had in my head since I first laid my eyes on her.

"I would take my time, love, explore your body and find every little spot I can kiss to make pleasure roll through you. I would go slow, use my fingers first, maybe that little toy you brought with you. I'd kiss and pleasure you until you're soaked for me and relaxed. Then, I'd bury myself deep inside of you, show you a pleasure you've never experienced before. I'd make you come over and over, *mami*, because I want to study what you look like when you fall apart," I say, watching her cheeks turn so red, they match the color of a tomato. Her breathing hitched every so often throughout my speech, but it's perfectly even now, merely fast.

"I want you," Scar says, and it takes everything out of me not to pick her up and throw her on the bed to do everything I just said I would. But we have to go. We have to stay on my dad's good side because he will introduce Scar to Robert Fuchs. This is important to her, so I fight past my desire.

"I crave you, *mami*, but we have to wait a little longer." She lets out a shaky breath, removing her hands from my pants.

"Okay," she mumbles, stepping away from me and toward her purse.

I watch her again, studying the graceful ways in which she moves. Hours, days, weeks, they are not enough to satisfy the part inside of me that wants to see everything she does. It would like to memorize the ways her body shifts, the birthmarks covering her skin, the way she comes. All of me wants to be around her at all times, see her smile and reassure her she doesn't have to do so at the same time. I want to do everything with her because she brightens up my life, hell, my entire existence.

Chapter 30
Scarlette

My heart is still thumping, *thud, thud, thud,* way too fast by the time Julián and I meet his father in the lobby. He gives me a weird smile, but it drops soon when he looks at his son. My eyes shift to Julián to see a scowl on his handsome face. I take his hand, bringing my chin to his arm and grinning up at him. A smile instantly slips onto his face then, and a sense of victory floods through me. I make him smile. It's the sweetest triumph I've ever experienced, so I beam up at him, happy beyond a doubt.

We follow Mr. Rodrick out of the hotel and toward a rental car with a driver. He gives us a brief nod before letting the engine roar to life. Then we're on our way to where the billionaire sitting in front of me is taking us to lunch. Julián slides his fingers through mine, studying the way they look together. He inspects the rings I wear on my hand, using his other one to trace the silver bands. He's smiling to himself as he brushes his index finger over the small birthmark on the back of the hand resting in his.

"What?" I ask, curious about his expression. His eyes, my new favorite pair in the world, skip to my face, glistening with that special something only I get to see.

"Your hand is so soft," he simply says with a slight chuckle, fixating on it again. Then he lifts it to his mouth, pressing a swift kiss to the back of it.

"You like holding it?" I ask, confused but content with how happy he is about this little display of affection.

"Nah, I just pretend, *mami*, that's all," he says, but he grins at me, revealing he's merely kidding.

"Was that a joke? I feel like this is the first time you've ever made a joke," I blurt out, and another chuckle vibrates off him.

I love his deep, husky voice when he's speaking, but there is something about the way he chuckles that sends a special sort of warmth over me. It inhabits my chest, spreading through my whole body until I can sense it in my toes and fingertips.

"Yes, love, I make jokes now, but don't tell anyone. This needs to be our little secret," he says, whispering the last sentence. I cover my mouth, promising I will keep this side of him quiet.

A few minutes later, we arrive at the restaurant where Julián tells me to wait in the car. I look around as he makes his way to my door. He opens it, holding out a helping hand for me. I shake my head and give him a breathless laugh as he guides me out of the vehicle and against his chest.

"Don't you think you're taking this a bit far? You don't have to fake it this much," I say, but it makes his lips curl downward.

"I haven't been faking anything with you from the beginning, Scar. Do *not* assume I do anything because I *have to* with you. I do it all because it makes me fucking happy, okay?" My next words spill from my lips faster than I can stop them.

"Then why haven't you kissed me yet?" I ask, causing his features to soften.

"Because I don't want you to think I'm doing it to play a part in our deal. When I kiss you for the first time, *mami*, it'll be completely separate. It will not be to fake anything. It will be real and honest. It will be everything," he says, leaning down to place his mouth on my cheek and kissing me softly.

"We should discuss what territory we've entered now," I say as he leans away again.

"Yes, later, when we're alone."

Alone. In bed. Naked because I want him and he wants me.

Oh my God, he really wants me.

Oh God, *we're really going to do this.*

But what if everything changes? What if he will have sex with me, realize it wasn't that great, and then break our deal? What if it will ruin my one chance at getting my foot in the door? What if I will lose him?

More what-ifs fill my head until I zone out, my anxiety creeping into my chest. *Great.* This one had a trigger at least. *But no!* I can't have an anxiety attack right now.

I'm already in it.

My hands are shaking. My head is disoriented as my breathing hitches and tears collect in my eyes. *No, no, no, not here, not now, please.* I don't know who I'm begging to, but at this point, I am willing to take anyone who's listening. I cannot have an anxiety attack. *What will Mr. Rodrick think? No. What will happen to Julián?* He's going to be so confused and scared. *I can't do this to him. Please. I can't—*

"Love, it's okay. Come with me. I've got you. It's alright," Julián says, guiding me somewhere I'm not processing. My lungs are burning.

"I can't—I can't," I repeat over and over again.

"I know you can't breathe, Scar. It's alright. You're going to be okay. I'm here," he says a moment before he pulls me onto the floor right into his arms.

"NO! You can't—can't see me—like this," I stutter, trying to push away the panic. It's not working. It's consuming every cell in my body, tightening my muscles until everything turns rigid.

"Actually, I physically can. I have pretty good vision, almost 20/20," he says, and in the midst of my attack, I manage to laugh. It's breathless and vanishes quickly, but he made me laugh. No one's ever been able to make me laugh during an attack.

"Leave me, please," I beg, feeling my lips trembling, a sign they are about to cramp into an ugly expression.

"No," he says, holding me close to him and stroking his hand down my hair and back. "I'm not going anywhere. I'm here, and we will get through this together, love. I promise. Now, where are your lavender and other remedies?" he asks, sending a wave of surprise through me.

"How do you—" I cut off, a tremble shaking my body. Julián holds me through it, kissing the top of my head. A wave of calm sweeps over me, but it isn't strong enough to stop my hands from shaking or my limbs from going numb.

"Let go of your purse, Scar. I need to check if it's in here," he says, and I realize he's trying to get it out from under my arm. I've been pressing it into my side without realizing, but it takes me a moment to unclench my arm for him. "Good, that's good. Thank you," he goes on, pressing a kiss to my temple.

"Julián, I'm scared," I whisper, another tremble shaking me.

"I know. Fuck, baby, I can't imagine how scared you are right now, but you've been through this before, and you've always come out of it. This time, I'm here. You don't have to do this alone. I'm here. Let me help you get through this."

For some reason, my body relaxes against his, giving fully into the attack. I was trying to hold it back, hide it from him, but this very second, I let it all go, knowing it'll make me feel better afterward. I cover my mouth when it cramps up, managing to rip my eyes open to see the confusion on his face. I'd ask why he's looking at me like that, but my brain doesn't have time for these sort of things. It's battling its biggest foe at the moment.

Julián rubs some of my lavender oil on my chest, behind my ears, and on my wrists. He takes his time, massaging it in until he feels my shaking settle a bit. He then tries to remove my hand from my mouth to give me my remedies, but I shake my head in response. He lets go of me, more confusion settling on his beautiful features.

"Let me see your mouth," he begs, but I tell him 'no'. "Why? Is it cramping?" he asks, and I nod. I don't know how he knows so much about anxiety, especially mine, but it's soothing right now. He's nothing but calm, which is refreshing and pleasant. It's like I already took my remedies. "Let me see, *arcoíris*," he says gently, tugging on my wrist ever so slightly. I let him remove it, watching him smile down at me. "I don't think you could ever understand just how beautiful I think you are," he says, brushing his thumb over my bottom lip.

"Yeah? Would you still kiss me like this?" I ask with a laugh I don't mean, still trying to slow my breathing. I already feel much better, but the anxiety hasn't quite left me yet.

"Yes. Let me prove it," he says, waiting for me to nod before he brings his mouth to mine.

Peace. It spreads through me all at once, starting where his lips envelop mine and settling everywhere. My insides turn and warm until nothing but desire and safety are left. Safe. I feel so safe and invincible, as if nothing can hurt me anymore. I relax in his arms, feeling the softness of his mouth, the heat radiating from him. My mouth uncramps until I'm kissing him back. I've never kissed anyone back like this, with need and desperation and desire. I'm slipping my hands into his hair, my attack subsiding as this distraction, the sweetest form of it, occupies my every thought.

Julián is gentle, but my body is exploding into a million sensations, pleasure like none I've ever felt taking charge of my nerve-endings. Bliss. This is pure bliss, and I never, ever want it to end. I feel free, even while I'm tethered to him. Happiness ebbs in my chest, back and forth, fighting with the darkness of my anxiety. I'm not sure which one will win, but when Julián presses the tip of his tongue against my mouth, I open without hesitation. I part my lips because nothing has ever felt this right to me.

He explores my mouth, and I let him, not quite sure how to kiss him back yet. I don't want to either, not while he's tasting me and groaning into my mouth in response. Not when my body tingles in every good way possible. Pleasure overwhelms me until I'm moaning so loudly, Julián pulls away from the kiss.

"Those sounds are just for me, *mami*," he says, kissing me once more while I tug on his hair, keeping him close.

"Please," I beg, unsure what I want him to do right here and now. Julián merely chuckles.

"God, I'm so glad we affect each other in the same way," he says, brushing my hair out of my face. There is something about him telling me how hot I make him that sends a thrill between my legs. "Not here, baby. Later. I promise. We will do so much later. For now, how are you feeling?" he asks, pulling me back to reality.

I just had an anxiety attack in front of him. *No, no, no, no, no.* This can't have happened. Now I've ruined his life, like I ruined Mom's, Dad's, and Violet's. He's going to be constantly worried about me now, interpreting every single thing about me as a side effect of my anxiety. We will never be the same. Everything's changed, and we can never go back.

I sit up straight, leaning away from him and burying my face in my hands to let out the sob of grief bubbling in my chest.

"Love, what's wrong? Talk to me," Julián begs, snaking his fingers around my wrists to drag my palms off my face. I let him.

"You weren't supposed to see me like this," I cry, knowing whatever was going on between us has to end. I won't drag him under. I can't. Violet was wrong. I did ruin her life. I see it in the way she watches me, checking me for any sign of anxiety when I'm around her.

"Baby, I really don't understand what's so bad about me see—" I cut him off.

"Because you weren't there, Julián. You didn't see the way my parents lost their minds over me. The number of times I fought with my mom because she didn't know what to do with me! Why do you think I started hiding my anxiety attacks? I did it so it wouldn't be such a burden for my parents. Not to mention, my father had absolutely no sympathy for what he called 'a weakness of the mind'. He blamed me, said I have to stop. Every time I started having an anxiety attack, he'd stare at me, disappointed, before screaming, 'Stop it! You're pathetic. You're worthless if you cannot get this shit under control. You're ruining everyone's lives, everyone who surrounds themselves with you. You're selfish. You're a selfish child, who needs to grow the fuck up and out of this *phase'*."

I stop abruptly when Julián's eyes go wider than I've ever seen before. His hands drop to his sides, shock all over his face. I get up while he's distracted, rushing toward where Mr. Rodrick must be inside. I wipe under my eyes, but I can tell how bad I look from the way he scans my features. I look around the fancy restaurant, sucking in a quiet, sharp breath.

"Where are the restrooms?" I ask, and he points me to a narrow hallway.

I hurry down it, stepping into the extraordinarily expensive restroom. It looks like it should be in a documentary about the lives of rich people, just like everything else I've seen on this trip so far. I've never felt more out of place than I do around Mr. Rodrick and all of his money.

"Crap," I whisper to myself when my reflection stares back at me.

My eyeshadow is smudged, but at least my mascara held up. Thank God for waterproof versions. I wipe away the remainder of my eyeshadow, but another wave of sadness storms through me without warning.

Julián and I blurred our boundaries. I didn't want to keep up this fake dating deal in private. I wanted him, but now, I need to end things as soon as possible. If this opportunity wasn't so important for my career, I'd fly home early. I'd do the right thing. But I can't. I need this.

I will just have to reestablish the boundaries and keep him away from me.

To keep him safe from the hell that is my mind.

Chapter 31
Julián

Scarlette and I hardly interact for the duration of lunch. She continues to ask my father countless questions to ensure the two of us don't have to either. What Scar doesn't realize is that I would never push her into a conversation with me when she isn't ready. She told me a lot of things, heartbreaking things, I need a minute to process too, so I can't imagine what she must be feeling. There is no doubt in my mind she's been carrying what her father said, inaccurate and horrible words, with her since it happened.

I want to kill him. I've never met the man, but I want to hurt him, inflict actual physical pain, for what he did to my rainbow. The way he treated her makes me sick to my stomach. The fact that Scar's parents made her feel like her anxiety was shameful, something she had to hide, is unacceptable. The amount of damage they've done to her self-esteem and self-worth... I can't begin to swallow those words Scar yelled at me. It makes me want to take her in my arms, hold her against my chest, and fight off anyone who dares to come close. I want to protect her from any further harm, keep her away from the parents who've hurt her deeply.

Scar and I need to talk. She thinks she will ruin my life if I'm with her, but she doesn't realize her anxiety doesn't take away from her value. It doesn't make her damaged or broken or pathetic, like her father said it did. If anything, she's stronger, more resilient, powerful, and extraordinary than I could have ever imagined. She can't see that because of her asshole father and selfish mother, but I will prove to her how perfect she is. Someone has to hold up a mirror for her, one capable of showing her exactly what kind of a brave person she truly is. God, this would be so much easier if she could see herself through my eyes.

The rest of lunch goes by quickly, and soon, we're sitting in the car again. Scar is staring out of the window, and, as much as I would love to take her hand and squeeze it, I stay on my side completely. I can sense her needing me, my comfort and safety, but I don't want to push her while she's vulnerable. It's hard, but she should reach out to me first, otherwise, I will only make her feel uncomfortable.

We get out of the car, Scar taking a deep breath when we're in front of the entrance. I know she is nervous. Fuck, she's probably never been more nervous, which is why I step in front of her, taking her shoulders in my hands and smiling with comfort. It relaxes her instantly.

"Listen, love, you will be amazing. I know this is nerve-racking, but I'm right here with you, okay? If you don't feel comfortable, or anything at all, tap my leg twice, and we will leave. Anything you need, *mami*, I'm here, always." She nods, staring past me.

Things feel so weird between us, like she's trying to push me away because of what I've seen earlier. Scar is distancing herself from me, and I hate it. I hate the fact that my feelings are so strong, they hurt. It hurts me that I can't touch her. It hurts me that she thinks she's protecting me by holding me at arm's length. It hurts me that no one's shown her the love I'm more than willing to offer her.

"Julián?" she asks, and I watch her closely. "You have to stop. You can't care for me," she whispers, dropping my hands from her body. The loss of contact sends a sharp pain down my spine, straightening out my back.

"Scarlette, *vida*, please, open your eyes. I can't stop, not now. I'm already in deep, and nothing can stop me from falling further," I say, making her eyes drop to the floor. "We will speak later, love. I will prove to you how much you've brightened up my life, *mi arcoíris*."

Then she does something I didn't expect. She wraps her arms around me, hugging me so hard, it knocks the breath out of me for a moment. But I melt into her. My body clicks into place with hers as I envelop her in my arms. It feels perfect, like I was made to hold her like this. I'll be fine if this is all we do for the rest of my life. I just need her. Like this. In any way, shape, or form.

"Okay," she says, and I celebrate internally.

We're going to talk later. We will make this work. I will even admit to her how I feel. I don't care. I just want her to see how breathtaking she is, inside and out. Someone has to help her rediscover her internal beauty. Her parents took it away from her, but I will help her find it again.

"Can I hold your hand while we do this?" I ask, desperate at this point. I hope she finds charm in it, and when a little smile slips across her face, I know at least a small part of her enjoys this side of me.

"Yes," she replies, and I jump up and down internally. This is all I fucking wanted, and she's giving everything to me.

Mi arcoíris, mi amor, mi vida. Mi perfecta Scarlette.

As expected, Scar is absolutely incredible. She charms every single person she meets, especially the engineers she talks to. Some of the drivers like Kyle Hughes and Andrew Beckett find her a bit too nice. They keep grinning and smirking at her, making the blood inside of me boil. I would never dare dream of saying something, this is too important, but I'd like to punch them in their faces. Scar, so oblivious to their attention, notices only how tense I am, not the reason for my body's reaction.

"Are you okay?" she asks after a while.

I give her a strained nod, glaring at Kyle Hughes as he walks up to us with the cap he'd promised he'd get Scarlette. The Dutchman gives me a confused look, but softness returns to my face when my rainbow presses her back against my chest, leaning into me. She takes my arm and wraps it around her stomach, resting it there before bringing her hand on top of mine.

Puñeta.

She's showing everyone she's mine. Fake dating or not, I don't care. Nothing has ever felt better than her realizing why I was upset and giving me exactly what I needed because she *wanted* to. I kiss the top of her head with a smile.

"Here you go, Scarlette. Wear it for me on Sunday?" he asks, and I give him a 'seriously, man' look. Can't he see she's not interested? For fuck's sake, she placed my hand on her stomach and pressed herself against me. If that doesn't speak volumes, I don't know what does.

"Actually, I will be rooting for Leonard. I'm sorry," she says with a little laugh, and I can't help but grin in response. Scarlette is nice to everyone, always so kind, but when it comes to people I can't stand, she makes less of an effort. I love it.

"Speaking of Leonard, I promised I'd introduce you," I say, leading Scar away from the man I wish I could kick in the balls.

"There is no way I will actually get to meet him," she says, shaking her head so her black hair dances from side to side. "You're being silly." I'm really not, but she's about to find that out for herself.

Scar takes my hand, grinning the entire way to the other side of the Meet & Greet area. Leonard is the busiest driver here, but we spoke over the phone a few days ago, from one racer to another, and he assured me he'd make some time for my wonderful girlfriend. Yes, I may have gushed over Scarlette a bit more than necessary.

We walk the length of the other eight tables, stepping toward the one Leonard and his teammate are sitting at. There are roofs made of cloth all over us, which is good because I didn't make sure Scar put on some sunscreen, and I didn't pack any in case she forgot. I'm not used to thinking about these things because I don't think about myself to that extent. Not like I think about her now. Her well-being is at the very top of my priority list, which is why my heart warms when she lets out an excited, low squeal in front of Leonard's table. He probably didn't hear her, but I smile at how happy Scar is.

"Storm," Leonard says, giving me a small nod. He then extends his hand to Scar. "It is a pleasure to meet you, Scarlette. Storm has told me much about you. Now, shall we talk about getting you into Formula One?" Straight to the point, a scowl on his face he must have practiced many years, and generous to a point I'd never expected.

"Getting me into Formula One? You make it sound so easy," she says with a small laugh, moving a step back again as if I'm a magnet that draws in her body. It's perfect.

"Actually, I did draw up a plan for you on steps you can take, giving you a list of contacts that can potentially help you in the future and answer any questions you might have. I had some help from my current race engineer, whose telephone number I put in there as well. Lana is very kind and forthcoming. She is a great person to speak to about how difficult it is to enter this career path. I put my own number in case there is anything else you need from me personally." He gives her a small nod. "However, Robert Fuchs will speak to you tomorrow. He can help you more in terms of planning for future jobs or maybe give you an internship in the summer between semesters. I'm sure he'd be happy to have you. You strike me as someone who is dedicated to her work." Scar nods eagerly in return, but no words leave her. This all must be a lot to try and process at once. It is for me. "I have to run, but it was a pleasure speaking to both of you. Scarlette. Storm," he says, nodding once at both of us, never cracking a smile.

I'm overwhelmed by everything Leonard just said. I asked him if there was anything he could give Scar to aid her in this process, but no part of me expected any of this from him. He wants her to succeed. He wants to help her reach her dream. My mind is crumbling from the best type of surprise, and I can see the same thing happening to Scar as she shakes his hand again and then watches him walk away.

"What just happened?" Scar asks, and I stare down at her, shrugging. I'm not sure either.

Leonard barely spent two minutes with us, but it accomplished more than any other interaction I've ever had. Then again, this is what he's known for. Leonard is a hard-working man, always focused on the task at hand and getting business done. He's not one to linger around and make small talk, especially not with people he does not know. His reputation precedes him.

"I met Leonard Tick. He gave me a folder to help me achieve my dream. If I could, I think I'd cry," Scar says, a little chuckle leaving me in response.

"I know, love. This was incredible. We should look over all of this information as soon as we get back to the hotel," I say, pressing a kiss to her temple while she stares down at the pages in her hand.

"Scarlette? Here you go. It should fit you," Andrew Beckett says as he hands her one of his team shirts. Completely startled by him approaching out of nowhere and offering her merchandise, Scar lets out a nervous laugh.

"That's really not necessary, Andrew," she says while I hold back the urge to tell him to fuck off.

Scar's a strong, independent woman, who most certainly does not need me to act jealous and possessive. As much as I would like to tell Andrew where he could shove it, it is not my place to intervene unless I feel like it's absolutely necessary. I might be watching her a bit too closely to find anything that would justify me stepping in.

"I insist, sweetheart. It'll look great on you," he says, his eyes trailing down her body. *Fucking pervert.* I'm going to destroy hi—

"Sorry, Andrew, I only wear my boyfriend's team shirt or jersey. Don't be offended, please, but I'm not comfortable wearing another man's number and colors," she says, stepping onto her tiptoes to kiss my cheek.

This isn't the first time Scarlette has blown my mind. I might be hers, but she isn't mine. I don't expect her to do things like this, not even for the sake of our fake dating arrangement. My father isn't here, which means she doesn't *have to* work this hard to make our relationship seem convincing. She does it for the sake of... *why does she do it?* She could be flirting with Andrew or Kyle. They're both good-looking men, and they are the most successful in their careers. I am not successful, at least not yet. I'm trying my best to get into MotoGP, but there are a million stepping stones I will have to get to first like Moto2 and Moto1. And who knows if I will ever make it to where I'd like to be. These men, on the other hand, they have it all. Money, power, influence, and success. Scarlette has the choice of flirting with them, do whatever she likes with them, but she doesn't. She kisses my cheek, leans into me, and smiles at me like I'm the best thing in her life. *God, I want to be the best thing in her life.*

"I understand. I apologize if I overstepped a boundary," Andrew says, first addressing Scar and then shifting his gaze to me. I glare at him, willing him away with my mind. I'm done with his presence, which is why I'm glad when he leaves.

"Alright, jealous man, where else can we go?" Scar asks, nudging me in the side as she grins at me.

"Wherever you want, *mami.*"

So, I take her everywhere we can possibly go. We walk through the pitlane where we get small glimpses of the covered cars in the twenty garages. Thousands of people are around us, chatting away happily, but we're too focused on walking the length of the pitlane and then along where a bunch of booths are to care. I buy her a Leonard Tick artwork she was eyeing as we walked past.

The sun sets soon, and we meet up with my father in time to go back to the hotel. I try not to think about the conversation Scarlette and I will have in our room, but a smirk slips across my face anyway. It's been a very long day. Hell, I don't think a day has ever felt this long for me, but I'm ready to spend the night worshipping Scar until she believes I mean every word I'm repeating over and over in my head. I can't wait to share every single one of my thoughts with her. Maybe not all of them. I don't want to overwhelm her.

A yawn slips past Scar's lips, but she quickly covers her mouth in response. I take her other hand in mine, pressing a kiss to the back of it. She gives me a sleepy smile, looking more content and happy than she's ever seemed. This isn't the fake joy she shows people. This is the genuine happiness I long to see on her face at all times.

We make our way to the hotel room where Scar kicks off her shoes and attempts to take off her dress when she realizes I'm right behind her. A shy grin skips over her lips as she takes her bag and disappears into the bathroom. A wave of nerves hits me, so I decide to step onto the balcony, taking in a deep breath of air. When my head doesn't stop spinning, I suck in another sharp breath.

I've opened my heart to this woman. My trust issues are constantly screaming at me to run from her, from my feelings, but she's... she's everything I wasn't looking for but needed. Scar is perfect, even if she thinks she is flawed. Fuck me. An image of her trembling in my arms storms into my head, weakening my knees. Then, her father's words come back to me, and I want to break the railing of the balcony.

I can't waste more time. I need to tell Scar how I feel now, prove to her how amazing I think she is. My feet bring me back inside the room while my mind runs to catch up with them. Everything seems to stand still as my eyes fixate on her sleeping form in bed, barely covered by anything but a tiny pair of shorts and a small tank top. Holy shit. I shouldn't stare, but I can't help myself. I stand in front of the bed for a second, studying every curve on her body, noticing the way her black hair is splayed across the pillow, her full lips resting on her face without her usual smile, and seeing her scar ever so faint on her mouth.

"I really wish you were mine," I whisper into the quiet room. Scar is fast asleep, her breathing even as she lies in bed. A bed we share.

I rush through my evening routine, lying down in bed next to her once I'm done. Unsure what she'd like, I stay on my side. It takes everything out of me not to cuddle her, but that'd be something she'd have to ask for.

"Hmmm," she moans in her sleep, turning to me and wrapping her arm around my torso. I melt into her touch, smiling as she snuggles her face into my chest.

Scar is cuddling with me. We're sharing a bed. I'm placing my lips on the top of her head and grinning as if I've done it my entire life, not feeling a single bit of the usual guilt.

"Good night, Scar," I say, pulling her tighter against my chest. Somehow, it's still not close enough, but I kiss her cheek and grin to myself anyway.

Soon, I fall asleep, joining her in the land of dreams, seeing nothing but the blue of her eyes and the shining of her smile.

Chapter 32

Scarlette

O h God. Crap! This... this feels so good. This feels like heaven. No. No, it's more than that. This feels like home. Julián's arms are around me, my back pressed against his chest. His breathing is so steady in my ear, it makes a wave of calm spread through me. I run my fingers over the back of his hand, smiling as I wiggle closer to him. *Too close!*

My butt grinds against his morning wood, causing a quick, surprised gasp to leave him. Julián sucks in a sharp breath, his hand slipping to my hips and grabbing tightly to keep me in place.

"*Mami*, careful, please," he begs, his voice raspy and husky from just waking up. His fingers slide down my lower abdomen until my clit swells uncomfortably, my whole body catching on fire.

"Julián, I know we have to talk, but, please, don't stop touching me," I reply before my mind processes the words. I mean them, I wanted to say them, but I have no idea where the heck all of that confidence came from.

"Tell me what you want," he says, pressing his hard cock against my ass as he inches closer to me.

"You, Julián. I want you, need you, crave you," I admit, grinding against him again. A low moan slips past his lips, sending a wave of arousal between my legs. I press them together in hopes to relieve some tension.

"God, there is nothing I'd love more than to fuck you with my fingers right now, love, but we have to talk first. You know that. After what happened yesterday, we have to clarify our situation," he says and removes his hands from me until I'm whimpering. Julián slips out of bed, disappearing into the bathroom while leaving me hot and unsatisfied, like all of our sexual interactions so far. Maybe I should point it out, see what he'd do in response.

I sit up in bed and run my fingers through my wavy hair, then over my face. My body is still vibrating from being worked up, but I don't think I'll have an opportunity to relieve it. Instead, I push the sheets off my body, standing up and stretching my tired limbs. I wait for them to warm up before stepping over to my suitcase. Julián appears in front of me, half-naked, and guides me back toward the bed by my shoulders. I let out a small giggle as I sit, watching him kneel in front of me. His face is serious, like it always is, so I lift my fingers to the birthmark on his left cheek.

"You don't smile a lot. Why?" I ask, and he rests his hands on top of my thighs, squeezing them tightly.

"Fuck the deal, Scar. I don't want you to think I'm pretending. I want this to be the real thing, love. I'm yours. I've been yours since the moment I saw you in that restaurant, and I have no doubt I will belong to you indefinitely. I want to kiss you, touch you, and love you without doubts circling your mind about whether or not I'm only doing it to keep up a pretense. It's not. It's because I *long* to do all of these things, baby."

Tears shoot into my eyes, dropping down my cheeks a moment later. Julián wipes them away without hesitation.

"My heart is yours. Even if you do not want it, it isn't mine anymore. It belongs to you alone, and I hope you will never try to give it back to me. We may have started off on bad terms, but even when we fought, I was a certain kind of happy, one I've never experienced before. I just wanted to be in your presence, in your mind, anywhere you'd allow me to be."

He pauses, sucks in a sharp breath, and then looks at the ground, thinking about what to say next. Meanwhile, I'm trying my best not to break down and scream at him to 'RUN'. 'Get out of here'. 'Save yourself'. I want to say all of those things, but words have left me.

"Your father was wrong," he goes on, and I slide onto the floor where he is, breaking down in tears. "You are *not* pathetic or a burden. You are not weak, and this isn't a phase, I know that. You may think I don't know what it means to be with someone with anxiety and anxiety attacks, but I promise, I know. I know, and it doesn't change anything, only how much admiration I hold for you. It was already high before, but even more so now," he says, and I let out a laugh combined with a sob. Julián grabs my face between his hands, smiling my favorite smile in the world. "Your anxiety is nothing to be ashamed of, love. Seeing you yesterday helped me understand you, but it didn't lessen my feelings for you or how desperate I am to be with you. It didn't ruin my life either. Fuck, Scar, if anything, you brighten up my life. I have so much darkness inside of me, but when I'm with you, it leaves. It vanishes in an instant, leaving only a rainbow in its wake. You're all the beautiful colors in the world, *arcoíris*," he says, making realization dawn on me.

"Rainbow. You've been calling me rainbow in Spanish," I say, my tears slowing as I watch Julián grin at me.

"Yes." One-word answers. They used to drive me crazy, but not anymore. After he just laid his heart out for me, how could they?

"You don't think I'm broken?" I ask, bringing the tips of my fingers to my scar. He leans forward, kissing the length of it while tilting my head back to get better access to the mark. I shiver involuntarily as he leans back again, studying my eyes.

"I think we're all a little broken, it's part of life. I also think we break so that when we meet our other half, the pieces can fit together. I think ours fit perfectly, love, don't you?" Julián asks, trailing the backs of his fingers over my cheek.

"There is a lot you don't know about me," I blurt out, earning me another small smile from him.

"When I was six years old, I had another best friend. His name was Jamie. He got sick, I don't remember with what, but I've never had the courage to ask my mom either." I scrunch my eyebrows together, sadness for Julián creeping into my chest. "The one thing I remember as if it happened yesterday is what he said the day he died. He said 'I will never get to smile or laugh again. That's a really weird thought.' I mean, we were six and eight, we didn't have a clear idea of death, but he was right. I also remember finding it so unfair that I would still get to do those things when he wouldn't be able to, so I stopped. I stopped because I always felt so guilty. Jamie was there the day I was born. We were best friends for six years, and losing him broke something inside of me. It hardened me. I stopped smiling and laughing but the guilt vanished when I met you.

"The first time I smiled at you, it didn't feel wrong. It felt more than right, especially because it made you happy to see me smile," Julián explains, and I allow the longing I feel for him to settle deep inside my bones. This beautiful, hurt man is mine. He's had a painful past, just like I did. Somehow, it makes me feel closer to him.

"I think Jamie would want you to smile and laugh for the both of you, Julián. He'd be happy to see you express all emotions of joy. Thank you for sharing it with me. Your smile has become my favorite," I admit, watching the lines in his cheeks appear as he grins at me. I trace them with my index finger. "I'm sorry you lost Jamie," I add, and Julián snakes his hand around my left wrist.

"It's okay. He brought you to me," he replies, and I can't help myself. I fling my arms around his neck, holding him against me.

"I don't know if I'm ready to share my dark times yet." Mostly because Violet doesn't even know the full story. My mom made me swear never to share it with anyone.

"You don't have to be. I didn't share mine to force yours to the surface. I wanted to tell you why I don't smile, well, why I didn't. That was my only intention, I promise." And I believe him because Julián is that type of person. A really good person. One of the best people I've ever met.

The man I've fallen in love with.

Shit.

I'm in love with Julián.

Why the heck am I smiling?

"If you don't want to be with me, Scar, we will keep going with this deal. I promise I will hold up my end of it and then leave you alone afterward—" Panic sears through me.

"No!" I say louder than necessary, pulling out of the hug. "No, Julián, I want you. You—You are—" I cut off, searching for the right words. He cups my face, kissing me briefly. It sends a wave of calm and confidence over me. "You are the man I want to be with in every way I possibly can. I want to explore it all with you, love, sex, relationships, everything. I didn't know I was waiting for you until my eyes found yours. I don't want this to be a deal either, but I don't think it ever has been. I never faked anything with you. It was real for me," I admit, and he kisses my lips again.

"It was real for me too, love."

Then his mouth claims mine with an intensity so strong, it knocks the breath from my chest. He takes his time, tasting me, exploring my lips and mouth with his tongue until a little groan slips out of him. I push off the floor, guiding him backward until he's sitting on the ground. My legs move to each side of him, straddling his lap while I hover over it.

"Is this okay? I'm not hurting you?" I ask, and Julián gives me a small complaining grunt.

"You are hurting me by not sitting down properly, *mami*. Now, sit," he commands, and I sink down on him completely.

He gives me an approving smile before grabbing my face and my lips again. His fingers drop to my hips, guiding them forward until—*Oh*. Julián grinds my clit against his hardness, a breathless moan leaving me.

"Fuck, Scar," he groans into my mouth, rolling my hips for me again.

My body melts into his completely, and I start grinding against him by myself. Pleasure rolls through me instantly. I slip my fingers into his hair, tugging on his curls as my head falls backward. His lips move to my neck where he places open-mouthed kisses along the length of it down to my collarbone. Julián's fingers dig into my hips as he moans, and I keep going, keep grinding my clit over his bulge. I've never been so happy about wearing pajamas that do nothing to hide my body or keep it warm.

"Julián," I moan, my movements never stopping. Having him press against me like this, it feels good. So good. Nothing's ever felt this good by myself.

"Let me see you, baby. I want to watch you come in front of someone for the first time," he says, tilting my head forward again. My eyes fixate on his as I ride him this way, clothed but closer than I've ever been to anyone before.

"I want your fingers," I manage to whisper, and Julián sucks in a sharp breath.

"You want my fingers on your clit, *mami*?" I nod, kissing him with desperation.

I've never been this needy for anyone, but, at the same time, I don't mind it. I like the way my body responds to him, the way goosebumps have covered every part of me. I like the arousal soaking my panties and the way my clit has swollen up for him.

Only for Julián. Always only for him. There's never been a man who has made me react to a single smile or look the same way he does. I'm a mess.

"I'm going to slip my hand into your panties now, okay?" he asks, and I nod, keeping eye contact with him as he trails his thumb over the waistband of my shorts. "Are you soaking wet for me, *mami*? Will I find you dripping?" he says, and I whimper as his hand disappears inside of my panties and he cups my pussy.

"Oh God," I moan, my forehead falling onto his shoulder in response to the pleasure setting my insides on fire.

"You'd be so ready for my cock right now, baby, it's driving me crazy," he says, pressing the ball of his hand to my clit. A cry of pleasure dances off my lips, filling the quiet room. "I want to make you come all of my fingers, feel you clench around them. You don't know how long I've waited for this," he says before picking me up off the ground and dropping me onto the bed, his hand moving back inside my panties.

"You're so strong," I say, his thumb tracing tight circles over my clit now. "It's really hot," I admit and let out a pleasure-filled laugh.

"Yeah? You like that I can lift you easily?" he asks, and I nod again, pushing the back of my head into the mattress.

"Yes," I say, moaning as his index finger disappears inside of me.

"You're so tight, *mami*, so tight. Do you think you can handle another finger?" he asks before kissing my lips, cheek, jaw, and neck.

"Yes, please," I beg, grinding myself into his hand to get more friction.

Julián slips two fingers inside of me, and I gasp in response. This is new. It's new, but delicious. I've fingered myself countless times, but nothing I ever did compares to the way he's touching me. Julián curls his fingers inside of me at a spot that curls my toes and arches my back off the bed.

"Woah," I say and grab his arms for support. He chuckles against my neck in response. "That felt—" I cut off when he does it again, moaning.

"Yeah?" he asks, caressing the same spot until I tremble under him.

He doesn't stop. He keeps going, keeps working that spot. The palm of his hand massages my clit with every stroke of his fingers until I'm a moaning mess underneath his strong, hot, naked torso.

"Julián, I'm going to come," I say a moment before his lips find mine. His tongue slips into my mouth, warm and welcome, dancing with my own while his hand does things to me I never imagined possible.

"Come, *mami*, all over my fingers. Let me finally feel it," he almost begs, and I give in, surrendering to the orgasm without a single care in the world.

My mind drifts into a haze, getting me so high on pleasure, my entire body shakes with relief and glee. Every hair on me raises itself as the knot in my stomach releases and spreads something hot and liquid through my veins. My chest presses against Julián's as more sounds of pleasure leave me. *God*, nothing's ever felt like... *this*. Nothing's ever felt so fulfilling and beautiful. It's as if waves were searching for a shore and they finally found it, allowing them to release all their strength onto the land, to finally let go.

"Julián?" I ask as I open my eyes. His find my gaze, a smile so bright it's almost blinding on his face.

"Scar?" he says while placing his hands on either side of me, his body fully on top of mine now. He's still holding himself up so his weight isn't on me, but I wouldn't mind having him envelop me right now.

"I adore you," I blurt out. His features soften before he briefly kisses my lips.

"*Siento lo mismo, mami.*" Then he kisses me again and again while I try to figure out what he just said to me.

Chapter 33
Julián

I break the kiss after another moment, standing up from the bed and smiling at her body still so high from the orgasm. Scar's cheeks are a wonderful shade of pink, and I could get fucking lost in the way her hard nipples are pushing against her little top and the smile lingering on her features.

"Where are you going?" she asks, and I let out a nervous laugh. Fuck me. I've never been so nervous in front of a woman because of a hard-on. A hard-on she gave me by grinding her beautiful pussy against me and moaning so loudly, I still feel the sounds in my bones.

"Give me a few minutes. I just have to take care of something, and then I'll be right back, I promise." Because if I don't release the build-up in my cock right now, a single graze from her later will make me explode.

Scar sits up straight and reaches for my hips, dragging my body back toward the edge of the bed.

"Show me," she says, and I cock an eyebrow.

"Show you what, love?" I ask because there is no way she means what my mind just thought of. Scar licks her lips, her gaze dropping to my bulge and then back up to my face.

"Show me how you take care of yourself so I can learn to take care of you," she explains, running her finger over my cock and making it twitch in response. I involuntarily lean into her touch, desperate to have her hands on me.

"Are you sure? You need to be a hundred percent sure because I don't want you to be uncomfortable seeing my—" Her hand trails down my bulge, palming me through my pants and knocking every single word from my mind.

"Show me, Julián. Show me how to pleasure you," she says, pulling her top over her head and exposing her big breasts to me. I can't help it. I sink onto the bed, my cock pushing unbearably against my pants. "What's wrong?" Scar asks when I let my head fall back against the mattress and sigh.

"Your body, your breasts, fuck, Scar, you're perfect," I say, pushing myself up by my elbows to see she's dropped onto her knees in front of the bed. She takes her tits into her hands and kneads them, making me even harder than before. Shit. I need to relieve this tension before I go crazy.

"You like it when I tease myself like this?" she asks with a smirk that tells me she knows exactly what she's doing.

"Yes. *Tú me tienes loco, mami*," I say and watch her eyes flame with desire at my words. She glides her hands over my thighs and squeezes them until I sit up. My fingers grab her face, holding it tightly in my grasp.

"Tell me what it means," she says as I cup one of her big breasts, massaging the nipple between my thumb and index finger. She's perfect.

"You drive me absolutely crazy with that body and confidence of yours, Scar. That's what I mean," I say, my cock aching in my boxers when she smiles up at me through those thick, black lashes of hers. The blue of her eyes looks faded in this light, but they are still the most beautiful in the world, especially with that ring of gold around her pupils.

"I want to see you," she says, tugging on the waistband of my pants.

"Are you desperate for my cock, love?" I ask with a smile, and she grins at me.

"Yes." No shame, no shyness, nothing. Scarlette is comfortable with me. There is no better goddamn feeling in the world.

"Then take it out, *mami*. I will show you how to use your hands on me," I say, and she wastes no second as she guides down the front of my pajama pants and takes me in her hands. *God.* I moan at the feel of her warm hands wrapping around me, something I have never done before. It takes more than that for me to moan.

Scar stares at my length, studying it because this is the first time she's ever seen a cock up close, first time she's holding one. I give her time, as much as she wants, even when my body is screaming at me to take over and release the tension that has built in my dick. I don't think it's ever been this sensitive to a woman's touch. Then again, with Scar swallowing hard at the size of my erection and her breathing so very uneven, I can barely keep myself from coming right here and now.

Her thumb trails over the head of my cock, making me suck in a sharp breath and grip the sheets in response. I know I'm supposed to show her how all of this works, but I don't want to pressure her either.

"Did that hurt?" she says, letting go of me immediately. I let out a low laugh I don't mean in the slightest.

"No, baby, it felt good, really good. Too good." I trace her bottom lip with my thumb before licking my hand and taking myself into it, smiling. "I like it like this," I tell her, stroking the length of my cock. I go up and down while she watches me with fascination, and I stare at her with lust. I've fantasized about being with her in any way, but I never thought she'd study me while I jerked off. Never in my wildest dreams did I let myself hope for this.

Her hands slip onto my thighs again while pleasure fills me from top to bottom, starting off in my erection and spreading through me in waves. I keep stroking myself until she sits up on her knees and lets out a little moan that throws me off-guard.

"I want to lick it," she says, and I barely keep myself from coming. "Can I?" she asks, almost pleading with me.

I let go of myself, and her hands move to the base of my cock. I adjust when I feel the orgasm building quickly, pushing it away. I want to give her time to explore me, not ruin it by orgasming before she even had the chance to do what she intends.

"You're so big," she says with a little grin, and I bite my bottom lip in response.

"Yeah?" She nods, stroking me with one of her thumbs. Fuck me. Pleasure storms through my body. "Don't worry, you will get used to it, *mami*, you will get used to me," I assure her, and Scar straightens out her back as her mouth inches closer to me.

"I wasn't worried," she replies, the confidence I got to see in our fights coming out now too. It's so hot. She's so hot. I can barely handle it. "Stand up for me," she instructs, and I almost laugh at her bossiness. This side of her is new to me, especially because this is not at all what I've been expecting. I didn't think she'd be so forward, telling me what she wants and taking it.

"You can take it slow, love, there is no rush or pressure," I assure her, but she's already taking the base of my cock between her hands again while her mouth closes the distance between it and my tip.

"I want you in my mouth. I want you to come in it, okay?" Fucking hell, she's perfect. In every way, this woman is perfect for me.

"Okay, baby," I respond a second before she darts her tongue out and runs it from the base to the tip of my cock. "Oh God, Scarlette," I moan, barely keeping myself standing upright.

Before I know what has hit me, I'm deep inside her mouth. One lick and she was ready to take me down her throat. Pleasure like I've never felt before rolls through me, and I have to grab onto her hair to keep standing upright. She's a little awkward at first, but I give her time to find her rhythm.

"Can you take me a bit deeper, baby?" I ask because she's been swirling her tongue around my head, and if she keeps going, I will come too soon.

"Like this?" she asks, taking my thick length into her mouth again until I hit the back of her throat and she gags.

"Oh God," I groan, so she does it again. And again.

Her head bops back and forth, her tongue playing with me while her hot mouth makes it impossible to fight off the orgasm. I don't want to let it seep through me, but after a few more moments, she has me undone in every single way a person can undo another. I spill down her throat, my cock pulsing while she sucks me off and moans in response.

"Fuuuuck," I grunt because it has never felt this good. I don't think anything has ever given me so much pleasure. Scar moans again, and I fall backward onto the bed, my knees too weak to keep me standing.

"I don't think I need you to teach me. I seem to be pretty good at it," she says happily as she crawls on top of me, straddling my lap.

Her black hair falls like curtains on each side of my face, but I guide her down to kiss her, taste myself on her lips. I can't help it. Knowing I'm the only man she's ever had in her hands and mouth sends a wave of hunger through me. I'm enjoying the thought a lot more than I should.

"You're mine," I blurt out between kisses, my voice breathless and needy. Scar smiles against my lips.

"And you're all mine," she replies, bringing her hands to my torso and kissing me fiercely. God, she's just the same level of possessive as me. I love it.

"We should get ready," I say while her lips find mine, her confidence now in her kiss too.

She was unsure the first time I planted my mouth on hers. It was new and she was inexperienced. Now, she's comfortable kissing me however she wants. Like most things in her life, Scar is incredibly quick in having picked up this new skill, driving me absolutely crazy.

"Okay," she says against my lips before sliding her tongue into my mouth.

Fuck the rest of the world. I'm staying in bed with her for the rest of the goddamn year.

Chapter 34
Scarlette

Somehow, Julián and I manage to separate our mouths long enough to talk about little things, topics I never saw us discussing. He shares his favorite coffee order with me, black without cream and sugar of course, and I tell him I don't like any. He chuckles in response to me scrunching my nose at the thought of the bitter taste of coffee before pressing a kiss to my temple.

"I can't function around Elias without coffee," he jokes, and I laugh, enjoying this playful side of him. He's never shown it to me like this, well, maybe once.

"Understandable. Then again, isn't he like a shot of espresso once he gets talking?" I ask, earning myself a heartfelt laugh from him. With my head on his chest, I get to hear it deep inside him and right over me. It's the sweetest sensation that I wish would last forever.

"Yeah, you're absolutely right, love," he replies and tilts my head up to kiss my lips.

"Are we dating now?" I ask, and a chuckle vibrates off him and through me.

"You want to be my girlfriend, *arcoíris*?" he replies, running the tips of his fingers down the length of my arm. For a moment, I get completely lost in the sensation and forget about him asking me a question.

"No, I want to be your rainbow, the woman you lose yourself in, the place you call home, the one you call *mami* when you're talking dirty, and so much more. I don't just want to be your girlfriend. I want to be more than that," I blurt out, not quite sure where the heck all of this just came from. Instead of freaking out, Julián guides me closer.

"You are everything you want to be to me and more, Scarlette. Every single position you desire in my heart, it already belongs to you," he replies, and all tension floods from my body as I melt into him.

We stay like this, in complete silence, for a little while. It gives me time to contemplate how we got here. This wasn't supposed to last. We gave ourselves a time frame and then we were supposed to be done. This wasn't supposed to be an epic love story. We didn't like each other when we first met. *How did we end up here?* Where I've fallen in love with him and he seems ready to hand me the world. It makes no sense to me, but, at the same time, I don't need it to either. I've never felt this at peace and on edge at the same time, as if anything could cause us to fall apart, but I'm happy to even have this time with him now.

It's messing with my head.

"Julián?" I ask after he pulls back. His different-colored eyes study my serious face, the hint of a smile resting on his features.

"Yes, *mami*?" Another kiss to my temple.

"We should get ready. Your dad is expecting us," I say, but Julián holds me close to his chest, groaning in complaint.

"No, let's stay here. Let's stay here forever and not worry about the rest of the world," he begs and buries his face in the crook of my neck. I breathe in, smelling the sandalwood coming off him and coursing through my veins.

"What about my career?" I challenge, and Julián sits up straight while pulling me with him.

"Go get ready, I will go after you," he instructs, and I salute him before stepping into the bathroom, the sound of his laughter following me inside.

Julián hasn't let go of my hand since we've sat down for dinner. I'd love to pay more attention to it, but all of my focus is stuck on Robert Fuchs. He's sitting in front of me, holding down a conversation about engineering and the subjects I'm currently taking. He asks me what got me interested in the sport of Formula One, so I share my story. Julián's eyes stay on me for the duration of it since this is also new information for him.

"My father used to make me watch the races when I was younger and I hated it. I thought it was boring, which I know I probably shouldn't tell you, but I swear Formula One is the most fascinating sport to me now," I start with a laugh, and Julián squeezes my hand reassuringly. A small smile lingers on his lips as he encourages me to keep going. "He had a mechanic shop when I was a child, and I used to help him. I knew how to disassemble an Internal Combustion Engine before I knew how to drive a car." Robert Fuchs looks impressed, so I keep going. "I also took apart my first bike and put it back together out of boredom." Everyone at the table lets out a small laugh, including the man I've fallen hopelessly for.

"So, engineering was the most interesting career path going from there?" Robert asks, and I give him a bright smile.

"Well, yes, but becoming a race engineer is even more fascinating. While I do like getting my hands dirty every now and then, I prefer doing analysis and the idea of working directly with a driver during race weekends," I admit, and the team principal leans forward on the table, studying me closely.

"You remind me of my daughter Nevaeh. She's just as strong-willed as you, stubborn almost," he says, making Julián chuckle beside me. I nudge him in the side so he wraps his arm around the back of my chair and leans back. "Don't get me wrong. I think it's a good trait to have in professions like this. This is a male-dominated field after all," he adds, and I nod.

"That's another reason why I've chosen this career," I explain. "I want to see more women pursue whatever job they want, and I hope to make a difference, even a small one, by becoming another woman to succeed in this path."

"I will tell you something, Scarlette. Finish your studies, and I promise you, I will give you opportunities to intern for my team during your summer break. It's the peak of the season in Formula One then, and it will give you great experience. Then, when you have your diploma and the internship goes well, we can see about getting you a permanent position, alright?" Robert says, causing my jaw to drop so far to the floor, I doubt I will ever bring it back up.

"She'd love that, sir," Julián says with a little nod when I don't find words. I snap out of my trance and give his hand a thankful squeeze.

"Yes, I would. I apologize. This merely caught me a bit off-guard. I didn't expect to be given an opportunity so quickly," I admit, mentally slapping myself for my inability to shut up when it is most crucial.

"You have Leonard to thank for that. He insisted I offer you all of this," Robert replies, and I raise both eyebrows in surprise. "Anyway, you all have a wonderful night. I have to get back to my hotel room. My daughters and wife are expecting me," he says, standing up and dropping a few hundred dollar bills onto the table. I barely keep from gasping.

It must be nice to have this much money. I always think that when I see the way my boss spends his money left and right. Julián dislikes his father's wealth, and I understand why now. The way he spends it, it's only ever for himself and what he wants. This trip, according to Julián, is the first thing his father has spent money on for someone other than himself or his family members. It doesn't make me feel any less guilty, but the opportunity I've just been handed by the team principal of Grenzenlos has eased it a little.

"That's kind of you, Robert, but I'm not letting you pay," Mr. Rodrick interrupts my thoughts, and I turn to Julián to find him watching me with an intense look on his face.

"What?" I ask, and he leans forward, brushing a loose strand of hair out of my face. He kisses me softly while the men across from us argue over who is going to pay for the meal. My lips melt against his while a small smile crosses my face.

"Do you like bumper cars?" he asks when he breaks the kiss, and I grin at him.

"I love them. Why?" I say, and Julián stands up, adjusting his blazer as he faces his father. He says something in Spanish to him before holding out his hand for me and leading me out of the restaurant. "Julián! I didn't even get to thank your father or Mr. Fuchs," I say, but he gives me a naughty look.

"You can thank them by thanking me in the car," he says, and a nervous laugh bubbles up in my throat. I manage to swallow it before it reaches the surface.

"You're impossible," I reply, and he squeezes my hand, acknowledging my comment in a way that says 'Yes, I am, and you love it'. Which I do. I love it more than I should.

"I want to take you somewhere, but it closes in an hour and a half, so we have to hurry," he explains, flagging down a taxi for us to get in.

"Will you tell me where?" I ask, staring at the clear blue sky without a cloud in sight. We had dinner early, so the sun is not even attempting to set as we leave the restaurant.

"No," he replies with his vague-response style, and I playfully frown at him. Julián starts grinning, which means so much more to me now that he's shared his story with me.

"What if I kissed and asked nicely?" I say as we settle down in the taxi. Julián covers my ears as he tells the driver where to go, and I burst into laughter. "Seriously?" I ask, still laughing. He joins me and shrugs in response.

"It's a surprise. Now, be a little patient," he says, and I cock an eyebrow.

"Twenty years I've been patiently waiting for something else, Julián. I think I can manage however long it takes us to get to wherever you're taking me," I say, but his reaction catches me a bit off-guard. He's amused and simultaneously desperate to be alone with me and put me out of my misery. I can see it in his eyes. I can sense the way he craves me.

Maybe I'm projecting because I desperately crave him.

"Tonight, *mami*. I will make it all worth it tonight."

And I have no doubt he will.

Chapter 35
Julián

S car might be a Grenzenlos fan through and through, but the way her eyes light up when we arrive at the *Velocità Rossa World* here in Monaco—they built a similar one to the one in Abu Dhabi in honor of the race weekend—would suggest she's the biggest Velocità Rossa fan. She twirls to take in every aspect of the theme park. People around us are chatting happily, filling the space with noise. Scar's eyes drop to the ground, which is made to mimic an actual Formula One track with lines painted on either side of the walkway. It's almost overwhelming how many different things are going on around us at once, but Scar takes it all in with that smile of hers, lighting up the entire space.

She brings me to the display of a bright-red Velocità Rossa and I watch her study the car with fascination. To her, this must all be new. To me, this is boring. I learned how to drive in my father's Audi R8, and he bought me a Grenzenlos when I turned eighteen. I sold it the day after, donating the money to charity. My dad was fucking pissed, but I almost smiled at him that day.

"Have you ever driven a car like this?" Scar asks, and I step toward her, so goddamn needy for her touch. I slide my fingers through hers and squeeze them gently.

"How hot would you find me if I told you I raced one around a track before?" I reply, making her eyes light up with desire.

"So hot, I feel like dragging you to the nearest bathroom so you can slip your fingers inside of me and find out," she says, and my jaw drops to the center of the earth. Fuck me.

"Damn, *mami*, why did you hide that dirty mouth of yours from me for so long?" I say, a little upset but mostly proud of her.

"Maybe having you come in it made it dirty," she says as she moves on her tiptoes and presses a kiss to my jaw. She walks away from me before I can hold on to her.

My feet follow behind her, and we spend the next hour exploring. We do every attraction she wants us to from the bumper cars to a fucking mary go round. Scar laughs the whole time, truly enjoying herself. I can't help but join her every single time. The way the sound falls from her lips reaches something deep inside of me. I never thought anyone would touch that part of my soul, of my existence, but now that she has, no one else will ever get the opportunity. I will make sure of it.

Eventually, we're kicked out of the event because they need to close it. Scar and I simply walk around for a while, enjoying the warmth of the night. Her hand rests in mine the entire time as she shares how excited she is to get back home and continue her studies. After the news she got tonight, I can't imagine how happy Scar must be. This is the best outcome either of us could have hoped for this weekend. On top of that, we're dating now without that fake aspect of our deal. Hell, even I'm giddy right now.

We move on to talk about other little things, like where my nickname Storm came from and what got her interested in riding bikes. She then asks me why I want to become a professional motorcycle racer, and I share the story of growing up and watching Marc Rodriguez, a Puerto Rican racer, win so many Grand Prixes. I always thought he was so cool, the way he leaned down in the corners until his knee touched the ground or how he rode on one wheel down the straight once he'd won. I wanted to be like him. I want to be the best.

"You will be," she says, sounding so convinced, I actually believe it too.

"Yeah, well, I haven't been taking it as seriously as I should have. I need to be deserving, which means no more getting distracted," I reply, not realizing how heavy this has been weighing on my chest until this very second. I don't think I'm deserving of a spot in Moto3, but it's my next stepping stone to getting into MotoGP, to get to where Marc was.

Scar stops in front of me, her hands moving under my shirt before they glide upwards. My skin catches on fire instantly.

"Am *I* a distraction?" she asks, both with worry and lust in her eyes.

"No, *mami*, you are a priority," I say and lean down to press my mouth to hers. A surprised little gasp leaves her, melting my insides.

"Julián," she whimpers when I nibble on her bottom lip.

"Can I admit something?" I say breathlessly, moving my kiss onto her neck.

"Yes," she replies, and I feel her swallowing hard.

"My parents were never on my ass for me to find someone. The reason why I agreed to fake dating was just to be close to you, love. That's all I wanted," I admit while wrapping my arms around her hips and bringing her close to my chest.

"You got nothing out of this agreement?" she asks, surprise all over her features. I take her face between my hands and wish I could make her see just how much she's given me.

"I got your attention, Scar. I got your affection, your compassion, a piece of your light. It's living inside of me now, nipping at the darkness to take over. I got something priceless out of it, love," I say as her arms slip around my neck. Her eyes soften in response to my words.

"And what's that?" she asks, her voice barely a whisper.

"I got you," I reply with a small smile.

"You're very good with your words, Julián," she says and buries her face in my chest to hide her blush.

"I'm very good with my hands, too, *mami*. Should we get back to the hotel room so I can remind you?" I ask, sensing she wants me to change the subject. Scar pulls out of the hug to reveal her naughty smirk.

"Actually, I would like to see how good you are with your other body parts," she says, and I grab her hand to lead her to one of the taxi pick-up areas.

The ride to the hotel is quiet, but Scar wiggles happily in her seat next to me. I furrow my brows, the smile slipping onto my face before I can stop it. I'm fucking excited too, but the way she's almost bouncing up and down is making me a bit nervous. This is going to be Scar's first time. She probably has a lot of expectations and—*Puñeta*.

What if I can't make it pleasurable for her? I know how to have sex, and I'm good at it too, but I've never been with a virgin. Shit. Oh God. What if it will be painful for her? What if I can't make her come? What if I come, but way too early?

"What? What's wrong?" she asks, grabbing my chin between her fingers. "You look like how I feel before one of my anxiety attacks," Scar says with a little laugh, probably to lighten the mood.

"I'm scared I won't be able to make you feel good," I admit, feeling extremely weird for sharing my feelings like this. Scar makes me feel like I can tell her everything, but it's new to me. I've never been able to be so open about my feelings.

"Julián, we don't have to have sex tonight if you don't want to," she replies, and it causes my eyebrows to furrow again.

"I've been fantasizing about having sex with you for a long time, Scar. Do you honestly think I don't want to do so tonight?" She shakes her head in response. "I'm just a little nervous. You probably have high expectations, as you should, and I'm worried I won't live up to them. God, by this rate, I will overthink so much, I probably won't even get hard," I say before I can stop the words from spilling from my lips. Damn this woman and her truth-serum-inflicting presence in my life.

"*Papi*," she says, leaning forward and sliding her hands up to my groin. I'm instantly hard. The way she addressed me combined with her lavender scent and hand on my bulge sends all of my blood straight into my cock. "We both know you're going to fuck me well. Don't start doubting yourself now," she adds, pulling the lobe of my ear into her mouth. Pleasure seeps through me, building a home deep inside my chest.

"You're going to make me come right here if you don't stop, *mami*," I reply, grabbing her wrist to keep her from palming me through my pants.

"Hmm, I would like that very much," she says with a naughty grin and leans back in her seat. It takes everything in me not to follow her and close the distance between us.

"We've arrived," the driver says a few minutes later.

Scar and I get out of the car before walking up the stairs of the hotel. We move through the lobby and into the elevators where I grab her face. I plant my lips on hers, slipping my tongue into her mouth and groaning in response to how sweet she tastes. There are no words for it either. It's just her, her flavor.

A moan leaves her as her hands slip under my shirt, and I press her into the wall of the elevator, trying to get closer. There are cameras in here, but I can't help myself at the moment. I need her. I need her taste, scent, and touch. I need her sound and the way she smiles in response to my gentle groping of her hips.

"God, how long does it take to get to our floor?" she says as I dart my tongue along the length of her neck. "Fuck, Julián," she moans, and I grin at her use of swear words.

"That dirty mouth of yours, *mami*, I love it. It makes me want to fuck it again," I say before nibbling on her soft spot. The elevator doors *bing* as they slide open.

I pick her up without hesitation, wrapping her legs around my torso and walking toward our room. Scar giggles in my arms.

"You're so strong." She always has the same response, but tonight, I smile at the way she says it. So happy. So proud. So fucking sweet.

"God, Scar, you have no idea how badly I want to be inside of you," I blurt out, and she claims my lips in response, showing me she feels the same need.

"Julián."

My senses go into high alert. I break the kiss to follow where the voice of my father came from. I drop Scar on her feet, panic flooding my chest when I see Dad on the ground in front of my room, his hand on his left arm.

"*Papá?*" I ask, dropping onto my knees. Sweat is rolling down his forehead.

"*Mi corazón,*" he says and points to his heart before his head falls backward against the wall.

"Call an ambulance," I yell to Scar, but she's already on it. "What the fuck do I do?" I ask because he's unresponsive now.

Scarlette hands me the phone and tells me to inform the person on the other line of our address. Then she guides my father onto the floor and performs CPR on him.

"Scar," I say softly because I've never been so terrified. She tilts her head in my direction, her attempts to save my father not stopping.

"I know," she replies, shifting her focus back to him. "Come on, Mr. Rodrick. Wake up," she begs, but he doesn't respond.

He's not fucking responding.

Please. Please, don't take him from me.

Chapter 36
Scarlette

I t's been two hours. Two. Hours. We've received no update. Julián pulled me onto his lap an hour ago, and he's been holding onto me ever since. His face is buried in my chest as he tries to hide and lets me protect him from the rest of the world. I wish I could. I wish his body didn't shudder every few minutes when a dark thought crosses his mind. I wish he didn't have to experience any of this pain. I wish, more than anything, that what I did to help Mr. Rodrick might have saved his life.

"*Tengo miedo, arcoíris,*" Julián says, but, naturally, I don't understand him. I run my fingers through his smooth hair, trailing my other ones over the birthmark on his cheek.

"You want to translate that for me?" I ask with a soft tone, and he nods.

"I'm scared, rainbow." He sucks in a sharp breath against my chest, and I wrap my hands around his head.

"Rainbow," I say, almost tasting the word. "Would you like to know something that's going to blow your mind?" Finally, he lifts his head, his different-colored eyes meeting mine in an instant.

"*Dime,*" he replies, and I give him a slight smile.

"The day I got this scar, I saw a rainbow." I trail the length of his jaw while his eyes watch me with a warm intensity.

"You did?" he asks, the hand that's been resting on my hip grabbing a bit tighter. I nod as I guide my fingers into his hair again and pull him closer. My lips brush over his, causing him to shiver.

"I was six. My dad, drunk as usual, took me to an ice cream shop even though he was supposed to take me to a friend's birthday party. He had forgotten, and when I tried to remind him, he'd said to me, 'Listen, you ungrateful little shit. I'm taking you for ice cream, and that is it. Stop fucking whining.' He could never remember what he said or done afterward because he was drunk out of his mind," I explain, watching Julián's eyes darken at my story.

"I hate him," he says, and I let out a small chuckle. He, on the other hand, is not even slightly amused.

"I did for a long time too, but he went to rehab, and we've worked a lot on our relationship in therapy. Yes, he hasn't contacted me since I moved, but Mom does enough checking in for the both of them," I reply.

Julián shifts me on his lap so I'm somehow even closer to him. Our breaths intertwine now, but nothing has ever felt more comfortable. He's hard underneath me, all muscle, but somehow there is no chair, couch, or other seating area in the world I would prefer over him.

"It had been raining when we went for ice cream, so as the sun came out, a beautiful rainbow was painted across the sky, hiding ever so slightly behind a few clouds," I say while he studies my lips as I talk. "After he bought the ice cream, we went back outside, and he stumbled over his own feet. To keep himself from falling, he tried to hold onto me, but all it did was cause him to take me down too. I heard something snap in my arm as he fell on top of me. My head hit the concrete floor and my lip split open, as did the side of my head." I lift my hair out of the way to show him my other scar. The tips of his fingers slide across it. "I was in a coma for a week, and they didn't know if I was going to make it because of the internal bleeding in my head."

"Scarlette," he says softly and squeezes my sides.

"Julián," I reply with a smile. He tilts his head back to show me his frightened frown.

"Is that what started triggering your anxiety?" he asks, unsure if this question is okay. "You don't have to tell me, of course," he adds, and I press my mouth to his with a smile.

"I'm not sure what was the trigger, to be honest. All I remember is getting my first anxiety attack in high school. I've always been someone who gets extremely nervous for tests, interviews, new situations, and even sometimes for no reason at all. Maybe it was bound to happen eventually, maybe it was nothing, or everything combined at once. I couldn't tell you," I reply, but he doesn't respond for a moment, simply stares into my eyes.

"Does it bother you? Not knowing why it started?" he asks, cupping my face and sliding his thumb across my bottom lip.

"It used to, but not anymore," I admit and feel his breathing hitch when I shift a little in his lap. His fingers dig into my sides to get me to still. "Sorry," I say with a small laugh which dies out as soon as his eyes flutter shut.

"Don't be. I wish this wasn't what we were doing right now. You didn't sign up for any of this drama. You wanted sex tonight, not a trip to the fucking hospital," he says, his head falling backward against the wall. Shock spreads through my chest.

"Julián, please tell me you're joking," I reply, but he opens his eyes to reveal he's one hundred percent serious.

"This was supposed to be a fake dating situation. I know we agreed to be more, but you shouldn't have to deal with this, with me when I'm terrified and scared to death," he says and lets go of me entirely. The loss of contact almost makes me complain, but my biggest concern is what he just said.

"You have no idea how I really feel about you, do you?" I ask, and his eyebrows scrunch together in response.

"You're attracted to me," he says, and I feel like shaking or slapping some sense into him.

"And you're attracted to me," I reply, but he scoffs in response.

"*Estoy enamorado de ti, mami.*" I roll my eyes so he grabs my chin. "I'm a lot more than attracted to you, Scarlette. I'm yours in ways a person shouldn't even belong to another. I feel things that should explode a heart. I breathe for you so much that my lungs crumble to dust when I'm not with you," he rants before letting go of my face again and screwing his eyes shut.

"Then you know exactly how I feel about you," I reply, but he shakes his head. "Julián, don't be stubborn, please. You're saying I didn't sign up for this, but I did. I signed up for it all the second I laid my eyes on you. I want you. I want all your feelings, especially when you're scared and helpless. I want to be the light that brightens up your dark times," I say as I look through my purse and pull out my lavender oil. My fingers catch a few drops before they massage it into his temples. He closes his eyes once more, a slight smile on his features.

"You already are, love," he whispers while I continue to place the lavender oil on his skin.

"Good. Now, open your eyes. Trust me when I say I care for you so deeply, it frightens me a little," I say, and before I know it, his lips are on mine and he's kissing me.

He's kissing me like never before. I can taste it on his tongue when he slides it into my mouth. I can feel it on his lips as they envelop mine with an intensity I sense going straight into my lower abdomen. I can hear it in the way he groans for me.

"Scar," he moans, and it makes me realize we're not alone. Other people can hear his little noises, and it unsettles me. They're for me and me alone.

"Julián," I warn, and he breaks the kiss, burying his face in the crook of my neck.

We stay like this for a while. Nurses, doctors, and patients pass by us, but all I see is Julián. I slide my hands through his hair, massaging his scalp because I can only imagine how badly his head is hurting. He's in a constant state of fear, and I know from experience that it has the awful side effect of exhausting your mind until it physically pains you. I've been there thousands of times and will probably get there a million more. For once, it doesn't bother me. It's helping Julián right now. It's allowing me to support someone else, which is one of the sweetest feelings.

"Do you like scones?" Julián asks eventually, and I smile as I watch him nuzzle his nose even more into my neck. He inhales deeply.

"That's really random," I reply, my eyes fluttering shut as he nibbles on my skin.

"I was thinking of making some for you when we get back," he says while a wave of pleasure seeps through me from his gentle assault.

"But only if you make some with chocolate chips. I hate blueberries," I inform him, and his lips disappear from my skin as he leans back with shock all over his features.

"You hate blueberries?" I nod, the smile on my face never leaving. His reaction is way too cute for me to stop. "But they're so good for you! And delicious." His eyes focus on mine before switching between them and my lips. He's trying to figure out if I'm joking.

"Is this going to be what makes or breaks our relationship?" I ask, and the corners of his mouth curl into the smile I know only I receive.

"No." He finds my question so amusing, he even shakes his head and chuckles.

"What if I told you I strongly dislike kale too?" His shoulders shake from a soundless laugh. "What? It's supposed to be good for you too, and I hate it. I'd rather eat a blueberry," I say, and a deep laugh roars from his chest and into the empty hallway of the hospital.

"Okay, I will make you blueberry-kale scones then," he replies, and I'm about to join his laughter when a nurse steps in front of us.

"Mr. Alvarez?" he asks, and I jump to my feet, feeling Julián's hands grab my hips to keep me in front of him with his chest pressed against my back.

"How is he?" Julián's voice is barely a whisper. The nurse gives him a reassuring smile.

"He had a heart attack, but he should make a full recovery. He's awake if you'd like to see him now," the nurse says before informing us of the room number. Julián laces his fingers through mine, sucking in a sharp breath. I pull him into a hug we both desperately need.

"He's going to be okay," I repeat, feeling his arms tighten around me.

"Thank you for being here with me," he says and plants a kiss to my lips.

"Always."

Chapter 37
Julián

It's strange. I've never been in a hospital because of my father before and seeing him like this, vulnerable and so unlike his usual invincible self, breaks me a little. It sends a chill down my spine, and I find myself clinging to Scar because she's the only one who can ground me right now. Not only does she smell like calming lavender, there is something fulfilling about having the woman I love by my side through this. Because I love her. I'm in love with my rainbow, and there is no more turning back.

She comforts me as I try to process what has happened tonight, what my eyes are focusing on right now.

Dad had a heart attack.

I swallow hard.

Scar squeezes my hand.

I relax instantly.

My feet bring me to where Dad is watching me from, the machine connected to him beeping in a steady rhythm. Scar's hand slips out of mine, but I'm too determined to check on my father to mind. At least that's what I tell myself when my body tries to turn back to grab her fingers again.

"*Hola, viejo,*" I say with a smile, something that brightens up his face.

"I'm still not used to your smile, but I guess I have this lovely woman behind you to thank for seeing it," Dad replies as he tilts his head to gaze past me and at Scar. I turn to her, extending my hand to tell her to come closer. She takes it, her smile, the genuine one I love so much, lingering on her lips.

"I'm glad to see you're okay, Mr. Rodrick." She saved his goddamn life but is too polite to call him 'Paulo'. He'd never tell her to address him by his first name either.

"I heard I have you to thank for that," Dad says, and I nod in agreement. Scar's face turns a bright red before she nuzzles her face into my side to hide from the attention.

"How are you feeling?" I ask instead, bringing the focus back to my father.

"Like I just had a heart attack. How are you?" he replies, and I frown at him.

"You scared the hell out of us," I say, but he brushes away my comment with a wave of his hand.

"I'm fine, no need to worry. And you two have to get back to the hotel and get some rest. It's been a long day, and Qualifying is tomorrow. Scarlette still has some mingling to do with all the famous people, and I made a plan for you both, where to go and such," he says, and my eyes go wide. Scar speaks before I have a chance to.

"No, Mr. Rodrick, we're going to be right here until they release you." *God, can I love her any more than I already do?* It seems impossible, but Scar makes everything possible, like falling in love when I've only known her for a little over two months.

"No, you two are going to enjoy yourselves. I'm fine here. I have the best doctors that money can buy." For once, I don't feel the need to roll my eyes at him showing off his money. I'm glad he has enough to get the best care. "You two, goodbye now," Dad says when neither of us attempts to leave.

I give him a single kiss to the top of his head before grabbing Scar's hand once more and leading her out of the hospital.

Scar and I haven't spoken in a while, but the silence between us is comfortable. She drops onto the bed with a small chuckle, and I lean against the wall, crossing my arms in front of my chest as I study her. Her attention drifts to my forearms, which I flex a little just to make her blush. She does.

"What should we do now?" she asks, and I let out a brief sigh.

"I feel disgusting from the hospital and tense. Only a bath can release the ache in my bones at the moment," I say, and Scar smiles at me.

"You like taking baths?" She seems amused, which is why I can't help but smirk at her.

"Do I not look like the type of person to enjoy them?" I challenge to which she blows raspberries.

"No, you look like a shower type of person," she says, and I furrow both of my eyebrows.

"You can't tell me you know if someone is a shower or bath person based on how they look." Mock surprise widens her eyes and drops her jaw.

"Wait, you can't do that?" she teases, and I push off the wall, making my way over to her and tickling her.

"No and neither can you since you didn't think I was a bath person," I defend, and more laughter leaves her.

Then, her body slumps into the bed while a sleepy smile takes over her features. I grin at her and kiss her lips, slipping my tongue inside her mouth to savor her sweet taste for a moment. She's got me addicted. I can't get enough, always seeking more, especially when she moans against my lips.

"Let's go take a bath," I say, and Scar nods. I push off the bed and walk into the bathroom, on my way to turn on the water when I hear her call out my name. Her voice is so soft, barely a whisper.

"Julián," she repeats, this time a bit firmer. Panic settles in my bones.

"Baby? What's wrong?" I ask, stepping back into the room. She's staring off into nothingness, her hands shaking and her breathing hitching until it's shallow and full of pain.

"Too tired. Happens sometimes," she says with maximum effort.

"Okay, hold on, I will get your stuff," I reply and rush over to her bag.

Her body starts shivering, and I curse at myself for letting it get to this point. I should have ensured she got some rest. *I should have thought about this!* Scar doesn't take enough care of herself. I can't believe I didn't make sure this wouldn't happen. God, I'm the worst boyfriend, and we've only been dating for twenty-four hours.

"Don't," she says, and I focus my eyes on the way she scolds me even during her attack.

"Don't what, love?" I ask while her entire body shakes violently once. I almost sprint toward her.

"Blame... yourself. I... see it... your eyes," she says, sinking to the ground and trying to fight off the attack. I drop to my knees. The way she senses my thoughts and feelings is beyond me.

"Can I take off your dress?" I ask to change the subject, and she furrows her brows with a smile. Her breathing is too uneven.

"You still—I'm still—" She cuts off, letting out a groan that sends a shiver down my spine. It's one of frustration and pain. "Sexy to you?" she finishes her joke, but I'm not laughing, even when she starts doing so breathlessly.

"You are, but that's not why I want to undress you," I explain, lifting her off the ground and her dress over her head when she raises her arms. I undress to get out of my disgusting hospital clothes, wearing only my boxers when I slip behind her on the bed. Her lavender oil rests in my right hand, my left one adjusting her position until she's between my legs.

"Julián?" she asks, her body shuddering again.

"I'm here, love. Don't worry. I'm going to make you feel better," I promise, applying some of the oil to her back.

Then, I take my time massaging it in everywhere. It works like a charm too. Her breathing slows soon before she sinks onto her chest and lets me knead the oil into her tensed muscles. I can almost feel the anxiety attack subsiding with every second I'm on top of her, easing her worries away.

Eventually, she lets out a satisfied hum, and I smile to myself as the sound echoes in my ears.

"Are you feeling better?" I ask, and she tilts her head, allowing me to see the tear slipping from the inside corner of her right eye.

"I don't want to be like this anymore," she replies, defeat all over her beautiful face.

"Come here," I say while opening my arms for her.

Scar wipes away her tear before shifting upright. Although she's sitting almost completely naked in front of me, I force my brain not to take this moment to admire how beautiful she is. It's not what she needs. Instead, I bring her close to my chest and wrap my arms around her until all of our limbs are tangled in one another.

"I'm tired, Julián. I can't keep going through this," she says as another tear rolls down her cheek.

"I think you underestimate your strength." I place my lips on the top of her head. "You've been fighting your anxiety almost completely by yourself for years, and it has only made you stronger. Now, you don't have to be alone anymore. I'm here and not going anywhere," I say, but she shakes her head in response.

"But you will. You will leave when you realize how exhausting it is to be around me. You will run, and I will understand because no one should have to feel so helpless and useless, the way my parents felt," Scar explains, and I just want to give her my brain so she can know exactly how highly I think of her. I want to give her my eyes so she can see herself the way I do. I want to give her my heart so she can experience everything I feel for her, so she can know how much it belongs to her.

"Love, you and your mental health are not a burden. Your anxiety is also not about me. It's about your journey with it, and no one else's, okay? I will never run because of it. It isn't heavy or exhausting for me." Scar looks up at me to show me her frown. I kiss her lips, kiss her sadness away.

"In two days, I've had two attacks. That's a lot, and it's not what *you* signed up for," she says, using my own words from earlier against me.

"I want you the way you are. I wouldn't change a single thing, Scar. Do you understand me? Not a single thing. I adore everything about you." *I'm so in love with you, any distance between us makes me physically ill. I want to be by your side at all times to make sure you're safe and comfortable. I want to be your everything.* I don't say any of those extreme thoughts because I have no intention of scaring her with them.

"I'm sorry I'm making such a fuss," she says, and I almost groan.

"You are not. I know people drilled it into your head that you have to feel like a burden, but you're not, Scarlette, please. You are the sunshine piercing through black clouds. You are all the colors of the rainbow in a gray world. You are perfect." And I need to shut the hell up before she gets overwhelmed by my love declaration.

"Why do you even like me, Julián?" she says, and I lean back.

"Please, don't tell me you're really this oblivious, Scar." She buries her face in my chest to hide her pink cheeks. "Scarlette, do you know how fucking terrified I was to open up to anyone after my ex cheated on me? Do you know how hard it was to allow the possibility of being vulnerable with someone else to settle inside of me? It was one of the toughest things I've ever had to do, but you made it so much easier. You aren't just a bright light, love. You are a genuinely good person, and there aren't many of those out there. And then, everything else about you is perfect too. So don't tell me you've given me nothing when I've gained everything by being in your presence." Eventually, all of this has to freak her out. *Hell, it's freaking me out.*

"I really like you, Julián, so much. I don't want to ruin this, not when we've just decided to try this thing between us," she says, and I tilt her chin upward so her eyes meet mine.

"You've ruined nothing, *mami*, not a thing. I'm yours." Just hers and never again anyone else's. I almost shudder at the thought.

I kiss her one more time before holding her close and listening to her fall asleep in my arms. Dreams consume me moments later, but not pleasant ones.

Nightmares of losing both her and Dad trouble me throughout the whole night.

Chapter 38

Scarlette

It's officially the day of Qualifying. I'm beyond excited. Mr. Rodrick is doing well, recovering at the hospital. Julián and I went to see him this morning and stayed until late in the afternoon. He complained about us being there instead of enjoying our time in Monaco, but neither his son nor I were prepared to leave him alone all day. We played a few card games and talked about everything I will have to take care of when we get back to Moonville. Julián scolded his father for making me think about work, but I didn't mind. After everything he's done for me, I owe him a lot.

"You owe him nothing," Julián said to me after we left the hospital, and I frowned at him.

"I got an in to my dream job because of him. I owe him so much," I replied, which only made my... *boyfriend* scowl. Boyfriend. The word feels funny in my head, even now, but strangely right too. I've never had a person to call mine before. I like it a lot.

Julián's been a bit distant from me since this morning, not physically but his mind is stuck on something else. I wish he'd share it with me because it obviously bothers him. He keeps checking his phone too, but as curious as I am, I won't pry. When he's ready to share what he's struggling with, I will listen.

We walk through the paddock, and I take in everything, all of my surroundings. Team members are running around, making their way through the crowds to get to wherever they're going. Julián's hand rests in mine as we stroll past the makeshift buildings that are used as headquarters for all the teams—Velocità Rossa, Grenzenlos, Spark, Hawke, etc.

"Ah, Ms. Roots, Mr. Alvarez, please, come with me," a man in a Grenzenlos team shirt says, grabbing our attention. Julián follows behind him, guiding me along. My heart is pounding in my chest.

When we step through the doors of the Grenzenlos building, I feel my heart jump in my chest. I'm excited and terrified at the same time, especially when I see Leonard Tick watching me approach him with his lips pulled into a thin line, revealing no emotion. Man, he reminds me of Julián when he looks this serious. I would point it out to the man holding my hand, but he seems to be completely in trance. This is new territory for him too.

"Scarlette, thank you for coming to see me," the Brit greets me, and I smile in return. I can't believe Leonard Tick knows me. My favorite Formula One driver in the world helped me get an internship and potentially a job in my dream field one day. My head feels dizzy and full and happy all at once.

"Of course. Thank you for having us," I reply, and he gives me a small nod.

"I won't linger too long on small talk so here it goes. Robert contacted your university this morning to verify your studies are going well, as you can understand," he says, and I nod in agreement. I completely understand. They might be giving me a contract today for an internship this coming summer. They have to verify I'm doing well, which I am. My grades are great, something I work very hard to achieve.

"So, what is the problem?" Julián asks, and I realize he's right. Something's wrong.

"One of your teachers, Professor Holden I believe, said your grades have taken a hit this week, that you aren't ready for such a big internship opportunity." Nausea instantly bubbles in my throat.

"What?" Julián's voice is loud and angry. "Please, tell me you spoke to her other professors too because that's bullshit. Scar's grades are perfect, and the only reason Professor Holden has a problem with her is because he's disgusting and she said no to his advances," he goes on, and I place a hand on his shoulder to calm him. Leonard stares at my boyfriend with a thoughtful frown.

"I will speak to Robert again, but he doesn't seem convinced anymore. I'm sorry, Scarlette, I can't guarantee he will change his mind again," Leonard says before walking away and leaving me to try and gather all of the broken pieces of my heart.

"Wait here," Julián says and presses a quick, soft kiss to my lips. He leaves the room, and I watch him, unsure what to do with myself right now.

I walk outside when oxygen has left my lungs. My one chance to make it into Formula One is slipping out of my hands, hands which feel too covered in soap to get a good grip. My breathing hitches uncomfortably, and I press my hand to my chest as I try to settle myself again. I won't have three anxiety attacks in three days. It's not happening. I won't allow myself to go back to how things were, not when I fought so hard to overcome the daily attacks.

"Hey, are you okay?" someone asks, and I spin around to see a young woman with blonde hair and green-blue eyes staring at me.

"Yes, sorry," I reply with a forced smile, but she doesn't seem to believe me.

"Here, sit down, and I will get you some water. Don't worry. I used to get panic attacks too, if that is what you're experiencing. Stay here," she says and disappears for a moment only to return with an ice-cold bottle of water. I expect her to give it to me, but instead, she places it against the back of my neck, sending a shock to my system. It pushes me away from the cliff, preventing me to fall into another attack.

"Sorry, I read once it's supposed to distract you if you're having a panic attack," she apologizes with a small smile after I sucked in a sharp breath.

"Don't be. It helped," I assure her with a little laugh and shake my head.

"I'm Valentina," she says a moment later, the sun shining in her eyes. I notice specks of brown in them, focusing on them as I search for words.

"Scarlette. It's nice to meet you." We shake hands, her smile never leaving her face. I can feel it right here and now. Valentina is a really good person. I've always had a good sense about people, and, so far, I've never been wrong. I also realize, the more I study her, the more familiar she looks.

"Yes, I'm Adrian Romana's sister," she says with a slight laugh, and I shake my head. "We look a lot alike, I know."

"Actually, you race in Formula Three, right?" I ask her, making her eyes light up.

"Yes! You watch?" I nod in response, deciding not to share the fact that I've only seen a handful of races. She's too excited for me to do that. "That's so cool. What brought you to this race weekend?" she asks, and I refocus on the moment.

"I was invited to come here by my boyfriend's father. I love Formula One. I want to be a race engineer one day," I say.

"You're kidding! Are you in university for that?" she asks, and I nod with a smile. "Have you been introduced to some of the other engineers yet? If not, I could ask my brother to introduce you," she says, but I stop her before she gets up.

"Actually, it's a long story," I reply, and Valentina looks at me with a curious frown. I decide to share what happened with this complete stranger because she's so nice, I feel oddly safe and comforted in her presence.

"I can't believe this. I'm so sorry, Scarlette," she says, squeezing my hand and forcing a smile. "Us women have it so much harder than men in these career fields. Do you think your professor would have done the same to one of your male peers? I don't think so." I nod in agreement. "But you can't give up. Please don't give up. I can help you. I can talk to my brother, and we will figure something out. Maybe Alfa Adrenalina is looking for someone to intern this summer. Okay? I will help you," she says, and there is something about *her* support that settles the shattered pieces of my heart back into place. An idea blooms onto her features. "Actually, I have a great idea. I know exactly who we should go to," she adds and stands up, holding out her hand for me.

"What do you need me to do?" I ask, taking her help and getting up too.

"Be yourself," she replies at the same moment as Julián steps out of the Grenzenlos building. He rushes over to me, scrunching his eyebrows together from confusion when he sees the hope in my eyes.

"Come," I say and grab his hand.

Both of us follow Valentina while my heart races in my chest. Maybe I will have another chance at my dream job. Maybe it isn't over just yet. Maybe I'm completely naïve, but I have faith.

The team principal of Alfa Adrenalina is one of the nicest men I've ever met. I spent hours talking to him, Valentina, and I even meet her drop-dead gorgeous brother Adrian. He gave me one of those smiles I'm sure have caused some people to faint or fall in love with him on the spot, but I simply snuggled against Julián's vibrating chest. Yeah, he wasn't too happy about the way Adrian initially looked at me. He's calmed down now since he's realized I'm only interested in him, and Adrian stopped offering me knee-weakening smirks.

When we're done with the conversation, it is time for Qualifying, and I thank the team principal for speaking with me. Alfonso seemed to like me, which gives me even more hope that I could still have a job opportunity here at Formula One after I'm done with my studies, or at least an internship for the summer.

Leonard takes pole, and Julián and I make our way back to the hotel room late at night. After the long day we've had, I'm ready to be all alone with him in that big comfy bed, naked and on top of each other.

"Scar? There is something we have to talk about," he says as soon as we step through the door. I spin around to face him, my hands flying up to his neck before I bring his lips to mine.

"Okay," I reply as I make my way across his cheek and jaw, planting my mouth on his neck. "*Dime*," I say, sucking on his soft spot and making a groan leave him.

"After," he breathes, and I smile to myself at the sight of him losing his composure because I'm pleasuring him. The ache between my legs becomes unbearable at the thought. "Can I take off that ridiculous top? I need to have you naked," he says, almost growls because he's losing control.

"I'm yours. Take all of me," I reply, and he rips the fabric off my body. I gasp in response.

"*Lo siento, mami*," he says before moaning as his hard cock pushes against my stomach. I take what I assume is an apology, smile to myself, and then let myself sink completely into the pleasure of his touch.

Chapter 39
Julián

"Julián," she moans into my mouth, and I take advantage of her parted lips to slide my tongue into it.

I know we shouldn't do this. There is something we need to discuss, something that could potentially throw everything we have right now on its head, but I can't stop. I can't worry about anything apart from the desperate need to be inside of her, to pleasure her, to lick my way down her body until she sees stars.

I guide her backward and turn us around before dropping onto the mattress and pulling her on top of me. A groan slips past my lips when she instinctively rubs herself against my cock, all the blood in my body rushing to harden it unbearably. My fingers dig into her soft hips as she explores my mouth at her own pace.

"You're so perfect," I blurt out between kisses, her fingers in my hair as she rocks herself back and forth. Dry humping shouldn't push me so close to the edge.

"I'm nervous," she admits, and I feel the orgasm drifting further away again as my mind fixates on her feelings.

"It's okay, baby, nothing has to happen. We can just make out a little longer," I assure her with a smile I mean with every piece of my soul. Scar slips her hands onto my cheeks and tilts my head back ever so slightly.

"I want you, Julián, so much. I'm just scared I will be too nervous and won't be able to relax," she explains, and I give her an understanding nod. Hell, I'm nervous about that too. The desire to make this experience good for her is stronger than anything I've ever felt. And so is the fear of fucking it all up.

"Where is your vibrator?" I ask, surprising her.

"In my suitcase," she replies, and I stand up, gently guiding her onto the bed. My mouth moves to hers for a brief moment before my feet bring me to her luggage.

There are two reasons why I want to use her vibrator. For one, she's comfortable with it and used to the pleasure. It will relax her, which leads me to my second reason. I want to help her get out of her head. Sex can be overwhelming the first time, I still remember how nervous I was. It will most likely be uncomfortable for her at first, which is why I want to make sure she's as relaxed as possible.

I find her vibrator, weighing it in my hands as I make my way back over to her. It's not very big, but I smile at the purple color of it. When I look up at Scar, she's completely undressed for me, showing off her beautiful body. My knees weaken at the sight of her breasts, so big they knock the breath from my chest as I let my gaze roam over her. Her legs are slightly spread, giving me a small glance of her pussy, already dripping wet for me. I swallow hard. God, she really is perfect in every single way imaginable.

"Julián?" she asks, and I do my best to meet her gaze. It gives my cock a moment to breathe too.

"Yes, *arcoíris*?" I reply and lift my shirt off my body. Then I slide my pants down, watching her gaze stick to the bulge in my boxers like glue. "I want to try something. Okay?" I ask, and she gives me an eager nod. Scar might be a little inexperienced, but she's not ashamed of sex in any way. She's not shy either, merely nervous about her first time, which is completely understandable.

"Where do you want me?" she asks, getting on her knees to present her body to me in a way that I can't handle. All of her curves, her wide hips and thick thighs and big breasts, everything is right in front of me, and it takes all of my willpower not to rush this. She needs me to go slow right now, which is why I ignore my throbbing cock.

"Between my legs, love." I move behind her on the bed and suck in a sharp breath when her backside grinds against my cock. "Fuck me," I groan as pleasure courses through me.

"Sorry," she says, and I let out a laugh I don't mean.

"You didn't hurt me, *mami*. Quite the opposite actually," I assure her and adjust her in front of me to create a distance between our bodies. This is about her pleasure. Her pleasure, which in return will give me a great amount of it too. There is nothing I love more than watching her fall apart from an orgasm I brought her. I realized it the first time I made her come.

"Oh," she says and giggles in front of me. All strength leaves me for a fraction of a second, but I refocus quickly.

"Lean back," I instruct, pressing her back against my chest. Her head moves onto my shoulder, which is when I realize how tightly I've been gripping her vibrator. God, I'm so far gone for this woman, I have no control over my body anymore.

"Touch me," she says after a moment, and I obey.

I bring my left hand up to her tit, kneading it in my head. It spills from my palm and fingers, making me almost come in my boxers. *Good God.*

"Julián," she moans when I squeeze her nipple, setting everything inside and out of me on fire.

My thumb presses the ON button of the vibrator, the humming sound filling the empty room instantly. I run it over her other nipple, tracing it as she moans so loudly, I feel the sound deep in my bones. It's close to making me vibrate.

"Oh God," she whimpers as I guide the toy between her legs, sliding it over the crease between her pussy and thigh. "Please," she begs, and I press it to her clit, making her back arch. Scar presses her tit even more into my hand, and I nibble on her shoulder to control my own aching erection.

"You're doing so good for me, baby," I say, sliding the vibrator down her heat and dipping it inside of her for a slight moment. It slips in with ease. "So wet and ready, Scar, just for me." She moans at my words, and I keep gliding the vibrator over her clit and then back inside of her. My mouth attaches to her shoulder, and I suck until she cries out with lust. "So ready for my cock, *mami*." She falls apart. Her body shakes and quivers as the orgasm pulses through her system.

"Fuck," she moans, and I chuckle to myself.

"What a dirty mouth you have, baby. I love knowing it's because of me," I say as she recovers from her high and joins me back in the now. Her breathing is so wonderfully fast and uneven, her chest pushing against my touch, I have to bite down on my bottom lip to keep from moaning. "I want to be inside you so fucking badly," I admit, using my fingers to trail over the folds of her soaked pussy. God, no one should be so soft and wet, so ready for me.

"I want you inside of me," she replies and digs her nails into my thighs. She wants me. She fucking needs me.

I flip us over until I'm on top of her, my mouth firmly placed on hers. A moan leaves me when the taste of Scar ignites my tastebuds. I've never been this hard in my goddamn life. Every inch of my body longs to be as connected to her as possible, but no matter how ready she seems for me, I have to take this slow. I don't want to hurt her, fuck, that's the last thing I'll ever want. Scarlette is relaxed under me, I can feel it in the way our mouths dance in perfect harmony. I can feel it by the way she lifts her legs and wraps them around my hips to guide my cock against her. I can feel it in the way she moans for me.

"I'm getting impatient," she complains, and I barely hold myself back from telling her just how in love I am with her. Oh God. She's too dangerous. "Get a condom," she instructs, grinding herself against me once more.

"We need to take this slowly," I manage to reply before she scrapes her teeth against my bottom lip.

"No more waiting. I'm ready. You got me ready."

I push off her in an instant and dig around in my own suitcase for a condom. The foil feels heavier in my hand than ever before, nerves now flooding my own mind and chest. There is no need to be nervous. I've had sex many times. I will be everything for Scar, no matter what it takes. If she needs me to last hours, hell, I'd fight hours to keep going at once. I don't care. Anything for her. Always.

My boxers cling to my cock for a second while I prepare myself for how tight she'll probably be. It's her first time after all. I've made her comfortable and ready, but she will hug my cock with a grip I've never experienced before, and it takes me a second to let that information sink in. God, I've never thought this much before having sex. I need to get out of my head, otherwise, this won't be pleasant for either of us. I'm anxious, yes, but when I see Scar grinning at me as she waits, I smile back. She makes me so happy.

"*Tú me tienes loco, mami*," I say, my favorite phrase to use with her, and she blushes with a smile because she knows what it means. I told her after she asked me a few days ago, and I've been waiting to say it again.

"Come here," she says and pats her chest instead of the bed to signal where I'm supposed to go. Yup. That's it. I'm going to be in love with her forever. I already knew it before, but now, I know it even more so.

"I will go anywhere for you," I blurt out, mentally slapping myself until I see her eyes flare with affection for me. I almost skip over to her.

"Anywhere, huh?" she teases, kneading her breasts to bring back the sexual tension. God, she's playing with me. She's playing a game I will never win, but I don't have to. I don't want to. I win just by getting anything from her.

"Yes, *mami*, anywhere." I slide the condom down my length, sucking in a sharp breath because I'm so worked up, I've become overly sensitive. Great. *No, don't overthink it!*

My lips move back onto hers, sending me straight back to heaven. Her body shakes underneath me as the tip of my cock lines up with her entrance, and I stop my movements, gliding over her folds for a moment.

"Ready, *mami*?" I ask, and she nods before giving me verbal consent once more.

Pleasure consumes me in anticipation, and then it knocks the air from my lungs when I'm halfway inside of her, her tight walls grabbing hold of me. I stop moving immediately when I feel resistance and her squirm a bit under me.

"Are you in pain?" I ask breathlessly, but Scar shakes her head, her bottom lip between her teeth.

"No, but I'm tense. I know I am. I'm in my head, sorry," she apologizes as she buries her face behind her hands.

"Don't be. It's okay. Take your time," I say, smiling through the exhaustion of keeping this position for her.

I kiss the backs of both her hands, trailing my mouth down her arms and cleavage until I reach her left nipple, sucking it into my mouth. Her body relaxes under my touch, causing me to sink completely inside of her. A gasp leaves Scar while I moan so loudly, it surprises both of us.

My body stills again while I wait for her to adjust to me. Every cell inside of me begs me to move, to thrust into her again and let her squeeze me as much as she's doing right now, but I feel Scar breathing heavily, and I'm not quite sure if she's in pain or not. The thought sends a horrible fear down my spine.

"Are you okay?" she asks me at the same time I do her, and we let out small laughs. "I'm okay. It doesn't hurt, it's just stretching. You're stretching me to fit your length," she says with a smile, and I can't help the thought crossing my mind. I'm the first man who gets to be inside of her. Fuck. It shouldn't make me as happy as it does. "You can move, Julián," she encourages me when I don't.

"I don't want to hurt you," I reply even more breathlessly than before. This position, while it gives her time to adjust, is taking everything out of me not to come, especially when she squeezes her walls around me. "Oh God, please don't do that," I beg, and Scar gives me a confused look.

"Do what? What did I do?" she asks, trailing her fingers over my cheek and the birthmark sitting there. I focus on her scar, then her eyes.

"You're squeezing my cock with your pussy, baby, and I won't last if you do that," I explain, and she shifts under me with a small smile.

"Sorry." Scar's hands move to my ass before she squeezes both cheeks and drags me completely on top of her, my chest firmly pressing against hers. "Move, Julián, please," she says with a firm tone, her teeth scraping over my earlobe. "Make me come," she whispers, and I lose all of my restraints.

I slide back out before thrusting inside again, slowly but strongly enough to make her moan. She's loosening up more and more with each stroke, which makes it easier for me to push back the orgasm I feel building in my cock. It wants to take over, relieve me of the uncomfortable tension that has now settled everywhere, but I won't let it. I want to make Scar come, and I don't give a single shit how long it will take.

"Oh God, yes," she screams when I angle her body a bit more up and to the side. Her G-spot... I smile to myself as I thrust against it over and over, making her scream into the quiet room. A wonderful slapping noise joins her voice, and I keep going,

246

keep hitting where I know she needs me the most. "Julián, yes, yes, yes," she moans, tugging on my hair as I suck on her perfectly hard nipple again.

Her body, completely under my control, is perfection. More. I want more. To hear everything she has to offer. To keep smelling the lavender scent coming off her. To feel her soft and tight walls around me. To taste her candy skin. To see her writhing in pleasure under me. Her blue eyes are closed and her black hair is all over the place, which is by far one of the most beautiful sights I've ever seen. Her tits bounce with every single pump, and her fingers curl around my hair, tugging to show me how good I make her feel.

"So close," I mumble without meaning to, my finger dropping to her clit.

"Come, Julián, I want you to," she says as the strongest wave of pleasure I've ever felt sweeps over me. Good God, this woman makes me the weakest man in the world.

"No," I groan, angling her even more to the side until I feel myself go so deep, there is no further to go. Scarlette screams, louder than I've ever heard before, so I do it again. And again.

"Shit," she moans as I squeeze her clit between my fingers.

Then I feel it. I feel her orgasm blindside her. I feel the way it works itself through her body and settles deep within her. Her back arches off the bed as I keep thrusting inside, letting her ride out the pleasure. Her walls clench around me in response, allowing me to fall apart too. And, fuck, I've never experienced anything like this pleasure. It's almost as if my body finds relief after years of being tensed up and swollen. I spill into the condom, my dick pulsing as my mind drifts into a high I never want to come down from.

"Julián?" Scar asks after we've been lying in bed for a while, me still inside of her and on top.

"Yes, *mami*?" I reply, my ear pressed against her chest so I can listen to the sound of her heartbeat.

"I need to check if there is blood. I don't want to ruin the hotel's sheets," she says, and I slide out of her to check if she is bleeding. A sigh of relief slips past my lips when I see she isn't. I didn't make her bleed, even if it would have been normal, I don't want to be the reason for that.

"Let's get cleaned up," I say and hold my hand for her.

We spend the next hour bathing, brushing our teeth, and smiling at each other like the two happiest people on the planet. It's easy to look that way when I feel it too. Scar makes me happier than I've ever been before, probably than I ever will be in a relationship. I trust her with all of me, which is something I've never done before. Something I know is stupid beyond reason.

"I love this," Scar says when we're in bed, naked, cuddling each other.

"So do I." *I love you. God, I love you. Why can't I tell you? Will you run? Is that why I won't say it out loud? Because I'm scared you don't feel the same and will leave me?*

"Can we stay like this forever, please?" she asks, and I kiss her stomach.

"Yes."

We both know it's impossible, but neither of us points it out. We simply stay this way, my arms around her and holding her close, sleeping through the whole night to wake up in the same position. In each other's embrace, protected from the rest of the world.

Chapter 40

Scarlette

The day of the race has finally arrived, and I'm vibrating out of my socks from excitement. Julián keeps chuckling because I'm all over the place, simultaneously thrilled about the thousands of people celebrating this sport and sweating because I hate big crowds. He makes sure to keep me close, shielding me from everyone else while we find our spots on one of the balcony areas. Mr. Rodrick is recovering well at the hospital and assured us they will discharge him tomorrow in time for our flight back home.

Every single one of the twenty drivers are lined up at the grid when I stare down at it, their teams working on their cars to prepare them for the race. I won't be there. That's not where I see myself. I will be sitting with the other race engineers in the box, looking at statistics on a screen and getting ready for the race there. Preparing the car *there*. Well, at least that's where I saw myself. Now, everything is so uncertain. I don't know if Alfonso will give me the same opportunity I could have had at Grenzenlos. All because of Professor Holden... what the hell is his problem anyway? What have I done to him? I know for a fact my grades are close to perfect. If he gave me bad grades because I wasn't in class this week, then he has another thing coming. He may have just cost me my only shot at making it into my dream career.

I push the thought aside to enjoy the way Julián drags me against his chest and holds me close. We're both looking out of the window, letting this moment linger for as long as the world allows it. People around us are speaking with loud voices, but everything quiets when he places his lips on my cheek. So much is happening on the grid, but I don't want to focus on anything other than the way Julián's fingers are placed on my stomach. He's happy. I know he is. I can feel it in my chest and bloodstream. I've made him so too, which is the best part of it all.

"Storm," I say, tasting the word on my tongue.

It feels like an old friend I've drifted apart from, replaced by something I have a much stronger connection to. But Storm is still one of his names, one of the things I love about him, and it makes me smile to experience it on my vocal cords.

"Yes, love?" he asks and kisses my temple.

"Julián," I say next, earning myself a small chuckle from him.

"*Mami*," he replies and sends a thrill straight down my spine. "What other name do you have for me?" Julián asks with a soft tone, which causes a grin to curl the corners of my mouth.

"Baby." He tenses in response, tightening his grip on me.

"Only yours," he says, and I let myself believe for the smallest moment that the rest of the world could vanish for good.

I let myself believe that my anxiety could ever disappear completely. I let myself believe that there is nothing that could ever tear us apart. It's all quite silly in reality, but I can't help it. It seems like we're invincible, no matter what's awaiting us next. Yes, I don't have a job or a future in Formula One anymore, I might not ever get the chance again. Yes, I still have anxiety attacks I don't know how to control. Yes, we're human and will probably make mistakes. But none of it poses a threat to us right now.

None, except...

"In four months' time, I will join the National Championship with Hawke," Julián blurts out, and I feel my heart sink and jump at the same time. It's a strange sensation I hope to never experience again. I spin around in his arms, forcing the side of me that's happy for him to take over.

"Congratulations! How long have you known?" I ask because this explains his reaction to whatever message he received yesterday morning, why he was so distant in his mind. His face reveals guilt.

"I've known for a while, but I got a reminder yesterday. I'm sorry I didn't tell you sooner. Before we were dating, I didn't think we'd be together by then. I'd hoped, but there was no way I could have known you felt anything but revulsion toward me," he says, and I start to speak, but he cuts me off with a kiss. "I'm sorry, I'm not done explaining myself. Hold on, please." He kisses me again, and I melt. "After we agreed to start dating, to give us a real try, it completely slipped my mind. It was so focused on you, on us, I suppressed anything that could be a threat," he explains, and a wave of panic turns my stomach upside down.

"I understand. I'm not mad, I promise," I assure him because it's true. I'm not upset about him forgetting to share this with me. I'm upset because of what this will mean for us.

"You should be mad! Hell, love, I kept something important from you, even if it was unintentionally. You should be furious. I know you're a good person, but still," he says and shakes my shoulders a bit, as if to shake some sense into me.

"Baby, no." He wraps his arms around me, and, suddenly, while we're sharing this intimate moment, I become hyperaware of every other person in here.

"I should have told you yesterday morning. I shouldn't have had sex with you without talking about this first. You had a right to know before giving yourself to me in that way. I'm so sorry," he says, and I shake my head, pulling him away and toward a bathroom. I lock the door behind us, spinning around to place my lips on his after.

"Feel this?" I ask and slide my tongue into his mouth to massage his. "I want you, Julián. I wanted you yesterday, I want you today, I want you always. What you just told me doesn't change anything. It made everything more difficult, but we will figure it out. I'm not going anywhere, okay?" Why does he think I'd leave him? Why would he— Because his biological father abandoned him. Because his ex cheated on him. Dang. How could I not think about that? "I'm staying," I assure him, and he picks me up, his hands moving to the backs of my knees to wrap my legs around him.

"You deserve so much better than this, a boyfriend who won't be gone most of the year," he says, kissing me more fiercely after. I sink into him, allowing myself to get lost for a moment.

"I want no one else." I don't think the words before they spill from my lips.

"You should," he says, and I groan in response.

"I don't." He calls me stubborn when he is the most stubborn out of both of us. "I want you," I say as he claims my lips in such a possessive way, it sucks the breath from my lungs.

"You shouldn't," he repeats, and I break the kiss, staring down at him from the high position he has me in. I'm heavy. I'm not ashamed to be, but he shouldn't be strong enough to hold me like this. Then again, Julián is pure muscle.

"You're mine," I say, squeezing his sides with my legs. "All mine. Now, put me down so we can go watch the start of the race," I instruct, and he drops me back onto my feet, heavy breaths coming from his mouth.

I know we're both hot now, after whatever we just shared, but it will have to wait. I don't know when I'm going to have the chance to watch the start of an F1 race again, if ever.

"Please, love, we have to talk about what it will mean for us if I'm not in Moonville for most of the year while you're in school and traveling the world for an internship," he says, but there is so much about that statement that unsettles me.

"I don't even have an internship anymore, and we will figure this out, I know we can," I promise, and he relaxes a bit against me.

"But if you had the internship—" I cut him off.

"But I don't, so drop it, Julián." Crap! I'm misdirecting my anger. "I'm sorry, I know you're worried, and you have every to be. It won't be easy, and I know I shouldn't dismiss it, but I'm scared, okay? I'm so scared because I've never felt this way about anyone and this whole thing with my job opportunity is kicking my butt because I have no idea how the heck I'm going to get into this sport without it, and everything just flipped upside down, and then your father having a heart attack doesn't make things any easier for you, and—" His lips wrap around mine before I can fall deeper down the rabbit hole.

"Breathe, love, please," he says, and I nod because if I keep going, an anxiety attack will wash over me.

"Can we just take things as they come? I don't want to lose you," I admit, and he wraps his arms around my center, nuzzling his face into my neck.

"Okay. We will take them as they come." I kiss him once more before we walk out of the bathroom just in time for the start of the race.

Chapter 41
Julián

S car was glued to the screens whenever the cars were out of sight. Then, as they raced by, she watched with absolute fascination. She'd seen races on TV, but it doesn't compare to the thrill of witnessing this sport live. Leonard Tick won by far, and we went back to our hotel room where both of us collapsed from exhaustion. Scar and I socialized a lot, trying to make connections with people, but we were, unfortunately, quite unsuccessful.

I know it bothers her. Even now, on our way back to her place, I can feel how upset she is about everything that happened this weekend regarding her career, her future in Formula One. Grenzenlos hasn't reached out to her again, and neither has Alfa Adrenalina. It's not looking great for her at the moment, and I've been racking my brain about ways to help her. Dad might have an idea. I'll have to speak to him once he's fully recovered and Mamá lets him out of her sight. Then again, I don't know if she ever will again. This weekend was horrible for her.

"Julián, I know we just spent almost a whole week together, but would you like to stay with me tonight?" she asks when we're about two minutes from her place. Surprise raises my eyebrows.

"What about Violet? She probably wants to be alone with you," I reply, wishing I wasn't so considerate. There is nothing I want more than to spend more time with Scar, all my time if possible.

"She's with Elias tonight," Scar explains, and, as much as I try to hide it, a bright smile slips across my face.

"I'd love to, *mami*," I say and squeeze her thigh. She shifts in her seat, pressing her legs together. *Puñeta*. All the blood in my body rushes to my cock when her eyes flutter shut and her back swiftly arches off the seat ever so slightly.

"We didn't get to have sex yesterday," she says, knocking all the air from my chest. *My horny girl.* I almost chuckle at how sweet she is.

"No, we didn't. We have a lot to catch up on," I reply and turn my head to wink at her.

We arrive at her place, the sadness I saw in her eyes now replaced with lust. I lead her to the door, dragging her suitcase and my backpack behind me. Scar slides her key into the lock but the door opens without her twisting it. Violet stands in front of my girlfriend, tears streaming down her face. Mascara is all over her cheeks, and I sense panic flooding my chest. Violet is Scar's best friend and my brother's girlfriend, so her well-being is important to me.

"Elias and I had a huge fight," Violet cries and throws herself into Scar's arms. Now I'm even more concerned.

My girl shoots me a confused look as she holds her best friend close, so I check my phone. One missed call from Elias. When I bring my eyes back to Scar, she mouths the word 'go', and I do as I'm told after a lot of hesitation. It feels wrong to leave without kissing her, but Violet needs her friend right now, and Elias needs me.

I get behind the wheel and rush home. One missed call is all it takes for me to know things are bad. Elias always does that, calls once but when I can't answer, he doesn't try to get a hold of me and 'bother me' as he puts it. If nothing's wrong, he will spam message me until I respond. No messages and one phone call mean shit has hit the fan. I curse under my breath as my foot slams down on the gas.

"Elias!" I call out once I'm inside our little place. He's on the ground, a bottle of beer in his hand and tears streaking down his face. My heart shatters at the sight. "*¿Qué pasó, Elias? Dime, por favor,*" I say as my knees hit the ground in front of him. He needs to tell me what happened. Seeing him in pain is one of the worst things for me. I have to figure out a way to make everything better again.

"I think Violet was using me to get over someone called Anna," he explains, and I lean backward until I'm on my ass, watching him closely.

"Why would you say that?" I ask, trying to figure out if this is jealousy or if Violet really was using him as a rebound.

The only reason why I'm questioning it is because he said 'I think' at the beginning of his explanation. That's not a good sign. Elias likes to overthink some things, especially when it comes to people he cares about. It was one of his triggers when he was struggling badly with his anxiety. Now, he rarely ever has attacks, something I wish I could tell Scar without making her think I have any expectations for her to stop having them. It's different for everyone.

Focus, my brain reminds me, and I shake my head to do just that.

"Anna showed up here two days ago, confessing her feelings to Vi. You can imagine how much that bothered me," he says, and I nod. If someone from Scar's past appeared out of nowhere and confessed their feelings to her, I'd lose it.

"What did Violet say?" I ask, trying to get more information. Sometimes I have to pull it out of his nose, offer him questions to organize his thoughts.

"She avoided me for a day. Then showed up here this morning, upset," he says. I sigh.

"Why was she upset?"

"Because she was in love with Anna for such a long time, and her feelings were never reciprocated. She was furious that now, after she moved away, Anna suddenly showed interest in her. I asked her why it bothered her so much since we only recently told each other 'I love you' for the first time. Violet said it wasn't about her feelings now, but because she's angry Anna thinks she can just come in now and expect her to drop everything and love her back. But I asked her again why it bothered her so much since we're happy. Then we started fighting, and she left," he explains in a rant I barely keep up with.

"Wouldn't you be angry? Let's say you weren't dating Violet. If you were in love with her, but she didn't reciprocate your feelings, and after you move away from her and start a new life, she comes back into it and tries to throw it all on its head? Wouldn't you be furious? And then, on top of that, the person she's really in love with doesn't sympathize but makes her feel bad about her feelings. I can understand why she's upset," I say, and Elias smacks his forehead with the palm of his hand, repeatedly. I stop him mid-slap and lower his hand.

"I'm such an idiot. How could I have been so stupid? You're so right! She was looking for comfort, and I made the situation worse. Of course she'd be upset about Anna, even when she's in love with me. *Por el amor de Dios, soy muy estúpido,*" he says, and I give him a compassionate smile.

"Fix it. We all mess up, it's okay, but you have to talk to her. Neither of you is doing well with this fight, and the longer you wait, the more she will think you're angry with her for having understandable feelings and reactions to what happened with Anna." Elias nods, getting up from the floor and grabbing his keys. I snatch them out of his hand and shake my head. "You're not driving intoxicated and emotionally overwhelmed," I say and walk toward the door. "Come on."

It takes us a long ten minutes to get back to Scar's place, and I notice Elias' legs bouncing up and down while he taps his phone against his right, upper thigh. It's distracting as hell, but I know it's his way of coping with the nerves of seeing Violet after what happened between them.

I told him to text Scar we're coming, and, as soon as we make our way up the driveway, I see both women waiting for us. Violet is still crying and Scar is holding onto her best friend's hand, comforting her. Elias lets out a shaky breath before we join the women we're in love with near the front porch of their small house.

"Vi," Elias says, and she shakes her head, her red hair bouncing from side to side.

"Don't 'Vi' me. You messed up so badly, you don't deserve to call me that right now," she yells, and I shift my gaze to Scar. She rubs her best friend's back.

"Vi, it's okay. Let him—" Violet cuts her off before she manages to finish that sentence.

"Don't tell me what to do! You have no idea how relationships work. The closest thing you have to one is that fake dating arrangement with Storm, and that hardly counts. So don't tell me what to do when you're too much of a nervous mess to ever experience life."

Too far. Violet has gone too far, and I'm angry now. Furious, actually. How dare she attack Scar, especially her anxiety, in this way? In any way? I want to punch a wall. Instead, I watch my girlfriend take three steps away from her best friend as tears fill her eyes. I move over to her, shielding her from Violet with my body, even if words are the redhead's choice of weapon.

"I know you're upset, Violet, but watch how you speak to Scarlette. I will not tolerate you lashing out at her, under no circumstances," I say, and Violet shoots daggers at me.

"Don't you think you're taking this fake dating thing a bit too far? We know it's not real. She's too damaged, and you're too fucking creepy with that frown always on your face." She's drunk. I realize it right then and there when she stumbles over the words. Oh God. She's drunk and attacking Scar. And I am incapable of holding back my next words.

"Violet," Elias warns now because she's insulted me as well, but I'm already speaking again.

"It's one thing to insult me, go for it if it makes you happy, but keep the name of the woman I love out of your mouth," I say to her.

That's when everything changes. All of the tension of the moment dissolves as Violet stumbles backward from my words, clearly surprised because she wasn't expecting them. Elias' eyes have gone wide because I've never fallen in love, let alone said so out loud. My shoulders tense in response, and I'm scared to turn around and check what Scar's face is doing. I'm so fucking screwed. This is not at all how I thought I'd tell her about my feelings for the first time.

"Let's go talk inside and get you a glass of water, Vi, please," Elias begs, and Violet is still so surprised about my words, my confession, she goes willingly with my best friend.

"Julián, look at me," Scar says, but I shake my head.

"I can't feel my body, so you might have to step in front of me," I reply, earning myself a soft laugh from her. It travels straight through my back, settling in my chest.

"Okay," she says and does as she's told. I watch the faint hint of a smile disappear as she stares into my eyes.

"I love you," I blurt out before she can say anything else. "I'm sorry it came out this way, but I do, I love you. I've never fallen in love, never wanted to either if I'm being honest, not until you. After I set my eyes on you, I fell faster than I could have ever imagined." *Cállate, Julián, you're going to freak her out.*

"Julián," she says, but I can't stop talking for some reason.

"You don't have to say it back. I mean, we just agreed to date and it would be too much of me to expect you to love me back, so, no pressure. I promise, I won't be upset if you don't say it back," I ramble, and Scar grabs my face, making me focus on her.

"Do you honestly think, after everything you've done for me, after everything you've made me feel and said to me, after putting me first from the moment we agreed to be anything, fake or not, that I wouldn't fall in love with you? Do you think I could have ever resisted falling right next to you when being by your side has become one of my favorite things? *Te amo,* Julián," she says, and I claim her mouth as soon as the words have left her, trying to taste them on my tongue.

I want to take this moment, shove it in a sparkling box, and place it in my pocket to carry it with me everywhere. I want it to last an eternity because I've never felt this full, this complete, in my entire life. I want to always remember how sweet she tastes right after the best words she could have ever said to me left her mouth.

I want everything with Scar, forever.

Chapter 42
Scarlette

Violet's words tore at my heart, but as Julián's lips press against mine, savoring me in every way he can, I feel the ripped piece move slowly back into place. I know my best friend. When she has that one drink over her limit, she becomes mean. It's why I'm not going to take what she said to heart, especially not when Julián just told me he loves me. My chest explodes into a million flowers.

"*Mi arcoíris*," he says, and I smile against his mouth.

"My Storm," I reply, snaking my fingers into his hair and tugging to get him closer to me. He groans in response, his hands falling to my butt and squeezing it with need.

"Tell me to stop and not take you right here, in my car." I moan in response to his words. "Oh God, *mami*, don't do that," he says while his grip on my ass tightens and brings me further against his chest. Another moan leaves me. "Scar," he growls, his tongue slipping into my mouth and massaging mine.

Julián guides us backward until my behind is pressed against his car. His right hand moves to the back of my knee, lifting it and placing it against his hip. I instantly feel his hard cock pushing against my clit. Oh, yes. I've never been more thankful for sweatpants in my entire life.

"Please, Julián, please," I beg when his erection merely pushes against my clit without moving. The ache between my legs is making my ears ring, especially when he nibbles on my neck and digs his fingers into my hips.

"We shouldn't be out here," he says, but I grab his ass and bring him closer to me. He groans against my throat when I ultimately rub him over my clit.

"Please," I say again, and Julián curses before thrusting against me.

"I like it when you beg for me, baby, and I promise, I will give you whatever you want, always. You ask for all the lavender in the world, I will buy it all. You ask for a Formula One team, I will start one for you. You ask for the world at your feet, I will make everyone worship you as their rightful queen."

He thrusts against me again, and I moan loudly as my head falls toward the car door. He places one of his hands behind it so my head doesn't hit the metal. My legs start to shake with every single one of his thrusts. I cling to him, enjoying the way his mouth is working its way down my neck to my collarbone. His breath is so unsteady and his low groans push me closer to the edge of my orgasm. It's not supposed to be this easy, is it? I shouldn't be ready to come from him rubbing his bulge against my clit, right?

"I want you to come right here, *mami*. Let me feel it," he says, rubbing himself over me again and again.

"Shit, your cock feels so good," I moan breathlessly, and he chuckles like he always does when I swear.

"My favorite dirty mouth," he says, digging his fingers into the back of my thigh to press me further against him.

One more firm thrust, and my orgasm ripples through me, blinding me. Little explosions of color flash in front of my eyes when I close them. Julián kisses me deeply, his tongue sliding into my mouth almost as if he wants to taste my orgasm. His chest is firmly pressed against mine as I shake. It feels so good to have him so close, devouring me like he's been starving for years. *I've* been starving for years, which is why I roll my hips to ride out the pleasure for as long as I can.

"Baby, I need more. A few more, a *dozen* more. I need to have you come on my tongue, on my cock, on my fingers, everywhere on me. Let me take you to my place," he begs, not quite letting go of my leg and mouth yet.

"Take me," I reply, not worrying about Vi or Elias anymore. I know I should be, but I'm a little too upset with my best friend to be too concerned.

That's a lie.

I want to go in there and check on her, but when my eyes drift to the kitchen window, I notice Elias' tongue down her throat. *Alright then.* I smile to myself while Julián opens the door for me, barely removing his lips from mine.

"Okay, fuck, get in the car, Scar, because I won't be able to tear myself from you," he says and grabs my face, kissing me again. A chuckle vibrates off me as I lean away but he follows me to delay the break of our skin contact.

"Come on," I say and sit down in the passenger seat. Julián shuts the door for me before rushing over to the driver's seat. He doesn't waste a second before putting the car in Drive and heading to his place.

He rips my sweater over my head as soon as the door closes behind us. His mouth, so hot and needy, is on mine, working its magic until I feel my second heartbeat again. He's demanding, dragging me with him to his room while undressing me with impatience.

"Naked, *mami*, I need you completely naked," he manages to say between kisses. I simply smile while removing my sweatpants. "Panties," he demands next.

"Okay, baby, give me a second," I reply and tug them down while he undresses too.

Once he's completely naked, he lies down on his bed, his cock in his hand and his eyes half-closed from desire. I watch him stroke himself for a moment, running my hands over my hard nipples and then down to my swollen, needy clit.

"No, *mami*, come here, on my face. I want you to ride my face," he says, and shock momentarily fills my chest.

"Ride your— I can't do that," I say with a nervous laugh, which makes him let go of his cock and hold out his hand for me.

"You don't want my mouth on you?" he asks once I've slipped my hands into both of his.

"I do, but I can't—I mean, I will suffocate you," I explain with another nervous laugh. Realization dawns on him, but it makes him smirk.

"Then I will die a happy man." I almost snort, but Julián places his hands on my ass and guides me between his legs. Desire envelops me in flames as he places his lips on my stomach and then nibbles on the skin there. "Please, love, don't deny me a taste of you because of that. I want to have you on my tongue," he says, and I can't help myself. I nod without another moment of hesitation.

Julián lies back completely and I make my way on top of his face, hovering for a moment. He's having none of it. His fingers dig into my hips, something he loves to do, and he brings me all the way down until his lips are wrapped around my clit. He sucks firmly, sending a lightning bolt of pleasure through me. Oh God. Why does that feel so good?

I try to sit up more, give him room to breathe, but it makes a groan leave him.

"All of you, *mami*, I want all of you. Now, sit down, and let me fuck you with my mouth." I shouldn't be so freaking attracted to this bossy side of him, but a moan leaves me anyway.

I lower myself onto his mouth to feel him lick across the length of my pussy. Luckily, he lifts his hands for me to grab and hold onto, otherwise, I would have fallen over from pleasure. He licks and kisses me over and over again. I've never experienced anything like this. What we've done before was heaven, and so is this, but in a completely different way. This pleasure has consumed my very being, sucked its way into every single one of my cells to work as a never-ending supply of euphoria.

"God, you taste so good," Julián says and moans, and I grind myself against his face, chasing my orgasm. It's in my grasp, oh so close.

"Julián," I scream as his tongue disappears inside of me. He licks over my clit a few more times before focusing completely on it.

"So fucking good," he repeats, pressing his tongue against my ache and then playing with it, tracing circles.

I fall apart, hard. An orgasm like I've never experienced storms through my body, knocking the breath from my chest. My toes curl, every part of me shakes, and I grind against him even more when he keeps going, keeps licking to prolong the orgasm. But even after it has passed, he continues his strokes, moaning against me. I'm shaking on top of him, unable to endure any more.

"Julián, please, I can't take the pleasure," I say right as another orgasm blindsides me. I grab his hands tightly to make sure I don't fall over.

He presses one more kiss to my clit before flipping us over so he's on top of me. I can feel his cock against my stomach as his mouth finds mine. A second ago, I couldn't take more, but now, that's all I want. More, more, more. Anything he will give me, I want it all. So I reach for his cock and slide it over my clit. Julián sucks in a sharp breath.

"You're going to make me come really quickly like this," he says with a slight laugh, but I don't care. I roll my hips to grind against his hard cock and feel the waves of pleasure wash through me.

"Where are the condoms?" I ask, not quite stopping my movements, even when he barely manages to hold himself up. His eyes are screwed shut and he's moaning so loudly, I feel it deep inside of me.

"Drawer," he replies and grabs my wrist to stop me. It allows him to take charge of his body again. He grabs one and slides it down his cock before moving back on top of me. "You ready, *mami*?" he asks, but I merely reach for him again and align him with my entrance.

"Fuck me," I demand, and he sinks into me with a hard thrust. It makes me see stars in the best way possible.

He slips out again and then back in, and I feel like my soul escapes me. I can't believe I waited so long to have this. I can't believe life made me wait so long for Julián. Everything about him, not just our incredible sex, is perfect to me.

He places a pillow under me, angling my body in such a way that when he slides inside me again, he hits my G-spot with complete ease. Strength leaves me. My muscles turn to putty as he continues his movements so steadily, it makes my head dizzy. His hands are on my breasts, squeezing my hard and sensitive nipples as he buries himself even deeper within me. A moan leaves him, then another, and another, until I'm lying underneath him with my eyes screwed shut, listening to the sweet noises coming from him.

"Scar, love, you're doing so fucking incredible. You take me so well. Shit, *mami*, how will I ever get enough of you?" he asks before thrusting so hard inside of me, I arch my back off the bed and push further into his hands.

His movements keep going, seconds turning into minutes, but I lose track of time. All I grasp of reality is when my orgasm hits me at the same time as his consumes him. He stays inside of me, pulsing and filling up the condom as he places his mouth back on mine and kisses me over and over.

"I love you, *arcoíris*," he says, and I smile against his mouth.

"I love you, Julián."

Chapter 43
Julián

S car sleeping in my arms is by far one of my favorite things in the universe at this point. The way she almost giggles in her sleep sometimes sends a warmth like no other down my spine and through my chest, almost like hot tea when you desperately seek heat during a freezing winter day. I love her. Yes. But there is something so much stronger about the feelings my heart contains for her. I'll forever be unable to describe it, but I think that's part of why it's so beautiful. It can't be tainted by words.

My phone vibrates on my nightstand, and I lean over to it, trying to turn it off before it wakes Scar. I furrow my eyebrows when I see Mamá is calling and slip out of bed to answer her call. It's the middle of the night. She doesn't call me at this hour.

Fuck.

She never calls me at this hour.

"What's wrong?" I ask in Spanish as soon as I hit answer. A sob leaves her, causing my knees to go weak.

"Your dad—he—he had another heart attack. He's—" She cuts off, and I blink hard trying to wake up. This isn't happening. This can't be happening. He was fine this morning, after the flight. Dad had his pills and everything else he needed to get better. This doesn't make any sense. This can't be real.

"Julián?" Scar asks, and I turn to her, my phone dropping out of my hand.

It feels like I'm going to faint but also strangely like I'm wide awake, more so than I've ever been before. She crawls across the bed and then slides off it to step toward me and place her hands on my chest. Her touch is like a jolt of reality straight into my system.

"My dad is dead," I blurt out. The words feel foul on my tongue. Part of me is too in denial to accept this information. How could I when I found out all of twenty seconds ago?

"Oh my God," she says and takes my hand, tears shooting into her eyes. "We need to go. Your mom needs you, and you have to call Elias. He has to know," Scar adds with tears slipping down her face. I should be crying too. Instead, everything inside of me is strangely numb. I can't feel anything, but what she's saying is bringing at least a bit of clarity into my foggy head. Mamá. I have to get to Mamá and let Elias know what happened. "Would you like me to call Elias?" Her question drags me out of my thoughts again.

"You would do that for me?" I ask, and she bends down to grab her clothes and my phone.

"Anything you need," she replies, and something about that small gesture, something I know she'd give me without hesitation, causes everything to crash down on me.

My heart aches unbearably. I can't breathe without pain surging through my veins because my dad, the man who raised me, took me in, and loved me from the day he met me, is dead. He's gone, vanished just like that. I sink to the floor and wrap my arms around my knees while I try to find a way to take in oxygen without experiencing the sensation of suffocation in my lungs.

It doesn't fade even a little until Scar kneels beside me and takes me in her arms, holding me close to her rapidly beating heart. Fuck. She's probably anxious. This is a lot to take in, and it can't be easier for her.

"Are you anxious, love? Do you want me to get your stuff?" I ask, and she tilts my head to her to show me the confusion in her eyes.

"No, baby, I'm fine." I don't believe her, which she sees. "I promise, I'm not anxious, just trying to figure out what you need," she admits, so I pull her into my lap and finally let my tears drop.

"Just hold me, please," I beg, sobs starting to leave me uncontrollably.

My dad is dead.

Fuck.

I was just beginning to be truly happy.

Chapter 44
Scarlette

Julián has been sitting with an arm wrapped around his mom for the past hour. Her tears have slowed, but she's still crying, and I wish more than anything that I could take her pain. This wasn't how I thought I'd meet Julián's mom, which is why I keep my distance from both of them. I'm a stranger to her and she doesn't need me to just show up in her life during such an inappropriate moment, at least not until my boyfriend decides it's okay.

Elias is sitting beside his best friend, Violet next to him as he leans his head against her shoulder and tries to process losing yet another father figure. Violet told me about the accident that cost him his parents when he was a child, and I can't imagine the grief hitting him as he experiences the same pain again.

My hands shake a little as I bring cups of coffee to them. Isabel, Julián's mom, doesn't even look at me as she takes it from my hands, her grief keeping her mind far from her body. She's staring into the distance with absentminded tears running down her face. Elias is clinging onto Violet's hand like he never wants to let her go again. Meanwhile, every time I get close to Julián, he leans away from me. So, I've been keeping my distance. I will give him everything he needs.

"Julián?" Isabel asks while I stay in the kitchen to clean up a little. Worry settles deep within me so I rush back into the living room to see him storm out of the front door. "Scarlette, do you mind?" she asks me, her accent strong and beautiful. It's the first time I've heard her speak English.

"Of course," I say and follow Julián outside.

He's kneeling on the floor, his breath rapid and uneven. His hands are shaking, and I realize exactly what's happening when he inhales sharply. Panic attack. Julián is having a panic attack. I rush over to him and sink to the ground, keeping my hands off him because I don't know what he needs in a situation like this. His eyes are wide and on high alert, and it breaks my heart to see him so disoriented.

"What's happening to me?" he asks, and I lift my hand to his cheek. He leans into my touch for a moment, then his whole body shakes and he moves away from me again. I drop my hand to give him space.

"You're having a panic attack, baby," I say softly, and he drops on all fours, forcing himself to snap out of this as if it were that simple. "It's okay, Julián, you're going to be okay," I assure him, still not certain if he'd like me to move closer or stay away from him.

"I'm not fine. I can't do this. He can't be dead. I can't deal with this, Scar, I can't— I can't even fucking breathe," he says before swearing in Spanish and wheezing.

"I know, it's alright. Let me help you," I say and reach out to take his arm, but he jerks it away from me and stands up on shaky legs.

"No, fuck, I can't do this. You need to—to leave. I don't want you here. I can't deal with you loo—looking at me like that. Go away," he says, still panicking and mostly disoriented. I can't imagine how overwhelmed he must be right now, which is why I ignore the stinging of his words.

"Let me help you, please. I can show you how to breathe to make this easier," I beg, but Julián has already decided to push me away and there is no stopping him now.

"No, I don't want your help. Leave me alone, Scar. Just because you deal with this shit on an everyday basis doesn't mean you can help me. Now, leave my house. Go. I don't want to be near you," he barks, and I take serval steps back.

"Okay," I mumble, moving toward the door to grab my things and do as he wishes.

I know this is not coming from a place of anger toward me. I know he is overwhelmed and didn't mean to hurt me. I would never hold his words against him while he's grieving. All I wish would be for him to want me to support him, but as long as he doesn't, I will stay away. My heart aches as I walk past him in the driveway again, but he makes no attempt to speak to me, so I leave him be. Almost.

"I love you, Julián. I'm only a call away, okay? Any time, night or day, you can reach me, and I will come to you. I promise," I say, reassuring him. I start on my way home, on foot since it is only a thirty-minute walk, and let the tears fall down my cheeks.

It's eight in the morning by the time I get home. My eyelids are heavy from exhaustion and my hands are shaking from anxiety I really don't need right now. I swear at myself for being so weak when I need to be strong. Julián just lost his father, and I can't even keep myself from falling straight into my anxiety because of what? Exhaustion? Fear of Julián and I breaking up? Sadness because I liked Mr. Rodrick and I can't believe he's dead? All of it combined? I wish I had a clue why my mind tortures me like this, why I can't have a moment without this illness to try and make sense of the rest of my life.

I take a shower to calm my body, but once I step out of it again, a fresh wave of anxiety weakens my knees. My hands find my sink to keep me upright, and I suck in a sharp breath of anger before letting out a scream. My arms slide across the marble, throwing down all my toiletries. I scream again and let myself drop to the ground as I break down.

Weak.

It's only a word. It shouldn't repeat itself over and over again in my head as a way to make me feel like nothing. It makes me feel like a waste of space, like I don't deserve the life that's coursing through my veins.

Weak.

My body and mind are both exhausted. This ongoing battle between them, it's dragging me to the depths of pain and chaos. They're at war, but, either way, I can't win. I can't do anything but fight my way to the surface to keep from drowning.

Weak.

I'm not weak. I won't let my brain convince me of that. I'm not a waste of space. I deserve this life, this body, and the breath in my lungs. I deserve to be happy. I deserve all the good things in the world. My mind might be battling with a mental illness, but it doesn't take away from my worth. I'm only human. Perfection doesn't exist, so I'm allowed to be struggling with finding the ground underneath my feet again. I'm allowed to fall, and I will catch myself as I have many times before.

A mental picture appears in my mind, one I haven't thought of since the beginning of my anxiety. I see myself. A younger me, sitting in the dark corner of my head and sobbing into her hands. I see the girl that almost died because her father was an alcoholic who couldn't care about her more than he could alcohol. My hands reach out to her. She slides hers into mine, so I can help her off the ground and smile at her.

"Let me help you," my voice rings in my ears, and I watch my younger self nod before wrapping her arms around the older me.

This picture used to ground me. I have to *fight* for myself. God, it can feel freaking lonely sometimes, but this is the only thing that helps me. I have to find it in me. I can't rely on anyone else. People can be unreliable, but I'll always have myself.

"I've got this," I say and run my hands over my face.

My phone rings a moment later, and I stare down at the e-mail from the Alfa Adrenalina team. *We currently have no position available for an internship.* It's the first line of a long e-mail I have no more interest in reading. They don't want me, Grenzenlos doesn't want me, and I have no connection to any other team. I'm screwed. My one opportunity to make myself known in the world of Formula One and gain anything from it to help further my career did nothing for me. All I got was disappointment.

And I still have to talk to Professor Holden, that slimy, disgusting man.

Great.

Life really doesn't hold back, does it?

Chapter 45
Julián

I never messed up so fucking bad. My body fell apart, and I lashed out at Scar. I'm the biggest asshole on the entire planet. Somebody should kick me in the balls repeatedly. I'd deserve it for what I said to her after she just wanted to help me. Instead, I've ignored her for the past three days, didn't invite her to my father's funeral, or did anything a good boyfriend is supposed to do. I've kept my distance from her because I'm so fucking overwhelmed, I can't face her and have her break up with me in response to being a dick. I know she will. No one deserves to be treated the way I treated Scar. She's going to leave me. So, I've avoided her. I don't have the emotional capacity to lose the woman I love right now. Nope. It's not happening.

I've processed my dad's death as well as I could in the past few days, but I'm nowhere near the acceptance stage of grief. Not that I'm supposed to be, I think. This whole thing also brought up the pain of when I lost Jamie, which is fucking phenomenal. I can't catch a moment to breathe, and it's causing my lungs to burn in response every time I'm merely walking up the stairs or too quickly down them. Even on my bike, I'm speeding down the highway, breathing harder than I should be. I do this for a living, after all.

Usually, being on my bike would bring me happiness of some sort. Now, everything is so fucking messed up, I feel like I'm suffocating instead. I'm too busy overthinking everything between Scar and me and wondering what in the hell I did to deserve losing my dad. I know life doesn't work like that, but my mind is stuck on it anyway as if I would ever find an answer to that unspoken question.

I turn off my bike in front of my dad's lawyer's office. He called Mamá and me yesterday, telling us we need to go over Dad's will again. Jeffrey, the lawyer, was still trying to figure out exactly what my father wanted to be done with his multi-billion dollar company. I don't want it. As a matter of fact, it is the last thing I want in this world. All of the responsibilities and duties that come with it are not for me. Luckily, Dad changed his will and put Mamá in charge, probably knowing the first thing I would do is sell it. Who am I kidding? I couldn't fucking sell the company now. It would break his heart if he knew I treated his legacy like something easily handed away.

"*Mierda*," I curse as I rip my helmet off and feel tears streaming down my cheeks.

Alright, they don't help this goddamn situation either. I wipe them away and bite down on the inside of my cheek to keep from shedding any more. I have to be strong for Mamá. She needs me to hold it together, and it's the least I can do for her after she's given me the world. Mamá deserves a son who can push his emotions back to focus on the business aspect for now. For fuck's sake, I didn't even cry at the funeral so I could take care of her. I'm not going to start falling apart now, before a meeting with Dad's lawyer.

Mamá parks her car next to my bike, dressed in all black. A tissue rests in her hand, as it has been since his passing, so she can wipe her tears as they roll down her face. I wrap her in a big hug as soon as she's out of the car. I expect sobs to leave her, anything to show me how much pain she is in, but, instead, she pulls out of the hug and gives me a small smile. The pad of her thumb runs over my cheek, and it sends a wave of emotions through me, one that throws me so off-balance, I start crying. I don't want to, I want to be strong for her, but Mamá comforting me prevents me from being capable of holding back my feelings. They spill to the front until they drop from my eyes.

"*Lo extraño mucho, Mamá,*" I admit before sobbing.

"*Yo sé, mi amor, yo sé,*" she replies, and I drop my face against her shoulder, letting a pain-filled sound leave me.

It takes me a few moments to collect myself, but then we walk up the stairs of the modern-style building with countless floor-to-ceiling windows. The receptionist greets us with a warm smile before leading us to the office on the fourth floor. He even opens the door for us, and Mamá thanks him as we step inside to meet Filipe. He's short, with a full head of silver locks, and a bright smile on his face. He knew my dad for forty years, which is probably why he's trying his best to figure out exactly what he put into his will.

"Take a seat," he says to us with his thick French accent. I pull out a chair for Mamá before settling in the one next to hers.

"Alright, talk to us, Filipe. What's changed in the last two days that we had to come as soon as possible?" I ask and watch his usual soft features harden into a frown.

"Listen, your dad was a complicated man when it came to his business. He left it to your mom under the condition that she—" Mamá cuts him off then.

"Don't," she says firmly, and I scrunch my eyebrows together as I turn to her. Panic flashes across her face, but she's avoiding eye contact with me at all costs. Fear strikes through me.

"Mamá?" I ask, but she's not even looking at me through her peripheral vision. Filipe clears his throat to grab my attention, but his focus is on Mamá.

"He deserves to know," he says, and I swallow hard. *Deserve to know what?*

"Someone better tell me what the fuck is going on right now before I lose my shit," I bark, grabbing Mamá's attention. Tears fill her eyes.

"Please, don't hate me for this," she says and takes my hand, holding it in both of hers. I have the urge to remove it from her grasp, but I have no reason to be upset with her. At least not yet.

"I could never hate you." Nothing she could have done would ever make me feel that way about her. She's my Mamá. I will always love her. Whether or not I'm going to be pissed at her, that's a different story.

"I—I can't tell him. You have to," she says, turning to Filipe and begging him to share whatever it is with me. I hold my breath while fear consumes me. Fuck. My hands are shaking again. Am I having another panic attack? No, I can't be. I just can't have one, not with so much uncertainty in the air.

"Your mother and father had an open relationship." Yeah, okay, sure. Try to swallow that when you have no idea how to feel about something like that.

"Okay?" I say, trying to get more information.

"In his will, your father stated that the company goes to your mother under the condition that she ended her relationship with José," Filipe goes on, and I forget how to breathe. That name sounds incredibly familiar. "Your biological father." I'm definitely going to throw up. "Since she doesn't want to do so, the company goes to you."

I'm on my feet before my brain has a moment to process his words. There is more Filipe wants to discuss, but a disgusting rage is spreading through my chest, and I have no idea how to stop it. It shatters my heart to see Mamá breaking down in tears, but there is a lot about this new information that doesn't sit right with me. Staying here and screaming at her out of a place of hurt and anger is the worst thing I could possibly do. Instead, I fixate my gaze on Filipe, keeping my voice steady and calm.

"I will take over the company. I will let the board know they have a new CEO."

I practically run out of the office and toward my bike. It's not a good idea to get on it in my current state, but I have no choice. I need to get out of here before

Mamá catches up with me and forces me to be ready to have a conversation without processing all of this information first. I have to think this all through so I can make sense of how I'm feeling. Being on my bike might even help me do so.

My mom and dad had an open relationship. That part I can wrap my head around. They were both adults, more than capable of making such decisions for themselves. I'm not mad they didn't tell me either. It was private to them, and I would never be upset about them withholding such information from me. Do I wish they felt comfortable enough to share that with me? Of course. I thought my parents and I had a more honest relationship, but they probably didn't know how I would feel about them seeing other people while being married. I couldn't give less of a shit. As long as they were both in agreement, that's their decision to make. Personally, I could never do the same because even the thought of another man touching Scar makes me want to tear down a building.

Scar.

I've been craving to see her, go to her since I mistreated her so badly last time, but that longing has intensified by a million now. Having her arms around me while I figure out what the hell I'm going to do with my life would soothe me in ways I can't even begin to explain. No. I can't go to her. She'll break up with me, and then I will be in worse condition than I already am. I'm not ready for that. Then again, I don't think I will ever be ready for her to leave me, even when I deserve it.

Instead of focusing on how badly I've messed up, I focus on Filipe's words. Mamá has been in contact with my biological father, the man who abandoned her and me when I wasn't even born yet. Better yet, she has a relationship with him, and not even my father approved of it. Why would he, after all? That man, José, left my mother to take care of herself and an infant without a job, money, or much knowledge of the English language. God, I want to punch a fucking wall. I can't believe she did this. I can't believe she let him in again after everything he put her through. Not to mention, he gave me unbelievable abandonment issues to the point where I'm avoiding the woman I love because I'm scared she will end our relationship and leave me for good.

I race home, not caring a single bit about the speed limit since no one else is on the road at this hour, and jump off my bike to make my way inside my place. Elias is sitting on the couch, going through the pile of paperwork from his job and bouncing his leg up and down. It's a manifestation of his work anxiety, but my mind is too busy freaking out to linger on it. He isn't the one I want to be with the most at this moment, but he is my brother in all ways that matter, and having him comfort me is more than good enough.

Elias looks up from the papers, his face showing he's on high alert when he sees mine. I walk over to him, my hands shaking from shock and anger. He stays quiet until I'm in front of him, fighting back the urge to scream at this situation. It might release some of the tension inside of me, but it would also be unnecessary and loud. No matter how much it would help me, I swallow down my scream and focus on sharing what happened with him.

"There is something we should talk about," I start, and Elias leans a little away from me, his brown eyes studying my face with an unsettling intensity.

"This can't be good. You look like you saw a ghost or something," Elias says, and I let out a laugh I don't mean in the slightest.

"I wish I'd seen a ghost. It would be easier to process than what I actually just heard," I reply, and he places his hand on my shoulder, squeezing it in an attempt to comfort me. Surprisingly enough, it gives me the courage to share everything with him.

"Whatever happened, we will face it together, okay? It's you and me, Storm, against the rest of the world," he says, and I give him a small smile, even if I don't fully mean it.

Chapter 46
Scarlette

Schoolwork has been keeping me occupied for the past four days. Julián hasn't reached out to me since his father died, but I haven't pressured him to either. I should assure him again that I'm here for him, but it feels like he doesn't want to be near me at the moment. Maybe I'm reading into things, after all, we're not broken up. He lost his father and is going through the worst time of his life. Not to mention, he probably has to take over the company now, something he doesn't want at all. He's all over the place and the least I can do is give him space until he figures everything out.

I walk into the lecture hall of my Introduction to Engineering class. I'm not too early, which is why I'm surprised to see no one is here yet. I check my e-mail to see if Professor Holden canceled class this morning, but there is nothing, except for a message from the dean. She's letting me know she will have a meeting with me tomorrow to discuss the unprofessionalism of Mr. Holden costing me a great job opportunity based on false information.

I contemplate leaving the lecture hall, but he isn't here either, so I decide to wait a little longer. In the meanwhile, I work on the assignment due by the end of the week. In order to make my argument even more convincing, my work has to be flawless. I can't give Professor Holden any reason to deduct points and give me a worse grade than I deserve. God, I freaking hate people who lash out and try to destroy another person's life because they were not interested in a relationship with them. That man has given me the ick since I first laid my eyes on him, and everything that's happened so far only proved my gut instinct right.

A *click* pulls me out of my thought trance, but when I look around, I don't see anyone at either of the entrances. I shake my head, clearly losing it, and stare at the page on my computer again. I'm almost ready to submit my assignment, just a few adjustments and then I'm done.

The minutes tick by, and I decide to text Halo and Victoria to see if they're coming soon. Usually, their whole group shows up together since they live in the dorms on campus. Neither of them responds by the time Professor Holden walks into the hall. It's only the two of us, and I stand up immediately, wanting to leave this room. I make my way up the stairs to the exit on the opposite side of where he's standing at the front, but his words stop me dead in my tracks, the worst type of shivers running down my spine.

"Stay put," he barks, and my muscles freeze in place at the violence in his voice. I have no desire to do as he requested. "Or I will tell the dean you came onto me and when I refused you, you lashed out and blamed me for getting rejected from job opportunities," he warns, sending a wave of disgust through me. Of course he'd play dirty. That man is a scumbag and revolting in every way possible.

"Tell the dean what you want. I don't care," I reply and keep walking toward the door. My phone suddenly feels heavy in my hand, reminding me I took it as I jumped out of my seat. Good. I should have it on me.

"Let's have a little chat about your behavior, Scarlette," Professor Holden says, but I continue moving.

I press down on the handle, trying to push the door open, but it doesn't budge. Oh my God. The *click* I heard earlier. He locked me in. He locked us into this room without windows or glass or anything where I could make myself seen by any passer-by. Damn it.

"Where are the others?" I ask, turning around to see he's been getting closer to me. A sick smile plays on his lips while fear sinks its teeth into my bones.

"I canceled class for them this morning," he replies, and I realize he must have sent out an e-mail to everyone but me. I'm going to be sick.

I call the police without another moment's hesitation. It rings three unnervingly long times before a man's voice comes through the speaker, asking me how he can assist me.

"Please, my professor locked me in a lecture hall with him and—" The person on the other side cuts me off.

"Ma'am, we already got a tip this morning that someone would prank call around this time from your current location. If we receive another call from you, there will be consequences," he says before hanging up on me. He hung up on me. Mr. Holden lets out a revolting laugh.

"You don't think I've thought of that, honey?" he asks, and I swallow down the bile rising in my throat. Shit.

My body turns back to the door where I push against it over and over. I stare down at my phone, quickly sending a message to the only person I know who can help me right now. I text Julián.

Scarlette: Professor Holden locked me in the lecture hall with him.

"Give me your phone," he says, but I'm not about to do anything he says.

He lunges toward me and rips it from my grasp. My head hits the wall behind me as he grabs the device from my hand and throws it at the ground. The screen shatters into a million pieces, but he doesn't give me time to linger on it before his hand wraps around my throat and he starts choking me.

"You've been giving me a lot of trouble, Scarlette. The dean wants to speak to me now because of you. Do you know what that means? I already had a student once who spoke ill of me. Another strike, and I will be fired. Is that what you want? To get me fired?" he asks, but I'm choking for air, his grip too tight on my throat. All that comes out is a wheezing noise. "That's not an answer, honey. I'm going to need you to use words," he says, his gray eyes staring into mine.

I claw at his hand, digging my nails into his skin. He curses, and I use that momentary loose grip on my throat to kick him in the balls.

"You fucking bitch," he screams as he falls to the ground, but I don't wait before kicking him in the face. He stumbles backward, nose bleeding and eyes watering.

I run toward the other exit.

"Shit," I cry out when that door is also locked. The only way to unlock it is with a key I'm pretty sure he's keeping on him.

Professor Holden stumbles to his feet, holding his bleeding nose as he makes his way to where I am. He's swearing and calling me every ugly name in the English vocabulary, but I'm too busy looking for anything to use as a weapon to defend myself.

"You know, you're going to ruin my whole life just because you couldn't give me what I wanted. You made me have to do all of this just to take what I want," he says, and I focus on him again. There are a few rows between us and the desk and speaker podium at the front.

"You're crazy. Because I didn't want to have private office hours with you, you're going to hurt me? Because *I didn't give you what you want*? Are you out of your mind?" I ask, trying to stall.

Then, I start screaming. If people can't see us, they will be able to hear me. I have no idea how far Professor Holden will take this, but I won't let him lay another finger on me unless it is while I kick him in the balls again, just to make sure he will never father any children. The world doesn't need more predators like him.

"I have been going out of my mind, yes. Seeing you sit in my classroom day after day, seeing those tight, big tits of yours without being able to touch them has been driving me crazy." A little bit of bile makes its way up my throat, but I swallow it down.

"I will never let you touch me," I spit, and he lets out a disgusting laugh. I feel it go straight into my bones, cracking them with disgust.

"Yeah, you will. Unless you would like to be expelled for attacking a professor, you will do everything I tell you," he says, wiping away the blood running out of his nose.

"Let them expel me. I don't care. You're not touching me," I say and walk around the podium when he comes closer to me again. He lets out another laugh before throwing it over and on top of me.

Before I know it, he wrestles me to the ground with his hands on my throat, choking me again.

Chapter 47

Julián

F ear. Raw, unfiltered, undeniable fear surges through me in waves as I race down the highway and toward Scar's university. I'm only two minutes away. Two minutes. She can distract him for two minutes, right? Fuck. Fuck. Fuck. I can't breathe, can't imagine what he's trying to do to her right now. I won't let anything happen to my girl. I'm almost there. Almost. I'm so fucking close.

I try calling the university over and over, but, for some goddamn reason, I will never understand, no one's answering. I called the police too, but they got an anonymous tip that someone would prank call the school so they won't send a car there. They even hung up on me, but I call them again as I run inside the school.

"Send a car to Moonville University right now!" I bark before hanging up and bumping into someone. I notice it's Violet.

"Storm? What's going on?" she asks, and I grab her shoulders, staring at her with panic.

"Take me to Scar's lecture hall. Now." She obeys without questioning my request.

We run down the stairs and toward the room. There are no windows or any way to look inside, but I don't linger on that before slamming my body against the locked door. Pain shoots through my side, but I ignore it. Violet helps me, and

287

soon, when people see what's happening, four more come to our aid. Halo fucking Henderson is one of them.

"What the hell's going on?" he yells as we throw ourselves against the door again.

"Holden locked them in," is all I need to say for his eyes to grow dark and anger to consume his features. He lets out a battle roar before hitting the door even harder, breaking it down.

For a split second, I admire his love for her. They're friends, and, although I hated him for how well they got along in the past, I like him for it now. He's ready to break his own body to get to her, just like me, and it allows me to go straight for Holden, knowing he will be there to hold Scar until I'm done killing the bald man.

I see him on top of Scar, nose bloody, his hand tight around her neck while she has his other one in a tight grasp in hers, holding it away from her body. She elbows him in the face as I run toward where they are on the ground, anger the dominant emotion inside of me now. *That's my girl*, I think, but the thought leaves quickly when I see him scramble to his feet to get back to her. Scar looks ready though. She kicks him in the balls before he can get close to her again, causing the bald man to drop to the floor with a loud pain-filled scream. Halo, Violet, and I place ourselves between Holden as a shield, ready to fight him if he tries to attack again.

The urge to hurt him even more than Scar already did crosses my mind for a second, but policemen fill the room a moment later. I turn to Scar to see Violet's arms already wrapped around her, comforting her while she cries. I sink to my knees next to her, my hands shaking. Fear has my whole body trembling, and I'm scared that after everything, she won't want me here. Tears fill my eyes, but she takes all my worries away as her arms fling around my neck. Now that the adrenalin has worn off, I'm a mess. I can't even think properly. Every part of me is falling apart at the thought of what Holden could have done to her if I hadn't shown up, all the things he did do.

"*Arcoíris*, where are you hurt? *Dime*," I beg, pulling back to study her face, arms, and legs. There are bruises on her throat, but, apart from those, I see no physical signs of injury. It doesn't settle me as much as I hoped it would.

"My throat," she croaks out, and I feel my heart sink at the sound.

Holden must have choked her for a long time with a lot of force for her voice to sound like this. The urge to turn around and kick him in the face repeatedly almost takes over, but Scar holds onto my arms, forcing my attention on her. Tears stream down her face, causing her mascara to run. I wipe it off her cheeks when she reaches for mine, shocking me by catching my tears. I hadn't even noticed I was crying until this very second.

"I can't believe you're here," she blurts out while staring into my eyes, and I realize something horrible. Scar didn't know if I'd show up because of the way I treated her last time.

"*Lo siento, mi amor*," I say and pull her into my lap. My heart is racing as I lean my forehead against hers, letting my fear slip from the corners of my eyes. "I am so sorry," I repeat, but she surprises me by pressing her lips to mine and sighing into my mouth.

"I love you," she whispers as she nuzzles her face into the crook of my neck. I slide my hands across her torso, resting them on her back to hold her close to me.

"I love you, *arcoíris*," I reply and kiss her temple, my eyes shifting to Violet, who is crying for her best friend. I understand completely. She's going to be okay.

Everything is going to be okay now.

Scar is in my arms on her bed. It's only been a few hours since she was attacked, but the paramedics cleared her. Apart from some bruising on her throat, she didn't sustain any injuries, not physically anyway. Emotionally and mentally? I can't imagine how much this has traumatized her. Holden trapped her in a room with him and tried to have his way with her. I shudder at the thought.

"I was really scared," she starts, almost as if she had heard my thoughts. Pain slices through me. "I knew something was off, but I didn't think he'd go that far," she adds, and bile rises in my throat. It takes everything out of me not to cry again.

"I'm so sorry, Scar. I should have been there faster. I should have—" She presses one of her perfect fingers to my lips to silence me.

"You shouldn't have done anything. You needed time to grieve your father's loss, I understand. You are hurting and overwhelmed, and this all must bring back what happened when you were a kid," she goes on, and I fight back my tears.

How does she know me so well? And why does she still want to be with me? After everything I put her through, I don't deserve her. I don't deserve us.

"I also know you're not the type of person who easily opens up to people about your own problems. You will take care of everyone else before yourself, but, I'm begging you, Julián, let me be there for you. All this weight on your shoulders, let me carry some of it on mine. I'm pretty strong, you know?" she says, and I wish I wouldn't lean away from her. I wish I'd wrap her up in my arms and never let go. Instead, I slide out of bed to create some distance between us.

"I know you're strong, *mami*, I have never and will never question that, but if you knew what was happening in my life right now, you'd run. No one wants to be burdened with the kind of bullshit my Mamá put on my plate," I blurt out, scolding myself for the drama I'm making after the day she's had. "I'm sorry, love, I know today was a lot and I'm making things worse. I'm sorry," I say, which only seems to frustrate her more. Scar kneels on her mattress, her hands on her hips.

"You listen to me, stubborn man. No matter what happened today, you and I are a unit. I know you're not used to that because your past relationships were one-sided, but I'm here now. And we're not leaving my room until you get it through your head that I don't want you to push me away. If you're not ready to speak about it, we don't have to, but if you are, please, confide in me. Let's find our way back to each other. Please," she says, and I sink onto the bed again, pulling her mouth onto mine.

Chapter 48
Scarlette

There is no aggression in his kiss. It's soft and careful, his tongue only swiping across my bottom lip before he seeks more comfort from my mouth. He's reassuring himself of my feelings this way, and I can't blame him. It's easy to say 'I love you'. It's easy to lie. There is nothing but honesty in our kiss, in the way our lips melt together in that longing need I know both of us have felt since our first intimate moment like this.

It settles my heart into an even rhythm. After what happened with Professor Holden, I've been having a hard time feeling anything. A strange numbness settled in after Julián took me home. It's preventing me from having an anxiety attack I know my mind and body needs. Without it, all my feelings are going to keep getting suppressed until I have a complete breakdown.

Julián pulls me out of my thoughts when he leans away from the kiss for a second, sucking in a sharp, painful breath, and then claiming my lips again. We're both a mess of emotions we need to sort through, but I get lost in him for a few moments longer. I can't leave the fantasy of being invincible yet, not when I have never felt safer than in his arms.

"I'm yours," Julián says between kisses, and I let out a little moan when his lips attach to my neck.

"I've only ever been yours," I reply, which causes him to stop kissing me completely. His arms wrap around my back and he pulls me into his lap, his face nuzzled into my neck.

We stay like this for a while, me running my hands through his hair and him running the tips of his fingers down my spine. I hum a random song, trying to sort out my thoughts while he gathers the strength to tell me what happened with his mom. Everything spins inside my head. The numbness in my chest is still there, but his body warmth is relieving some of it now. I'm okay. We're okay. Everything will be okay. We're going to figure out what to do, and he's going to let me in so I can finally be there for him.

"I think I'm going to go back to therapy," I blurt out after a while of silence. Julián raises his head to study my face.

"Yeah?" he asks, and I tug one of his curls behind his ear, my eyes on his different-colored ones before I run my finger along the length of his birthmark.

"Yes. It will help me work through what happened today," I explain, and he gives me an agreeing nod. I miss his smile. I haven't seen it in a long time, and it reminds me of the days he kept it hidden from the world. "Do you think therapy could help you too?" I ask, caressing his cheeks with the pads of my thumbs.

"Maybe. I don't know. I've never thought about going. Plus, whoever has a session with me is not going to know what hit them when I explain what's going on," he says and chuckles. I know the sound is humorless, which is why I frown at him. "Something really bad happened," he adds, and I press a quick kiss to his lips.

"*Dime*," I say, and, finally, he gives me a small smile.

"My mom and dad had an open relationship." That's like a slap to the face, waking me up. "She can't inherit my dad's company because she's in a relationship with my biological father." That feels more like someone poured a bucket of ice water over my head. It's a cold, creeping pain, pain for him.

"And she never told you?" Of course she didn't, but I have no idea what else to say. Julián cups my face with both of his hands, staring into my eyes as his next words follow.

"No. She never told me, but it doesn't matter now. That's a problem for when I have calmed down enough to let her explain. In the meantime, I've just inherited a multi-billion dollar company, and I do not want it. I want to go race with my team next season. I want to win the National Championship and make it all the way into MotoGP. I am not a businessman, I never have been. I'm an athlete, but how the fuck can I sell my dad's life's work? I can't betray him like that." He lets go of my face only to take my hands in his. "I don't want to disappoint him any more than I would like to give up my dream," he whispers, squeezing my fingers with his.

This is a lot of information I'm not sure how to process and turn into a solution this very second. So, I slide my hands into his hair and massage his scalp to calm him. His eyes flutter shut in response while he lets me comfort him. It also gives me a moment to chew on his words.

He doesn't want to run his dad's company, but he's also been unhappy with the way it was taking advantage of people. He has to follow his dream, but it must be without giving up everything his dad accomplished. Julián can't see a way out of this... *but I can!*

"Keep your share of the company, but make Elias the CEO," I say, and he lifts his head, confusion on his features

"Elias? Why Elias?" he asks, and I give him a small smile.

"Because he's been frustrated with his job for a few weeks now, and he always talked to me about how much he admired your dad for creating such a powerful empire. Plus, he will immediately start implementing your ideas of giving back to the people and investing some of the profits in environmentally conscious companies." I slap his shoulder when an idea strikes me. He chuckles at my enthusiasm, but I'm on a roll and not ready to stop just yet. "We could even work with him to come up with ideas to be more environmentally friendly. Your dad's company has so much money and influence. It has great potential to do good in the world, and this is your opportunity to do that. Put Elias in charge, I know he'd thrive in a CEO position since he will finally be able to use that business degree of his and let him implement your ideas."

Julián watches me with an intensity that makes me question whether or not I stepped over a line. This is a sensitive topic. I'd hate to give him hope if this is an impossible idea. I just wanted to give him something, anything to show him there is another way. He doesn't have to take over his dad's company. It's the last thing he would ever do willingly. Like he said, he isn't a businessman. He's an athlete through and through. He belongs on a bike, on a race track, something he's been working toward for years of his life. Julián deserves to live his dream.

"You don't think it's too much to ask of Elias?" he asks, rubbing the pads of his thumbs over my wrists.

"I think he'd love it, but, to be safe, make him an offer. A job offer. If he turns it down, we can find someone else. You can still have controlling shares without having to be the one to call all the shots. Okay? We will do it together. I am your assistant for now, after all," I say with a smile, which makes him raise both his brows.

"My assistant, huh?" he asks and squeezes my ass, simultaneously rubbing me against him.

"Yes," I say and swallow hard.

"Then my first order of business is to give you a big raise, big enough to pay for your studies, and fire you directly after," he replies, and it pulls me out of the pleasure trance he just put me in.

"No, thank you. You know I won't take your money," I reply and grab his chin between my fingers. Julián looks thoughtful for a moment.

"Alright. You're fired. You will get your severance pay soon," he says, and I wrestle him backward onto the mattress.

He flips us over, a serious look on his face, a smile hidden underneath, one I know wants to come to the surface if he wasn't upset with me for being stubborn about this.

"I've never wanted you at this job, Scarlette. Let me pay you a severance pay big enough to cover your courses for the next two or three years. Maybe even for the rest of your studies. You want to know why?" I flash him an easy grin.

"Enlighten me, baby," I reply, watching his muscles flex in response.

"Because you deserve it." He leans down and kisses my lips. "Because it's pennies to me now." Julián swipes his tongue over my bottom lip. "Because I would like to, very much," he says and places his body fully on top of mine, his cock firmly pressed against my clit. Oh God.

"Okay," I hear myself reply, snapping me back to reality. Julián merely chuckles. "I mean, no! I'm not just taking the money without earning it. Not to mention, Elias is going to need me to help him. I know the company better than him," I add, trying to convince him. He looks unhappy with me, so I go on. "Let me help you make a difference," I say, and he lets out a loud groan of frustration.

"How could I say not to that tone?" he asks, and I lift my hips to grind myself against him.

"You can't," I say, smiling when he loses his composure on top of me. A slight moan leaves him, but right before he gets lost in what I'm doing, his eyes flicker to the bruises around my neck, and he stops my movements.

"I'm going to make you something to eat," he says and kisses me so fiercely, it tells me leaving this bedroom is the last thing he wants to do right now. I also know he's only doing it because neither of us is in the right mindset to have sex. I still have to deal with what the hell happened today, and Julián has to do the same.

"Wait," I blurt out right as he is about to slide off me. "Are we okay? Are we us again?" I ask, and his eyes soften.

"We've always been us. I'm so sorry I ever made you doubt it. I'm so sorry for everything, *mami. Lo siento mucho*," he says and kisses me over and over. "I don't ever want to lose you, Scar. You're my rainbow, *mi arcoíris*," he says and sits up, wrapping me up in his arms.

"I love you," I say and listen to his racing heartbeat.

"I love you more than will ever make sense to me. I love you more than my heart can take. I love you with everything I will ever have to offer. It's all yours, and it's non-refundable too, in case you're wondering."

We smile at each other for a long time after his words, until my stomach growls from hunger and he jumps out of bed to take care of my needs. He almost throws me over his shoulder to bring me to my dining room area, where he tells me to stay put. I watch all of his muscles on display for me as he prepares the food and then places it in front of me with another one of those breathtaking smiles of his.

"Oh, I've missed you," I say as I take in the scent of the food.

"I've missed you more, love," he replies, and I suck in a sharp breath.

"No, baby, I meant your food. Having a break from you was kind of refreshing." I wish I'd have filmed his reaction because it's priceless. His jaw drops so far to the floor, I think about bending down to retrieve it for him.

"You're mean," he says and takes my plate away again. I burst into laughter.

"Give it back," I complain, still laughing because he's pouting now. "I'm just teasing. God," I add, and Julián hands me the plate once more, stealing a kiss at the same time.

"Eat," he commands, and I cock an eyebrow in response. "Maybe it will make you nicer," he says, and I fall into another fit of laughter. This time, he joins me, and the melodic sound of his amusement fills my soul.

I really have missed him, so much.

Chapter 49
Scarlette

Julián and I have been sitting at his desk in the office for the past eight hours, trying to come up with more environmentally friendly solutions, find charities to invest some of the profit in, and create the contract for Elias' job offer. Everyone else has left, and my boyfriend rubs his temples with the pads of his fingers, probably fighting a headache. If I already have a headache from staring at the screen for so long, I can't imagine how bad it is for him. I'm used to it more than he is since I was working for his father for the last few months.

"My head is throbbing," Julián says after a few more minutes of us silently working.

"Let me get you a painkiller," I say and get up, but Julián's fingers wrap around my wrist to stop me. He pushes his chair back and tugs on my arm until I'm standing between his spread legs.

"I have a better idea," he says and lifts his fingers to my thighs. I'm only wearing a skirt, giving him easy access to my skin. "You know, I never had the fantasy of boss and assistant, but, right now, I can't think of anything better than to put you on my desk, spread your legs, and bury my face in your pretty pussy," Julián says, and my heart skips several beats from his words.

"What about your headache?" I ask while he trails his hands up my legs and his fingers curl around the waistband of my panties.

"There is no better painkiller than feeling you come on my tongue," he replies, standing up and bringing his lips close to mine. My breathing is heavy, my skin flushed with heat, and desire courses through me in steady waves. "Will you make me beg, *mami*? Or can I get on my knees and take what I want?" he asks, his lips brushing over mine, but he's not kissing me.

So, I kiss him instead.

Our lips melt together, but his hands remain on my panties, patiently waiting for my permission to remove them. I wish I could tell him to take them off, but I'm too distracted by the way his tongue slips into my mouth and explores it with need. The taste of him lights my tastebuds on fire until I'm whimpering slightly in his grasp.

"I've been thinking about ripping these panties off you all day," Julián says and I moan when he does just that, tearing at the waistband until the fabric drops from my body.

"What if someone sees?" I manage to ask, but he's already reaching behind me and wiping everything off the table.

"No one's here," he replies, lifting me onto the desk. He grabs my chin to force my gaze to his. "That ridiculously sexy blouse needs to be off, but this skirt, *mami*, I need it on while I fuck you with my tongue. These heels too," he says and lifts my leg to press a kiss to my ankle. Anticipation courses through me until it makes my clit ache unbearably.

"Please," I beg, and Julián drops my leg to step between them and kiss me again. My hands roam over his hard stomach, tugging at his shirt to get him closer. His bulge rubs against my bare sex, forcing a moan from my lips.

"I need to taste you," he says, biting down on my bottom lip and trailing kisses down my neck. His fingers slip through an opening between the buttons of my blouse before he rips it apart too.

"I need you," I moan when he cups my breasts and tugs down the lace of my bra with his teeth.

"Is your pretty pussy ready for me?" he asks, sucking on my hard left nipple and dragging another moan out of me. Pleasure explodes inside my body until I see stars.

"Yes," I reply while he gives my right nipple the same amount of attention.

"Hmmmm," he moans, licking down my body until he's on his knees and guiding my legs onto his shoulders. "Such a perfect sight," he says as he stares at my pussy, but then his eyes lift to mine, and I shudder with need and pleasure.

"Please," I repeat, and he inches closer, keeping eye contact with me at the same time.

"I love it when you beg, Scar," he says right before licking along the length of me. "God, this is the sweetest pain reliever in the world," he groans, and I let out a breathless laugh, which turns into a moan as soon as the tip of his tongue starts playing with my clit.

"Fuck!" I moan, my back arching off the desk as he drags his tongue along the length of my pussy again.

"My favorite dirty mouth," Julián says with a small chuckle, and I can't help but smile. "Play with your tits, Scar, I want to watch," he commands, so I reach for my nipples, pinching them together until I cry out his name. "That's my girl," he praises, and another wave of pleasure goes through me.

Everything in my lower abdomen tenses as heat spreads through my bloodstream, lighting me on fire. He flicks his tongue over my clit again and again, sliding it inside me every so often to make my toes curl. The tips of his fingers dig into my bare thighs as he moans against me. Every cell in my body starts vibrating as he pushes me closer to the edge with his mouth.

"Julián," I scream right as he sucks on my clit and causes an orgasm to shatter through me.

He drags his tongue along the length of me once more, almost as if he's savoring the taste. My heart skips several beats while I do my best to come down from my high. Julián traces kisses along the inside of my right thigh and up to my stomach while I push off the desk to get closer to him. I need more of him. My hands move to his cheeks, cupping them so I can guide his face to mine and kiss him fiercely. I taste myself on his lips, making me grin. Julián is mine.

"I want you to come inside me," I blurt out, catching myself and him off-guard. He hesitates for a fraction of a second before grinning from ear to ear and capturing my mouth with his again. His tongue pushes inside, exploring me until all my muscles have turned to putty.

"Let me get a condom," he says, but I hold onto his dress shirt to keep him in place. I start undoing his buttons while I gather the courage to say what I want.

"No condom. I want to feel you without anything between us," I admit, so he cups my face and forces my whole attention on him.

"Are you sure?" Julián asks, and I give him an easy smile.

We talked about not using a condom a few days ago. I'm on one of the safest birth controls, and we're both tested and clean. He wants to, he told me so, and so do I. He's the only one for me, and I want us to be one in every way we possibly can be.

"Yes," I say, and he kisses me again.

My fingers push his dress shirt off his body and then drop to the button of his pants, undoing it before palming his hard cock through his boxers. He groans into my mouth before grabbing my hand and giving me a wicked grin.

"Turn around, *mami*. I want to watch your ass bounce on me," he says, and I don't hesitate.

I give him one last kiss before turning around and bending over at the waist. I let out a little squeal when the coolness of the wood presses against my hard nipples, the sound quickly morphing into a moan. Julián drags his fingers along the length of my pussy, giving an approving hum.

"You're so wet for me, *mami*, I'll slip right into my paradise," he says, running his hands over my butt cheeks before giving my right one a swift smack. It's not painful, but a small part of me wishes he'd do it again. Harder.

I move my ass backward, looking for him and earning myself a low chuckle from him. A second later, the head of his cock presses against my entrance, sending a wave of anticipation through me. He slips inside as easily as we both knew he would, dragging gasps from both of our mouths. Julián kneads my butt cheeks once more, spreading them ever so slightly.

"God, this sight, Scar, it's perfection. The way you're pussy hugs my cock is the sexiest thing I've ever seen," he says, making me moan from his words. He thrusts into me again, a lot harder than the first time, causing me to scream so loudly, I cover my mouth with my hand. "Don't muffle your screams. I want to hear how good I make you feel, *mami*," he says, slamming inside of me even harder. "Bounce your ass on me, baby, let me see you chasing your pleasure," Julián instructs, and I obey. I move backward, slamming onto his hard cock and finding the spot inside of me that will get me off. "Fucking perfect," Julián moans, slapping my right ass cheek again as I bounce it against him.

A few minutes pass, both of us in a trance of bliss and pleasure, when he suddenly grabs my hips, flips me around, and places me back on the table. I mourn the loss of his hardness for a moment, but he doesn't give me time. Julián's mouth is on mine as he guides me to the edge and slams back into me again.

"Fuck," I cry when he picks up speed, going harder and faster than my body can keep up with. Pleasure blindsides me until my vision blurs and everything inside of me tenses again.

"You feel so fucking good, Scar," Julián groans, and my body lights up from the way he moans over and over again. It does feel incredible without the condom. His skin rubbing against mine is heaven on Earth. "Look at the way we fit together, *mami*, look how perfect," he says, and I look down at where his cock slides inside of me like we were made for this, for each other.

"I'm gonna come," I cry out right as he fills me up by thrusting inside harder than before.

The sight of him fucking me combined with the pleasure of his movements sends me straight over the edge. My orgasm ripples through me, grabbing hold of every cell in my body. My nails dig into Julián's biceps as my head falls back and the pleasure consumes me. Colors explode behind my eyes until I feel absolutely euphoric. His movements continue until his orgasm takes over too, so I clench my walls around him, trying to get as much of his pleasure out of him as possible. His whole body shakes, and his cock pulses inside of me, filling me with his cum for the first time.

"You're mine," Julián says before his hand carefully wraps around my neck to drag my lips back onto his.

I'm his. All his. Just like he's mine.

Chapter 50
Julián

"Are you kidding me? I'd love to, Storm! This is my dream job." Elias is out of his chair and stepping toward me a moment later, happiness all over his face. Scar and I worked on the contract I handed him a moment ago for the past week. I'm glad he seems to like what I've laid out for him in the pages.

"Are you one hundred percent sure?" I ask, and Scar chuckles in the chair next to me. I flash her a frown before Elias' arms wrap around me and pull me out of the chair.

"Thank you for this, seriously. I watched Dad build this from the ground up, and I was secretly hoping he'd let me into the business one day, but right as he and I were about to come to an agreement, he passed away," Elias explains, and I feel the need to frown at the secret they were keeping from me.

How come I never knew? Why did neither of them tell me? Does it really matter? No, no it doesn't. I didn't have to know everything that went on between the both of them and this business. The thing to be glad about is Elias wanting this job opportunity. He's ready to make changes and turn this company into something I can be proud of. Maybe it isn't what Dad would have done, but he'd be proud of both of us, I'm sure of it.

"This calls for champagne," Violet says before waving at the waiter with a smile and asking for a bottle of the most expensive champagne. "Since you guys are billionaires," is the only thing she says with a shrug of her shoulders.

"You're impossible," Scar says with a smile, which I return as effortlessly as breathing nowadays.

Scar is doing much better. It's been a week since everything happened, but she's been to therapy once already, and she came back feeling lighter, she said. Professor Holden was kicked out of the university and is now facing prison time for what he's done. With so many witnesses—Halo, Violet, me, and the dozen people helping us break down the door—he didn't get a trial. He got a sentence, just like that motherfucker deserves.

My girlfriend leans toward me and kisses my cheek, smiling like there is no tomorrow. I have a surprise for her later, something I've been working on since we came back from Monaco, even if I was interrupted in getting everything settled for her. Now, everything is set and ready, and I can already see how happy she will be. *She's going to be happy, right? Fuck. What if she doesn't like it? What if this is the last thing she wants?* I won't pressure her into anything, it's all up to her, but now, doubts fill my head.

Puñeta.

"Where is Mamá?" Elias asks, and I let out a sharp breath that sends a wave of pain through my chest.

"She should be here soon," I assure him while Scar grabs my hand and laces her fingers through mine. Her touch sends a wave of comfort through me instantly.

I haven't spoken to Mamá since our meeting with Filipe, but I know this is taking a toll on her, just like it is on me. Silence between us always hurts both of us, especially when that silence comes from being in a fight. I invited her to lunch with Scar, Violet, Elias, and me because it's neutral ground. My anger has faded enough to make me want to be in her presence, to figure out a way to repair our relationship. Not that it's damaged. I don't think. I hope not. I don't know anything anymore. It sends waves of dread and grief through me because there is nothing I'd love more than to speak to Dad. He'd be able to explain to me why he ever agreed to be in an open relationship with Mamá when the man she's hooking up with is the man who abandoned her and her son.

Why didn't he tell me?

That question also repeats itself in my head over and over again. I was so upset with Mamá for the first few days, I didn't even think about Dad's part in all of this. He also kept my biological father's presence in Mamá's life hidden from me. Unfortunately, I can't stay angry at him because it won't lead anywhere. He's not here to explain himself to me. Dad will never get the chance to answer all of my questions, so there is nothing to do but let go of whatever anger that's trying to settle inside of my chest. I don't want to be angry at my dad. I want to hold onto the good memories I have with him without them getting tainted by whatever he kept hidden from me.

"You're going to get wrinkles from frowning so hard," Scar whispers and squeezes my fingers. I see a smile dancing onto her full lips and sparkling in her blue eyes.

"I haven't gotten any so far," I reply and return her grin.

"Well, you're still young, but that won't last forever. If you keep frowning at this rate, you'll be covered in wrinkles in a few years," she teases, and I nudge her shoulder with mine.

"Will you not find me attractive anymore then?" I ask, guiding her closer to me.

"I will always find you attractive, Julián, don't be silly," she replies and pouts, but I only take advantage of the position of her lips and press mine to hers.

"You're so beautiful," I blurt out when I lean back and see her blue eyes half closed and full of love for me.

"I'm sorry I'm late," Mamá says, her voice filling my ears.

Yeah, I thought I was ready to hear her excuses, but I'm not. I'm so mad at her, merely being in her presence angers me. But it can't keep going on like this. So, I straighten out my back, give Scar one last kiss on her temple, and then turn to Mamá. It's a good thing my smiles are reserved for Scar because I don't feel like forcing one at my mother right now. She doesn't deserve to see the side of me only my girlfriend brings out.

"Julián," Mamá greets me while Elias pulls out a chair for her.

"Mamá," I reply and watch her sit down, her brown-gray hair in a tight bun on her head, like always. She's still wearing black, which only angers me more.

"Vi, can you come with me to check on my bike? I think I forgot to—" I disregard the rest of Elias' sentence, my focus on Mamá.

"Do you want me to go with them?" Scar asks, but I shake my head once.

"We should talk," Mamá says in Spanish, but I won't have it.

She's trying to exclude Scar from our conversation, and it's not happening. I tell her everything, so Mamá might as well use the English she was forced to learn so quickly because the man she's fucking abandoned her. God, I'm going to be sick.

"Why him, Mamá? Why the man who caused us so much pain?" Tears fill her eyes, and I feel sick to my stomach.

"Would it make you feel better if I told you that he left me again? He didn't want to deal with my grief," she replies, and my heart shatters into a million pieces for her.

This isn't what I wanted either. Hell, I even thought about meeting him for the first time, trying to understand why he could have left, but, apparently, that's not going to happen. He left. Again. *Ese cabrón.* I would love to punch him in the face.

"Please, answer my question," I plead, and she stares at the table, her brown eyes tired of getting hurt.

"Your father and I agreed to have an open relationship when he almost cheated on me ten years ago on a business trip," she explains, and I swallow hard. Okay, good. Almost is good. He came home and told her, and they decided to do the adult thing and find an arrangement that worked for them. "José and I ran into each other at the airport a few years ago. I think he talked me right back into a relationship with him, made me dependent on the way I felt about him, the way I *feel* about him," she explains, her accent thick. I let out a silent breath.

"I don't understand," I admit, so Mamá goes on.

"I thought he was the love of my life. When he left me, left us, I thought I'd lost my other half forever. When he came back into my life, I was so desperate to feel whole again, I ignored what had happened between us before," she says, and I feel like slapping my forehead with the palm of my hand. *Por el amor de Dios, Mamá.*

"Why didn't you tell me? Why didn't you introduce me to him?" I challenge, and a tear finally drips down her face. That fucking hurts more than I would like for it to.

"Because he didn't want to meet you. It was part of our deal. He stayed as long as I kept you away from him." *Ouch.* God, why does that hurt me even more?

"He was manipulating you, you see that now, right?" I ask, and she gives me several nods, more tears leaving her eyes. "You also understand how much this hurt me, yeah? How this broke my trust?" Again, she nods.

"Baby," Scar says and rubs my forearm with her fingers.

She's reminding me that, even though Mamá fucked up really badly, she's only human. This toxic relationship José dragged her into created an emotional dependence she didn't know how to live without. I can understand that, but I also need more time.

"I'm so sorry for the pain I've caused you, Julián. I love you so much, and this was never supposed to be something you had to deal with. I'm deeply sorry for the way and when it came to the surface." Damn it. How the fuck am I supposed to stay mad at her when she's hurting so badly too? We need each other. Hell, I need Mamá and me to be on good terms again.

"I'm not a child you need to protect anymore, okay? You have to tell me things," I say, and she nods, breaking down in more tears. For fuck's sake. I get up and pull her against my chest, letting her fall apart.

My eyes shift to Scar, who is mouthing the words 'You are amazing' to me. Everything inside of me flutters in response, and a smile slips across my face. I don't try to hide it or deny it. I let it take over my features, just like I know Jamie would want me to. Scar was right. Every smile he can't give the world anymore, I'm supposed to offer for him. Too bad they all belong to Scar now, just like the rest of me.

Chapter 51
Scarlette

After we came back from lunch, I decided to fix the rain gutter outside of Vi's and my house. She's been bugging me about fixing it for the past three days because she's scared the water won't run through properly and it will cause problems inside of the house. Julián said he'd pick me up later again to go for a ride, something we've been doing more and more recently. Him on his bike and me on mine as we let freedom course through our veins has become like a drug to me. It's a source of happiness I never knew I needed.

Julián took a big step today with his mom, and I couldn't be prouder of him. I spoke to my mom right after lunch, wanting to catch up and see how she's doing without me around. Dad even came to the phone to check up on me too. It was... nice. I really enjoyed my conversation with both of them, which is a rarity in itself, but I will take it.

Everything seems to be going well, and I don't trust it one bit. I haven't had an anxiety attack in almost a week, and I'm still waiting for everything to settle more for it to hit me, but, so far, nothing. Maybe I'm learning to cope a little better with it. I know it will never leave me. Anxiety has become a part of me, but for the first time since I started having my attacks, I feel strangely at peace with it. Yes, they will forever exhaust me and try to break me apart, but I've found a place of strength inside of me, a well it seems, and I will draw from it to the best of my abilities. Going to therapy might also help. All I have to do is be patient and believe in myself.

I will never again let my anxiety try to take away from my worth. It is part of me, but it doesn't define me. It's something I struggle with, but it will not be what tears me apart. It's my nemesis, but it also feels strangely like a friend.

I shake my head and finish fixing the gutter. Vi comes outside with a bright smile and hands me a glass of water once I'm done, thanking me a million times for being such a badass. Her giddy mood rubs off on me until I'm grinning at her. Violet has apologized to me a hundred times about what she said, but I was never really mad at her. I knew what I signed up for when we became best friends. One drop over her alcohol limit, and she turns into a mean woman. Usually not toward me, but I also should have known better than to step in when she was drunk and angry at Elias.

The roaring of Julián's bike tears us out of our conversation about what we're going to do during summer break, even if it's still far away, and I shift my whole body to the driveway. My boyfriend parks his bike right next to mine, taking his helmet off and smiling at me like he's never done anything else. A bundle of lavender is sitting on the top of his bike, causing heat to flood my cheeks. I saw him two hours ago, but I can't help rushing over to him and wrapping my arms around his neck, breathing in his warm scent.

"Let's go?" he asks after giving me a long kiss, and I nod eagerly.

We get on our bikes and drive toward the highway, letting the warm wind hit our equipped bodies. Safety first, after all. Julián tells me to follow him, picking up speed and racing down the empty road. I'm right behind him, smiling like there is no tomorrow. This is all I will ever need to feel happy. No matter what is going on, this, him and I like this, will never fail to make my chest fill with joy.

Julián points toward an exit, and I follow behind him. He keeps driving until we arrive at the beach, parking our bikes in the designated spots and taking off our gear.

"You should have told me we were going to the beach. I would have put on a bikini," I say, and he smiles at me, his birthmark so dark and beautiful on his face.

"Don't worry, it's a nude beach," he replies, and my eyes widen. "Kidding. I would never take you to a nude beach. The only cock I want you to see is mine," he replies, and I smack my forehead, earning myself a chuckle from him, my favorite sound. "Here, this is for you," he says and hands me the lavender bundle. I take it from him with a kiss.

"Thank you."

He kisses me again before taking my hand and strolling along the beach with me. We stay silent for a while, my eyes glued to the ocean and the waves as they crash onto the shore and wrap around our feet. We left our shoes at the bikes because, as Julián said, nothing happens in this town without someone knowing.

"Thank you for fake dating me, Scar," Julián eventually blurts out, and I raise an eyebrow at him.

"I believe you were the one fake dating me to help me," I remind him, and he chuckles at the ground. Two chuckles in less than ten minutes. It was unthinkable a few months ago. I love that it's normal now.

"I agreed to because it allowed me to be near you at all costs. It was all selfish," he says, and I smile up at him. He wraps his arm around my shoulders and brings me close to his chest to kiss my temple. "I have to tell you something," he says as he steps in front of me. I stop dead in my tracks.

"Uh oh," I reply, but he waves away my worry when he laughs.

"No, it's a good thing, I promise," he says, but I hold my breath anyway. Julián runs his fingers over the backs of my hands before cupping them. "My team, the one I'm racing with next season, would like to have you as an intern for the entire duration of the summer. I gave them your resume and bragged a little about how smart you are, and they almost hired you on the spot." I almost choke on my own breath. "Which means we don't have to be apart *and*, most importantly, you get engineering experience in a motorsport field," he goes on, but I can't process anything at this point. "There is no pressure, but I thought it would help you eventually get a job in Formula One. Having experience is always good," he adds, suddenly unsure of himself because I haven't responded yet. "No pressure, Scar, I promise," Julián says, and I lift my hand to cover his mouth before he can reassure me once more.

"Are you kidding me?" I start, and panic fills his eyes. *That's probably not the right way to go about this, Scar.* "I would love to, Julián! Oh my God, I can't believe this. This is incredible. You're incredible. I—I have no words. Thank you so much," I say and attack him by wrapping my arms around his neck and jumping into his arms. He catches me and holds onto the backs of my legs to keep me in place.

"It was all you, love. I just gave them your resume." I drop back onto my feet and guide his head down so his lips meet mine.

I can't believe this. I have an internship in a racing sport. It may not be Formula One, but I'm going to work my way up there. I will never stop fighting for my dream, but I've got time. It doesn't have to be at this very second. I haven't even finished my degree yet. For now, I'm going to travel the country with Julián. I'm going to gather field experience while cheering on the man I love.

I can't think of anything better.

"My Storm," I mumble against his lips a moment later, making him smile.

"*Mi arcoíris,*" he replies, capturing my mouth with his again.

Epilogue
Julián

Four years later

"Scarlette Alvarez," I say after I take off my helmet.

She's standing in front of me, her arms crossed in front of her in a way that pushes her breasts together so beautifully, I can't resist staring at them for a moment. Then, her blue eyes grab my attention completely. The way her sundress, with lavender drawn all over it, flies around her curves almost brings me to my knees. Her scar is faded and beautiful in every way possible. I still can't believe she said yes to marrying me a year ago. I can't believe she's my wife.

"Roots-Alvarez," she corrects me, her frown bringing a smile to my lips. I know she isn't upset with me. I just put in my best lap time since we started testing the new bike for... for my first season in MotoGP. Damn, I still can't believe that either.

"No, *mami*, our last name is Alvarez," I reply while making my way to her and attempting to wrap my sweaty body around her. This suit is tight in all the wrong places, but I don't care about any of that when she flashes me a smile so bright, it settles deep inside of me.

"You need to be more careful going so deep into the corners," she scolds in Spanish, leading me inside a second before I could have my arms around her. She's so bossy when she's in work mode, and it's fucking gorgeous.

"Yes, boss," I reply and trail behind her to check the footage of my lap. She's right. It was risky to go so deep into the corner. I have to be more careful.

"Your lap times are great," she says, pointing at the sector times I put in during my practice laps.

"What's my reward?" I ask, earning myself a weird look from some of my other team members. I offer them an apologetic shrug, not ashamed in the slightest.

"This," she says, holding up the hand with her wedding ring around it. Fuck. That is my reward. It will forever be my reward.

Her phone *dings* from an incoming message, and she picks it up, her eyes going wide in response to whatever it is that lit up her screen.

"Is it Vi? Is the baby coming?" I ask, but Scar simply shakes her head.

"No, no, it's way too early for that. She's only seven months along," Scar reminds me, and I let out the breath I've been holding. She's right, and I'm glad it's not what I thought. Elias made me swear that I would be there when my niece is born. "This is an e-mail from Valentina Romana," Scar goes on, and I refocus on her. *Valentina Romana?* The girl she met years ago, who tried to help her get an internship at one of the teams. The first female Formula One championship contestant in Formula One history is e-mailing Scar.

Holy shit.

Holy fucking shit!

"She wants you as her race engineer," I blurt out, and when Scar looks at me, eyes filled with tears of happiness, I realize I'm right. Her nod only reassures me of what I already figured out. "My love. You did it!" I say, and Scar covers her mouth as tears drop down her cheeks.

"I did it," she says softly, and I pick her up and spin her around.

"You did it!" I cheer and, even though they might not know what the hell is going on, my whole team joins me. We're clapping and congratulating her because Scar fucking deserves this. She's been working her ass off for the last four years, and she finally did it.

Scar reached her dream.

And with her in my arms, I will forever have mine.

Translations

Mamá me va a odiar. = Mama is going to hate me.

Ay, qué preciosa. = How sweet/precious.

Esa mujer me tiene loco. = This woman drives me crazy.

Puñeta. = Fuck.

Ella monta motocicletas. = She rides motorcycles.

Lo escuché. = I heard.

No creo que sea verdad. = I don't think that's true.

Te voy a matar. = I'm going to kill you.

Qué dramático. = So dramatic.

La comida está lista. = The food is ready.

Te extrañé. = I missed you.

Yo sé, mijo. = I know, son.

Vámos, la comida se está enfriando. = Let's go, the food is getting cold.

Perdóname. = Forgive me.

Y tú me tienes loco. = And you drive me crazy.

Pendejo = Asshole Cállate, mentiroso.

La vas a hacer sentir incómoda. = You're going to make her uncomfortable.

Eres una traviesa. = You're naughty. Relájate. = Relax.

¿Qué puñeta? = What the fuck?

No sé, mami, pero— = I don't know, mami, but—

Arcoíris = Rainbow

Eres la mujer más bonita en todo el mundo =
You are the most beautiful woman in the world

¿Qué pasa? Dime. = What's wrong? Tell me.

THE INSIDE OF A RAINBOW

Nada = Nothing el arcoíris de mi vida = the rainbow of my life

Quiero ser tu todo, arcoíris. = I want to be your everything, rainbow.

Quiero mi lengua en tu piel. = I want my tongue on your skin.

Tú eres perfecta. = You are perfect.
Dios mío = My God

Muéstrame. = Show me.

Siento lo mismo. = I feel the same.

Mi corazón = My heart

Tengo miedo. = I am scared.

Estoy enamorado de ti. = I am in love with you.

Viejo = Old man

Lo siento. = I'm sorry.

¿Qué pasó, Elias? Dime, por favor. = What happened, Elias? Tell me, please.

Por el amor de Dios, soy muy estúpido. = For the love of God, I am so stupid.

Cállate, Julián. = Shut up, Julián.

Te amo. = I love you.

Mierda = Shit

Lo extraño mucho. = I miss him so much.

Yo sé, mi amor, yo sé. = I know, my love, I know.

Ese cabrón. = That dick.

Lo siento mucho. = I am so sorry.

Sneak Peak

Jump-Start

Chapter 1

Leonard

Another race. Another win. Another critic probably ready to jump on the mistake I made in the third corner during the opening lap.

I felt it in the car as soon as it happened. I didn't leave enough space for my rival, and teammate, so he went off track and lost first place. I can already see the headlines. 'Leonard Tick Only Wins Races By Cheating'. My entire life has been like this. Since I was a kid, people have attacked me and tried to tear me down. That's what happens when you're the first black race car driver in a predominantly white motorsport. I fucking love this sport, but there are so many things wrong with it. We still have a long way to go before we can truly be proud of it.

I jump out of my Formula One car, briefly appreciating the sleek black colour my team went with this year. My eyes fixate on the Mercedes symbol on top of the nose, a wave of nostalgia running through me. I won my first World Championship with this team and hope to win more in the future. We've come a long way over the years I've been a racer at Mercedes, and I couldn't be prouder of the team I have.

"Leonard!" the post-race interviewer—Jason Dirk, I believe—starts, and I stare at him with my lips pulled into a thin line.

Formula One has hardened me to the point of no return. One smile is all it takes for people to spin things out of proportion like I'm happy about the move I pulled in corner three, which inevitably led to my win. Sometimes shit like that happens, it's normal in an aggressive sport like racing, but reporters don't care about that when it comes to *me* making the mistake. I'm judged a lot more harshly than other drivers.

"You drove a great race today and managed your tyres well. What a way to start the season! How do you feel coming back as a World Champion?" he asks, and I suck in an inaudible, sharp breath.

"I feel great. My team and I have worked hard and restlessly over the break, which is why it's great to see it paying off already," I say, shaking my head at his next comment.

"That incident in turn three sure did help. How do you feel about that?" *I feel like I want to punch you in the face,* I think to myself, but except for me grabbing my towel a little harder, no one would suspect how much his question bothers me. That's why it's great to have a reputation for never smiling. It allows me to hide how I truly feel.

"I will have to review the incident before I can comment on what happened. From the car, it felt like a normal racing incident," I explain, wiping away the sweat dripping down the side of my forehead.

I'm exhausted.

Today was a hot and long race, and I can't wait to get back home and spend time with my family. After test-driving the car for the past few weeks and putting every available hour into training to get ready for the start of the season, I've barely seen them. My brothers, Mum, and Dad all miss me too—they make sure to remind me every day—and I have to get back to Benz, my three-year-old pitbull. I miss her. I miss everything about my home. Even that pain in the arse, Chi—

"Well, congratulations on your win. Let's move onto our second place," Jason says, and I step over to where my performance coach, Quinn, is standing.

"Great drive, kiddo," she says before my hand slips onto her shoulder. Quinn is my best friend in the entire world. She's hardly five years older than me, but insists on keeping that nickname.

"Yeah, you liked my move in corner three?" I ask, which causes her to laugh. We both know I'm joking in the only way I do—without showing it on my face—but she's enjoying my playful attitude very much.

"I did. Now go get your trophy, kiddo. I haven't got all day," she teases, and I pinch her side in response. She laughs loudly, the sound making a wonderful warmth spread through my chest.

Before I can make my way to the cool-down room, Adrian Romana, a Formula One rookie I've only met a few times, comes up to me, still wearing his helmet. He holds out his hand for me as he calls out a 'congrats' before pulling me into an excited hug and telling me how well I drove—from what he could see as I lapped him. I don't usually show affection to people, but this barely eighteen-year-old gives me no choice, and I don't mind it as much as I thought I would. Adrian's a good kid, maybe that's why.

"I'll see you later!" he says before letting himself get weighed, just like every driver has to after a race.

I wonder what the fuck has him so happy all the time, but it's nice. Having someone positive like him in my life might be good for me. The thought is pushed away by my pessimistic side before I can linger on it.

My tired and sore feet bring me to the cool-down room, where my teammate, Jonathan Kent, is taking small sips from the bottle of water they have ready for us. There are three podium-style tables at the front of the room, and I walk toward mine, seeing the cap with the number 1 on it. I place it on my head before taking my bottle and joining the other drivers.

Cameron Kion, Adrian's teammate, managed to come in third, and it has him smiling so brightly, I wish I knew if he's always this fucking happy too. Whoever paired them up wanted a sunshine driver line-up. They must be quite popular with the fans.

"Nice defence in the eighth corner on the second lap, Leonard," Cameron says, and I shift my attention to his blue eyes, giving him a slight nod.

"Nice work on your start," I reply, not used to anyone making small talk with me after the race.

The other drivers mostly keep their distance from me. It's always been like this, but I can't blame them either. My facial expression doesn't communicate 'hey, I'm approachable'. It communicates 'fuck off', I've made sure of it over the years.

"My throttle was fucking stuck in the first corner," Cameron goes on, and I raise both eyebrows in response. "Yeah, it was crazy. Thank God it unstuck itself after a terrifying five seconds," he says with a slight laugh that makes his chest move. I give him a thoughtful nod, so he moves over to his water bottle.

Dreadful silence fills the room, and I'm convinced I can hear Jonathan's stomach rumble from hunger. It makes me want to kick him. We don't have the closest of relationships. He can't stand me, and I've fantasised about strangling him on many occasions. He's a spoiled, arrogant brat, and I'm too serious for him. We don't match on any level, but fans go crazy for our rivalry. Last year, we were head-to-head in the Driver's Championship, but I beat him in the second-to-last race for good. The title fell on me, and he's hated me more since. I couldn't give less of a shit. As a matter of fact, I often have to suppress a grin when he tries to talk behind my back about how I cheated to get the title. He's such a bloody sore loser, it's hilarious.

"Let's go," someone says, and I stand up from the seats at the wall to follow them toward the podium area.

First, Cameron steps onto the podium, taking his place. Then follows Jonathan, who bumps his shoulder against mine on his way out knowing full well I won't be able to trip him in front of all of these people. I would love to though. I would also very much enjoy it if he fell right on top of that nose job he had five years ago. Arsehole.

I walk onto the podium, standing on the highest spot because I'm the winner of the fucking race. I should be happy. Starting the season off like this is what every driver dreams of, but, for some reason, a numbness has spread through my chest. It's incredibly unsettling and makes me suck in a sharp breath. *What the hell?*

A frightening question crosses my thoughts a second later.

Am I falling out of love with racing?

Acknowledgements

First and foremost, I would like to thank my family and friends for always supporting me and my dream. I wouldn't be where I am today without them. For my sister/ editor/ photographer, I am especially grateful. Thank you for continuously putting hours and hours of your time into perfecting my stories with me. Thank you for your patience. Thank you for seeing things I don't sometimes. Thank you for everything.

I would also like to thank my readers, especially Sophie, Emma, Amy, Megan, and Franzi for your continued support with every book that I write. Your support will forever mean the world to me, and I am more than grateful for the love you continue to show my stories. Thank you.

About the Author

Bridget L. Rose is a half-German, half-Italian author, who was born and raised in Germany until the age of thirteen. She fell in love with books from a young age, and soon discovered her passion for writing as well. She likes to spend her free time with her family, reading a book, or writing one herself. She also adores the sport Formula One, which led her to write her Pitstop Series.

Books by Bridget L. Rose

The Pitstop Series

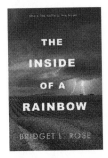

Jump-Start

The Inside of a Rainbow

Rush: Part One & Two

Chase: Part One & Two

From Angels to Devils Series

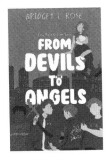

From Devils to Angels

Made in United States
Orlando, FL
17 June 2024